# Death Panel

## A Medical Thriller

Charles J. Hemphill

DEATH PANEL- A Medical Thriller

Copyright © 2011 by Charles J. Hemphill

Email: deathpanelbook@gmail.com

Printed in USA

# Dedication

To all the hard-working mental health professionals who shovel against the tide every day.

# CHAPTER 1

A terrified George Cobb ran through the quiet residential neighborhood carrying his high powered rifle clutched tightly in his grasp. He frantically raced through the darkened streets too scared to even look back. When he reached the safety of his porch, he almost tore the hinges off the front door as he rushed inside his unassuming three-bedroom stucco house. Cobb was afraid, very afraid. He had just been threatened by a demon from hell. The beast had flashing red eyes and screamed like a banshee. Cobb, a tall scruffy forty-four year old man with a three day beard and dark circles under his brown eyes, was determined to not let Satan's spawn claim him as his next victim. Even though he was safely inside his home, Cobb knew demons were tricky so he quickly searched the house for any fiends that might have slipped in while he was gone. When he found that he was alone, he breathed a loud sigh of relief. Still wired and wary, he returned to his living room to wait out the night. Cobb sat on the floor in the middle of the living room and prayed he would go undetected by the demons he knew were gathering outside. Experience had taught him that they never traveled alone and preferred to hunt in packs.

The only light that entered the living room crammed with second hand furniture was from slivers of full moon seeping through the gaps in the curtains. They created ghostly shadows that covered the clothes on Cobb's lean six-foot frame like natural camouflage. After silently seething for over two hours, Cobb could no longer contain himself and exploded. He jumped off the floor and with all the righteous indignation of a tent preacher he screamed at the top of his lungs, "You spawn of Satan. You'll never take me alive." He then broke into a rhythmic chant of, "God is on my side, God is on my side," as he rearranged the furniture in the living room. He shoved the big fabric covered sofa against the front door and pushed the rickety recliner chair in front of the coffee stained sofa. He set the oak veneer coffee table in front of the big bay window and stacked the two matching end tables on top of it. After he finished turning his living room into a rickety makeshift fortress, he stepped back to admire his handiwork, "Try and get me now you demons from hell," he smiled.

Proud of his feat, Cobb let out an animalistic howl and then quickly ran out to the garage. His strength bolstered by adrenaline, Cobb made three round trips to his cluttered garage and returned with three military surplus footlockers and set them down on the stained beige carpet in the middle of the living room. He flipped open the wooden lids to the olive drab containers, gazed at their contents and then reverently made the sign of the cross over each one. When he finished, a maniacal grin appeared on his face. Cobb knew the contents stored in the three wooden boxes were more than a match for the evil gathering outside. The old footlockers contained a mini-arsenal complete with enough ammunition to repel a small invasion.

Cobb carefully removed the weapons from each footlocker and gently placed them in three neat rows on the living room carpet, The Father, The Son and the Holy Ghost. He then scattered fully charged ammo clips and extra individual cartridges among the assorted weapons. Most of the weapons in Cobb's arsenal were purchased before he was placed under psychiatric care, the other half were purchased at gun shows where lax firearm regulations were the norm. Cobb had many firearms to choose from tonight, everything from an AK-47 to a nice assortment of nine-millimeter handguns.

However, if there was any killing to be done tonight Cobb would use the lever action thirty-odd-six of his youth. When Cobb was a pimple-faced kid, he went hunting with his father who always carried the big rifle slung over his right shoulder. "You had to be a real man to carry and shoot something like that," Cobb would often think to himself as he trudged through the hills with his father looking for white tails. When his father was sent to Vietnam, he gave the hunting rifle to George as a present.

After his father returned home six months later in a hermetically sealed casket, the rifle became young Georges' most prized possession. A tear trickled down Cobb's cheek as he remembered that awful day, but it was short lived. As he wiped the tear from his eye, Cobb froze and his face grew pale as a flashing crimson light filled the living room. In his mind it only meant one thing, the demons had found him. He ran to the bay window and peeked outside. "Oh, God," he said as he confirmed his worst fear, it was another demon only this one was green and white.

"Oh, the tricks of the devil," Cobb whispered as he watched the blood red eyes of the beast angrily flashing at him. "Time to feel the wrath of God," he uttered coldly to the demon as he raised the butt of his trusty rifle and smashed out a pane of glass in the bay window.

George Cobb was not himself today. He had not been himself for the last couple of days, ever since he stopped taking the Stelazine prescribed for his paranoid schizophrenia. When he was on his medication, it improved his sleep, stopped the voices in his head that were constantly telling him to prepare for Armageddon and made him feel pretty good about life in general. That would have been a blessing for most people but not for George Cobb. Because in his own form of twisted logic, as soon as he started feeling better, he stopped taking the Stelazine rationalizing that since he felt better he no longer needed to take the pill that was making him feel better.

This delusion was further bolstered by his fanatical fear of becoming addicted to pills. His mother constantly warned him about the evils of taking drugs after his younger brother died of an overdose. She literally beat it into young George that taking pills was bad. Ironically, like most people, she didn't view alcohol as a drug and used it copiously to deal with the loss of her husband and son. This mixed message was not lost on George and he quickly developed a substance abuse problem of his own as he grew older.

Despite his fears of becoming a drug addict, George needed his daily blue pill. Without it his hypothalamus would be unable to stop the chemical imbalance from taking place in his brain that would rekindle his psychosis. The Stelazine was crucial for keeping Cobb's paranoid schizophrenia at bay. Yet, he routinely stopped taking it and as soon as he did his liver would dutifully remove it from his blood stream. It took time for Cobb's liver to completely filter out the Stelazine, but one thing was certain. As soon as the therapeutic levels of his Stelazine decreased, Cobb's bizarre behavior would increase. When the Stelazine cleared his system this time, Cobb began to read his Bible.

He read and re-read the sacred verses of chapters twelve and seventeen of the Book of Revelation until he was finally able to interpret the message God had placed in the book of the end times exclusively for him. It told him to protect his neighborhood from Lucifer's demons until God's Son returned. Cobb had received similar messages in the past, but this was the strongest he'd ever received, so it had to be from the Lord Himself.

Cobb remained cloistered inside his home for the next two days pondering God's message, the missive percolating in his paranoid brain during the day and keeping him awake at night. By the time the sun began to set on the third day, Cobb's paranoia was boiling over. After a meal of raw hot dogs and cold cereal, Cobb grabbed the rifle of his youth and went to the front door. He was now ready to carry out God's personal mandate and protect his neighborhood. As he stepped into the cool night air he scanned the neighborhood for any signs of Armageddon, "So far, so good," he thought. He then made a smart military left turn and proceeded down the sidewalk on his delusional mission.

It didn't take long for the first reports of, "a man with a gun" to come into the San Salina Police Department, after Cobb started his psychotic patrol. The first officers to arrive at the scene saw George Cobb walking smartly down the sidewalk with a hunting rifle draped over his shoulder. From their patrol car they could also make out he was wearing a long-sleeved camouflage shirt and matching pants with the cuffs tucked military style inside the tops of his black leather combat boots.

"Well, there's our gun," said Sergeant Duane Branigan, a beefy third generation Irishman, second generation police officer and fifteen-year veteran of the force, as he scrutinized Cobb from the open passenger window of his black and white patrol car.

"Maybe he's just a hunter who got lost," quipped Staci Morgen as the petite six-year veteran and divorced mother of two slowly steered the car in Cobb's direction.

"We could only be so lucky," Branigan half jested even though he could feel his stomach tightening, his veteran instincts were telling him something didn't add up about this guy.

When George turned the next corner, Branigan saw Cobb also had a full bandoleer of ammunition draped over his shoulder. "Oh, my God," Branigan said under his breath.

"What's wrong?" Morgen quickly asked.

"He's got a bandoleer full of ammo with that rifle," Branigan replied. Cobb had just upped the ante. Branigan grabbed the microphone to the patrol car's two-way radio and called in, "This is Twenty-One Delta. That man with a gun call we got over at West Lakes is a man with a rifle, lots of ammo and dressed like Rambo. We're gonna need back up."

Branigan then looked over at Morgen and said, "Light him up."

Morgen reached over and briefly flipped on the car's siren, its loud burst warbled through the quiet neighborhood. She then turned on the switch that activated the bar of red and blue lights on top of the police cruiser.

"Roger, Twenty-One Delta," came the female voice over the radio's speaker. "State your location."

Branigan raised the microphone to respond, "We're south of the eighteen hundred block of Maple just before you reach. . ."

"Kapow!" The windshield in front of Branigan exploded in a spray of glass before he could finish his sentence. He instinctively ducked and took cover behind the dashboard.

"Kapow!" Another gapping spider web appeared in the windshield spraying more glass on the dashboard. Branigan felt something heavy fall on top of him. It didn't register at first then a chill ran down his spine. "Oh, my God, Staci," he thought with dread.

It was Staci. However, she was also diving for cover behind the dashboard. Fortunately the bullet fired at her missed and she received only superficial cuts on her face when the windshield exploded.

"Staci," asked Branigan, his voice filled with both apprehension and dread. "Are you all right?"

"I'm okay," Staci answered as tiny rivulets of blood trickled down her face.

"Thank God," Branigan sighed gratefully.

As the two officers hid behind the dashboard, two more bullets from Cobb's rifle hit their cruiser. One high-powered slug tore into the flashing lights on the roof of the car. Pieces of red plastic rained down on top of the car's hood and onto the street from the impact. The second round ripped into what was left of the flashing lights and permanently extinguished them.

Branigan spoke with controlled professionalism into the microphone of the still functioning police radio. "Shots fired. Shots fired. Officers need help at this location."

"All units. All units. Officers need help. Shots fired," the instant response came from the dispatcher over the open radio channel.

Every available police officer, Sheriffs' deputy and Highway Patrolman within a two-county radius responded to the broadcast and converged on the location. However, by the time reinforcements arrived, Cobb had fled into the growing darkness. It was now up to law enforcement to find him somewhere in the quiet tree-lined streets of the middle class subdivision. However, it didn't take long for them to find their suspect because as soon the first patrol car passed in front of Cobb's house, it came under fire.

The punched out pane of glass in the bay window allowed Cobb to easily slide the barrel of his powerful hunting rifle through the opening and aim it at the green and white demon passing slowly in front of his house. He looked through the rifle's telescope and took careful aim at what his delusional brain told him was a demon from hell. But, in reality it was a Dentin County Sheriff's patrol car, its overhead lights casting an eerie red glow along Oak Street. The two deputies inside were intent on finding the heavily armed man who fled into the night and didn't notice the rifle barrel poking out the window of Cobb's house.

Deputy Roger Armstrong thought he heard the sound of glass breaking as the patrol car slowly passed in front of a house with the big bay window. However, before he could turn to investigate the first bullet from Cobb's hunting rifle entered the driver's side door of the patrol car narrowly missing his leg. "What the hell," Armstrong shouted as he slammed on the brakes and unbuckled his seat belt. A second bullet ripped through the flashing light bar on top of the cruiser showering the street with pieces of plastic. "Get out," Armstrong yelled at his partner sitting next to him.

Dave Siegel was way ahead of him. Siegel, in one adrenaline-pumping move, unbuckled his seat belt, bailed out the passenger side door before Armstrong even finished his sentence and took cover on the driver's side of the car. Siegel, a veteran of Operation Desert Storm, knew the sound of a bullet hitting its mark. Both deputies were able to take cover alongside their iron horse as another bullet tore into the light bar overhead permanently disabling it.

"Son of a bitch! Where did those shots come from?" Armstrong excitedly asked.

Siegel cautiously peeked over the car's trunk and surveyed the houses along the street. "I don't know I didn't see anything." The loud crack of a rifle along with a muzzle flash from the bay window gave Cobb's position away. "The third house from the end, the one with the bay window," Siegel shouted as he ducked behind the car.

Both deputies lifted their heads from behind the cover of their patrol car, took quick aim at the house and returned fire. Each deputy emptied half a clip of nine millimeter ammunition in the direction of Cobb's house before their nerves settled down. In response to their fusillade, two more bullets from Cobb's rifle ripped into the side of patrol car with metallic thuds.

"He's a good shot," said Armstrong as he pressed up against the cold metal of the patrol car. Armstrong and Siegel quickly responded to Cobb's last volley by empting the rest of their seventeen round Glock magazines at his house. Armstrong then spoke calmly into the radio microphone clipped to his epaulet, "This is Baker Twenty-Nineteen. We've found the suspect. We're at the fifteen hundred block of Oak Street. Shots fired."

Armstrong and his partner quickly reloaded their pistols and waited for Cobb's next move. But nothing happened, there was only silence. No shots fired, no muzzle flashes, no noise of any kind. Armstrong prudently waited a couple of minutes longer before he cautiously peeked over the hood of the patrol car, still nothing. The only thing he could hear was the distinctive wail of an army of sirens converging on their location.

"Maybe we got him," Siegel said optimistically.

"Yeah, right," Armstrong skeptically replied.

Then without any provocation they heard the shouts of a deranged man yelling from inside the house they had been shooting at, his irrational rant apparently directed at them.

"You spawn of Satan," Cobb yelled at the top of his lungs from inside his living room, "Go back to hell where you came from. God is on my side."

"Oh great," a disgusted Armstrong said out loud, "We've got a nut job on our hands."

"Not just a nut job," replied Siegel, "A nut job with a rifle that can shoot pretty damned good."

Cobb shouted again from inside his house, "You will not take my soul. You will not take my soul. You spawn from hell. God is on my side."

Both deputies looked at each other and just shook their heads because they knew it was going to be a long night.

In less than an hour, Cobb's once quiet residential neighborhood was surrounded by a cordon of law enforcement officers and filled with a phalanx of police cars. Nearby homes were evacuated as a precaution and members of the San Salina S.W.A.T team were strategically deployed around Cobb's house waiting patiently to take action in the event the standoff required their services. Assistant Police Chief Mark Garland, a street cop who worked his way up through the ranks was in charge of the scene. The lean five eleven, grandfather of two was also the department's hostage negotiator. He sat in the back of the S.W.A.T. team's van on the phone with Cobb.

"Mr. Cobb, I've read the Book of Revelation," an exasperated Garland said for the third time. Garland had been verbally fencing with Cobb over the phone since he arrived on scene and was getting nowhere with the delusional man. Garland knew after the first few minutes of trying to negotiate with Cobb the chances of establishing a rapport or even a rational dialogue with him were slim to none. The man was irrational and crazy as a bed bug. However, Garland had to try and talk him out because it was department policy. The department's former policy of tossing in tear gas, breaking down the door and asking questions later was revised in response to losing two costly civil law suits. Garland, like it or not, had to follow the department's stringent new protocol to the letter or there would be hell to pay.

"Mr. Cobb, please listen to me," Garland tried again.

"No, you agent of Satan," Cobb screamed at the phone in his hand, "I will never fall into the hands of Lucifer's army." Cobb then yanked the connection out of the wall and violently threw the phone across the room. He then began to rhythmically chant again, "You'll never take my soul. You'll never take my soul. You'll never take my soul."

Garland looked at the skipper of the S.W.A.T. team standing on the bumper of the van. Captain Tony Tonelli a six-foot, hundred and ninety pound fifteen-year veteran of the force was also frustrated and tired of waiting, but he knew the rules.

"He's broken off contact," said an exasperated Garland.

Tonelli was dressed like the rest of the members of his team in black police assault gear, complete with a mat black Kevlar helmet. "So all we do now is sit and wait?" asked an annoyed Tonelli.

"Not much else we can do under the new guidelines, unless he starts shooting again."

As if on cue, two shoots rang out. Tonelli listened intently to the information coming into his earpiece. "That was Cobb. He took two shots at a Sheriff's Deputy." He then smiled at Garland knowing his men could now move in.

Garland smiled back at him because according to the new protocols they could now assault the house. "Go ahead and send your men in."

"You got it," said Tonelli as he jumped down from the bumper.

The four closest S.W.A.T. team members left their concealment and slowly crept closer to Cobb's house. After the four-man squad arrived along side the house they split up into two-man assault teams and positioned themselves on either side of the front door. Their movements went unnoticed by Cobb as he went back to his mindless ramblings inside the living room. The men put on their gas masks and the lead S.W.A.T team member raised his left arm to signal they were ready for the tear gas. Captain Tonelli saw the signal as he squatted down behind the trunk of his police car. He then stood from behind his black and white police car and quickly aimed the tear gas gun at Cobb's house. A loud thump announced the gas filled canister was on its way and heading towards the bay window. Tonelli then promptly ducked behind the car and waited to hear if the gas shell found its mark.

Cobb pulled back the curtain of the bay window when he heard the loud thump outside. Despite his best efforts at barricading the big window, his defenses left much to be desired. The tear-gas canister came crashing through the top portion of the window and landed on the living room carpet. The large bullet shaped projectile performed as advertised and ejected the contents of its canister into the room. Cobb rushed over and picked up the spewing canister and angrily threw it at the bay window hoping it would find its way outside. "Get the hell out of here," he screamed.

Either because of the gas stinging his eyes or because of his clouded mind Cobb missed the window and the canister hit the wall. It then bounced back into the living room and landed on top of the arsenal strewn across the carpet.

"Damn it all to hell," Cobb choked as the room continued to fill with tear gas. Cobb hacked and coughed as the gas burned his lungs and stung his eyes. Disorientated and psychotic, but still filled with an innate sense of self preservation, Cobb dropped his rifle and stumbled to the front door. He pushed away the recliner chair shoved the sofa out of the way and unlocked the door. As the defeated warrior stepped onto the porch to surrender he stretched his arms out as if being crucified and yelled for all to hear, "Forgive them, Father, for they know not what they do."

In less than a heartbeat, the four S.W.A.T team members standing by the front door jumped Cobb and forced him to the ground. "Get down!" The largest man of the assault team bellowed through his gas mask, "You're under arrest!"

Cobb put up no resistance but kept quoting verses from the Book of Revelation as they pulled his arms behind his back and handcuffed him. After he was handcuffed and on his feet, Cobb was led away by two S.W.A.T team members along with two uniformed San Salina Police Officers and two Sheriff's Deputies.

As Cobb and his law enforcement entourage maneuvered their way to a waiting patrol car, the entire group fell under the glare of half a dozen news' cameras. Each shoulder-held camera had an intrusive television news reporter attached to it. En mass, the reporters pounced on Cobb and his escorts like a school of piranhas.

Cobb stared unblinkingly into the bright camera lights, the brown nickel-sized birthmark on his left cheek clearly visible and yelled at the reporters with spittle flying from his mouth, "Go to back to hell, you demons of Lucifer! You'll never take my soul. As God is my witness, you'll never take my soul."

The reporters followed Cobb all the way to a waiting patrol car with its back door open as he continued to rant about Lucifer's army taking his soul. The eager press recorded every minute on tape as he was put in the back of the caged patrol car. Cameras stayed on him until the car pulled away from the curb, its destination the Psychiatric Triage Department at Dentin County General Hospital.

# CHAPTER 2

Dentin County General Hospital or simply County General, as the locals call it, has seen better days. Like many of the hospitals built in the early Seventies County General, despite regular preventative maintenance and continuous painting, had lost some of its luster. The once proud eight-story building that greeted the public at the hospital's festive ribbon cutting no longer exists. Now a cosmetically-challenged edifice stands in its place with urban blight slowly encroaching upon it like weeds in a rose garden. Before the neighborhood's demographics changed County General was the hospital of choice for the well heeled who also had Cadillac health insurance plans. Today, however, it serves a radically different patient population than it did when its doors first opened.

The flotsam and jetsam that now streams into County General have medical problems ranging from a sucking chest wounds, courtesy of the latest drive by, to a destitute child with a fever. An additional consequence of shifting demographics also made those now seeking treatment at the hospital very unlikely to have any money to pay for their treatment, much less have any type of health insurance. Leaving the taxpayers of Dentin County to pick up the shortfall and County General always struggling to stay out of the red. If this wasn't bad enough, adding to County General's financial burden was the county ordinance that mandated that indigent patients should receive more than just emergency care. No matter how grave or trivial their illness, the indigent received the best comprehensive medical treatment regardless of their ability to pay.

County General not only provides treatment for those with physical injuries, it also provides treatment for those with psychiatric problems. County General has only one psychiatric wing and it's always full, such is the demand for free inpatient psychiatric care. Oh, to be sure there are other psychiatric beds available in San Salina. However, they belong to the for-profit hospitals chains that are notorious for financially screening potential patients with the scrutiny of a bank auditor. The general rule at the profit driven hospitals was that if a patient was found lacking they were sent packing to County General. Unfortunately, County General didn't have the luxury of the same policy. They had to screen everyone who walked into psych triage regardless of ability to pay. The hospital relied heavily on their assessment skills because they determined who was admitted to the limited number of beds on the hospital's psychiatric floor or were sent to a lesser level of care.

Psych triage is the gatekeeper for the psychiatric floor. It is in a tiny room on the first floor and is inundated daily by those seeking free psychiatric care. Triage, from the French, means to rank things in terms of importance, and it's practiced at psych triage twenty-four hours a day, three hundred and sixty-five days a year. On average the staff in psych triage sees between four and five hundred potential patients a month. Their job is to determine who really needed inpatient psychiatric care from those who could use a less restrictive form of treatment. All the while walking a legal tightrope between the endless streams of street-wise deadbeats, malingerers and derelicts looking for three hot meals and a bed from those who were truly in need of care. If it weren't for the staff's screening expertise, County General would have to build two additional psych wards just to accommodate all those seeking to get off the streets during the cold of winter or during the sweltering heat of summer.

Today, the "on call" psychiatrist for psych triage is Dr. James Corrigan, a lean six foot two, third-generation Irishman in his late thirties with soft blue eyes and salt and pepper hair, the kind of hair endowed with the genetic code guaranteed to turn Corrigan's hair prematurely gray just like his father and his father before him. Corrigan's, otherwise pleasant features were marred by a three quarter inch scar over his left eyebrow. The vestige of a beer bottle he caught in the face during a nasty bar fight while matriculating at Harvard Medical School.

Corrigan will be the, "on call" for psych triage for the next seven days. He will be responsible for admitting those given the green light by the triage staff for admission, as well as setting up a preliminary treatment plan and prescribing medications. He will do this from the minute he walks into the hospital at seven in the morning until he goes home, some eight to ten hours later. The down side of being on call is that he's also required to maintain a full patient case load and perform his regularly assigned duties at the hospital no matter how many assessments come in. Because there's not an upside to being on call, the unpleasant duty is rotated among the five psychiatrists who work at the hospital. Little did James Corrigan know that when his name appeared at the top of innocuous rotation list it would change his life forever?

When not seeing patients, Corrigan can usually be found sitting behind his desk digging through the endless mounds of paperwork required by managed care companies and government agencies attached to each of his patients like umbilical cords. Like most large Bureaucracies, County General also generates its own enormous amount of paperwork so the old axiom that a case is not finished until the paperwork is done equally holds true no matter the workload. Corrigan's windowless office is located on the fifth floor just off the hospital's psychiatric ward. Today, as usual, he wore his wrinkled physician's white coat over his street clothes. A hospital identification badge dangled from the left breast pocket of his physician's coat, which still has the original picture that was taken when he arrived at County General seven years ago. Above the badge his name was embroidered in blue, James Corrigan M.D. While in the middle of dictating his fifteenth patient progress note, the unwelcome sound of the phone ringing on his desk interrupted his concentration. "What now?" When you're on call and the phone rings, especially near the end of your shift, it can mean many things, most of them bad.

"This is Dr. Corrigan. How can I help you?" He rolled his eyes when the triage nurse identified herself. He knew he shouldn't have answered the phone. "I had a feeling you'd call." When the nurse asked why? He chuckled, "Oh, I guess I'm just psychic." The triage nurse informed him they had a male walk-in that needed an assessment. Even though he'd be officially off duty at the top of the hour he agreed to do the assessment anyway. "Okay, I'll be right down."

Corrigan dutifully put away the confidential medical records lying on his desk, locked his office door and made his way to the elevators. Before long, he was in front of the faded blue pastel psych triage door. As he knocked on the heavy door he noticed there were some new black scuffmarks on the battle scared entry.

Mute testimony to those literally brought kicking and screaming to psych triage for an assessment. Corrigan glanced at the security camera mounted on the wall above the door. The staff on the other side saw him in their color monitor and buzzed him thorough the electrically locked door.

Not knowing if there was a flight risk on the other side of the door, Corrigan took his usual precaution of opening the door quickly, entering and then pulling it shut behind him. If there were a door anywhere in the hospital where you could literally say, "You never knew what you were going to find when you opened it," it was the door to psych triage. Most of the patients behind the door were under some kind of stress or duress, which made them unstable and very unpredictable. Today everything seemed peaceful in the large faded beige waiting room with the gray amorphous patterned floor tiles. Then the stench hit him.

It was the pungent odor of unwashed street people combined with a faint smell of urine and just a hint of vomit. Corrigan knew the waiting area was cleaned daily but for some reason, no matter how often the room was disinfected, that distinctive smell always hung in the air. A special ventilation system would have remedied the problem, but it was never installed and most likely never would be due to continual budgetary constraints.

Since Corrigan knew he'd been called down to assess a male patient, he scanned the room and saw all the men had gravitated to chairs along one side of the room. The three men sat quietly among the other patients in the room. Corrigan recognized some of the patients from when he came on duty, waiting with the patience of Job, for a bed to open up on the psych floor. Corrigan shook his head in disbelief when he recognized the derelict dozing off on the end chair. "Not him again," he groaned.

The man nodding off in the triage chair was Gary Ellis, a well-known and frequent visitor to psych triage. Corrigan prayed it wasn't him. He walked over and stood in front of the half wall and half Plexiglas shield that separated the triage office from the waiting area. Looking like a reinforced box office ticket window, the thick Plexiglas shield acted as a barrier to protect staff from belligerent patients while allowing an unobstructed view of the waiting area. Strategically located in the Plexiglas barrier was a five-inch diameter circle for easier communication. This along with a metal trough underneath so papers could be passed back and forth also added to the box office window effect. The strength of the Plexiglas window had been tested many times by irrational people of both sexes. Corrigan saw a man run head first at it, only to land on his butt with a throbbing headache for his troubles when he bounced off.

Nurse Linda Zerbee, a pleasingly plump brunette in her mid-forties sat at the long counter top desk behind the thick Plexiglas window. Corrigan nodded to the two male psych techs standing behind the barrier, a big beefy African- America man and a tall man with short blonde hair, they both nodded back.

Corrigan tilted his head in the direction of Ellis as he spoke to Zerbee through the hole in the window. "Don't tell me you want me to assess him again?"

Zerbee looked up and simply gave him a thin-lipped smile that said it all.

Corrigan sighed loudly.

As far as Zerbee and Corrigan were concerned, Mr. Ellis had worn out his welcome at psych triage a long time ago. However, it was department policy that anyone who came through the door of psych triage would be assessed regardless of the number of previous visits, so Ellis would be assessed again. Zerbee had already retrieved Ellis' medical chart before Corrigan arrived. It was two inches thick.

Corrigan suspected he could predict with uncanny accuracy Ellis' current appearance in psych triage would be a carbon copy of his last twenty or so visits. Each of his previous visit having generated an assessment form placed in chronologically order in his chart. He was such a frequent flyer that when Zerbee saw Ellis walk in, she felt all she had to do was change the date on his last assessment, make a copy and put it in his chart and no one would be the wiser.

"Sorry, he's all yours," said the jaded nurse. She placed a brand new assessment form inside Ellis' chart, rolled it up as tight as she could and squeezed it through the hole in the Plexiglas.

Corrigan unrolled the chart, walked over and woke Ellis from his alcohol-induced slumber. As Ellis walked to the assessment room, Corrigan could tell from the man's unsteady gait that an Axis One diagnosis of chronic alcoholism-continuous, would be in Ellis' future, again. The two men entered one of the four Spartan windowless interview rooms that opened up to the waiting area. The rooms provided some privacy but very little security. Corrigan invited the inebriated Ellis to sit in the chair in front of a well-worn battle ship gray metal desk that took up most of the room. Corrigan stepped behind the desk, plopped Ellis' chart down and sat on the wooden chair across from the latest frequent flyer to land in psych triage. As soon as Ellis sat down, he started to drift off again.

Corrigan knew Ellis' story by heart so he filled out most of the assessment form without having to consult the practicing alcoholic. Gary Warren Ellis, white male, age forty-two, an unemployed delivery truck driver who looks much older than his stated age due to years of uninterrupted alcohol abuse. Gary used to deliver packages all over town and also drank while he delivered his packages. He played a cat and mouse game with his employer for years until he was finally busted before setting out on his morning route. On that fateful day Gary was caught in the cab of his truck sucking vodka from a tube he kept hidden under the dashboard that was connected to the truck's windshield wiper reservoir. A flip of the switch on the dashboard and Gary got a shot of vodka any time he wanted. His employer rewarded Gary for his ingenuity by letting him go. After he was fired, everything went down hill from there. Gary is now a divorced smelly, disheveled man with dirty brown hair rummy eyes and a strong odor of alcohol on his breath most of the time. He had no job and very few prospects of finding one. He was also out of money again and looking for a place to stay.

"We meet again, Mr. Ellis," Corrigan cheerfully greeted the frequent flyer as he looked up from the half filled out assessment form.

Ellis lifted his head, opened his eyes and tried to focus on Corrigan, "Do I know you?"

"Gary, you were here just last week. Don't you remember me?"

Ellis stared at Corrigan and shook his head, "Nope."

"Of course you don't," Corrigan sighed, feeling like a ticket taker on some bizarre merry go round where nobody ever got off. "Okay then. What brings you to the hospital today, Mr. Ellis?"

"I need to be admitted to the hospital real bad," Ellis replied.

"Why is that?" Corrigan asked with feigned curiosity.

"Because I want to kill myself," Ellis casually replied.

"And how do you plan to kill yourself this time?"

"Uh," Ellis hesitated as he tried to think of a convincing answer. However, before he could connect the dots his alcohol soaked brain blurted out, "I'll jump in front of a car or something."

"Really?" Corrigan replied with numbed skepticism.

"Say, have you got anything to eat?" Ellis asked out of the clear blue. "I haven't had a bite to eat in three days."

"This is not a restaurant, Mr. Ellis, it's a hospital," Corrigan curtly replied.

"I know my rights. You're supposed to feed me," Ellis complained.

"Only if you're a patient. We haven't even finished your intake assessment, yet."

"Oh," Ellis meekly replied. He'd had little time for food during his latest three day binge and knew the staff at triage always had some sandwiches stashed away from the hospital's cafeteria for hungry patients so he figured it was worth a try.

Corrigan flipped open Ellis' thick chart. "How much alcohol have you had to drink today?"

"What makes you think I've been drinking?" Ellis asked indignantly.

"I can smell the alcohol on your breath all the way over here. How much have you had?"

Ellis figured since he couldn't really deny it, he'd shift gears and use a tried-and-true alcoholic defense mechanism called minimization. "Not much."

"Mr. Ellis you smell like a brewery. How much have you had?"

"Damn, this guy is good," thought Ellis.

Ellis was oblivious to the fact that Corrigan having dealt with hundreds of alcoholics, he was well aware of the defense mechanisms they used to hide their disease. So Corrigan asked again firmly, but without confrontation. "How much have you had, Mr. Ellis?"

"Oh, I don't know. A case, maybe a case and a half of beer," Ellis estimated.

"When did you have your last beer?"

Ellis contemplatively scratched the stubble on his chin before he replied, "When I ran out."

"How long ago was that?"

"A little while ago," Ellis replied, his foggy brain short on details.

Corrigan figured it would have taken about an hour to an hour and a half for Ellis to walk from his stomping grounds on the east side of town to the hospital. So he estimated out loud as he wrote his best guess down on the assessment form. "Patient's last drink was approximately an hour to an hour an a half ago."

Ellis nodded his head indicating he approved of the estimate.

"What have you been doing since the last time you were here?" asked Corrigan.

Ellis didn't respond.

"Let me guess. Living mostly on the streets, right?"

"The shelters close too early for me," Ellis complained. "Then they've got all those damned rules, might as well be in jail."

"You got a job yet?" asked Corrigan.

"Don't need one. I get Medicaid and SSI from the government now," Ellis smugly replied.

Corrigan shook his head. He'd seen the same scenario countless times before, government subsidized alcohol and drug abuse. "Tell me again why you need to be admitted to the hospital."

Ellis looked directly at Corrigan for the first time and with blood-shot eyes replied, "I told you I want to kill myself."

Corrigan then casually thumbed through Ellis' chart. He stopped at Ellis' psycho-social history and began to read from it. "Let's see, January 2008, patient states he wants to kill himself. March 2008, patient states he wants to kill himself. 2009, patient stated he wanted to kill himself, one, two, three, four, five times. Ah, then there was 2010. That was a banner year. Patient stated he wanted to kill himself eight times. 2011, patient stated he wanted to kill him self six times. And so it goes, on and on and on. Forgive me if I don't believe you this time."

"But I really mean it this time," Ellis said as he tried to sound convincing.

Corrigan ignored Ellis' attempted manipulation. "Mr. Ellis, do you know what your problem is?"

Ellis pretended he didn't hear the question. However, deep down Ellis knew he had a problem with alcohol but he wasn't about to admit it to anyone, especially someone like Corrigan. It's central to being a practicing alcoholic; everyone has a problem but you.

"You need to stop drinking," Corrigan obviously revealed.

"Like hell I do," Ellis shot back. Ellis then resorted to another standard alcoholic defense: rationalization. "It's my wife's fault. If she hadn't left me I'd..."

Corrigan cut him off in mid-sentence, "Mr. Ellis, your wife probably left you because of your drinking. You just don't get it, do you?" Corrigan was systematically stripping away Ellis' defense mechanism.

Ellis' lip curled as a spasm of irritation crossed his face. He wanted to curse and lash out at Corrigan however he wisely held his tongue. Because Ellis knew that Corrigan was the only one who could greenlight his admission to the psych ward. A place with a bed, clean sheets and hot food; a paradise compared to living on the streets.

"Mr. Ellis, you're an alcoholic. You just don't realize it. Unfortunately, you're probably not going to realize it until you've hit bottom. And who knows when that will be?"

"Screw you," Ellis bellowed as the truth hit home and he finally lost his temper.

Undaunted Corrigan continued, "When you finally decide to stop drinking, and God only knows when that will be, then come and see me."

"Asshole," Ellis said angrily through clinched teeth. "When I want a lecture I'll go back to school."

"Mr. Ellis, I call um as I see um."

"GRRRRRRR," Ellis spat. With his SSI money already spent and no place to stay, his objective of getting three meals and a place to sleep on the county were fading fast.

Corrigan had heard enough and made his final notation on Ellis' assessment form. He closed Ellis' chart with the new assessment tucked inside, rose from behind the desk and opened the door.

"I really mean it this time. I'll kill myself."

"I know Mr. Ellis," Corrigan sighed sadly.

"Then you're going to keep me, right?" Ellis smiled optimistically. He then quickly asked, "Have you got any sandwiches? I'm really hungry."

Corrigan stepped out of the room and walked over to the Plexiglas window where Zerbee sat waiting for the results of Corrigan's assessment.

"Well?" asked Zerbee through the hole in the thick safety glass.

"I'm not going to admit him, it would take up a bed for someone who really needs it. He belongs in a drunk tank. But, since he's not under arrest and since we'll be the ones who'll be held liable if we let him leave in his present condition we'll have to keep him here until he sobers up." Corrigan then rolled up Ellis' thick chart and squeezed it back through the Plexiglas hole.

"I know," Zerbee grumbled. She knew the drill because she'd been forced to be an ad hoc drunk tank matron many times. "I'll put a mattress down in one of the interview rooms until he sobers up and then send him on his way."

"Thanks," said Corrigan. "Would you also try and get him a couple of sandwiches. I think he'll be less of a problem if you do."

"Sure, Dr. Corrigan, will do."

Corrigan walked over and stuck his head back inside the interview room. "See you next week, Mr. Ellis."

"Are you going to admit me?"

"No."

"Up yours, butthead," Ellis cursed.

Finished with Ellis' assessment and his shift over, Corrigan walked towards the triage door. Even though he had just completed another unnecessary, albeit abbreviated, assessment he could at least take solace in the fact that he'd saved a psych bed for a patient who would really need it. Not that he was getting cynical or anything, but it seemed like when the local alcoholics ran out of money or booze, they were drawn to psych triage like moths to a flame.

When he reached the triage door, he was buzzed back into the busy hallway. He stopped for a moment and looked through the sliding glass doors of the north entrance, it was dark outside.

"Crap," he grumbled softly under his breath. He remembered the weatherman said there was going to be a full moon tonight. He knew from experience that if the Big Luna were out tonight so would be the lunatics. By morning, psych triage would be filled to the gunwales with the latest catches of the night, courtesy of the San Salina police department and every catch needing an assessment.

As he started back to his office to retrieve his stuff, Corrigan was blissfully unaware that one of the lunatics being brought in tonight would be George Cobb and he would regret for the rest of his life the day that he met him.

# CHAPTER 3

Despite the fact George Cobb, for some reason, still had private medical insurance; his arrival at County General wasn't an accident. County General's psychiatric triage department was the only hospital left in the county where the police could bring a person on a mental health warrant for an evaluation. The for-profits opted out of the money-losing venture a long time ago after they made the startling discovery that most people brought in on mental health warrants didn't have any money or medical insurance. The for-profits still provided mental health evaluations but only for those who could produce a valid insurance card.

When Cobb arrived at psych triage, blood was quickly drawn for a toxicology screen and then he was given a shot of Haldol. There was no point in trying to talk to him in his agitated state. Cobb was no stranger to psych triage having been brought in dozens of times by the police for some kind of aberrant display of behavior in public. Even though his delusions blossomed mostly at night, he'd been brought in during all three shifts at psych triage, the true hallmark of a platinum level frequent flyer.

Cobb was checked every fifteen minutes by triage staff during the night to insure his safety. Around quarter to seven in the morning, Marlin Brown turned on the light in the small interview room where Cobb lay loudly snoring on a mattress. Marlin, a state licensed therapist, was assigned to the graveyard shift at psych triage as a family counselor. His job was to deal with the dysfunctional families that always seemed to have a crisis in the middle of the night and came running to psych triage looking for a quick fix. He did crisis counseling and provided links to outpatient services for family members who didn't need inpatient psychiatric care.

Marlin reached down and shook Cobb's shoulder. "Time to get up, Mr. Cobb." Cobb stirred, briefly groaned and went back to sleep, the Haldol coursing through his veins was still doing its job. "At least I tried," Marlin, said as he turned off the light and left.

Two hours later a bleary-eyed George Cobb woke up, spent some time in the bathroom had a box of cold cereal and was led to an interview room by a psych tech. Cobb plopped down in a chair in front of a dinged up gray metal desk and waited for his umpteenth assessment to begin. Cobb still had on his camouflage shirt and pants minus his belt, combat boots and the contents of his pockets. "Where the hell am I?" Cobb mumbled to no one in particular. The psych tech standing outside the room didn't answer because he saw Dr. Corrigan enter the waiting room. Corrigan picked up Cobb's voluminous chart and walked towards the interview room. The psych tech gave Corrigan a knowing grin and a nod of the head as he greeted Corrigan, "Good morning."

"Good morning," Corrigan replied as he stepped into the interview room carrying Cobb's chart ready to assess the new, old patient.

Corrigan stepped into the interview room and greeted Cobb, "I saw you on television this morning, George. Thank God, you didn't hurt anyone." Corrigan placed Cobb's thick chart on the desk, pulled up a wooden chair and sat down across from his not so alert patient. "Let me guess. You stopped taking your Stelazine again."

"I didn't stop taking it," Cobb replied defensively.

"Come on George, it's me you're talking to," admonished Corrigan as he casually opened Cobb's chart and pulled out a blank assessment form. Corrigan asked again even though he knew he'd probably get the same response, "When did you stop taking your Stelazine, George?"

"I told you I didn't stop taking it," Cobb snarled, without even looking up.

Corrigan pulled a copy of Cobb's toxicology report from the chart. "According to your toxicology report the Stelazine you're supposed to be taking wasn't found in your blood stream. So cut the crap, okay? When did you stop taking your Stelazine?"

Cobb looked up from the floor. He thought about protesting again but reluctantly confessed in light of the evidence, "About a week ago."

Corrigan placed the toxicology screen back in the chart and asked the obvious question, "And why did you stop taking it?" Despite the fact he had heard every excuse in the book, who knows? Maybe, Cobb would come up with something new this time but he doubted it.

"Cause I didn't need it anymore," Cobb replied matter-of-factually.

"You didn't need it anymore," Corrigan dubiously repeated. He wasn't surprised. If he had heard the same exact reason once, he had heard it a thousand times.

"That's right. I was feeling a whole lot better so I stopped taking it," replied Cobb, as if it were the first time he had ever stopped taking his medication.

Corrigan leaned forward to get Cobb's attention. "George, the reason you were feeling a whole better was because of the Stelazine you were taking."

Cobb lowered his head and looked at the floor again because he'd been scolded like this before.

"Mr. Cobb," Corrigan began, knowing his admonishment would fall on deaf ears. "Do you realize this is the tenth time you've been here in this year? And each time it's because you stopped taking your Stelazine."

After a long silence Cobb rebuked Corrigan. "It's not natural to put drugs in a person," he spat bitterly. "The first chance you get all you damned doctors do is dope people."

Corrigan brushed aside Cobb's foolish accusation. "George, you can't stop taking your medication whenever you feel like it."

"Screw you. I can do whatever I want," Cobb shot back. He then muttered cantankerously under his breath. "It's a free country. I got my rights."

Corrigan leaned back in his chair and countered with, "If you won't take your medication, then we'll just have to start injecting it."

"You can't do that. I've got my rights. You do and I'll sue your asses big time. I'll own this hospital and everything in it before I'm through."

Corrigan ignored Cobb's flare up as he leaned forward and casually flipped through the irrational man's chart. He'd encountered this type of behavior countless times before and unfortunately there was a kernel of truth in what Cobb said. He had the same rights as any citizen and could not be forced to take his medication. The hospital could engage in a costly legal battle to force Cobb to take his medication, but because of the expense it was seldom done. Therefore the odds were stacked in Cobb's favor that he'd be allowed to continue to enjoy his psychotic civil liberties just like any non-medicated citizen.

Corrigan pulled out a copy of the police report that accompanied Cobb to the hospital. "It says here that you were seeing demons."

"Who says?"

"It's in the police report. Among other things you were calling the police, Lucifer's army and Satan's spawn."

"They're lying," Cobb said defensively.

"Do you realize you could have killed someone last night?"

For the first time Cobb looked directly at Corrigan and replied with a smirk on is face, "I guess I didn't though or I'd be in jail, huh?"

"That can still be arranged," Corrigan shot back.

"Like hell. You've got to keep me. I'm still on my ex-wife's insurance."

"You seem to forget, insurance or not, I decide who gets admitted to this hospital not you," Corrigan countered. "And I think you belong in jail."

"Go to hell," snarled Cobb.

"You know, Mr. Cobb, all this could have been avoided, if you'd just taken your medication."

Cobb flipped Corrigan the finger.

Corrigan could feel his face turning red with anger. For some reason, Cobb's gesture bore a hole through his professional detachment and he uncharacteristically replied, "You asshole, all you have to do is take one pill a day and you can't even do that."

Cobb became indignant, "I don't like your attitude, asshole."

"I'm not the one who put an entire neighborhood in jeopardy last night. That alone, is enough for me to send you to jail."

Cobb had spared with other psychiatrists at County General and knew how to counter punch. He smiled at Corrigan, "You can't send me to jail."

"And why not?"

Still smiling, Cobb pulled out the ace high card of every manipulative psychiatric patient and calmly announced, "I'm suicidal. I'll kill myself."

"Oh, really?" Corrigan replied with sarcastic disbelief.

"You know the jail won't take me if I'm suicidal. They're afraid of being sued since they lost their liability insurance." Like a game of chess, Cobb had just checked Corrigan.

"Well two can play at that game," Corrigan thought smugly. He took a pen from his shirt pocket and began to write on the assessment form. As he did, he read out loud, "Patient denies any suicide ideations, plan or intent," said Corrigan as he thought he had just checkmated Cobb?

"Hey, that's not what I said," Cobb protested.

"You suicidal? Yeah, sure, you've been saying that," Corrigan took a quick glance at Cobb's psych history in the chart. "For the last five years. And look you're still alive. Amazing isn't it?"

Cobb jumped out his chair. "You son of a bitch!"

Corrigan remained seated and slid his hand under the desk where he pressed a hidden duress button. "Now, now. Mr. Cobb. Temper, temper."

Corrigan's snide remark infuriated Cobb even more and he angrily lunged at Corrigan. He desperately wanted to silence the antagonist seated in the chair across from him. Corrigan dodged Cobb's out stretched arms as a salt and pepper team of psychiatric technicians rushed in. They grabbed Cobb and restrained him.

Cobb fought back, but the veteran techs expertly maintained control of the situation.

"Let go of me you bastards! I've got my rights," Cobb yelled as he tried to kick one of the techs restraining him. "If you don't let go of me, I'll sue you and this whole damn hospital."

Corrigan stood from behind the desk and told the psych tech with the short blonde hair, "Take him to seclusion. I'll write the orders."

"Yes, sir."

"You prick, I'll get you for this you bastard," screamed Cobb.

"Yeah, yeah, get in line," Corrigan replied with professional indifference. He'd been threatened so many times before he'd lost count. It came with the job.

"I'll get in line, asshole, to cut your heart out," Cobb shouted as he continued to struggle.

The two muscular techs efficiently pulled Cobb out of the interview room. They escorted him down the hall to one of the seclusion rooms designed for such explosive outbursts. After he made sure Cobb was securely tucked away, Corrigan stepped back inside the interview room, finished Cobb's assessment and wrote the seclusion orders for his recalcitrant patient.

Psychologist, Dr. Juanita Cortez, late twenties an attractive Hispanic woman with raven-black shoulder-length hair, caramel skin and dark brown eyes, popped her head into the interview room. "What's the matter with Mr. Cobb? He sounds pissed off."

Corrigan looked up. "Oh, he's just a little upset that things didn't go his way."

"Sounds like you recommended he be sent to jail rather than the state hospital after last night's little incident."

"You got that right," said Corrigan as he put his pen back in his shirt pocket and closed Cobb's chart. "He's a menace to society."

"You can say that again."

"I guess I should have recommended a spa treatment at some mountain resort, instead. Maybe then he wouldn't be so upset," Corrigan wisecracked as he stood and picked up Cobb's chart. He then stepped out into the waiting room with Cortez.

"Why not? He's been everywhere else," Cortez chided. She then glanced at her watch. "I came by to see if you're on for staffing this morning."

"Yeah, I'm Mr. Intake and Staffing today," Corrigan grumbled.

"Oh, mi pobrecito," Cortez replied without a hint of sympathy.

"I need a cup of coffee. How about you?" Corrigan asked.

"No thanks, I've already had two cups. I don't want to be too wired before staffing."

"Suit yourself, but I need one."

They both walked over to the triage door and Corrigan handed Cobb's chart to the nurse on duty and the two were buzzed out. As they stood in the well-traveled hallway Cortez cynically observed, "It seems guys like Cobb are on some kind of bizarre conveyor belt, doesn't it? They get on and keep getting dropped off on our doorstep over and over again."

"I know," said Corrigan, "Shoveling against the tide comes to mind."

Cortez looked at her watch again. As staff psychologist her life revolved around being some place at the top of the hour, every hour. As result, she was now a habitual clock-watcher. "Well, I got get going. I've got a group starting in five minutes. Adios."

"I'll see you at staffing," said Corrigan as he turned and headed for the cafeteria, where his morning caffeine fix had been percolating before the sun came up.

# CHAPTER 4

Corrigan passed the psych nurses' station at the end of an exhaustive two-hour patient staffing and was handed a stack of phone messages. There had to be at least a dozen of the pesky things from managed care companies and government agencies wanting updates on their patients. "Must be a slow day," Corrigan mused as he walked to his office.

He unlocked the door to his windowless office tossed the phone messages on his cluttered desk and sat down. Displayed on the wall behind his desk were the requisite framed diplomas, licenses to practice medicine and psychiatry, framed certificates of achievement and a couple of plaques for volunteer work done in the community. Corrigan didn't embellish his office with lots of personal touches like some of his colleagues. He followed the old axiom of never bringing anything to work that you could not afford to lose.

It had served him well over the years and was underscored by the recent firings of two janitorial staff caught pilfering items from desks and staff offices. His office decor consisted of a gray hospital issue metal desk, a wooden veneer bookcase, two putty colored filing cabinets and the two wooden chairs. The only things that belonged to him were his black high back swivel chair behind his desk, the two Impressionist art prints hanging on the wall, the two water-starved potted plants and the antique wooden coat hanger, the rest was hospital issue.

Corrigan had been promised an office with a window when he agreed to come to work for County General. However, he learned after he arrived that offices with windows were handed out only to those with the rank of director or above. Or used like coin of the realm and given out to those who found favor in the eyes of the hospital's administration. Since he was clearly not the apple of the administration's eye and he wasn't the director of anything, he knew his chances of obtaining an office with a window were slim and none. Once he settled into his comfortable leather chair he rummaged through the middle drawer of his desk until he retrieved his trusty micro-tape recorder. "Time to get started," he sighed. He then leaned back in his chair and started plowing through the discharge summaries that had accumulated in his absence. A quick glance at his watch told him he would be having another late night dinner at home.

Corrigan had been dictating for an hour when one of the recessed neon lights over-head began to flicker. "Damn not again," he muttered to himself. It was times like this he really, really wished he had a window. He longed for the day when he could work by natural sunlight, as God intended, and not the glow of neon tubes. However, since a window was not in his foreseeable future he'd have to call maintenance and have them replace the annoying neon tube. As he reached for the phone, there was a knock at the door.

"It's open, come on in," he bellowed.

The door opened and Dr. Cortez walked in.

Corrigan smiled. "Well, what do I owe the pleasure of your visit to my humble abode?"

Cortez rolled her eyes. "Please," she said with mock irritation. She shut the door and sat down across from Corrigan. She squinted at the flickering neon light. "You need to get that fixed."

"I was just about to call maintenance."

"Good. Cause something like that could drive you nuts," she said with a half smile.

"I know. It's like a Chinese water torture. So, what brings you here?"

"I thought I'd better tell you before you got the phone call that Dr. Lang wants to see you."

"What did I do now?" Corrigan asked knowing he probably already knew the answer to that question.

"He wants to see you about Cobb."

"Crap, I guess no good deed goes unpunished," Corrigan, sighed loudly.

"Hey, for what it's worth I agree with your recommendation."

"Thanks. But, I have a feeling that our fearless leader doesn't," Corrigan bluntly speculated.

"Yeah, you're probably right."

"Damn," Corrigan cursed as he leaned back in his swivel chair and resigned himself to another ass chewing.

Hoping to change the subject Cortez asked, "Did you hear about David Rockford?"

"You mean old Rockfish? No, what happened?"

"He hanged himself last night in his garage," Cortez replied with practiced professional detachment. A detachment born not only from years of professional seasoning, but also from knowing that if someone really wanted to kill himself, they would eventually find a way.

"And another frequent flyer bites the dust," replied Corrigan with equal detachment and candor. "I'll bet his managed care company is happy. He must have cost them a fortune."

"Do you think they'll go after Dr. Writhe?" asked Cortez out of concern for another mental health professional.

Corrigan leaned forward and replied with cynical bluntness, "Of course. It's standard procedure in our litigious society. No matter how screwed up the patient was or how many times he didn't follow his treatment plan, it's always easier to blame someone else. The relatives will sue anyone who came within mile of him before he died. It's like winning the lottery."

"I hope he has enough malpractice insurance," Cortez worried.

"Me too."

Cortez then mused out loud, "You'd think with all the time and money spent on that man he'd..."

"What?" Corrigan interrupted. "Get any better? I doubt it. You and I both know that ten percent of the patients we treat will never get better. He was one of them."

"I know," Cortez sighed with fatalistic acquiescence.

"Besides, Rockford was a frequent flyer, who stopped taking his medications so many times it was ridiculous. What did you expect?" Corrigan reminded Cortez.

"I know."

"Remember what they say about frequent flyers," Corrigan quipped.

"I know," Cortez grinned. "You can lead a frequent flyer to his meds."

"But you can't make um take um," Corrigan finished the parody of the old bromide.

"God, I wish it weren't so true," Cortez sadly lamented.

"Well," said Corrigan as he stood. "I better not keep the boss man waiting and enter the lion's den before I get summoned."

Cortez looked at her watch and stood to her full five feet, ten inches, "I better get going too. I've got a group. Let me know how it went with Lang, okay?" She then turned and started toward the door. Corrigan stepped from behind his desk and slipped in behind her.

"I can already tell you what he's going to say," Corrigan grumbled as they reached the door. Corrigan then did an impression of his Germanic boss using an exaggerated accent. "Vat in da hell do you sink your doing sending Mr. Cobb to jail?"

Cortez giggled as they stepped into the hallway and quipped, "Oh, you of little faith."

"Oh, ye of little reality," Corrigan cynically replied as he shut the door.

# CHAPTER 5

The office of Dr. Markus Lang reflected his title as Director of Psychiatric Services at Dentin County General Hospital. His spacious office had not one, but two windows, carpeted flooring, an oak desk with matching credenza, two bookcases and a high back swivel chair that would be the envy of any judge. It also had a small conference table complete with six chairs. Into this already plush setting Lang added his own personal touches: Bric-a-brac here, bric-a-brac there and two surrealistic prints on opposite walls. He hung the prints shortly after he became Director of Psychiatry five years ago. Lang sat behind his polished oak desk with George Cobb's medical chart in front of him when the anticipated knock at his door came.

"It's open, come in," Lang called out with a slight German accent. Lang parents, Adolph and Ulla, left Germany just before the Nazis invaded of Poland. Lang's father hated the Nazi party so much that he changed his name from Adolph to Donald after he and Ulla settled in Pennsylvania. After America entered the war he changed the family name from Langendorff to Lang. Markus was born four years later. He was an only child and went to the best schools where he accrued enough academic honors to attend college on a full scholarship. He became interested in medicine during his sophomore year of college and declared it as his major the following semester.

While at Johns Hopkins School of Medicine, he became intrigued with the field of psychiatry and decided to make it his life's work. After he graduated from Johns Hopkins, and finished his residency, he returned to Pennsylvania and went into private practice. Where he lived until a strange incidence forced him to leave under a dark cloud. Although, nobody really knew all the facts about whether or not he had an affair with a patient, there were a couple of telling signs: his wife left him and his practice slowly dried up. However, with no formal charges filed against him and his license to practice psychiatry still intact, he still looked good on paper.

After he left Pennsylvania, he applied for the director's job at County General. The search committee grabbed him and quickly put him in the director's position that they had been unable to fill for over a year. After he was hired, Lang quickly learned why nobody wanted the job. However, he stayed and with Germanic tenacity and discipline he soon became the hospital administration's wunderkind because he did their bidding without question. But, more importantly he kept his department well within its budgetary guidelines, which, he knew was the best way to curry favor with those above him.

Corrigan opened the door and walked up to Lang's desk ready for a fight. "Maybe I'll win one today," he thought optimistically as he stopped and squared off in front of Lang.

Lang, a stately gentleman in his mid-sixties with gray hair and trim features could easily be mistaken for a foreign diplomat if it were not for his physician's white coat. Lang looked up and briefly studied the thorn in his side standing in front of him.

"I take it you wanted see me about Cobb," asked Corrigan. His words sounding more like a challenge than a question.

"How intuitive," Lang sarcastically replied. "Please have a seat," Lang graciously offered.

"That's all right; I'll stand if you don't mind."

"Suit yourself."

Lang tapped his finger on the page in Cobb's chart where Corrigan recommended the paranoid schizophrenic be sent to jail. "It says here that you're recommending Mr. Cobb be sent to jail rather than the state hospital."

"Yes, sir," Corrigan curtly replied.

"I disagree with your recommendation. Mr. Cobb does not belong in jail. He belongs in the state hospital at Crown Point."

"He could have killed someone last night."

"That's no reason for him to be sent to jail. Mr. Cobb is a mental patient not a criminal," Lang firmly asserted.

"I disagree," Corrigan replied with equal firmness.

"Was anyone seriously injured last night?" Lang inquired knowing full well from the police report in the chart that except for some minor facial cuts to a police officer no one was killed or seriously injured.

"No," Corrigan responded weakly.

"Then we must give Mr. Cobb the benefit of the doubt."

"What are you saying? Corrigan asked incredulously. "No harm, no foul?"

"Don't be ridiculous," Lang snapped.

"He deserves to be punished for what he did," Corrigan insisted.

Lang swiveled around in his chair, opened the door to the credenza behind him and pulled out a hardback book. He placed the book on top of Cobb's chart. "So you really do believe the stuff you wrote in your book, huh?" Lang picked up the book and read the title out loud. "Public Safety verses Patient Rights. A new look at the treatment of chronically ill mental patients." He then dismissively tossed the book back down on the desk. "Either you're extremely callous or burned out. I don't know which, maybe both."

"Sir, with all due respect," Corrigan began as he defended the premise of his book for the umpteenth time. "The crux of my book is that at some point in a person's life they must take responsibility for their own actions and the same holds true for mental patients."

"But that's my point," Lang countered. "Mr. Cobb was not responsible for his own actions. That's what separates him from the common criminal. He doesn't know the consequences of his behavior."

"The only thing separating him from a common criminal is that he's supposed to take Stelazine once a day," Corrigan replied with increasing frustration. "And he can't even do that."

"Which only underscores my point," Lang confidently replied. Then hopping to scuttle Corrigan's argument he asked. "Was Mr. Cobb on his medication when he was brought in last night?"

Corrigan knew Lang wouldn't have asked the question if he didn't already know the answer. "His toxicology screen showed no Stelazine in his system," Corrigan feebly replied.

"Then don't you think it's safe to say that since he was not on his medication, he was not responsible for his actions? And therefore the M'Naghten rule would apply?"

Corrigan knew Lang was going in invoke the M'Naghten rule at some point as they argued, it just came faster than he anticipated. The M'Naghten rule has been used for decades by courts to determine the sanity of a criminal. It states, in essence, that at the time of a criminal act if a person as a result of a severe mental disease or defect was not able to appreciate the nature and wrong fullness of his or her act the person, to use the court's terminology, should be found insane. Ergo, they are not culpable for the crime they committed no matter how heinous. While sound in principle, the rule didn't take into account the increasing number of frequent flyers like George Cobb, when it was written.

Corrigan agreed with the rule except for one minor point. He felt the conscious decision by a patient to stop taking his medications while he was lucid was tantamount to premeditation. It made them culpable for any actions or behavior that followed. If that person should put society in jeopardy by their ensuing behavior, Corrigan felt their actions should not be mitigated because they voluntarily stopped taking their medication. They had to be in some way held accountable for their behavior. This was especially true for patients, like George Cobb, who had a long history of not taking medications after being discharged from the hospital.

"Maybe if he were on his Stelazine at the time," Lang said as he offered a half-hearted olive branch. "A jury would see it differently."

"But he's never going to appear in front of a jury, because he is never going to be on his medication when he commits a crime, which means he'll never be held accountable for anything. The man is a menace to society," Corrigan bitterly replied as he rebuffed Lang's olive branch.

"I'm sorry, Dr. Corrigan. I'm afraid I'm going to have to overrule your recommendation and refer Mr. Cobb to Crown Point, because that's where he belongs. Thank you for coming in." As far as Lang was concerned, the conversation was over. Lang had made his unilateral decision and there would be no rejoinders from this point on. He had won again, case closed.

Corrigan knew no matter what he said or did from this point on, his words would fall on deaf ears. Lang had won, again. Damn him.

As Lang calmly started to write the reversal order in Cobb's chart he thought, "Das unterrichtet das Arschloch. You'd think he'd learn by now."

Corrigan silently stood and watched as Lang countermanded his order. Corrigan had taken another professional slap in the face. What made it especially irritating, was the reversal came from a man whose current professional career no longer consisted of seeing patients or the practice of medicine. It consisted of spreadsheets, budgets and cost containment strategies. To Lang patients were no longer people, but numbers to be crunched into mathematical ratios used to calculate inpatient illness day's verses diagnosis and authorized insurance days or days remaining to discharge. All of which fit nicely into Lang's obsession to stay within or below his authorized budget each year.

Lang continued writing in Cobb's chart oblivious of the fact Corrigan was still standing in front of him. He then casually looked up and asked, "Anything else?"

"No," Corrigan replied flatly.

"Good day then," Lang said curtly as he wrote his name with a flurry on Cobb's new medical orders.

As Corrigan walked down the hall towards his office, Charge Nurse Anne Sokolov, late fifties, and standing all of five foot two, appeared with a chart in her hand. She handed it to Corrigan. "You've got another assessment."

Irritated, Corrigan grabbed the chart and asked. "What have they got going on down there, a two for one sale?"

Corrigan then looked at the name on the chart. "Oh, crap. Not her again."

"I'm afraid so," Sokolov replied with a hint of aggravation and sympathy.

"Isn't she Dr. Manguvada's patient?"

"Yes."

"Then why isn't he doing the intake?"

"We called his office," Sokolov replied. "He's out for the rest of the afternoon."

"Oh, the joys of private practice," Corrigan contemptuously jeered. He then made his way to the elevator that would take him back to psych triage.

# CHAPTER 6

Corrigan walked up to the heavy triage door and was about to knock, when the lock buzzed. He walked in and did his customary quick door-shutting technique and brief risk assessment. Satisfied no one was trying to flee, he walked up to the Plexiglas window and spoke to Nurse Barbara McCarthy.

"Where is she?" asked Corrigan unenthusiastically.

Nurse McCarthy, a trim, attractive brunette in her late thirties, pointed to the interview room with the door half open. "She's in there." McCarthy then slipped the frequent flier's chart under the slot in the Plexiglas window.

Corrigan made his way through the odoriferous waiting area and back to the same interview room where he previously interviewed both Cobb and Ellis. When he opened the door he found frequent flyer, Mindy Blackwell, waiting patiently for her assessment. Corrigan entered the room and carefully left the door half open. While it afforded less privacy, it reduced his chances of being accused of sexual misconduct. A precaution not only needed in light of today's litigious society but also because patients were known to lie, just to get staff in trouble. A male, female situation was always ripe with potential abuse, especially if things didn't go the way the female wanted.

Corrigan set Blackwell's chart on the well-used metal desk, pulled up a chair and sat down. Mindy Blackwell, a ditzy blonde in her late twenties, part-time crack user and part-time prostitute sat quietly in the chair across from him. She wore blue jeans and a red tank top that showed off the tattoo of a witch riding a broomstick on her right arm and a tattoo of a rose on her left arm. Corrigan noticed her bright red finger nail polish was peeling.

"Good morning Miss Blackwell. How can I help you today?" Said Corrigan, as he politely began his interview with the latest female frequent flyer to set down in psych triage.

With rote exactness bordering almost on boredom Mindy replied. "I've got S.I. and H.I. with major depression and I need to be hospitalized."

"Suicidal ideations and homicidal ideations along with depression," Corrigan repeated skeptically.

"That's right," said Blackwell as she causally confirmed her litany of problems.

"And how are you planning on killing yourself?"

Before Blackwell answered, she was distracted by one of her peeling finger nails. She nonchalantly peeled off the offending piece of polish from her index finger and then responded, "An overdose."

"And whom do you wish to kill?"

"My boyfriend," she replied with casual indifference as she continued to work on her finger nails.

Corrigan then asked the next obvious question. "Why?"

"Cause he's an asshole that's why."

"Could you be a little more specific please?"

Mindy looked up from her impromptu manicure repair and replied annoyingly. "Cause he's using crack again. And he's letting some slut stay with us."

"And how long has this been going on?"

"The crack or the slut living with us?" asked Mindy.

"I guess both," replied Corrigan.

"The crack, he's never really stopped using. He's tried to stop before, but he can't. The slut, he picked up about a week ago." Mindy bit down on another nail spat the red polish on the floor and then added resentfully. "And he's even letting the bitch use his crack. That really pisses me off."

"Then why don't you leave?" Corrigan suggested.

"Cause I don't have any place else to go."

"Don't you have any friends or relatives you can stay with?" Corrigan asked. "Of course she doesn't," he thought bitterly. Mindy Blackwell has burned more bridges behind her than Sherman's march to the sea. Corrigan knew it and she knew it, but it was required on the assessment form. A blank space can be interpreted as an incomplete assessment. And an incomplete assessment was not tolerated by Dr. Marcus Lang, who recently sent out a flurry of memos on the subject.

"No," Mindy resentfully replied. The truculent crackhead was becoming annoyed with Corrigan. She wanted to be admitted to the hospital and the stupid doctor was getting in the way of her objective with all his dumb questions.

"What about a shelter?"

"None of them will take me anymore."

"Why not?"

"Because," came Blackwell annoyed response as her voice went up an octave.

"Because why?" Corrigan naturally asked again.

Blackwell looked at Corrigan and angrily shouted, "Because they won't, all right!"

"Okay. I believe you. Calm down," Corrigan replied with practiced professionalism.

Blackwell went peacefully back to work on her nails and didn't make eye contact with Corrigan. She then asked the only thing that mattered to her, "When are you going to admit me?"

"I'll have to contact Dr. Manguvada first. Since you're his patient, he'll have to make the decision."

Blackwell looked up at Corrigan. Then like a spoiled child she arrogantly said, "You have to admit me. I've got Medicaid." She then reached into her purse and pulled out her Medicaid eligibility letter and waved it in front of Corrigan, "See."

Corrigan glanced at the letter, it was current. "Damn," he thought, it looked like she had her ticket already punched.

Corrigan stood, "If you'll excuse me for a moment."

"Sure, no problem," Mindy replied. "Just make sure I'm admitted before lunch, okay?"

Corrigan left the malingering manicurist, stepped into the next interview room, shut the door and pulled out his cell phone. He punched in Dr. Manguvada's phone number and waited. He got his answering service.

"Yes, this is Dr. Corrigan over at County General. I need to speak with Dr. Manguvada. I have one of his patients' here that I need to talk to him about . . . Yes. I'll hold."

Dr. Ghupta Manguvada was driving his new BMW home for the first time. He smiled as he inhaled the new car smell of his latest status symbol. Private practice had been good to him. He owned a beautiful home in a fashionable part of town along with a membership in the best country club money could buy. The forty-year-old psychiatrist always dressed like he just stepped off the cover of a men's fashion magazine, complete with gold bracelet and Rolex watch. Today, he took the afternoon off to drive his new

BMW home and show it to his wife. He was half way home, when his cell phone chimed and he answered it.

"This is Dr. Manguvada. . . .How are you Dr. Corrigan? It's been a long time."

"Yes. I know," Corrigan cordially replied. "Listen. I've got one of your patients' here at County General named Mindy Blackwell."

"Oh yes," Manguvada acknowledged. "I know her well. Major Depression. What is she doing there?"

"She's looking for a place to stay."

"She's what?" Manguvada asked somewhat mystified.

"Apparently her drug-using boyfriend brought home a new girlfriend and he's sharing his crack with her. So Mindy's pissed off and doesn't want to stay there anymore." "Is she suicidal?" Manguvada inquired.

"Not really."

"Is she depressed?"

"No. She's more pissed off than anything else," Corrigan said to his high paid counter-part.

"Does she have any friends or relatives she can stay with," Manguvada asked as he began to grasp at straws.

"Apparently not," Corrigan countered. "She's even worn out her welcome at the local shelters."

"What do you think we should do?" Manguvada asked as he differed to Corrigan as a last resort.

"She doesn't meet any criteria for admission. All she wants is three meals and a bed to sleep in until her boyfriend dumps his latest love interest. I'd say we set her up with an outpatient appointment with you and then send her on her way," Corrigan truthfully replied.

"Does she still have the Medicaid," Manguvada asked hoping Corrigan would say yes and instantly solve his problem.

"Yes," Corrigan reluctantly replied. There it was, the magic word: Medicaid. Corrigan could now predict with confidence the outcome of his conversation with Manguvada. The psychiatric floor of County General would soon receive a new patient. "She waved her current eligibility letter in front of my face like it was a hotel reservation."

"Then I think we should admit her."

"Why?" She doesn't meet any inpatient criteria," asked Corrigan even though he already knew the answer.

"As a precaution," Manguvada said as he tried not to sound disingenuous.

"As a precaution for what?"

"Dr. Corrigan, please," Manguvada arrogantly replied. "I know my patients better than you. And I want her admitted."

"Jeez," Manguvada thought. "How dare a psychiatrist working for the county question my judgment."

Manguvada's admonishment only confirmed what Corrigan already suspected. Manguvada felt a twinge of guilt knowing Corrigan knew he wasn't going to let a Medicaid customer slip through his fingers. It meant money in the bank. For private practitioners, the old adage still held true: Medicaid is as good as gold.

"All right," Corrigan replied as he held his tongue. Another battle fought. Another battle lost. "What diagnosis do you want to give her?"

"Major Depression, recurrent."

"What about meds?"

"She can continue taking the ones she's already on. A list of her meds should be in her chart."

"Okay. Any Axis Two you want to add? Say like borderline personality disorder?" Corrigan asked as he took a subtle professional jab at Manguvada.

"No," Manguvada replied curtly. "And I will be the attending."

"Of course," Corrigan answered without much surprise.

"Anything else?" asked Manguvada.

"No, Doctor. That about covers it."

"Then good-bye," Manguvada said briskly as he ended the conversation. He slid his cell phone into his coat pocket just as he pulled his BMW into the drive way of his two story Mediterranean house.

Corrigan put his cell phone away, walked over and stopped in front of the Plexiglas window where he could see McCarthy working on her daily reports.

She looked up and asked, "Well, do we keep her?"

"Manguvada wants to admit her. Again," an exasperated Corrigan replied.

"You're kidding," McCarthy responded as she wondered what admission this would make for the blonde frequent flyer.

"I wish I were."

"Let me guess?" The veteran nurse asked. "She still has Medicaid."

"Bingo. Give that nurse a cigar," Corrigan half joked.

"Jeez," McCarthy sighed loudly. "Medicaid: don't leave home without it." She then shook her head in frustrated resignation. "I'll start the admission packet."

"Thanks," replied Corrigan. "Dr. Manguvada will forever be in your debt."

McCarthy slid an admission packet under the Plexiglas window to Corrigan. "No use for you to hang around. Just sign your name in the usual places. I'll page the second on call and have him come down and examine her."

Corrigan quickly went through the ten page admission packet and wrote his name on every line that required his signature. He slid the papers back to McCarthy then looked at his watch. "No wonder my stomach's growling. I'm going to go get something to eat."

"The cafeteria is having mystery meat today," McCarthy offered.

"No thanks. I think I'll go out for a bite to eat. If anyone needs me tell them to go take a hike," Corrigan sarcastically smiled. He then added seriously. "Better yet, have them call me on my cell phone."

"Will do," McCarthy replied as she started toward the interview room where County General's newest psychiatric admission peacefully waited.

Mindy smiled broadly when McCarthy opened the door to the interview room and she saw the nurse carrying an admission packet in her hand. Mindy got her wish. Another frequent flyer had played the system and won.

# CHAPTER 7

The sliding glass doors to the north entrance of County General parted and Corrigan stepped outside. He was greeted by a cool fall afternoon. The trees in the parking lot islands were beginning to lose their leaves and the yellow and red flowers planted underneath them were starting to wilt. It always amazed Corrigan how the simple act of stepping outside the confines of the hospital seemed to revitalize him. Feeling the cool crisp outdoor air on his face was like plunging it into a cold mountain stream. "Nothing could spoil a picture post card day like this," thought Corrigan as he made his way to the physician's parking lot. As he approached his car, he saw a small envelope tucked under the left windshield wiper of to his brand-new Ford Mustang. "Oh crap! That's all I needed."

He took excellent care of his fully loaded Mustang. It was the unattainable goal of his youth that he was now able to afford. It was his pride and joy and his one guilty pleasure. After completing a three hundred and sixty degree inspection of his beloved set of wheels, much to his surprise, he found nothing wrong. There were no nicks or dings to be found and the paint wasn't even scratched. With a sigh of relief he pulled the envelope from under the windshield wiper, opened it and read the type written message inside: If you're not busy tonight I would like to meet you at Mason's on 1197 South Grand. Signed, a fellow professional. "Weird," was Corrigan's first reaction.

He looked around to see if the note writer was observing him and waiting for his reaction. He didn't spot anyone vaguely suspicious or even nearby. He read the note again and scanned the area more closely to see if he had been made the butt of some practical joke. Nothing, it appeared the mysterious note was a genuine invitation of some kind. After scrutinizing the invitation again, the next thought that came to mind was, bizarre. Without giving it another thought, Corrigan stuffed the envelope in his back pocket, slipped behind the wheel of his Mustang and drove out of the parking lot.

It didn't take long for Corrigan to arrive at his favorite gastronomic destination for lunch. A small corner hot dog stand with the name Hot Dog Heaven emblazoned in red neon above the front facade. Corrigan pulled up and carefully parked his Mustang along the curb in front of the dingy stucco food stand. As soon as he got out of the car the aroma of hot dogs and warm French fries greeted him. He found Hot Dog Heaven by accident three years ago and has been a loyal customer ever since. His loyalty, however, was not based solely on the tasty food the little hut served. The real reason he found Hot Dog Heaven so enjoyable was because of the solitude. He could sit al fresco at one of the little white plastic tables alone and undisturbed. It was a way to recharge his batteries and get away from the pressures of the hospital. In a profession that used a lot of talk therapy, it was nice to be alone and not have to converse with anyone. Not once during the five years he'd been patronizing Hot Dog Heaven did he ever run into anyone he knew, and he liked it that way. Even though a mustard and mayo dog with fries and a diet soda made for a good repast, enjoying it alone always elevated it to a five star experience. And he needed a five star experience today.

Corrigan walked up to the window counter and was greeted by the owner who Corrigan only knew as Paco. The Hispanic man in his late forties, with an affable grin, pot belly and bushy mustache, was there the day Corrigan placed his first order. Paco knew Corrigan's name and that he was a doctor at County General because he inadvertently left his physician's coat on one day while ordering lunch. Today Corrigan wore a wind breaker against the chill afternoon air sans his white coat.

"Hey, Doc, how's it going?" Paco happily greeted Corrigan when he saw him at the counter, "Haven't seen you in a while."

"Been busy," Corrigan truthfully answered, "How you doing?"

"Can't complain," said the rotund Paco. "You want the usual?"

"Of course," Corrigan smiled, feeling buoyed as the stress of the last few hours began to melt away. "Why else would I patronize such a fine eating establishment?"

"Okay, then," Paco acknowledged. "Two mustard and mayo dogs with onions, a small order of fries and a diet soda."

"A fine feast if I do say so myself," Corrigan cheerfully replied as he smelled the aroma of hot dogs and fries drifting through the window where Paco stood.

"That'll be five, sixty-five," Paco advised as he wrote down the order.

Corrigan pulled a ten out of his wallet and handed it to Paco. "Sorry I don't have any change. I don't like it rattling around in my pockets."

"That's okay," said Paco as he opened the cash register and handed Corrigan his change. "It'll be just a minute." Paco then went back to the grill to prepare Corrigan's order.

Corrigan walked over to a cheap white plastic table and sat down on an equally cheap white matching plastic chair. He then settled back and watched the parade of normal everyday people pass in front of him on the sidewalk.

It wasn't long before Paco stuck his head out the counter window and bellowed, "Your order's up, Doc."

Corrigan fetched his order and returned to his seat. He unwrapped the first hot dog and poured the hot fries onto a napkin to cool off. Then with great relish he proceeded to wolf down the tasty tube steak. While unwrapping the second hot dog, he spotted a derelict walking down the sidewalk towards him. The man had a scraggly beard and carried a small cardboard sign. As the man drew closer Corrigan was able to make out the block letters of the hand written sign. "I'll be damned," he said out loud to himself. The sign read: "Unemployed. Need money for beer."

Corrigan signaled for the man to come over. The derelict pointed at himself in disbelief, "Who me?" He was used to being chased off rather than asked to join someone.

"Yeah, you, come on over," said Corrigan as he extended a friendly invitation to the man down on his luck.

The derelict walked over and stood next to Corrigan. "What can I do for ya?"

"Nothing," Corrigan replied. "You're just the first honest person I've met all day."

"What?" replied the bewildered derelict?

"It's a long story," replied Corrigan as he reached into his wallet and retrieved a five dollar bill. He handed the five spot to the surprised man. "Here, the next six pack of beer is on me."

The man couldn't believe his good fortune. "Thanks, man." He then quickly stuffed the five dollar bill into his pant's pocket. "You got any more where that came from?"

As Corrigan replaced his wallet he said. "Hey, don't press your luck."

"Okay. That's cool man," the vagrant replied as he slowly backed away. No use pushing it. Besides he now had enough money for a liquid lunch. With a smile on his face and flush with cash, he started to leave. As he did Corrigan said to him,

"When you see Diogenes tell him I said, hi."

The man gave Corrigan a quizzical look, "Who?"

"Never mind," Corrigan smiled.

The derelict smiled back and then ambled off in search of the nearest liquor store.

Corrigan returned to his lunch and as he bit down on the second hot dog his cell phone rang. He quickly swallowed the morsel in his mouth, "Damn, can't a guy even have lunch?"

He grabbed his cell phone and recognized the number. "This is Dr. Corrigan what do you want?" He asked, with more than a hint of irritation in his voice. He listened intently to the person on the other end of the line and then grimaced. He was needed for another assessment. "Isn't there someone else around there that can do it? I'm in the middle of lunch," he protested. The response he got was not what he wanted to hear, but it said it all. "Oh, Dr. Lang insists because I'm the on call," said Corrigan as he parroted back the charge nurses reply.

"He's sticking it to me again," thought Corrigan. No use fighting it. Lang was obviously finding new ways to show the thorn in his side he was still boss. So he told the triage nurse, "Okay. I'll be right there."

Corrigan wolfed down the rest of his lunch and rolled the trash into a ball. He then stood, aimed and tossed the trash ball at a nearby garbage can like a basketball player shooting a three pointer. Much to his surprise he sunk the trash ball. Paco, who was watching from the counter window and yelled. "He scores!"

Corrigan raised his arms in a victory salute and smiled broadly at Paco. He then waved good-bye.

"Don't be a stranger," Paco shouted.

"I'll try not to," said Corrigan as he walked triumphantly to his car. He opened the door to the Mustang and slid behind the wheel. He put the key in the ignition, fired up the big eight cylinder engine and pulled away from the curb. Off to psych triage, again. The place was like an evil magnet that kept pulling him back. As the Mustang accelerated down the street he could feel his shoulder and neck muscles already tightening.

# CHAPTER 8

The sliding glass doors opened and Corrigan walked down the hallway to psych triage. He knocked on the big door and was buzzed inside. This time he noticed the waiting area was surprisingly empty. "They must have had some beds open up," he thought.

Then he saw the room's sole occupant, a woman who appeared to be in her late thirties strapped to a hospital gurney parked against the back wall. The woman's eyes were closed and she was mumbling quietly to herself. Corrigan could see she was only wearing a flimsy hospital gown under the blanket that covered her. When he saw the bulging white plastic bag underneath the gurney that contained her street clothes it confirmed what he suspected. The patient was an M.O.T. from a for-profit hospital and was, unbelievably, still hooked up to a catheter, its bag half full of urine. That catheter broke a cardinal rule regarding Memorandums of Transfer.

Corrigan went over to the woman and did a cursory exam. He shook his head and walked over to the Plexiglas window and looked at Nurse McCarthy through the thick barrier. "What's she doing here? She's not medically stable. For crying out loud, she's still hooked up to a catheter."

"I know," McCarthy replied with resigned frustration. "She's an M.O.T from Briarwood ER. What can I say?"

"Let me guess," Corrigan asked. "We had some beds open up."

"After I admitted Blackwell, we had six discharges. I sent up the ones we had down here and then magically I started getting phone calls from hospitals all over town."

"How do they know when we have empty beds?" Corrigan asked. It was like some kind of a mysterious grapevine that telegraphed to the world they had empty beds.

Federal law required that before a patient can be transferred from one hospital to another a protocol known as a Memorandum of Transfer had to be completed. Prior to the law going into effect, patients without money were bounced from one hospital to another like ping-pong balls. The unwritten GOMER policy or the, "get out of my emergency room" philosophy reined supreme and unchallenged for decades. Patient dumping, as it's called, finally came to the public's attention when a reporter discovered pregnant women with no medical insurance in major metropolitan cities were delivering babies in record numbers inside ambulances while being transferred from for-profit hospitals to nonprofit County Hospitals. After the law went into effect, it protected not just pregnant women, but all patients. The M.O.T. law set up a stringent protocol that had to be followed to the letter before any patient could be transferred from one hospital. And it applied to psychiatric patients as well. Now money, or what used to the lack of it, could not enter into the equation when a patient needed to be transferred.

Under the new law one of three criteria must be met before a transferring hospital can send a patient to another hospital. The first was that the transferring hospital was unable to provide the specialized treatment the patient needed, such as a medical hospital without a psychiatric unit. Second, there had to be no beds available to admit the patient at the requesting hospital and that beds were available at another hospital. Third, the patient made a specific request to be transferred to a specific hospital. However, in all three cases a patient had to be medically stable before he or she could be transferred. Failure to stringently follow M.O.T. regulations could result in a fine of up to fifty thousand dollars. Psych triage, however, was used to being dumped on by other hospitals despite M.O.T protocols, especially when psych beds became available.

As soon a psychiatric bed becomes available at County General, every hospital in town raced to fill it. ER staff at transferring hospitals viewed it as a golden opportunity to rid their respective emergency room of unruly patients. Staff on medicine floors campaigned to have uncooperative patients transferred out. Hospital staff who work on medical floors work there for a reason. Their hearts are with the sick of body not of the mind. They don't particularly like treating psychiatric patients or they would have gone into that line of work. It is not that uncommon for staff to pester doctors about specific patients so they can get them removed from their floor, especially if they were uncooperative. Their rationale being that there must be something wrong with a person who doesn't want medical treatment. It's just wasn't natural for people not to want help. The argument to transfer was always made better if the patient had even a suggestion of previous psychiatric care in their history. Emergency rooms did their best to transfer patients, which explained the woman from Briarwood ER with urine slowly dripping into a plastic bag hanging underneath her gurney.

"Let me see her M.O.T. papers," said Corrigan as he wondered who the doctor was that dumped on psych triage again.

McCarthy picked up a clipboard, removed the M.O.T. papers, rolled them up and stuck them through the opening in the Plexiglas.

Corrigan studied the five pages of standardized forms. He paid particular attention to the signature that signed off on the patient being medically stable for transfer. When he recognized the chicken scratching on the form as his old nemesis, Dr. John Freestone, he snarled. "It figures." The reason there was an M.O.T. law was because of callous ER physicians like Freestone.

Dr. John Freestone is the Director of Emergency Services at Briarwood Hospital. Freestone is a jerk that wouldn't give a psychiatric patient the time of day and views them as ER clogging rabble. Freestone made it very clear to his staff that he didn't want psychiatric patients taking up valuable bed space in his emergency room. And most of his emergency room staff concurred with his unwritten policy. Freestone was also a master of obfuscation when it came to M.O.T. forms.

Corrigan debated whether or not to call Freestone and argue the finer points of M.O.T. protocols with him again. He knew it probably wouldn't do any good. But, he was upset and wanted to let Freestone know he hadn't slipped another one past him. But more importantly he wanted to let him know he didn't appreciate the M.O.T catch twenty-two he'd just been put in. Because the way the M.O.T. law was written, Corrigan was now unable to send the patient back to Briarwood's ER because she was not medically stable. And because she was not medically stable and now on County General property they were required to treat her or face a stiff fine. Patient dumping was still alive and well, despite M.O.T. regulations. Corrigan handed the M.O.T. forms back to McCarthy. "I think I'll give Freestone a call."

"Why?" asked McCarthy, knowing the futility as well.

"I guess I'm just a glutton for punishment," he loudly sighed. However, part of his motive for calling Freestone was to let him know that, even though James Corrigan was a psychiatrist, he was still a medical doctor and he knew a medically unstable patient when he saw one. "While I'm doing that," he said to McCarthy, "page the second on call. We'll probably wind up having to send her to our own ER."

It was County General policy, written by the hospital's ER physicians, that before a patient could be transferred from psych triage to their own ER, a second opinion from another physician on staff had to be obtained. It infuriated Corrigan to think County General's own ER had the same mindset as the other ER's in town when it came to psychiatric patients. It also demeaned him as a physician because even though he didn't wear a stethoscope around his neck like his hot shot colleagues in the ER, he was still a medical doctor.

County General's ER doctors complained long and hard until they got the change they wanted in the internal transfer policy. The ER doctors sighted the steady stream of psych patients that came into their emergency room and crowded out those with real traumas and injuries. They also complained there were only so many ER beds and those with injuries to the mind rather than the body should be treated by psychiatrists, thus freeing up bed space for real trauma victims, both valid points. But it also stereotyped psych patients and didn't give them the benefit of the doubt when they might have an actual medical problem. Realistically, Corrigan understood why the ER staff felt the way they did. They didn't need a lot of psychiatric frequent fliers in their ER pretending to be ill for secondary gain. But he also knew that even though they were a pain in the butt they still deserved better.

McCarthy picked up the phone to have the second on call, paged.

"Do you know who's on call?" asked Corrigan.

"Dr. Stanley."

"She's good," replied Corrigan with professional respect.

"I know," said McCarthy as she punched the zero on the phone.

Corrigan walked around to the locked door that separated the triage office from the waiting area and was buzzed through by McCarthy. The door automatically closed behind him. Corrigan went over to the nearest desk, sat down and punched in the number to the offending ER. He waited patiently for Briarwood ER to answer. "Yes," this is Dr. Corrigan from County General. I'd like to speak to Dr. Freestone please."

As he waited for Freestone to come on the line, Corrigan reflected on how it always galled him to think physicians like Freestone thought less of psychiatry just because psychiatrists were not up to their elbows in blood and guts. Psychiatry, he grumbled, always seemed to be at the bottom rung of the medical profession's pecking order. At the top of the pecking order was Freestone and his ilk. They were also the ones who took seriously that their MD's meant Major Deities. Well, major deity or not he was going tweak Dr. Freestone's nose.

"This is Dr. Freestone," the curt voice over the phone responded.

"Dr. Freestone this is Dr. Corrigan over at County General psych triage. We just got one of your patients over here and she's not medically stable. In fact she still has a catheter in place. I was just wondering how something like that could have happened."

Dr. John Freestone, late thirties, trim athletic build, and type "A" personality, stood next to the nurses' station of the busy emergency room as he talked on the, phone. "She was medically stable when she left here."

"What about the catheter?" Corrigan pressed.

"I wrote an order for that to be taken out before she left. I guess someone must have screwed up. I'll find out who it was and talk to um."

Corrigan knew that was a lie. Then hoping to learn more about the patient he asked. "What did she present with?"

"She was lethargic, tremulous, slightly disorientated, and had some nausea, a head ache, and rashes on her arms. We gave her an I.V. and when she finally came around she complained of insomnia. Her condition improved well enough for us to transfer her to you guys."

"Well, she's not well now."

"All I know is she was medically stable when she left here. So I don't know what happened."

Corrigan then asked the sixty four thousand dollar question. "Why did you send her to us?"

"Because she's a psych patient," he answered without hesitation.

"How do you know that?"

"Because we found a bottle of Xanax in her purse. From the number of pills still left in the bottle it looks like she's been taking it for about three weeks."

"A bottle of Xanax!" Corrigan asked incredulously. "That could mean anything." He then calmed down before asked. "Who wrote the prescription?"

"Someone over at the free clinic."

"Did you call the doctor to find out why she was taking the Xanax?"

"We tried. The lines were busy. I can't spare someone to keep making phone calls. I've got an ER to run."

"A bottle of Xanax doesn't make a person is a psych patient," Corrigan advised. "She could be taking it for anything."

"Maybe so," said Freestone. "But since we don't have a psych unit we felt she would be better served over there. You guys can sort things out over there rather than have her take up bed space here. We're pretty full."

"Why didn't you admit her to one of your own medicine floors so they could sort things out?" Corrigan asked.

"Like I said she's a psych patient. She belongs over there. We don't have a psych unit, remember?"

"So you're telling me the only reason you sent that woman over here was because she had a bottle of Xanax in her purse?"

"That's not what I'm saying," said Freestone as he became a little irritated.

"Oh, yes you are," thought Corrigan.

"The woman was disorientated when she presented," continued Freestone with practiced skill. "She's on a known psychiatric medication. And we don't have the resources at this hospital to help a psych patient. After we stabilized her, we sent her to the appropriate facility."

"She may not be a psych patient. She could be taking the Xanax for anything for crying out loud," Corrigan indignantly countered.

"Well, then this will be an easy one for you," Freestone arrogantly replied. "Look. I've got to go. They just brought in two traumas from an MVA." The line went dead.

He did it again. Corrigan hung up the phone, sighed and shook his head.

McCarthy looked at Corrigan. "Well, what did he say?"

"She had a bottle of Xanax in her purse," Corrigan replied incredulously. "That automatically made her a psych patient. Forget about any of the other legitimate medical reason for taking Xanax as far as Freestone's ER was concerned, she was a psych patient."

Freestone and his staff had put on their professional blinders the minute they saw the bottle of Xanax and immediately made the woman unwelcome in their ER.

# CHAPTER 9

Corrigan could see Dr. Ellen Stanley standing in front of the triage door from the color monitor mounted on the wall above the counter. The tall, brunette with the holly green eyes wore blue scrubs under her white medical coat. Stanley, who stood six foot one, played basketball in college and was always picked first when the residents got together for a pick up game. When she played, she gave no quarter and didn't expect any in return. Corrigan saw her lift her arm, which was quickly followed by a knock at the door. McCarthy checked the monitor and buzzed Dr. Stanley in. Stanley saw Corrigan sitting in the triage office and waived at him. McCarthy buzzed her through to the office and she gracefully walked over and sat down next to Corrigan.

"What have you got?" she asked.

"I've got another M.O.T. dump from Briarwood ER."

"Let me guess. The lady on the gurney," she asked.

"Boy you're good," he joked. "I guess that's why you're a doctor and I'm just a psychiatrist."

Stanley smiled at the good nature joke. "What's going on?" she asked. It was time to get down to business.

Corrigan explained to Stanley how the patient on the gurney wound up in psych triage interlaced along with a few epithets directed at Freestone. When he finished, Stanley shook her head in disbelief and said as she stood, "I'll check her out."

She was buzzed into the waiting room and began her examination of the M.O.T. dump. She checked her blood pressure looked at the rashes on her arms and examined her as well as she could, considering the lack of privacy in the middle of a waiting area. Thankfully there were no other patients in the room. When she finished examining the woman, she was buzzed back into the triage office. She walked over and sat down next to Corrigan again.

"Well, what do you think?" asked Corrigan.

"You say she's been on Xanax for about three weeks?"

"Yes, according to Freestone."

"No previous psych history?"

"I checked on that while you were examining her. I couldn't find her in any of our patient data bases," Corrigan replied. "I personally don't think she's taking Xanax for psychiatric reasons."

"You're probably right," Stanley agreed. "In my opinion it she looks like she's having an allergic reaction to the Xanax. She's right on schedule if it were going to happen. Symptoms start about two to three weeks out."

"So in your opinion she has a medical problem and not a psychiatric one at the present time, right?" Corrigan cautiously asked.

"Yes," Stanley confidently replied.

"You'll back me up, right?"

"This woman belongs in the ER," Stanley said with unwavering assurance. "We've got to get her medically stable. Then we can find out for sure why she's taking the Xanax."

"The medical problem supersedes the psychiatric one right now, correct?"

"Yes. So make the damn call," said Stanley with mock irritation, knowing full well why she was being crossed examined.

Corrigan wanted to make sure before he called the ER he had everything lined up. Because he knew from previous attempts how difficult it was to transfer a patient from psych triage to their own ER. Something about squeezing a camel through the eye of a needle came to mind as he picked up the phone to call the ER pit boss. However, this time he felt confident he had all his ducks in a row. But, like a practiced skeet shooter, an experienced ER boss could shoot down his arguments and block the transfer. Corrigan punched in the number to the ER nurses' station. He didn't have long to wait before Dr. Iorgos Mackopoulos or Mack as he's called, a big Greek with curly black hair, a barrel chest and muscular arms came on the line. Mack stood next to the nurses' station in the busy ER as he spoke to Corrigan. "What can I do for you, Dr. Corrigan?"

"I've got a patient I need to send to you. She's not medically stable and appears to be having marked side effects from the medication she's on."

"What medication is that?" Mack inquired.

"Damn," Corrigan said to himself. He knew as soon as he said Xanax, Dr. Mack would launch into a skeptical game of twenty questions with him. "Xanax," he said reluctantly.

"Xanax," Mack dubiously replied. "If she's on Xanax it sounds to me like she's already in the right place. She doesn't need to be here."

"But, she's not medically stable," Corrigan countered.

"Do you have a second opinion on that?"

"Yes I do. Dr. Stanley concurs with me. She feels that before we can do anything on our end she needs to be medically stabilized first," Corrigan added as he pled his case.

"I see," Mack replied trying to think of another roadblock.

However, before Mack could reply, Corrigan took the initiative. "We've followed departmental policy. You've got my recommendation and a second opinion for another physician on staff. And we'll gladly take her back once she's stable. We'll even supply the gurney."

"Oh, all right," Mack begrudgingly relented. "We'll send someone over to get her."

"Thanks," Corrigan sincerely replied. He then turned to Stanley and smiled as he hung up the phone. "They're going to take her."

"Man, you're getting good at this," said Stanley as she congratulated him. She was impressed. She also thought it was ridiculous for them to have to practically beg their own ER every time they wanted to transfer a patient. During her residency she developed a more compassionate view of the patients who came through the doors of psych triage because of her frequent visits to the unit. Unlike some of her colleagues who dreaded receiving a call from psych triage, she didn't mind coming down.

"It helps to have everything lined up before you call. It leaves them very little wiggle room," Corrigan could now brag.

"Very astute."

Stanley's pager went off. She pulled it out her coat pocket, turned it off and quickly glanced at the LED display. "Looks like I'm needed in labor and delivery. You need anything else from me?"

"No. That's it for now," Corrigan replied as he reached for the paperwork to transfer the patient to the ER.

Stanley stood to leave.

Corrigan looked up at her before he started writing. "Thanks for coming down and helping me out. I really appreciate it."

"Any time," smiled Stanley.

Corrigan sorted through the transfer papers and found the form he needed Stanley to sign. "Better sign this before you leave."

She took her pen, signed her name on the form and was buzzed through to the waiting room and buzzed out of triage.

As Corrigan finished signing the last transfer form he heard McCarthy buzz the triage door. A male and female ER nurse wearing blue scrubs entered the waiting room. The male nurse went over to the patient and the female nurse walked over and spoke to McCarthy through the hole in the Plexiglas. "I assume this is our patient," she asked with a hint of annoyance.

"Yes she is," replied McCarthy in a succinct, yet professional manner. "Dr. Corrigan is finishing up the paperwork."

Corrigan stood with the completed hospital forms in his hand and announced. "Dr. Corrigan has finished the paperwork."

Corrigan reached over and handed the forms to McCarthy, who rolled them up and handed them through the Plexiglas opening to the female ER nurse. The male ER nurse pushed the woman's gurney to the triage door and waited for his partner to take the front end. She indifferently tossed the completed transfer forms on the patient's stomach and went to the front of the gurney. McCarthy buzzed the door open and the trio left.

"Don't you get tired of them being so damned arrogant?" Asked McCarthy.

"Yeah, but you've got to remember. Over there, they're legends in their own minds," Corrigan chuckled.

McCarthy agreed, "Yeah I guess you're right. They get all the glory while we get all the guff."

"Well, I better get going. I don't want to press my luck down here," said Corrigan as he prepared to leave.

Suddenly there was a loud bang at the triage door. Corrigan and McCarthy both looked at the door monitor. Standing in front of the door in living color were two police officers struggling with a screaming wild man in handcuffs. The monitor showed the man kicking his legs at anything in sight and occasionally hitting the triage door.

"Yippee," Corrigan sarcastically exclaimed.

McCarthy buzzed the door open and the policemen wrestled the scrawny, disheveled man with bloodshot eyes into the waiting room.

"Let go of me!" screamed the dirty vagrant as he fought with the police officers. "The president will hear about this. I work for the Secret Service!"

"I thought you said you worked for the FBI," said the bull-necked police officer, who stood well over six feet six inches, as he pushed and pulled the man toward a chair in the waiting room.

Corrigan looked at McCarthy and quickly ordered, "Call security and get fifteen cc's of Haldol sent down here, stat."

McCarthy picked up the phone and had security paged. She then buzzed Corrigan into the waiting room and called the psych floor for a syringe of Haldol to be sent down.

Within minutes two hospital security guards, one a fireplug of a man and the other with a blonde crew cut, dressed in matching gray slacks and white shirts with hospital district badges came rushing into the room. They wore thick black leather belts with handcuffs along with other items of their trade minus handguns. They immediately went to the assistance of the police officers. It took the brute force of all four men to finally secure the wild man to a chair and put him in hospital authorized four point restraints.

Corrigan was always amazed at how even the smallest psychotic patient, when they were agitated, possessed such Herculean strength. "Man, I'd hate to meet that guy in a dark alley when he's off his meds," thought Corrigan.

The wild man now secured to the chair couldn't weigh more than a hundred and twenty pounds, yet it took four men to restrain him. Corrigan walked up to the bull-necked cop to learn about triage's newest occupant.

"What have we got here?" asked Corrigan.

The wild man in the chair kept cursing and screaming at them. Insisting he was an FBI agent that he worked for the CIA and was a member of the United Nations and anyone who touched him would be in trouble with all three agencies. He also hinted he was on a secret mission to get space aliens out of the United Nations.

"We got a disturbance call at the convenience store over on Dakota street," said the bull-necked cop. "When we got there, we found this guy standing by the front door yelling, pretty much what you're hearing now, at anyone going in or out of the place."

"I didn't smell any alcohol on him," observed Corrigan. "Did you notice any when you picked him up?"

"No but he sure acts like he's on something. I'd say he's probably on crystal meth."

"Do you know his name?"

"He had no I.D. on him but the guy at the store said he goes by the name of Rusty."

"Any last name?"

"Nope, just Rusty," replied the cop

"I wonder why? He doesn't have red hair," Corrigan briefly pondered.

"You got me," said the officer. He then reached into his back pocket and pulled out the admission ticket for psych triage's newest challenge, a mental health warrant. "Here you go, just to make it nice and legal."

Corrigan took the papers and tucked them into his coat pocket. No use reading them now, it was pretty obvious why the man was put on a warrant. Besides he had more important things to do right now, like calming the man down.

Rusty continued his rant about how he was being unjustly detained and as an FBI and Secret Service agent he was entitled to some professional courtesy. And as an ambassador to the United Nations, he should be treated with more respect. He was also adamant that once the United Nations was notified about his detention; a representative would be dispatched to set him free.

"He's all yours Doc," the taller of the two officers said with a wry grin on his face.

"Thanks," Corrigan sarcastically replied. Just then Rusty's left foot restraint broke and Corrigan received a blow to his right shin.

"Ouch!" cried Corrigan as he backed away and automatically grabbed his shin. "Damn that hurt."

The two security guards quickly retied wild man's ankle. "There, that should hold him," said the fireplug shaped guard. "Sorry about that Dr. Corrigan."

"You want to press charges?" asked the bull neck police officer. "It won't be any problem."

"Nah," said Corrigan as he shook off the injury. "It comes with the territory."

"Suit yourself."

The two police officers then walked out of triage and back to the relative peace and quiet of street patrol leaving the two hospital security guards in charge of wild man.

Nurse Julia Nester from the psych floor arrived and was buzzed through to the waiting room. The petite nurse carefully carried a syringe of Haldol. She walked over to Corrigan and handed it to him. "Fifteen cc's of Haldol," said Nester as she verbally confirmed Corrigan's order.

"Thank you," Corrigan courteously replied. Corrigan then turned to the security guards. "You want to hold his right arm down so I can give him this."

The two guards went into action and secured wild man's arm.

"The CIA will get you for this," screamed Rusty as he saw the syringe coming towards his arm. "J. Edger Hoover will hear about this. He'll tell the president. Then you'll be in trouble."

"I'll take my chances," said Corrigan as he injected the man with the Haldol. "There, that should do it." He then handed the empty syringe back to Nester who turned and quickly left. Not even veteran psych nurses liked working in psych triage. Too many crazy things happened down there and you could get hurt.

The wild man continued to rant and rave for about another five minutes. Then the Haldol kicked in and he settled down and he fell sound asleep while still tied to the chair. The security guards removed the restraints and laid out a mattress in an interview room so Rusty could spend the night. He could be assessed later. The Haldol would make sure he wouldn't disturb anyone for quite a while. When the two security guards were finished, the one with the blonde crew cut entered the triage office and walked over to Corrigan who was filling out the obligatory paperwork on wild man.

"You need anything else Dr. Corrigan?" The conscientious security guard asked.

"No. Thanks for your help."

"That's what we're here for. You have any more problems with him just page us."

"Will do, but hopefully I won't need to see you guys again today."

The security guard turned and left. He joined his partner in the waiting room and the two were buzzed out of triage. They then went back to patrolling the busy hallways of the hospital and when time permitted the exterior grounds.

When Corrigan finished the paperwork on wild man he looked at his watch. His shift would be over in less than an hour. He stood and went over to McCarthy and handed her the finished paperwork. "If you need me I'll be in my office. I'm going to try and finish some paperwork before it's time to go home."

The phone rang on the counter in front of McCarthy.

Corrigan froze and his stomach tightened. "Will I ever get out of this place," he thought.

McCarthy answered the phone. She listened intently and then shook her head as she continued to talk, signaling that Corrigan could leave.

Corrigan's stomach unknotted, he smiled and waved good-bye. McCarthy buzzed Corrigan through to the waiting room and then through the triage door. When he stepped back into the hallway, he automatically glanced at the sliding glass doors. This time to see if there was another example of extreme aberrant behavior being brought in, fortunately the coast was clear. He finally reached the elevators that would take him back to his office and the mounds of paperwork that always seemed to pile up on his desk while he was gone.

# CHAPTER 10

It took Corrigan longer than he thought to finish the pile of mandatory paperwork he found waiting for him. It consisted mostly of Medicare and Medicaid red tape the hospital had to comply with in order to make the government happy. While he was sure his efforts would delight some non-elected bureaucrat back in Washington, what it really did was take time away from his patients. It really aggravated him to see how much time he now spent on paperwork rather than seeing patients. Just a few years ago he could practice the kind of medicine he thought was best for his patients. Now he had to justify everything he did to some faceless bureaucrat or penny pinching managed care case manager.

When he finally made it out of the hospital, the sun was just setting. He zipped up his wind breaker as he made his way to the physician's parking lot. He found his Mustang and slid behind the wheel. As he sat down he felt the envelope in his back pocket that he had taken from the windshield earlier. He retrieved it and read the note again. "Hmm," he thought as he mulled over the idea of whether or not he should respond to the mysterious invitation. In a way it was kind of flattering. But, why the secrecy? He looked at the address again. It was downtown and in the opposite direction of his home. However, curiosity got the better of him so he pulled out his cell phone, punched in a number to his speed dial and waited.

He expected to hear Diane's voice but got her voice mail instead. He quickly composed a message and then after the beep said. "Hey, it's me. I just wanted to let you know I'm going to be a little bit late tonight. I've got a meeting that just came up. I'll be home as soon as I can. You don't have to wait up. Love you, bye."

He slid the cell phone into coat pocket and started the engine to his high performance car.

By the time Corrigan arrived downtown, the store front windows on south Grand were on and the street lights were brightly lit. Corrigan pulled his Mustang up to the curb of 1197 South Grand. He put the car in park and looked out the window. His eyes narrowed as he studied the building. "This can't be right," he said out loud to himself. Mason's was a combination gun store and indoor shooting range. The two big glass storefront windows even had reinforced burglar bars on them. Corrigan looked at the note again. "It's the address all right." He slipped the note inside his coat pocket and with some trepidation got out of his car. He locked the doors and made his way to the front door of Mason's gun shop and indoor shooting range.

Painted in white block letters on the glass door were the store's hours of operation. It was open 12 hours a day, six days a week and was closed only on Sundays. "How admirable of them," Corrigan thought. "They ceased fire on Sundays."

The aroma of gun oil, new leather and just a whiff of cordite hung in the air as he walked into the well lit store. "What have I gotten myself into," Corrigan said, as he sized up the interior of the store. The store appeared to be stocked with every type weapon on the face of the earth. Including some firearms he didn't even know existed. One wall was devoted completely to specialty knives and leather sheaths. Another wall carried a variety of leather holsters. A big American flag was nailed to the wall behind the cash register. Pro gun bumper stickers were plastered everywhere.

A man appeared from behind the cash register seemingly out of nowhere. The man appeared affable. He looked like he was in his in his mid-fifties, with a sock of grey hair and bulbous nose greeted Corrigan. "Can I help you?"

Corrigan walked over to the man behind the display counter. He could have been mistaken for someone's grandfather, except for the leather holster strapped to his hip that held a chrome plated forty-four caliber revolver. The name tag on the man's shirt identified him as Bill.

"Ah, yes. Is this the only Mason's on south Grand?" Corrigan asked.

"The only one I know of," said Bill with a friendly smile.

"I'm looking for someone."

"What's their name?" Bill politely asked.

"I don't know. I've really never met them," Corrigan answered awkwardly.

"Then how you gonna know if they're here or not?" asked Bill, a little puzzled.

"I was hoping they would introduce them self to me when I walked in."

"Anybody walked up to you, yet?"

"No," replied Corrigan now feeling even more self-conscious since he was the only customer in the store.

"Then I guess they're not out here. You might want to try the gun range. There are some guys back there shooting," Bill suggested. He pointed to the door in the corner of the store. "It's through that door over there."

Corrigan looked in the direction Bill was pointing and could see a door with the sign painted on it. Gun Range: Authorized Personnel Only.

"Thank you," said Corrigan as he turned and started towards the entrance.

"What a sec," said Bill as he reached under the counter and pulled out a noise suppression headset and yellow tinted safety glasses. He handed them to Corrigan. "You're gonna need these. It gets kind of noisy back there."

"Thanks," smiled Corrigan awkwardly as he took the protective equipment. He walked over to the door and stopped. He saw printed in black marker under the larger gun range sign the warning: Enter at your own risk. "Nice," thought Corrigan as he put on the protective headset and glasses. He slowly opened the heavy sound proof door and stepped inside. He was immediately greeted by a cacophony of sporadic gun fire.

Three men were firing handguns from individual high panel firing booths. Corrigan could only see the out-stretched arms of the shooters from where he stood as each man discharged his pistol at a paper target hung down range. The remaining six firing booths were unoccupied. Corrigan hoped one of the shooters was the person that sent him the invitation. If not he'd been made the butt of someone's very unfunny practical joke.

With mixed feelings, Corrigan slowly crept along the wall behind the row of shooting booths. The first man he came to appeared to be in his early thirties, well over six feet tall, medium build, with coal black hair. He was wearing casual clothes and protective equipment. Corrigan watched the man expertly put a cluster of bullets from his nine millimeter Glock 17 dead center in the paper target some twenty feet down range. When the man finished shooting, he turned and looked briefly at Corrigan. The man's face was badly scared from acne. The man ignored Corrigan, ejected the empty magazine from his pistol and replaced it with a fresh one. Corrigan politely smiled and moved on.

The second man was also in his early thirties, but a little shorter, and had a neatly trimmed mustache and short brown hair. He also wore protective equipment. Corrigan thought even though the man was in civilian clothes, he had a distinctive military bearing about him. The man shoved a full ammo clip into his nine millimeter Beretta, as Corrigan walked up. He gave Corrigan the once over with practiced eyes. Apparently satisfied Corrigan didn't pose a threat; the man turned and opened up with his Beretta on the paper target down range. Corrigan saw the center of the paper target shred from the nine millimeter slugs ripping through it. "I guess it's not him either," Corrigan mused as he pressed on.

There was only one man left. He was in the last stall and was firing at the paper target in front of him with a smaller seven round capacity Walther PPK. The bullets from the venerable semiautomatic were hitting the target but not expertly clustered in tight groups like the other two shooters. When Corrigan walked up behind the man the first thing he noticed was that, unlike the other to two men, he was wearing a business suit. He had well-groomed black hair and stood around five foot, five. When the man's clip ran out of bullets he turned, saw Corrigan and smiled.

"I'm glad you could make it, Dr. Corrigan," said the Japanese man with the pleasant smile.

"Nice shooting," Corrigan remarked, not knowing what else to say to the man he never met.

"I just pretend that it's a frequent flyer," the man joked. He then placed the Walther on the counter, lifted up the right side of his suppression headset and extended his hand to Corrigan. "I'm Doctor Saito Ozawa."

As he shook Ozawa's hand Corrigan was pleased to know his invitation was real and not a malicious prank. "Nice to meet you,"

Corrigan graciously replied. Corrigan lifted the right side of his headset in order to better hear Ozawa.

"I'm with Global Behavioral," said Ozawa.

"That's a pretty big managed care company."

"It is," Ozawa proudly replied. "We're the second largest psychiatric managed care company in the country."

"Why would someone from a company like Global Behavioral want to talk to me?" Corrigan asked with genuine curiosity.

Before Ozawa could answer a rapid burst of gun fire filled the room as bullets tore into a paper target down range from the man using the Beretta.

Corrigan winced. "You could have picked a quieter place to meet."

"I know," replied Ozawa. "But, I figured I wouldn't run into very many psychiatrists here."

"You got that right . . . Say. Are you trying to recruit me?" Corrigan asked.

"Yes and no," Ozawa cryptically replied.

"Then give me the yes, first and the no second," Corrigan suggested.

"Yes, I'm trying to recruit you. But, no, not for Global Behavioral," came Ozawa's even more enigmatic reply.

"Then for who?"

"By a group," Ozawa was cut off in mid-sentence. The two men had reloaded and were firing again. Corrigan and Ozawa winced at the noise, waited and then picked up their conversation after the shooters finished.

Ozawa began again. "By a group of psychiatrists who share your views about the treatment of chronically ill mental patients.

They have read your journal articles and were very impressed by your book."

Corrigan was flattered, "Really?"

"My colleagues sent me to ask you if you would be interested in joining our chronic care team."

"Chronic care team," Corrigan parroted back. "What's that?"

"As you know, being a psychiatrist, one third of the patients we treat will get better. One third will get better without our help. And one third will never get better," Ozawa expertly recited from the multiple studies done on the topic.

"True," Corrigan's one word response confirmed.

"Our team deals with the one third who will never improve."

"You mean the frequent flyers." Corrigan concluded.

"Yes."

"How come I've never heard of your group before?" asked Corrigan.

"We prefer to keep a low profile. As you know when dealing with chronically ill patient, there are always risks. Especially when implementing, shall we say, new and unconventional treatment techniques."

"Of course, that's a given," Corrigan acknowledged.

"But not to those whose sole purpose in life is to litigate the medical profession into bankruptcy."

Corrigan gave Ozawa a knowing nod, damned malpractice attorneys.

"In order to keep from being sued," Ozawa continued. "We work as quietly and discreetly as possible. So far we haven't had one malpractice suit filed against us."

"That's pretty damn good," Corrigan replied admiringly.

"Yes it is, that's why the secrecy and that's why we're meeting here. The less visibility the better."

"I see," said Corrigan. Then he asked just to make sure. "And these people are really interested in me?"

"Very interested," replied Ozawa.

"Is this a full time position?" asked Corrigan.

"No. It would be more like a consulting job. We only meet once a month. You can continue working at County General."

"I see. What about compensation?"

"You will be well compensated for your time. I can assure you."

"What kind of new and unusual treatment techniques do you use?" Corrigan pretended to naively ask hopping to garner a secret or two.

"If you attend one of our meetings you'll see," Ozawa politely countered.

"Touché," Corrigan smiled.

"Well. What do you say? Are you interested?" Ozawa pressed hopping to get Corrigan to commit.

"I don't know what to say."

"How about, yes?" Ozawa encouraged.

"I guess it couldn't hurt to talk to them."

"Excellent," a delighted Ozawa replied. "They'll be glad to hear you've accepted their invitation."

"What now?" Corrigan asked.

"Like I said, we meet only once a month, on the last Monday of each month. I'll contact you before our next meeting about the time and location." Ozawa then turned serious. "There is one caveat, however."

"There always is," sighed Corrigan as he waited for the other shoe to drop.

"I would ask that, for now, you not tell anyone, including your wife, about this invitation."

"Aren't you being just a little bit paranoid?" asked Corrigan. An alarm should have gone off in his head, but it didn't.

"Not when you swim in an ocean full of malpractice sharks," Ozawa responded with his expertly crafted reply prepared in advance.

Corrigan nodded his head in agreement. "True."

"We haven't been sued yet. And we want to keep it that way," said Ozawa.

"I guess that makes sense," replied Corrigan as his ego got in the way of his better judgment. "Anything else I should know?"

"No. I'll be in touch. And thanks for accepting our invitation."

"You're welcome. I look forward to meeting your group," Corrigan warmly replied.

One of the shooters opened up again, but this time with a series of rapid three shot bursts from his handgun. Corrigan winced again.

"Don't worry. I promise the next time we meet, it will be at a much quieter location," Ozawa apologized.

"I hope so."

Ozawa extended his hand. "Until me meet again."

Corrigan shook his hand. "Good-bye."

"Good-bye," smiled Ozawa.

When Corrigan finally made it to the gun range door, he opened it and disappeared inside the store. The heavy door closed behind him.

As soon as he felt Corrigan would not return, Ozawa called out. "It's all right, he's gone." The two shooters left their firing booths and joined him.

When Corrigan pulled into the driveway of his three-bedroom residential ranch house, he could tell his wife was already in bed. The porch light was on and the rest of the house was dark. He parked his Mustang in the uncluttered garage next to his wife's Mercedes. He then made his way through the living room filled with contemporary Mediterranean furniture to the entrance of the master bedroom. The door to the bedroom was open and Corrigan's wife of eight years was asleep with the lamp still burning on the night stand. A romance novel lay across her swollen belly. He smiled. In about a month, Corrigan would be a father for the first time.

Diane was an established television news producer and recipient of several prestigious local news awards. She enjoyed the excitement of the news room. Although she might not admit it, she probably was an adrenaline junkie and working in a fast-paced news room environment sated her need to be active. She also wanted a baby. So after some discussion and a close examination of their budget, they decided this would be the year they would start a family. It had been a fun-filled eight months as the couple prepared for their new arrival. Everything in the baby's room was ready except for the crib. Corrigan promised Diane he would put it together before the baby arrived. However, he was running out of time. He pledged, and crossed his heart and hoped to die, that he would put it together this weekend.

Corrigan stepped noiselessly to his dresser. He quietly placed his keys in the small slightly imperfect ceramic bowl that Diane made him, when pottery was her latest form of artistic expression.

He smiled every time he saw the deformed little bowl. He then stripped down to his boxers and made his way over to his side of the bed. As soon as he lifted the covers and sat down, Diane woke up.

"Hi, honey. How'd your meeting go?" asked Diane as she opened her eyes.

"Fine," Corrigan replied with a purposely nebulous answer hoping it would discourage any further conversation. "Sorry I woke you."

"That's all right," said Diane as she sat up and fluffed the pillows behind her.

"How are you feeling?" Corrigan innocently asked.

Diane ran her hand through her auburn hair and looked at her husband with her cobalt blue eyes and groaned, "Like an old cow."

"Oh, come on now," Corrigan gently responded.

"But, I do," Diane grumbled. "I feel like I'm never going to have this baby."

"Dr. Potter said you'd feel like this during your last month."

"Yeah, but knowing it and living it are two different things."

Corrigan leaned over and kissed Diane on the forehead. "You're more beautiful than the day I met you."

"Yeah, sure," Diane grunted sourly.

"No, you honestly have a glow about you. I think it's really true what they say about women who are pregnant."

"I bet you say that to all the pregnant T.V. producers you meet," Diane mischievously grinned.

"Only the ones I sleep with on a regular basis," Corrigan jokingly responded.

"Why you," said Diane as she playfully popped her husband in the head with a pillow. "There better not be anyone else."

Corrigan put his hands up in mock defense. "You're the only one." He then crossed himself. "Cross my heart and hope to die. Honest."

"You nut," Diane eyes crinkled mirthfully as she laughed.

Corrigan scooted closer to Diane as she lay back on her pillow. He pressed his face close to hers and hovered over her sensual lips. Diane looked up at him and they kissed. When their lips finally parted they both looked at each other and said at the same time. "I love you."

Corrigan then softly patted Diane's stomach. "And I love you too."

"I'll bet our daughter is going to have you wrapped around her little finger."

"I don't care," Corrigan said lovingly.

Diane yawned and re-fluffed her pillows. "Man, I can't believe how tired I've been these days."

"Well, you are sleeping for two, remember?" Corrigan joked.

"Yeah, I guess you're right," Diane smiled as she looked at what used to be her slim waistline.

Corrigan slid back to his side of the bed and pulled the covers up to his waist. Diane turned off the light and made herself comfortable.

As they both settled in for the night, Diane turned and looked at her husband. "Do you think they'll miss me at the station after tomorrow?"

"I don't know how they'll be able to stay on the air without you," Corrigan grinned.

"Yeah, sure," Diane said sarcastically.

"Honestly, I'm just glad tomorrow's your last day."

"Me too," said Diane as she nestled her head next to her husband's shoulder. "Carrying this baby of yours is a full time job."

"And I appreciate it," Corrigan honestly replied. The two kissed again and then slowly drifted off to sleep.

# CHAPTER 11

Corrigan had just finished his morning rounds at venerable County General when his cell phone rang. "Doctor Corrigan," he answered. It was Diane, she just wanted to talk. Ever since she took her leave of absence three weeks ago the hard charging television producer quickly grew bored puttering around the house and watching soap operas. Since all her friends were at work and they didn't have time to talk, she began calling her husband just to chat and see how things were going.

"I'm fine," said Corrigan. "Diane, I can't talk right now I'm doing rounds . . . No, I'm not angry at you. But, I've got to go, okay. All right, dear. Good-bye."

He returned his cell phone to his coat pocket as he walked past the nurses' station where he was handed a stack of phone messages. He scanned them as he walked down the hallway to his office. Once inside his office he tossed the messages on his desk and sat down. He now had to dictate progress notes on all the patients he'd just seen. As he opened the first patient's chart, there was a knock at the door.

"It's open. Come on in," Corrigan bellowed.

Dr. Cortez walked in. She looked particularly attractive this morning in her white blouse and dark blue skirt. Corrigan could see that she was carrying a hand full of mail as she shut the door and walked over to his desk. "I hope you don't mind. I picked up your mail on my way up."

"No, not at all, thanks."

Cortez placed the stack of mail on the desk and sat down across from Corrigan. Cortez was troubled this morning and her face reflected it. She'd been debating all morning about whether or not to be the bearer of bad news from the rumor mill. She felt obligated to tell her friend even though she knew it would upset him.

Corrigan sensed that Cortez was not her usual easy going self as he looked at her from across the desk. "What's the matter? You seem to be a little distracted."

"What?" asked Cortez as her internal debate continued?

"What's the matter?" Corrigan asked with genuine concern. "Are you all right?"

"I'm sorry. I'm just thinking," she apologized.

"I thought I smelled something burning," he joked.

However, the joke only got a wane smile from Cortez. "I hate to be the bearer of bad tidings," she finally decided to tell him. "But, I heard something through the grapevine you might be interested in."

"What's that?"

"I heard that Cobb was discharged from Crown Point."

"You've got to be kidding," said Corrigan, his voice filled with resentment. "Are you sure?"

"I'm pretty sure." Cortez replied feeling relieved that she told him even though she got the reaction she expected. "One of the hospital security guards told me. He has a friend who's a security guard at Crown Point. His friend said he saw Cobb get on the bus home a few days ago."

Corrigan glanced at the calendar on his desk and quickly calculated. "That means they kept him for only two weeks, for God's sake. I knew it. Damn it. I just knew it," Corrigan said as his face flushed with anger. His prediction had come true. Cobb was back on the streets. "When will they ever learn?"

Cortez let Corrigan's anger run its course. She had seen him like this only a couple of times. Very few things set Corrigan off, however, at the top of his list was being second guessed by Dr. Lang. Cortez watched Corrigan's ears turn red as he fumed and verbally took Lang apart. Done venting his flushed cheeks slowly returned to normal as did his temper and professional objectivity. Corrigan sighed and looked at Cortez. "Sorry."

"That's okay," replied Cortez.

"I wonder how long it'll be before we see him back here again," Corrigan openly speculated.

"I don't know," Cortez replied. "I wish there was something we could do about him. Permanently."

"Me too," Corrigan half-heartedly agreed.

"Maybe we can take up a collection and hire a hit man," Cortez said with gallows humor.

"That's not a bad idea," Corrigan agreed.

"You know, I've got a fiend who knows a friend who's in La Familia."

"What's his name? Maybe I'll call him," Corrigan asked as he fantasized about her offer.

"His name is Antonio," smiled Cortez, her red lips parted to reveal pearl white teeth.

"What's his last name?" Corrigan asked as he continued the joke.

"Cortez."

"Is he related to you?"

"I'll never tell," Cortez said with a mischievous grin. She then glanced at her watch. She always had to be some place at the top of the hour during her eight hour shift and today was no exception.

"Sorry about the bad news," said Cortez as she stood to leave. "I've got to get going. I've got a group starting in a few minutes."

"You never shoot the messenger you know that." said Corrigan, "and thanks for bringing the mail."

"No problem, catch you later." She then let herself out and shut the door. However, the sent of her perfume lingered in the room.

When Corrigan reached over and picked up the stack of mail, the exotic bouquet of Cortez's perfume filled his senses. He breathed the fragrance in deeply. "Damn, that's good stuff," he thought. He exhaled slowly and leaned back in his chair. He then shook his head to clear the lingering effects of the perfume and began to sort through the mail.

He automatically made two piles. One pile for the letters of return addresses he recognized and a pile for those he didn't. He could fill a trash dump with all the professional junk mail he got every week. As he sorted through the letters he saw an envelope similar to the one he found on the windshield of his car. The envelope had no return address although the post mark showed that it was mailed within the city. Corrigan opened the envelope and inside there was another typed written invitation. The note gave him the time and location of the next chronic care team meeting. "Looks like I finally got my invitation."

As he studied the note the phone on his desk rang. "Hello, this is Dr. Corrigan." It was County General's emergency room calling him. Corrigan listened intently to the nurse on the other end of the line. "Yes, she's my patient. No, she's never had a panic attack before in her life Sure, tell Dr. Mack, I'll be right down. Bye." Corrigan hung up the phone and headed down to the ER.

County General's twelve bed emergency room is a state of the art facility. The rest of the hospital may go underfunded but never the ER. It's the sparkling jewel in the lackluster crown of County General. Whenever there was a hospital fundraiser, the ER was always trotted out as the showpiece and it worked. The ER was always stocked with the finest life-saving equipment to deal with any medical trauma that came through its doors.

Corrigan entered the busy ER and stopped the first nurse he saw. "What room is Dorothy Madison in?"

The ER nurse looked up at the big white board that had the name, tentative diagnosis and room number of each patient currently in the ER. "She's in room ten."

"Thanks."

As Corrigan stepped inside room ten, he saw his psychiatric patient, Dorothy Madison lying in bed with her eyes closed. The slightly obese fifty-year-old woman with black hair and gray roots was having trouble breathing. She wore an out–of-date pant suit and tennis shoes.

Dr. "Mack," wearing blood speckled blue ER scrubs, entered the room. "Thanks for coming down."

"No problem," said Corrigan. "What's going on?"

"She came in about twenty minutes ago. The guys in the ambulance couldn't find anything grossly wrong." He then quickly rattled off Madison's litany of symptoms. "She presented with shortness of breath, nausea, some dizziness, an accelerated heart rate and some chest discomfort, along with anxiety and a feeling that she was going to die; a classic panic attack if I ever saw one."

"Are you sure?" asked Corrigan knowing Mack's proclivity for dismissing psychiatric patients as hypochondriacs. "She's never had a panic attack while I've been treating her."

"Well, there's always a first time," Mack countered.

"Have you run any tests?"

"No need to," Mack said bluntly. "She's having a panic attack. Nobody's ever died from a panic attack."

"May I talk to her?" Asked Corrigan feeling like he was back in medical school and Mack was talking to him like an intern.

"Of course, that's why you're here. We need the bed. So as soon as you work your magic on her we'll discharge her." Now that Mack had revealed to Corrigan the real reason he'd been called down to the ER, the legend in his own mind felt free to leave. It was punt, pass and kick time.

However, before Mack could make it to the door Corrigan verbally stopped him. With tempered acrimony in his voice Corrigan asked Mack. "So what you're saying is that because she's a psychiatric patient she can't have any medical problems, right?"

Mack choose to ignore Corrigan's question because, Corrigan was now in Mack's domain. "We need the bed," he responded with detached aloofness and abruptly walked out of the room.

Corrigan gritted his teeth and said under his breath, "You pompous asshole." He then turned his attention to Dorothy Madison. He walked over and stood next to her bed. Her eyes were closed and her breathing was still labored. "Mrs. Madison. It's me, Dr. Corrigan."

Madison's eyes slowly opened. She looked up at Corrigan and smiled. "Dr. Corrigan. I'm so glad you're here. I told them you were my doctor."

Corrigan could now see the chain of events. "The bastards," he thought to himself. "As soon as they found out she was my patient they pushed her in here and called me. Not bothering to do any medical work up or anything else. Just another psych patient, heaven forbid she actually had something medically wrong with her." Then with the bedside manner of an old country doctor, Corrigan tenderly asked Dorothy. "How are you feeling?"

"I feel awful. My chest hurts and my arm aches."

"Mrs. Madison, I need to ask you a question. We've known each other for a quite a while now so I want you to answer me honestly, okay?"

Dorothy nodded her head. "Sure."

"Have you ever had a panic attack?"

"Never," she honestly replied. Suddenly her breath became more labored. She groaned in pain.

Concerned, Corrigan swiftly went to the door and as he stepped into the hallway ER Nurse, Pam Kobayashi walked up with a clipboard in her hand. She asked Corrigan with aloof bluntness. "Is she good to go?"

"I don't think so."

"But, Dr. Mack has already signed her discharge orders."

Corrigan took Kobayashi by the arm and led her into Madison's room. "This is more than just a panic attack."

The nurse looked at Madison unconvinced. "I don't know," she said.

Suddenly with both of them watching, Madison went into full cardiac arrest. "Oh, no!" said Kobayashi as she pressed the red button on the wall next to the bed. She then started CPR on the unconscious woman.

"Anything I can do," asked Corrigan.

"Just stay out of the way when the crash cart gets here," Kobayashi ordered as she kept up the CPR.

Seconds later a Code Blue Team rushed into the room. It consisted of Doctor Benjamin Foster, and two additional ER Nurses. The shorter of the two nurses pushed the crash cart up to Madison's bed. The red tool chest on wheels was filled with all the life saving technology needed to pull a patient out of cardiac arrest. All three staff members joined Kobayashi at Madison's bed side. The taller of the two nurses' expertly inserted an I.V. in Madison's right arm. Dr. Foster, the youngest doctor in the ER, grabbed the cardiac paddles from the cart. "Charge to three hundred joules," he ordered.

The shorter ER nurse parroted back, "three hundred."

Dr. Foster placed the paddles on Madison's now exposed chest and shouted, "Clear!" All three nurses held up their hands as they stepped away from the patient.

Madison's body jerked from the electrical shock. The cardiac monitor now hooked up to her still showed a flat line.

Dr. Foster shouted to the ER nurse standing closest to the new I.V. line. "One hundred milligrams lidocaine push."

The ER nurse quickly introduced the medication into the patient's I.V. line.

Dr. Foster then shouted. "Charge to three sixty!"

"Three sixty," the nurse on the defibrillator shouted back. "Charged."

"Clear." He jolted Madison again. This time the cardiac monitor registered a blip and then a sinuous wave appeared.

"She's converted," the taller ER nurse thankfully announced.

"Good," said Dr. Foster with a sign of relief. "Set a dopamine drip, ten mikes per minute."

The excitement of the moment over, the Code Blue Team was able to momentarily relax.

"Good save," Kobayashi told Foster.

"Thanks," he replied. "Okay let's get her up to CCU."

Dr. Foster volunteered to push the crash cart out the door while the two ER nurses prepared Madison for the trip up to CCU. Kobayashi was now going to have to shred Madison's already signed discharge order. She was also going to have to call CCU and tell them they had a new patient coming up.

Corrigan, who had been standing against the wall watched as they wheeled Madison from the room. Her color was back to normal and she was breathing on her own.

As the two ER nurses pushed Madison's gurney out of the room Corrigan followed behind. As he walked out of the room, he spotted Dr. Mack and Dr. Foster standing next to the red crash cart half way down the hall. Corrigan walked down the hall and caught the last half of their conversation.

"She'll be fine," said Dr. Foster confidently.

"Good," replied Dr. Mack. "Does CCU know she's coming?"

"Yes. Nurse Kobayashi has already called them."

"Excellent" the burly Greek replied. "Good job."

Dr. Foster graciously accepted his mentor's praise and then continued pushing the crash cart down the hall.

Corrigan took the opportunity to step up and get into Dr. Mack's face. "How come you didn't run any tests on her?" he demanded.

Mack's eyes narrowed with contempt as he angrily replied. "Do you know how many of your hypochondriacs we see down here every week? Not including those who come in seeking drugs or the malingerers?"

Corrigan was startled by Mack's stinging rebuke. However, he wisely decided to let Mack continue uninterrupted. Even hospital administrators listened when God spoke in the ER. And on this shift Mack was God.

Mack answered his own question as his diatribe continued. "We see one hell of a lot, that's how many. And every one of them takes us away from a patient who really needs help. Don't climb up on your moral high horse and tell me what to do down here."

Corrigan was flabbergasted. All he could muster was a weak. "Sorry."

Fortunately for Corrigan another ER Nurse came running up to Mack and interrupted him. "We need you in trauma six, a G.S.W. just came in. He's bleeding out."

Unable to finish his tirade Mack scowled at Corrigan, "If you'll excuse me. I have real patients to attend to." Mack then abruptly turned his back on Corrigan and ran down the hall with the ER nurse to trauma room six.

Stunned, Corrigan just stood there. He ran his hand through his hair and slowly shook his head. He knew psych patients were treated poorly in emergency rooms but this was the first time it had been so bluntly confirmed. However, after a little soul searching he had to begrudgingly agree with Mack. If it weren't for those damned frequent flyers clogging up the ER, patients like Madison who were truly sick, would get better attention. It was another awful trait of frequent flyers. They had a nasty habit of soiling anyone's nest they landed in. In a funk, Corrigan wondered back to the psych floor. Mack's tirade stayed with him like a bad case of indigestion the rest of the day. When it was time for him to leave, Corrigan was tired and emotionally drained and ready to escape.

When he arrived home, he saw the lights were on inside the house telling him that Diane was still up. Last week had been a particularly rough week for her. She didn't sleep well and she felt big as a house and thought she'd be carrying their baby for the rest of her life. He wondered as he pulled into the garage whether or not he'd be sent back out on a junk food run to satisfy one of Diane's increasingly unusual food cravings.

Someone hiding in the bushes along the side Corrigan's house also saw him pull into the garage. When Corrigan stepped from his car, the silhouette of a man left his concealment and crept toward the front door. When the light from a window briefly splashed across the silhouette, it illuminated the face of George Cobb. He was there for only one reason, to extract revenge. His anger silently smoldered while he was in the state hospital and upon his discharge it exploded red hot. Cobb was armed again and, by any police standards, he would be considered dangerous. After he was sent to the state hospital, the police confiscated the arsenal they found in his home. However, their search failed to find the replica Bowie knife he had taped behind the refrigerator. The big razor sharp knife was now strapped to Cobb's belt.

Since his discharge from the state hospital all Cobb could think about was pay back. "Get in line. Get in line." The sentence ran through Cobb's unstable mind like a broken record and would not give him peace until Corrigan was dead. "Get in line. Get in line. Get in line." Cobb whispered as he briefly fondled the handle of the big Bowie knife. He watched Corrigan make his way to the front porch. "Looks like I'm first in line tonight, asshole."

Just as Corrigan put his house key into the dead blot Cobb jumped him from behind. He quickly put Corrigan in a choke hold. "I've got you now, you bastard." Energized and pumped full of

110

adrenaline, Cobb lifted Corrigan off his feet. "Get in line. You get in line." Again, like so many previous times, there was no medication in Cobb's system to curtail his madness. He stopped taking his Stelazine immediately after he was discharged from the state hospital. He'd show those bastards he didn't need to take any drugs. His mother would have been proud of him. Cobb had deliberately missed his two required post discharge appointments. They would have caught the fact he was running around un-medicated again. Unfortunately, the overworked staff at the outpatient clinic didn't have time to follow up on him and simply put his name in a pending box.

Corrigan immediately used both hands and grabbed the arm that was choking him. He knew if he didn't quickly release the pressure on his carotid artery he'd have less than three minutes before his brain would be starved of oxygen. He'd then pass out and might not wake up again. Corrigan tugged with all his might, but the arm that was choking him wouldn't budge. Cobb had Corrigan in a death grip. Cobb smiled, his plan was working perfectly. As soon as Cobb rendered his tormenter unconscious, he'd remove Corrigan's heart and render it unto Caesar. Cobb was almost euphoric as he continued to strangle the man he despised. However, his exhilaration was cut short by a sharp pain in his left rib cage.

Corrigan had summoned the last of his strength and shoved his left elbow into the rib cage of the man standing behind him. It immediately resulted in a supply of fresh blood reaching his brain. As he felt the man's grip loosen, he jabbed him again and was able to free himself.

Cobb was stunned at the last minute counter attack by Corrigan. He let go of Corrigan's neck and bent over from the pain in his ribs. "You bastard, I'll get you for that," he snarled. Corrigan had upset his plans.

Regaining his senses, Corrigan recognized the man under the glare of the porch light. He also saw that Cobb was reaching for a knife strapped to his belt. It was the biggest knife he had ever seen. Although he had been in a couple of scrapes as a young man he'd never been in a knife fight, much less a one-sided knife fight. When Cobb removed the Bowie knife from its sheath it looked like he'd pulled out a sword. Corrigan knew he had better go on the offensive rather than try to fend off that lethal weapon bare-handed. He quickly landed a round house punch to the side of Cobb's face, the blow staggered him and he dropped the big knife. Corrigan smashed Cobb in the face again. "You son of a bitch!" Corrigan shouted as he felt the warm blood on his knuckles. He continued to angrily punch Cobb in the face. Cobb lashed out, his arms flailing in front of him hoping to hit something solid. Just then the front door opened.

Standing in the door way was Diane. She was wearing red sweat pants and a matching top that had an arrow pointing at her pregnant belly with the words: Under Construction. "What's going on?" she innocently asked before she realized what was playing out in front of her.

Corrigan looked at his wife and shouted, "Call the police!" That was the last thing he remembered. Cobb used the distraction to land a haymaker to Corrigan's jaw sending him spinning unconscious to the ground. Cobb looked at Corrigan's limp body and began to savagely kick him in the ribs. "Take that you bastard!" He kicked Corrigan again and again as he vented his anger on the inert body lying in front of him. He also kicked Corrigan in the head a few times for good measure. "How do you like that asshole? How does it feel to get in line now?" he snarled. His anger momentarily quenched he noticed the front door was still open. A terrified, Diane had forgotten to shut it when she ran to the phone to call the police. Cobb looked down at Corrigan. He wasn't moving. He could cut out his heart later. Right now Cobb had an unexpected bonus fall into his lap. And he damn sure wasn't going let the opportunity go to waste.

Cobb picked up his knife and slowly pushed open the front door. As he entered the house, he held the Bowie knife in his right hand and let the tip of the sharp weapon lead the way as he searched the house for his antagonist's wife. He looked in the living room, nothing. The kitchen was empty as well as Corrigan's office. "She has to be here," Cobb mumbled as he entered the master bedroom. The bedroom was also empty however the door to the bathroom was closed. A sinister smile appeared on Cobb's face. Now he knew where his prey was hiding and he was going to pay her a visit.

Cobb tried the door knob to the bathroom. It was locked only confirming what he suspected. He then forcefully tried the door knob. It didn't budge. "Open the door. I won't hurt you," Cobb said smoothly. He then waited for a response, but none came. "Open the door," he repeated. No response. "Open the damn door!" he shouted as he banged on it with his fist. He stopped and waited for a response, nothing.

"I know you're in there." Again silence. "If you don't open this door I swear to God I'll break it down." Cobb snarled. He then waited to see if his threat worked. It didn't. There was only silence on the other side of the door. Angered, Cobb smashed his shoulder up against the door. The door held but Diane screamed. "So you are in there," Cobb smiled. Confident his search was over Cobb stepped back and kicked the door with his big black military boot. Diane screamed again. Cobb kicked the door so violently the door started to splinter. He could now see Diane through a crack in the door. She was standing in the bathtub pressed up against the wall. "I told you to let me in!" Cobb angrily shouted.

Diane screamed for all she was worth. "Jim, help! Help!" Cobb now stood in the bathroom. Diane saw the huge knife in his hand. "Please don't hurt me," she sobbed. She instinctively wrapped her arms around her pregnant belly. Cobb advanced toward her. "Please don't hurt my baby. Please God, no!"

Corrigan was still lying on the ground by the open front door, his brain trying to crawl out of the murky blackness induced by Cobb's beating. As the neurons in his cortex reintroduced consciousness to his body a strident noise impinged upon his ears. It was high-pitched and sounded vaguely familiar. When he tried to identify the sound, his throbbing head hurt even more. Where was that familiar sound coming from? As he slowly regained his senses, the numbness that had mercifully engulfed his body while he was unconscious was replaced by excruciating pain. His rib cage and upper torso felt like it he had gone fifteen rounds with a heavyweight boxer. He also found it hard to breathe and felt warm blood in his mouth, both not good signs. There was that high pitched wail again. This time it was louder and closer.

San Salina police officer, Odell Washington's patrol car skidded to a stop in front of Corrigan's home, its siren still wailing. Washington, an African-American in his mid-thirties and a former local high school running back of some notoriety turned off the siren, but left the red and blue lights flashing as he jumped out of his police cruiser. He was the first officer to respond to the frantic 911 call of a home invasion at the Mockingbird address. As

Washington approached the front door with his nine millimeter Glock drawn, he saw Corrigan lying on the ground. He moved swiftly to Corrigan's side while keeping a vigilant eye out for any suspects still at the scene. He reached down and checked Corrigan's neck for a pulse. Corrigan moaned.

"That answers that question," Washington said softly to himself. He then reached for the microphone on his epaulet. He spoke quietly and succinctly into the radio. "This is Twenty-One, Thirteen. I need an ambulance at the break in on Mockingbird."

"Roger, Twenty-One Thirteen." The female dispatcher acknowledged.

Washington didn't know if the man lying in front of him was able to hear him or not but he had to ask. So he leaned down and spoke softly in Corrigan's ear. "Is there anyone else in the house?" No response.

"An ambulance is on its way," the dispatcher responded over the radio.

"Twenty-One Thirteen," Washington quickly replied and clipped the microphone back onto his epaulet.

"Is there anyone else in the house?" Washington asked the now semiconscious Corrigan again. Corrigan just moaned. "Okay. Just sit tight," said Washington. "An ambulance is on the way." The six year veteran of the force stood and scanned the entrance to the house. He then slowly entered the quiet house, his senses alert and his gun at the ready.

Although he couldn't respond to Washington's question, the police officer's voice did pierce the fog of Corrigan's temporary amnesia. The question brought memory circuits on line of the events that preceded the darkness that had enveloped him. As the scenes played out in his head, they became clearer. Then a feeling of urgency and dread started to well up inside him. Suddenly like a jolt of electricity, he remembered the last thing he saw was Diane standing in the door way, she looked scared. "I've got to help Diane," was the first sentence that formed in Corrigan's half-conscious brain.

Racked with pain and barely able to remember his own name, Corrigan forced his body to move. He had to get to Diane. He cursed his body for not responding fast enough. "Got to get to Diane," became his mantra as he struggled to stand. When he was finally able to stand upright he slowly put one foot in front of the other, an effort that felt like he was scaling the last leg of Mt. Everest. As he entered the house he called out in a raspy, barely audible voice. "Diane." Corrigan didn't hear the second police officer enter the house.

Police Sergeant, Alan Kubek, a giant of a man with short black hair and hazel eyes, could tell the man in front of him was dazed and hurt just from the way he walked. "Sir, are you all right?" asked Kubek as he approached Corrigan from behind. Corrigan turned and silently looked at the sergeant. "Yep, you're hurt all right," Kubek said to himself as he took stock of the injured man.

Corrigan focused his eyes and recognized the man was a police officer. "My wife, where's my wife?" Corrigan asked weakly.

"I don't know," Kubek answered honestly.

Washington shouted from the master bath room. "Is that you Kubek?"

"Yeah," he replied.

"We're going to need another ambulance," shouted Washington.

"Did you clear the house?" Kubek yelled back.

"Yes. Whoever, did this is long gone," Washington responded.

Corrigan turned his head in the direction of Washington's voice and moaned, "Diane." Corrigan then summoned up the last of his strength, ignored the pain shooting through his body and awkwardly made his way down the hall to the master bedroom. When he finally reached the entrance he leaned against the door jam to hold himself up. He looked in disbelief at the entrance to the master bathroom. The door was smashed in and the lock around the door jamb was splintered.

Officer Washington came out of the bath room. He didn't expect to see Corrigan standing there. "What are you doing here? Man, you need to sit down until the ambulance gets here."

"Where's my wife?" Corrigan asked him. Before Washington could come up with a neutral response, Corrigan inched his way toward the bathroom.

Washington immediately stepped in front of Corrigan. "I don't think you should go in there."

Corrigan, his face bloody and swollen, looked directly into Washington's eyes and snarled. "Get the hell out of my way."

"The paramedics are here," yelled Sergeant Kubek from the living room.

"Send them back here. And hurry!" Washington shouted. He then turned his attention back to Corrigan. "Look, I know how you feel."

"Like hell you do," said Corrigan. He tried to push Washington out of the way, but he didn't have the strength.

Washington effortlessly deflected Corrigan's efforts. "Just hold on, man. The paramedics are here."

117

A male and female paramedic team walked briskly down the hallway and entered the bedroom where the distraught husband and waiting police officer were standing. The paramedics carried red plastic boxes containing the lifesaving equipment used in their profession. The female paramedic, a short stocky woman in her late thirties, arrived first and asked Washington. "What have you got?"

"An injured female in the bath tub," Washington quickly replied.

The male paramedic, a tall man with curly brown hair, glanced at Corrigan. "What about him?"

Corrigan snapped at the paramedic. "Get in there and help my wife, damn it!"

"Okay, relax," the paramedic replied.

The female paramedic entered the bath room first. The male paramedic pushed the broken door out of the way as he followed his partner inside. "Damn," he said under his breath as he looked at the damage to the door. "Whoever did this must have been really pissed."

It then became agonizingly quiet in the bathroom. Except for the movement of the paramedics, Corrigan couldn't tell what was happening. After what seemed like an eternity, Corrigan finally summoned up the nerve to ask the question he dreaded. "Is my wife alive?"

"She's alive," the female paramedic's voice echoed from inside the bathroom. "She's hurt. But she's alive."

A flood of relief swept over Corrigan. "Thank God," he whispered. He then quickly asked. "What about the baby?"

"How far along is your wife?" asked the female paramedic.

"The last trimester," said Corrigan. "She's due any time."

"The baby's alive and kicking. I'm no obstetrician but you might be a father before morning."

"Thank you God. Thank you," Corrigan said softly as he looked upward with tears filling his swollen eyes.

The male paramedic walked out of the bath room. As he passed in front of Washington he said to him. "I'm going to get the gurney."

"If you see any other paramedics out there," said Washington. "Send them back here, will you? I don't know how much longer this guy's going to be able to keep standing."

The paramedic nodded his head and quickly made his way down the hall.

Knowing that the two most important things in his life were safe, Corrigan's brain told the rest of his body it could finally see to its own needs. The pure force of will that had been sustaining him was no longer needed. Diane and the baby were alive and in good hands. His energy depleted, Corrigan relinquished control of his legs and slowly slid down the wall that had been supporting him and passed out.

# CHAPTER 12

When he opened his eyes again, Corrigan found himself lying in a hospital bed. When his vision cleared he recognized his surroundings. He was on a medical floor at County General. He reached for the nurse's call button and pressed it. The movement was painful. His body felt like it had been used as a punching bag. Nurse Jack Spooner, a pleasant man in his mid-thirties with a shiny shaved head, entered Corrigan's room. He walked over and stood next to Corrigan.

"How we doing this morning, Dr. Corrigan?" asked Spooner with a cheerful smile.

"Where's my wife?" was the priority question Corrigan wanted answered.

"She's on the OB/GYN floor," he replied. "Dr. Potter wants to keep her there until she delivers just as a precaution."

"Is she all right?"

"She got pretty banged up. From what I heard, she's doing fine. She's a real fighter."

Corrigan breathed a sigh of relief. "What about the baby?"

"You should be a father any day now," Spooner replied with a smile on his face.

"Thank God," Corrigan audibly sighed. "How long have I been here?"

"Two days. You were in and out most of the time."

"Jeez," said Corrigan as he slowly continued to orientate himself.

"You had a pretty bad concussion," said Spooner.

"When can I see my wife?" asked Corrigan.

"You'll have to ask Dr. Amati. He's your attending."

"Where is he?"

"He should be here shortly. He's making rounds," Spooner answered professionally.

"Tell him I'd like to see him right now," Corrigan demanded on the verge of being rude. Seeing Spooner wince, Corrigan apologized. "Sorry."

"That's all right. I understand," said Spooner.

Corrigan then politely asked. "Could you ask Dr. Amati as a professional courtesy to stop by and see me as soon as he can?"

"Sure," Spooner quickly replied. "He's just down the hall. I'll go ask him."

"Thanks."

"Can I get you anything before I leave?"

"Maybe the number of the truck that hit me," Corrigan painfully joked.

Spooner smiled and left the room in search of Dr. Amati.

A few minutes later Dr. Amati walked into Corrigan's hospital room. The short trim man in his late forties with thinning black hair made his way over to Corrigan's bed with a medical chart in his hand.

"Nurse Spooner said you wanted to see me."

"Yes. I'd like to see my wife. She's on the OB/GYN floor."

"I know, but first things first." Colleague or not, Amati wasn't going to take any chances. His personal patient risk protocol had served him well over the years and kept him out of a lot of litigation and he wasn't going to abandon it now. "How are you feeling this morning?" Dr. Amati began.

"My ribs are sore. My head aches. But other than that I feel fine," Corrigan replied with a touch of humor, hopping it would make Amati think he was feeling better than he actually did so he could reach his goal of seeing Diane.

"Any blurred vision?" asked Amati.

"No," replied Corrigan.

"Any trouble breathing?"

Of course he had a little trouble breathing. He'd been kicked in the ribs for Pete sake. But he wasn't about to let Amati know. "Some," Corrigan said nonchalantly.

Amati flipped trough Corrigan's medical chart. He then asked. "How are the pain medications working?"

"They seem to be doing okay."

"Do you want me to increase the dosage?"

"No. I'm good." Corrigan lied. He didn't want to feel any groggier than he already did.

"Any dizziness?" asked Amati.

"No," Although the room did spin for a little while when he first woke up. But he told himself that was to be expected.

"Have you tried to stand?"

"Dr. Amati, I'd love to go down your check list with you. But I can tell you as a fellow physician that my condition is more than stable. I feel sore, which is normal for someone who was beaten to a pulp. Internally everything seems to be working okay."

"I'm just trying," was all that Amati could say before Corrigan started up again.

"Unless I'm pissing blood or have an embolism somewhere," Corrigan continued firmly. "I am going to see my wife, whether or not I get your clearance."

Taken back my Corrigan's ultimatum, Amati quickly scanned Corrigan's medial chart. "Let's see. According to the X-Rays you must have some pretty strong ribs because you've only got a hair line fracture on one rib and some tearing between the third and fourth intercostals."

Amati flipped to the next page in the chart. "According to your MRI you must have a pretty thick skull too. You were given a clean bill of health. There were no signs of any gross anatomical or structural changes in the brain. However, you did have a concussion, just for the record."

"Which is to be expected," Corrigan interjected. "What about my blood work?"

Amati flipped through the pages of the medical chart until he found the results of the latest blood screen. "Hmm," was his first reaction as he studied the blood work, "Looks like everything is within normal limits and your kidneys seem to be working just fine? However, your cholesterol is a little high. You might think about taking something for it."

"So what you're saying is that except for eating too much red meat, I'm fine," Corrigan replied. He had Amati where he wanted him.

"After what happened to you, I'd say yes," Amati, thoughtfully responded.

"Good," said Corrigan as he tried to minimize the pain as he sat up in bed. Like an attorney that already knew the answer to his next question, Corrigan asked. "Then there's no reason why I can't see my wife, is there?"

"No," said Amati. "You are one lucky man, Dr. Corrigan. You took a beating that would have put many a man out of action for a long time."

"I guess you can chalk it up to good clean living," Corrigan smiled.

"Do you have any idea who did this to you?" asked Amati.

"No," Corrigan honestly replied. Temporary amnesia was not uncommon after having such a terrible brain trauma. Hopefully, as he got better, he'd able to piece together the events that took place that night, but then again he may never remember. God was not the only one who worked in mysterious ways, so did the human brain. It had its own timetable for working things out.

Despite Corrigan's brave front, Amati knew Corrigan was stretching the truth and was still in a lot of pain. But he also didn't want to stop him from seeing his wife. "I'll tell you what. So the nurses won't get on your case, I'm going to write in your chart that you're able to ambulate. So whatever you do or wherever you go after that is strictly up to you."

"Thanks," Corrigan gratefully replied.

"Well, I've got other patients to see," said Amati as he closed Corrigan's medical chart and started towards the door. When he reached the door he turned and looked at Corrigan and said with unusual candor for a physician. "I hope the son of bitch who did this puts up a fight when they try to arrest him. That way they can skip the ER and take him directly to the morgue."

"I couldn't agree with you more," Corrigan also bluntly replied. "I just wish I could be there when they find him."

Amati nodded his head and left the room.

A few minutes later nurse Spooner walked into Corrigan's room with one of the hospital's venerable old black wheelchairs. "I thought you might need this since Dr. Amati said you can get out of bed now. You really must have really fooled him."

"Thanks. But, I don't think I really did," said Corrigan with a wry smile.

Spooner rolled the well-worn wheelchair up to Corrigan's bedside and stopped. "Here you go. Hop in. I'll take you up to see your wife." Corrigan got in the wheelchair and Spooner pushed him into the hallway and down to the elevators.

The door to Diane's room was closed when they arrived. As is the custom in all hospitals, Spooner knocked on the door before he entered. Corrigan anxiously waited in his wheelchair, as Spooner entered the room.

Diane was in bed, her eyes closed with an I.V. hooked up to her arm. She had bruises on her arms where Cobb grabbed her and her left eye still looked pretty nasty even though its changing colors indicated it was really getting better. Diane opened her eyes and was momentarily startled when she saw Spooner.

"Hi, I'm Nurse Spooner. I've got someone here to see you."

Before Diane could respond, Spooner stepped outside and wheeled Corrigan into the room. Diane's face lit up when she saw her husband. However, it was quickly followed by a look of shock when she saw him in a wheelchair. Tears started to flow down her checks, "Oh, Jim."

When Corrigan saw his wife, a surge of elation swept over him. However, his joy was tempered as he drew closer and he saw what Cobb did to his beautiful wife. An anger as intense as he ever felt before welled up inside him. However, he kept it in check. This was neither the time nor the place for it to surface. Instead he reached out and softly touched Diane's face and tried to stop the tears running down her cheeks with his finger. As he did he broke down and cried, "Oh, Diane."

Spooner decided it was time to leave. "I'll leave you two alone." He then quietly walked out of the room and shut the door.

Diane took her husband's hand and kissed it. She then gazed tenderly into his soft blue eyes. With tears running down both their cheeks they said at the same time. "I love you."

Corrigan kissed Diane's hand. "I'm so glad you're all right."

The two then hugged the best they could as she leaned down from her hospital bed and he reached up from his wheelchair. It was important for them to reestablish physical contact. As they continued to hold each other, their bodies silently reestablished that intimate bond only known to those who are deeply in love. When Corrigan's tears subsided he looked at his wife. "Boy, don't we make a fine pair?"

Diane smiled as she tried to dry her eyes with her fingers. "Boy, I'm glad I'm not wearing mascara." She took some tissues from the box on the bed stand and patted her eyes.

"The baby's fine," Diane said as she anticipated her husband's next question. She softly placed her right hand on top of her pregnant stomach. "They want me to have complete bed rest just as a precaution until she's born."

"I agree," smiled Corrigan as he softly placed his hand on top of hers. "You two have been through enough."

Their daughter kicked. "Did you feel that?" He asked.

"Of course I did," Diane grinned.

"God, I'm so glad you two are all right."

Diane laid back on her propped up hospital pillows and finished wiping the last of her tears.

Corrigan made himself as comfortable as possible in his wheelchair and then reached out and rested his hand on top of Diane's arm. He wanted to maintain physical contact with her. It felt good to feel her warm presence next to his skin. There was something about the closeness of skin against skin. It was the most intimate form of communication.

As he sat silently touching his injured wife's arm, a new emotion seeped into his psyche: guilt. He was now beginning to feel guilty for not being able to protect his wife and child. His wife and child were in the hospital because of him. No matter how he tried to rationalize it the guilt still won out. In his mind he had failed as a husband and as a man. He silently promised that hell would freeze over before he would let anything like this ever happen to his wife and daughter again.

"Have they caught the person who did it?" Corrigan asked softly.

"I don't know. I talked with the police after they brought me to the hospital. But I haven't heard anything from them since. I also spoke to a detective. He gave me his card. It's in the drawer."

"I hope they catch the S.O.B. who did it," said Corrigan.

"I'm sure they will," said Diane. She knew she'd sleep better when they did. "Jim," Diane asked.

"Yes."

"Do you think the man who did this could have been one of your patients?"

"I don't know," he honestly replied. Suddenly a hepatic (touch) memory, that should have been extinguished long ago, suddenly flickered inside Corrigan's brain. "I have no memory of what happened that night," he confessed to Diane.

Diane reached out and softly touched her husband's head. It was her way of saying it was all right. "I gave the police a description of the man from what I could remember."

"What did he look like?"

Diane described an average man of above average height and build with brown hair and brown eyes, a description that could literally fit thousands of men. It also wasn't much for the police to go on.

After she finished describing the man, another hepatic memory flickered to life in Corrigan's post concussive brain. This one linked itself with another memory buried in a nearby neural circuit.

"Did he say anything?" Corrigan asked.

"He did say one thing I didn't understand," Diane replied as her arms blossomed with goose bumps as she remembered that horrible night. "When he broke into the bathroom and was coming at me, he kept said something like, "I won't wait in line or get in line, something about a line." She briefly shuddered at the memory. "God, I hope they catch him."

An iconic (visual) memory awakened in Corrigan's occipital lobe. This one connected itself to a series of other iconic memories that were slowly awakening and joining forces to create a memory strand. They were also linking up with new hepatic memories as they sprung to life. Together both types of memories were slowly forming the initial structure of a complete memory. When they finished combining their information, they would slowly transfer it to Corrigan's short term memory bank where it would be stored until it was ready to up link to his long term memory.

Diane watched as her husband's face took on a distant look as if trying to remember something. "Are you all right?" She asked.

"Uh, yeah," replied Corrigan as Diane broke into his thoughts. "I thought I remembered something." More short term memory circuits were coming on line and impinging on his long term memory circuits.

"Jim."

"What?" Corrigan asked.

"I just remembered something. He had a brown spot on his left cheek, like that actor on TV who lived on a mountain back during the depression with his family. It was round and about the same size."

"Where have I seen one of those before?" Corrigan thought. His capacity to remember information about past patients was like having a large collection of old cassette tapes in his head. Once a key word or characteristic of a patient was remembered it activated the rest of the tape. He could remember in stunningly detail everything about a patient down to the smallest minutia. So Corrigan began to rummage through his internal tape collection to see if he could find a match for a man with a brown spot on his cheek. A he concentrated the hepatic and iconic memories of that horrible night finally came together in his short term memory and made the leap to his long term memory. The leap brought enough information for Corrigan to finally recall the first fuzzy pieces of that awful event. As the events of that night came into focus, he saw the snarling face of George Cobb. "Oh, my God," he said out loud.

This time Diane's asked with apprehension in her voice "What's the matter?"

"I know who it was," he replied, between clinched teeth. "Was it one of your patients?" she asked.

Corrigan silently nodded his head.

Then the memory of Cobb beating him senseless exploded into his consciousness, his face turned red with anger. He could feel the rage swelling inside him.

Diane responded by crying. Corrigan started to feel light headed. Then everything turned gray and he passed out.

# CHAPTER 13

When Corrigan woke up, he was back in his hospital bed with Dr. Amati standing over him.

"What happened?" asked a baffled Corrigan.

"You passed out. Your blood pressure was off the charts. You're still recovering from a concussion, remember?"

"Sorry," Corrigan replied as the events leading up to his passing out came back into focus. "I guess I was pretty pissed off."

"You need to be careful. You mustn't let your anger get the better of you at least not for a while, anyway. Anger and high blood pressure are a bad combination. Your brain needs time to heal."

"I'll remember that," Corrigan said repentantly.

"I kind of figured you weren't telling me the whole truth about your condition anyway. Do both of us a favor and take it easy, okay?"

Corrigan smiled and embarrassingly nodded his head.

"Your wife told me that you remembered who attacked you."

"Yes."

"Good. Cause I've got a couple of detectives waiting outside who'd like to talk to you."

"And I'd like to talk to them."

"I thought you might say that," Amati smiled.

"Send them in," Corrigan eagerly replied. "If you think I'm up to it, doctor," he added with professional deference.

Amati accepted the compliment with a smile. "I don't see why not." He then left the room.

Detective Jack Norwell, late thirties, short black hair and hazel eyes, a two day a pack smoker and former jock whose once athletic body had turned spongy, walked into the room. His partner, Detective Wanda Joiner, a tall chocolate skin African-American, in her late twenties, with a short trim haircut who had the distinction of being San Salina Police Department's first female minority hire followed Norwell into the room.

"I'm Detective Jack Norwell," the senior detective advised Corrigan as he walked up and stood next to the bed. As Norwell flashed his badge Corrigan could smell the odor of stale cigarette smoke. "And this is Detective Joiner."

Joiner smiled politely and nodded her head.

Corrigan cordially replied to both of them, "How do you do?"

"We spoke to your wife when she first came in," Norwell began. "And she gave us a description of the guy who attacked both of you. But, to be honest with you, it could have fit a lot of guys. When she called us and told us you remembered who attacked, you we came right down."

"I'm glad you're here."

"Who was it?" asked Norwell, not wanting to waste any time getting an APB out on the man.

"It was George Cobb," Corrigan replied quickly and firmly.

"You're absolutely sure," asked Norwell knowing Corrigan had a suffered a concussion and no doubt some memory loss as a result. The last thing Norwell needed was to build a case, take it to court and then have it tossed out because the victim's memory was faulty.

"Yes. I'm absolutely sure."

"Are you're willing to testify to that in court?" Norwell asked just to make sure.

"Yes."

"Good," smiled Norwell. Now that they knew who the perpetrator was all they had to do now was pick him up. And in no time at all this case would be closed.

"Isn't he the guy that barricaded himself in his house last month and shot at the police?" asked Joiner.

"The same," Corrigan replied matter-of-factually.

"I thought they sent him to the state hospital," Norwell wondered out loud.

"They did. But apparently he got better so they discharged him," Corrigan responded, his voice dripping with sarcasm.

"What can you tell us about Cobb?" asked Norwell.

"I can't tell you much because of Federal confidentiality laws. I am a doctor and he's still a patient. Ironic isn't it?"

"Then what can you tell us?" pressed Norwell.

"As you've probably already guessed, he's a paranoid schizophrenic. And he stops taking his medication the first chance he gets. And that's when he becomes dangerous."

"Why would he stop taking his medication?" Joiner asked.

"Because when he feels better, he doesn't think he needs it anymore," Corrigan replied.

"That's stupid," said Joiner.

"Tell me about it," Corrigan concurred.

"Anything else you can tell us?" Norwell asked.

"That's about all I can tell you without getting into trouble," Corrigan said with more than a hint of frustration.

"Well, at least we know where he lives. We can stake out his place and catch him there."

"I don't think he'll go back to his house," said Corrigan.

"Why not?" asked Norwell.

"He maybe crazy but he's not stupid. He's probably hole up some place where he feels safe. My guess is the only way you're going to find him is when his delusions become so overpowering that he acts on them."

"Meaning?" asked Joiner.

"Meaning, he'll do something to attract the attention of the police, when he's paranoid enough. Unfortunately it will also be when he's at his most dangerous."

"Damn," said Norwell, knowing his case just got a little more complicated. "Then I guess we better catch him before that happens."

"I hope you do," Corrigan honestly replied.

"Are you sure there's nothing else you can tell us about him?" Norwell prodded. He was well aware of the sacredness of the patient-doctor privilege, but this was the first time he'd ever saw an honest to God practitioner of it.

"I promise that whatever you tell me will not leave this room," Norwell added hoping to encourage Corrigan to divulge anything else that might help him catch Cobb.

"Sorry. I wish I could," Corrigan regretfully replied.

"That's all right," said Norwell. "At least we know who we're looking for now. That's more than we had when we came in."

"I hope you catch the son of a bitch and throw away the key," Corrigan said coldly, his face hardening

"We'll catch him. Don't worry," Joiner confidently replied.

"Thank you for your help, Dr. Corrigan," said Norwell as he automatically reached for the pack of cigarettes in his shirt pocket. He always lit up a cigarette after an interview. His body could only go so long without nicotine. Then remembered he was in a hospital and stopped. "Damn," he thought. Old habits die hard.

"Let me know when you catch him," Corrigan requested of both detectives as they departed.

"You'll be the first to know," replied Norwell.

"Thanks."

Their interview at an end, both Joiner and Norwell made their way out of the room.

Corrigan was tired. It had been a long day. He closed his eyes and would sleep better knowing the police were looking Cobb.

When Corrigan woke the next morning, he swung his feet out of bed and set them on the floor. He carefully made his way to the bathroom. When he finished, he walked out and pushed the nurse page button.

In a couple of minutes Nurse Spooner walked in. "What can I do for you, Dr. Corrigan?"

"You can get Dr. Amati," Corrigan said evenly. "I think I'm ready to be discharged."

"I'll go get him. He's just down the hall." Spooner then left the room.

After running through his patented patient discharge protocol and Corrigan, this time, giving him truthful answers, Amati agreed his patient could be discharged. He advised Corrigan to take it easy for a few days and call him if he had any problems. Other than that, he was free to leave.

"Thanks, Dr. Amati for everything," said Corrigan as he extended his hand and the two men shook.

"You're welcome," Amati graciously replied.

"Well, I better get dressed and get going," Corrigan hinted openly to Dr. Amati. He didn't want Amati to change his mind. But more importantly he still had a score to settle with someone before he left the hospital.

Dr. Amati took the hint, said good-bye, left the room and continued his rounds.

Corrigan was focused on one thing now. He was going to kick some psychiatric director's butt. He showered, shaved and got dressed as quickly as he could. When he finished, he closed the door to his hospital room for the last time and started towards the elevators. Nothing was going to stop him from having a little one-on-one time with Dr. Lang.

"This should never have happened. Damn it!" Corrigan shouted as he began his verbal assault on Lang.

Lang sat behind his fortress-like desk trying not to look uncomfortable as Corrigan verbally assaulted him from only a few feet away. His decision about Cobb had come back to haunt him. That didn't bother him as much as the unjustified tongue-lashing he was receiving from a subordinate.

"Cobb should have gone to jail," Corrigan continued, each word filled with bitter resentment. His Irish temper was up and he was fighting mad.

Lang should have known better and sat patiently behind his desk and let Corrigan's diatribe run its course. However, Lang wasn't known for his people skills. Corrigan was a subordinate and it galled him to think he could walk into his office and talk to him like that.

"We don't have a crystal ball, Dr. Corrigan," Lang interrupted. "We cannot predict human behavior."

"Hell, I know that. But, good God almighty, what does it take to keep someone like Cobb off the streets?"

"The police will catch him," said Lang hoping to assuage Corrigan's anger.

"And when they catch him. Then what?"

"We then let the system do its job," Lang offered with an edge of impatience creeping into his voice.

"Yeah right, just like last time," Corrigan spat sarcastically.

"It may not be a perfect system, but it's the only one we have," said Lang as he arrogantly threw out the effete platitude.

"Well, the system sucks as far as I'm concerned," Corrigan angrily fired back.

"I'm sorry you feel that way."

"You are? Hell. I didn't know you could feel anything," Corrigan hissed venomously.

Lang was stung by Corrigan's insult; however he tried to remain calm. "I will overlook that last outburst, Dr. Corrigan, because I know you're upset."

"Hey, if the shoe fits," Corrigan pushed.

"Don't push me."

"You're nothing more than a bureaucratic pain in the ass," Corrigan said, his voice dripping with contempt. "A paper-pushing bureaucrat. When was the last time you even saw a patient?"

"Dr. Corrigan, that will be enough out of you," ordered Lang as he raised his voice.

"What's the matter? The truth hurt?" Corrigan replied.

Corrigan had reached his breaking point. His life, the life of his wife and his unborn daughter had been put in jeopardy by the pompous ass sitting in front of him.

"Dr. Corrigan, please, I will not tolerate such insolence."

"Well, that's too damn bad," Corrigan fired back.

"Then Dr. Corrigan you leave me no choice."

"What are you going to do? Fire me?" challenged Corrigan.

"No," Lang calmly replied. "I'm going to place you on paid administrative leave until you've had time to put this terrible incident behind you. It's obvious that you need to regain your composure and professional objectivity before you can work with psychiatric patients again."

"My objectivity," Corrigan shot back. "Screw you!"

Lang stood and shouted. "That's enough, Dr. Corrigan!"

Corrigan eyes narrowed with contempt.

"Get out of my office!" Lang screamed as he pointed to the door.

Corrigan held his ground and gave Lang an acerbic stare.

"How dare this subordinate challenge my authority," thought Lang. Yet, Corrigan stood there and glared at him with the veins in his neck standing out in livid ridges.

Lang picked up the phone and punched in a number. "Security, yes, this is Dr. Lang."

"You bastard," said Corrigan through clenched teeth.

Lang looked at Corrigan and he thought he noticed a slight change in Corrigan's facial expression. He waited before he spoke again.

Corrigan could feel himself starting to get light-headed. He could no longer hold his withering stare. Lang had raised both his ire and his blood pressure a bad combination, especially with the effects of a concussion still swirling around in his head. He didn't want to pass out in front of Lang. "Calm down," he admonished himself. The last thing he wanted to do was make a spectacle of himself and be taken out of Lang's office on a gurney. He started to feel faint and his field of vision began to narrow. Then he remembered an old axiom: Better to retreat now and live to fight another day.

"I've got no choice," he thought. "I've got to get out of here before the room starts spinning." On slightly rubbery legs, Corrigan turned to leave.

"Never mind, that's all right. Everything's fine," a relieved and almost cheerful, Lang said to the security guard on the other end of the line as he saw Corrigan retreating. "Sorry to bother you. Goodbye." Corrigan reached the door, as Lang hung up the phone.

"Be sure to stop by Human Resources on your way out. I'm sure they'll have some papers for you to sign," Lang said casually as Corrigan reached for the door knob.

Corrigan stopped. He thought about saying something, spiteful but instead he opened the door. As he walked out with his back turned, he didn't see the grin appear on Lang's face.

"I'll call them and let them know you're coming," Lang added almost too cheerfully.

"You asshole," Corrigan said under his breath as he left, and shut the door behind him.

Corrigan's anger slowly drained away as he made his way back to his office. Fortunately, he didn't meet any colleagues along the way. When he finally sat down behind his desk, his blood pressure was back to normal. Unsure of how long he would be exiled, he went through his desk and placed some personal things in a seldom-used briefcase. When he opened the middle desk drawer, he saw the invitation from the chronic care team. He picked it up and studied it for a moment. He then looked at the calendar on his desk. "Hmm, tomorrow night," he thought to himself. "Looks like I'll have plenty of time to make it now." He tossed the invitation into the briefcase, closed it and left.

# CHAPTER 14

As Corrigan parked in the driveway of the two-story mansion, he noticed only the lights on were on the first floor of the stately residence. However, their warm glow even behind closed curtains was inviting, especially on a cool crisp evening like tonight. Corrigan noticed his car was the only one in the driveway. He looked at his invitation again to reassure himself. "I guess this is the right place." Satisfied he was at the correct address, he stuffed the invitation into the inside pocket of his Navy blue blazer, adjusted his tie and got out of the car. He walked up to the front door and rang the bell.

The door opened and Dr. Ozawa greeted him with a friendly smile. "I'm so glad you could make it. I was so sorry to hear about what happened to you and your wife. I trust she and the baby are okay?"

"Yes. They're both doing fine, thank you. Although Diane will have to stay in the hospital until after our daughter is born just as a precaution."

"Sounds prudent, I'm glad they are both doing well," Ozawa sincerely replied. He then stepped back and invited Corrigan in. "Please come in."

Corrigan walked into the mansion's elegant foyer. It had marble flooring, a magnificent white spiraled staircase, patterned wallpaper and oil paintings hung around the room. The whole place shouted opulence.

Ozawa shut the door. "We meet in the study. It's this way."

Corrigan followed Ozawa as he led him through a luxurious living room and down a sumptuously carpeted hallway. They stopped in front of a pair of solid oak doors.

"Whose place is this?" asked Corrigan.

"You'll find out in due time," replied Ozawa as he opened the door to the study.

When Corrigan entered the room, he was immediately struck by how plush, yet cozy, the room felt. It had two floor-to-ceiling bookcases filled with an assortment of books. In the center of the room sat a mahogany conference table surrounded by six black comfortable high-back, swivel leather chairs. A long Tiffany style lamp shade filled with soft florescent neon lights was suspended down the center of the table. It reminded Corrigan of the kind found in pool halls. The neon provided the only light in the room. Corrigan noticed all the curtains in the room were tightly drawn. Already seated around the conference table were two men and two women. Each was wearing business attire, coats and ties for the men and professional pantsuits for the women.

"Please have a seat," invited Ozawa as he pointed to the empty chair next to the man seated at the head of the table. Corrigan sat down and Ozawa took the seat opposite him.

Dr. John Zilker, mid-fifties, a friendly but aloof man, with a receding hairline, double chin, and green eyes was the first to speak. As the director and founder of the Chronic Care Team, Zilker always sat at the head of the table. "Thank you for coming, Dr. Corrigan. I think I can speak for all of us when I say we we're terribly sorry to hear about what happened to you and your wife."

"Thank you. I appreciate your concern," replied Corrigan as he graciously acknowledged the kind words.

141

Zilker then got down to business. "I think the first order of business should be introductions," said Zilker. He went around the room starting with the comely woman in her early forties seated next to Ozawa. "This is Doctor Anne Gatway."

Dr. Gatway nodded her head at Corrigan, "Doctor."

Zilker then pointed to a distinguished looking Hindu man in his late thirties. "This is Doctor V. J. Marapudi."

Marapudi smiled at Corrigan, "Doctor."

Zilker then introduced the next woman on the team. Doctor Virginia Blair, a tough looking, no-nonsense woman in her early 50s, wearing black horn-rimmed glasses. "This is Doctor Virginia Blair."

Blair just nodded her head.

"You've already met Dr. Ozawa and I'm Doctor John Zilker."

"The John Zilker of Multi-Group Managed Care?" asked Corrigan.

"The same," smiled Zilker, sounding proud of the name recognition but not wanting to sound too vain. "I'm sure you have a lot of questions. Let me see if I can answer a few of them before we get started, if that's all right with you?"

"Yes please," said Corrigan as he nodded his head approvingly.

Zilker leaned back in his chair and got comfortable. "Doctor Ozawa has already told you that we are a group of psychiatrists who deal exclusively with chronically ill mental patients."

"Yes," Corrigan replied affirmatively.

"We deal with the one third who will never get better," Zilker continued. "About a year ago, the four leading psychiatric managed care companies in the United States got together and secretly formed the chronic care team you see in front of you. We were created for the sole purpose of reducing the amount of money spent by our respective managed care companies on frequent flyers."

"A noble undertaking, I'm sure," Corrigan interjected.

Zilker smiled and continued. "Indeed. Patients who are referred to us have to meet three criteria." He counted off the necessary criteria using his fingers for emphasis. "First they must have had multiple hospital admissions. Second, at least a half a million dollars or more spent on them by their managed care company. And third, they must show no signs of improvement."

"Sounds like you do get the dregs of the DSM-VI," said Corrigan.

"We deal with a very unique population to be sure," Zilker replied.

"Statistically, the patients sent to us are the ones who have cost our companies the most money," added Ozawa.

"What's your success rate?" Corrigan inquired.

"I can honestly say that not one patient referred to this panel has ever been readmitted to a psychiatric hospital," Zilker said proudly.

"Damn. You must have one hell of a magic wand," an astonished Corrigan replied. He had never heard, seen or read of any program having such a high success rate. These people must truly be miracle workers.

"That we do," Zilker replied as he hid a sinister smile. "That we do."

"What's your secret?" Corrigan naturally asked.

"May I ask you a question first?" Zilker inquired.

"Sure," said Corrigan, not knowing he was being lead down a path he would soon regret.

"Knowing our criteria, do you know of any patients who would benefit from a referral to our panel?"

"Several," Corrigan replied enthusiastically.

"How about those you think need to be punished rather than coddled with more psychiatric care?"

The question caught Corrigan off guard and it made him a little uneasy. "Punished rather than coddled? I'm not quite sure I understand what you mean."

Zilker spoke more bluntly. "You recommended George Cobb be sent to jail. Yet, he was sent to Crown Point and after he was discharged, he attacked you and your wife. If he had been in jail like you recommended, he wouldn't have been able to attack you and your wife. You wanted him punished, didn't you?"

"Yes," Corrigan hesitantly replied. "But, how did you know that?"

"We have our sources," Zilker answered cryptically. "Do you still want to see him punished?"

"Yes, of course."

"And do you still want him to be held accountable for his behavior?" asked Zilker, as he weighed each of Corrigan's responses.

"Of course," replied Corrigan. "But what does that have to do with this panel?"

Zilker casually removed the top medical chart from the stack in front of him. "If you'll allow us to review a case I think you'll see." Zilker looked around the room at his colleagues and then opened the chart. "Shall we begin?" They all nodded.

Zilker began the review process using psychiatric shorthand, as he read from the patient's medical chart. "Frank Wellington, a single thirty-five year old Caucasian male admitted to Manchester

Psychiatric Hospital in Ohio last month with a diagnosis of paranoid schizophrenia. No family, no job and little prospects of finding one. He was placed on the usual meds upon admission."

"What brought him in this time," asked Gatway.

Zilker read from the chart. "He was caught trying to steal a set of steak knives from a department store. He said he needed them to protect himself from some kind of an alien life form. Apparently he's a Star Command fan. Sadly, when a sales clerk tried to stop him from leaving, he punched her in the face and broke the poor girl's nose."

"Damn," said Blair.

"This makes his 15th psychiatric admission in three years," Zilker continued. "He's been sent to the state hospital outside Cleveland by court order six times, where they keep him an average of three weeks."

"Wait a minute. You mean this guy is already back on the streets?" asked Dr. Blair.

"I'm afraid so. He spent 14 days at the state hospital and was discharged."

"Damn. With his track record, why in the hell didn't they keep him longer?" Marapudi lamented rhetorically.

"The same reason they always do," Blair bristled. "As soon as he was able to walk and chew gum at the same time, they kicked his ass out because they needed the bed for someone else." Blair added from first-hand experiences while in private practice when she battled with state psychiatric hospitals.

"Push um in and push um out," Gatway quipped as she shook her head.

Ozawa and Marapudi nodded their heads in agreement.

145

"How much has he cost Psych-Group Mutual," asked Ozawa?

Dr. Gatway looked at what appeared to Corrigan to be a spread sheet in front of her. "Over $800,000."

"Wow," said Ozawa. "That's got to be a record."

"Not really," Gatway casually replied. "One of the first patients we reviewed broke the million dollar mark, remember? I believe his name was Josh something."

"Yeah, I think you're right."

"He was beyond saving," Marapudi interjected.

"How much does Wellington have left on his policy?" Zilker asked as he interrupted the walk down memory lane.

"He's got parity diagnosis written into his policy so there's no cap," Gatway answered.

"So your company will just have to keep shoveling money down a rat hole, too bad."

"I know," Gatway sighed.

"What about his medications, any recent changes or additions?" Dr. Blair asked.

Zilker flipped to the patient's medication page in the chart. He quickly scanned it. "Yes. Apparently, they tried him on something new while he was at the state hospital and he responded well to it. But alas, I'm afraid Mr. Wellington has already missed his first and second follow-up appointments since his discharge, which can mean only one thing."

Everyone around the table except for Corrigan nodded their head knowingly. Wellington had stopped taking his medications, again.

146

"The old, "I feel better so I don't need to take them, syndrome," Dr. Blair voiced what everyone was thinking, "What about family support?"

"Married twice, divorced twice, one child, living with his last ex-wife. Two brothers, and one sister, both parents are dead. From reading the notes in his psycho-social it appears his entire family, for all intense and purposes, have disowned him."

"I would too," Dr. Gatway glibly seconded.

"Sounds like nobody wants a paranoid schizophrenic with a history of violent behavior living with them," Ozawa quipped.

"What about any other arrests?" Gatway asked.

"According to a rap sheet I obtained from a private detective friend of mine," Zilker said with a wry smile on his face. "He's been arrested twice for assault on a police officer and three times for spousal abuse. In my opinion it's only a matter of time before he kills someone."

"It does sounds like he's getting more violent over apparently less consequential things," Ozawa surmised.

Zilker turned and looked at Corrigan. "In addition to his numerous inpatient hospitalizations, the patient has been in individual therapy, three residential programs, two structured outpatient programs and even an experimental state program for schizophrenics with violent behavior."

"And I take it, he failed all of them," Corrigan concluded.

"Yes," Zilker sighed. "I'm afraid so." Zilker then closed Wellington's chart to indicate there was no need for any further discussion. "Psych-Group Mutual sent us this case, frankly, because they said it would be like flushing money down the drain if they continued paying for his treatment. I'm open to recommendations."

"I don't think he should be admitted to another psychiatric hospital. It would be a waste of time and money," said Ozawa as he made, what seemed to Corrigan, an unusually harsh recommendation.

"Amen to that," added Blair,

"He's cost Psych-Group Mutual way too much money," Marapudi chimed in.

"As the representative for Psych-Group Mutual, I concur," said Gatway. "I think it's time we revoke his frequent flyer card."

There were silent nods of agreement from everyone sitting around the table. Except for Corrigan who was still not sure what was going on.

"Then I think he needs a new diagnosis," suggested Ozawa.

"I agree," Zilker concurred.

"Any objections?" asked Zilker. Everyone remained silent. "Very well then, his new diagnosis will be terminus en extremes."

Corrigan couldn't believe what he just heard. His Latin was a little rusty, however, it was good enough to figure out that they just sentenced Wellington to death.

"As always, our friends will make it look like an accident or a suicide," Ozawa added perfunctorily.

"I know they will," Zilker said with confidence.

Corrigan was stunned. He just witnessed a death sentence ordered by a group of psychiatrists. This had to be some kind of macabre joke.

Zilker looked at Corrigan and said, "That's how we do it. What do you think?"

Apparently, it wasn't a joke. Zilker was serious. This group sat in judgment of patients and handed out death sentences like they were treatment options. "Damn," he thought. A million things raced through his mind. Murder, however, kept coming to the forefront. He sat and stared at the group as if they had suddenly grown horns and pointed tails. "They want me to join this?" Corrigan said to himself.

The group was hand-picked by Zilker and they came from the four managed care companies that funded the chronic care team. He based his selection on each doctor's individual history of outspoken disapproval of frequent flyers and their success at implementing effective cost containment strategies. Until Dr. Leonard died in a plane crash in Alaska, Zilker hadn't given much thought about a replacement.

Since he couldn't put an ad in the newspaper, it fell upon Zilker to do the research and come up with a suitable candidate to replace Leonard and then present him to the group for possible induction. He purposely wanted an outsider this time in order to test the viability of adding new staff if his pilot program proved successful and he needed to expand it.

After several weeks of going through biographical information on potential candidates, Zilker picked Corrigan's name to present to the group. When he presented his findings and rationale to the group they agreed Corrigan would make an ideal candidate to replace Dr. Leonard and that Corrigan should be contacted. They also knew it wouldn't be easy to sell their deadly concept to an outsider when they sent out their invitation. They prepared a well orchestrated strategy in advance, hoping it would bring Corrigan into the fold. And now they were about to implement it.

"Dr. Corrigan," began Dr. Blair as she looked directly at the still speechless psychiatrist. "Some patients will never improve and should be treated accordingly. Isn't that the essence of your book?" she asked disarmingly.

"What?" responded Corrigan, his mind still reeling from what just happened?

"I'm talking about your book," Blair reiterated.

"What about it?" Corrigan replied as he prepared to defend the book's basic tenets like he'd done so many times before in front of skeptical, almost hostile, colleagues. However, Blair's comment didn't sound accusatory but more like she was agreeing with him.

"Isn't what we're doing only a logical extension of your thesis?" Blair frankly asked.

Corrigan wasn't prepared for that kind of question. "It's more of a corruption of what I wrote," he finally countered.

"You know as well as I do some of our patients are never going to get better," Blair added bluntly.

"Of course some people never get better," Corrigan thought to himself. But killing them? His book didn't advocate that.

Blair took advantage of Corrigan's momentary silence to make the conversation a little more personal. "What about George Cobb? He's been in every treatment program under the sun, multiple times. Yet, he's not getting any better."

Zilker, on cue interjected. "Can I ask you a personal question, Dr. Corrigan?"

Corrigan looked at Zilker and simply nodded his head.

"Do you think George Cobb has the right to injure another human being? Or even kill someone?"

"Of course not," Corrigan said empathically. The flow of the conversation was making him uncomfortable. However, the introduction of George Cobb suddenly made it more tenable. It got his attention, as the group intended.

"If Cobb hurt someone else, I wouldn't want that on my conscience," Blair added for effect. Her well-practiced words flowing smoothly.

"Surely, you must have entertained the thought of wanting to see Mr. Cobb, you know?" said Zilker purposely leaving the sentence hanging to see how Corrigan would respond.

"What?" Corrigan replied. "Dead, of course I have, especially after what he did to my family."

"A very natural reaction I'm sure everyone here has entertained at one time or another," said Zilker.

"What gives you people the right to play God?" Corrigan asked contemptuously.

"We don't play God," said Zilker as he delicately rebutted Corrigan. "We're more like the police. We get dangerous people off the streets."

"And you have to admit that Cobb is dangerous," Ozawa quickly tossed out. Each person in the carefully planned script knew when to nudge Corrigan a further along.

Corrigan shook his head in disbelief. "I can't believe this is happening," he said to himself. When he accepted the innocuous invitation, he didn't expect to walk into a psychiatric star chamber.

"A man like Cobb shouldn't be walking the streets," Blair added bitterly.

"I know if I had the chance to do something about him, I would do it," Marapudi said coldly.

"Well, I'm not you," Corrigan shot back.

"I guess we were wrong," Gatway spitefully quipped. She then spat, "You hypocrite."

They were getting a rise out of Corrigan and that was part of the plan. They wanted him to make him angry because they knew his anger would work to their advantage. Because when a person becomes angry, they don't think rationally and when logic is removed, emotions replace it. They wanted to play heavily on Corrigan's emotions.

Marapudi then interjected. "Have you been living under a rock or something?"

"No," Corrigan replied, "I'm quite aware of what's going on out there. That's why I wrote my book." Corrigan's ears were turning red.

Zilker saw Corrigan's ears turning red. It was time. "Enough talk," he said as he removed the cell phone clipped to his belt and punched in a number. He held it up to his ear, waited for the connection and then spoke, "Hello, yes. Good. I'll let you talk to him. Our men have located Mr. Cobb. They await your instructions."

"My instructions?" asked Corrigan with a puzzled look.

"Go on. Talk to them," Zilker encouraged as he handed the cell phone to Corrigan.

Corrigan took the cell phone and put up it to his ear and then spoke to the unknown person on the other end of the line. "Hello? . . . .Then why don't you call the police?"

"They won't. They've been instructed not to," interrupted Zilker. The trap was set.

Corrigan looked at Zilker in disbelief. "What kind of mad game are you playing?"

"It is not a game," Zilker said soberly. The group was now going to find out just how good Zilker was at picking a replacement.

"Dr. Corrigan," said Zilker. "You can let Cobb go or you can tell our partners in the field to take care of the problem. It's up to you and God knows what Cobb will do next?" The trap was sprung.

"What partners?" Corrigan asked.

"I think you've already met them," Zilker replied as he looked at Ozawa, "hasn't he?

"Not formally," Ozawa replied.

Corrigan then remembered meeting Ozawa at the gun range. "You mean the two men at the gun range?"

"Yes," Ozawa replied. "The wife of the man with the mustache was stabbed and slashed over two hundred times by a frequent flyer, who thought she was a robot intent on killing him. When the animal went to court, he was found not guilty by reason of insanity. The other man you saw also lost his wife. She wore an Arkansas baseball cap and some frequent flyer thought the "A" stood for Antichrist, so he killed her. They both have made it their life's mission to prevent similar tragedies from happening. They're both ex-military and are very good at what they do. They have no children so they are free to travel where ever we send them using the cover of traveling salesmen. They believe in the mission of this group one hundred per cent."

"My God," Corrigan thought to himself. He had made life and death decisions during his medical career. But this was totally unprecedented. They were asking him to authorize the premeditated murder of another human being by a hit squad.

One of the psychiatric team's assassins must have gotten tired of waiting for a response from Corrigan. "I'm still here," replied Corrigan.

"Think of your wife and child," Zilker said tenderly.

"The police won't be around to protect them all the time," Blair not so subtly added.

"Even if they arrest him, he'll only be found guilty by reason of insanity for anything he did and then be let go down the road," added Zilker. "If I remember correctly in your book, you advocated for a new court classification called guilty by reason of insanity. That way a person could still be found guilty of a crime and later it could be used in a court of law and for determining punishment after they've been treated."

Corrigan simply nodded his head in agreement. He couldn't deny it because he outlined the concept in chapter 15 of his book.

"Your wife and child deserve to be safe and that won't happen as long as Cobb is on the loose," Gatway added as she upped the emotional ante.

"You already know the system can't protect you," Zilker said.

With the trauma inflicted on his family still fresh in his mind, coupled with the expertly crafted lines spoken by those around the table, Corrigan was beginning to be swayed. What they were saying was now resonating with him.

Each person around the table watched Corrigan intently. They could see they had stirred up some genuine feelings and hoped as they manipulated his emotions, they could bring him into their camp.

The memory of how Diane cried at the hospital for their unborn daughter flashed through Corrigan's mind. He remembered the guilt he felt, as he sat next to her and how he was unable to protect them. The group had stirred up guilt and anger in Corrigan. The two emotions had now entered into the equation and began to cloud Corrigan's judgment.

"You recommended that Cobb be sent to jail after your assessment, didn't you?" asked Zilker.

"Yes," replied Corrigan.

"But, it didn't happen, which meant your recommendation was overturned," Zilker verbally jabbed, as he fanned the emotional coals now burning inside Corrigan. "Hell of a thing to have one's professional judgment overruled. I know I wouldn't like it," Zilker sniffed haughtily. Zilker could see his carefully crafted remarks had not been lost on Corrigan. They had stung him.

"Lang," Corrigan thought to himself, "The bastard." The scene of him pleading with Lang to send Cobb to jail played out in his mind. Corrigan's lip curled noticeably with disgust.

The assassin on the other end of the cell phone must have said something, because Corrigan responded. "I don't know what to say. . . .I know that's not what you wanted to hear."

"You let him get away, the police may never find him," said Zilker. "We're not talking about the citizen of the month here. We're talking about a potential killer that has been given every chance in the book." Zilker could see Corrigan's face hardening. Their carefully-worded script was having the desired effect.

"Look at all the times he's been hospitalized," chimed in Marapudi. "And what good has it done?"

"I think we've established the fact he's never going to get better," said Blair.

"If you don't act now, he could potentially kill someone," said Zilker, letting the sentence hang in the air.

"God, I'd hate to wake up in the morning and read in the paper that he killed someone," said Blair. "And knowing I could have done something to prevent it. That would be hard to live with." Blair slowly shook her head and also let her last comment hang in the air for effect.

"You know he's never going to change," said Ozawa. "He stops taking his meds as soon as he gets out of the hospital. Then he gets arrested and walks away a free man for things if you and I did, we'd be sent to prison and never see the light of day again."

"What was it that you said in your book?" Zilker asked. "That when a lucid patient stops taking his medication it's tantamount to premeditation, when he commits a crime."

"It's obvious Cobb committed a heinous crime and it was premeditated because he stopped taking his medication," Gatway piled on.

"They were right," Corrigan found himself agreeing. The man was a menace and his actions were premeditated because he stopped taking his medication.

"I promise whatever action you decide to take, it will not leave this room," said Zilker, assuring Corrigan he was not only among sympathetic friends, but confidants.

Corrigan's mind set off on a torturous self examination of his conscience. Everything they said about Cobb was true. Cobb was a psychopath. He was still on the loose and capable of murder. He knew the police couldn't protect his wife and daughter forever. Which, meant, how could he?

Ozawa started to say something but Zilker cut him off with a wave of his hand. He held his finger up to his lips to indicate everyone should remain silent. Zilker could tell something had resonated within Corrigan and he was wrestling with his conscience. He didn't want anyone to disturb him. They had dealt Corrigan their best cards. It was now time for him to play or fold.

Corrigan finally broke his silence and with deliberate cool detachment spoke into the cell phone. "Take care of the problem." He then tossed the cell phone back to Zilker as if it was red hot coal burning his hand.

Corrigan's decision was met with smiles of approval and nods from those sitting around the table. Corrigan had just joined the dark side.

Zilker finally spoke up. "Oh, come now, Dr. Corrigan. You can't tell me that somewhere deep down inside of you there wasn't a little part of you saying the bastard got what he deserved." He could see Corrigan's stony expression change. The furrows in his brow relaxed and the look in his eyes said the rest. Zilker was right. "Break out the brandy. We need to officially welcome our newest member." Their plan had worked and Corrigan had just inducted himself into their unholy order.

As he sat among his joyous colleagues, Corrigan didn't feel like celebrating as it started to sink in that the chronic care team had not only won him over but they now owned him.

Ozawa stood and fetched a brandy decanter and set it down on the conference table. It was quickly followed by six brandy snifters.

Corrigan leaned over and whispered to Zilker. "What if I were to go to the police about this?"

"First off," Zilker responded. "This panel doesn't exist. Second, you'd have a hard time proving that it did. Third, who would believe you? We're doctors. We're supposed to help people not harm them."

"But what if I could convince the police otherwise?"

"Then I'd send them a copy of the tape you just made ordering Cobb's death. Anonymously of course," Zilker smiled.

"Of course," Corrigan wanly smiled, knowing his fate had been sealed.

Ozawa poured generous amounts of brandy into each snifter and passed them around.

Corrigan asked Zilker. "How many patients have your partners in the field…?" Corrigan couldn't bring himself to say murdered. He struggled to find an appropriate euphemism.

"We like to say permanently discharged," offered Zilker as he helped Corrigan finish the sentence. Euphemisms were such nice things. Especially for Zilker, who could reduce the murder of another human being into simple hospital jargon?

"We get cases from all over the country," Zilker continued. "We review an average of about five or six cases a month. We've been in business for about a year. So I'd say roughly sixty."

A brandy snifter was set in front of Corrigan.

Zilker stood and raised his glass, "To our newest member."

The panel members stood as one and happily raised their glasses. Corrigan, still uncomfortable about what just happened, slowly stood and weakly raised his glass. Each panel member made it a point to clink their brandy snifter against Corrigan's glass. They then took a healthy sip of the warm liquid as they welcomed their newest member.

Corrigan enjoyed a good brandy. But, tonight for some reason, the brandy in his mouth tasted bitter.

# CHAPTER 15

Corrigan didn't need the alarm clock to wake up the next morning. He lay in bed and stared at the ceiling most of the night. Sleep had not come easy as he tossed and turned, his mind still trying to absorb what happened earlier. Was he, with the dawning of a new day, really a murderer? Or was the whole chronic-care-team encounter just a dreadful nightmare? No, he was there. He remembered it all too vividly for it to be a bad dream. It really happened. He couldn't believe it.

Only a few hours earlier he sat at a table where death sentences were handed out like prescriptions to five psychiatric patients. And he participated in the grisly event. How could he? What made him do such a thing? He then quickly rationalized that George Cobb made him do it. Damn him. He wished to hell he'd never met George Cobb.

He glanced at the alarm clock for what seemed like the hundredth time. The red digital numbers appeared to be frozen at seven, fifteen. "What the hell," he said to himself, "I might as well get up." Spending the day with Diane at the hospital would help take his mind off things. He got out of bed and walked into the bathroom. After he showered and shaved, he went to the closet where he picked out some casual clothes and got dressed. He then checked his cell phone for any messages and clipped the electronic leash to his belt.

He felt better as he walked into the kitchen. Maybe it was the psychological lift of knowing Diane was truly safe now that Cobb had been eliminated or maybe it was just the hot shower. Either way, he felt better. As he put on a pot of coffee, he glanced at his watch. Diane would be having breakfast about now. "Poor thing," he thought to himself. Diane was such a finicky eater and the food at the hospital wasn't exactly five-star fare.

When the hot water finished draining through the coffee filter, Corrigan poured a cup and sat down at the kitchen table. As he sat staring at the hot cup of coffee, the events of the previous night kept intruding into his thoughts. He shook his head to try and exorcize the scenes, but they wouldn't go away. "Can't have this," Corrigan said to himself out loud. "Physician, heal thyself." He took a sip of coffee cup and shook his head again. The last thing he needed was a case of PTSD, so in order to distract himself he stood and went to retrieve the morning paper. Reading the paper would surely take his mind off what happened.

When he opened the front door, he was shocked to see Detectives Norwell and Joiner standing there. The detectives were both just as startled and Norwell quickly took the cigarette out of his mouth and hid it behind his back. It was department policy to discourage smoking when interacting with the public. The San Salina Police Department wanted to present a clean cut, wholesome image to the public. Not to mention the city also wanted to save money on its health insurance premiums.

Norwell was the least health-conscious detective on the police force. He'd gained more than a few pounds around his waist since he last played college ball and although he had seriously tried to stop smoking a couple of dozen times, he just couldn't kick the nicotine habit. He was able to rationalize each time he returned to smoking that if he didn't continue to smoke, who would pay all for the government funded programs his cigarette taxes supported? Despite his physical shortcomings and his chain smoking, Norwell was a damned good detective. Therefore, his bad habits were overlooked.

Joiner was the first to speak. "We didn't mean to startle you. We were just about to ring your door bell. We have some news about George Cobb that might interest you."

Corrigan's mind went into overdrive. A sense of dread, guilt and fear swept over him. And for an instant his face revealed the thoughts swirling inside his head. The cops were at his front door and they had news about George Cobb. It could only mean one thing. Somehow, they found out he was responsible for Cobb's death and they were there to arrest him. What should he do? Run? No, they would catch him before he got ten feet. They might even shoot him and justify it by saying he was a fleeing felon. Should he call an attorney? He didn't know any. Damn it.

Zilker had promised him that whatever happened around that table would stay there. How could he do this? He didn't want to spend the rest of his life in jail or worse yet, be given a lethal injection. What would happen to Diane? Would he ever be able to hold his baby daughter in his arms? A million permutations about his future ran through his mind in the seconds before Norwell finally spoke up.

"George Cobb died of a drug overdose last night," Norwell said without any emotion. To him, a scum bag was a scum bag.

When Corrigan heard the words, "drug overdose," his mind stopped racing and he allowed himself an internal sigh of relief. Then he remembered what Ozawa said. "They would make it look like an accident or suicide." Apparently the detectives didn't know he ordered Cobb's murder after all and they were looking at Cobb's death as an accident. "Thank God," he selfishly thought. He was off the hook. He wouldn't be going to jail after all.

However, he still had to remain calm and play it cool. Detectives were just as intuitive as psychiatrists at picking up subtle behavioral clues given off by people who felt guilty. Corrigan had to concentrate on not feeling guilty.

"We just came from the scene and thought you'd like to know," Norwell continued.

"I'm not going to deny it, but it's a relief," Corrigan said honestly. "That's it," he said to himself. Be honest and they'll never suspect anything. "How did it happen?" he asked.

Norwell answered as he let the cigarette behind his back fall from between his fingers and land on the porch. He quickly crushed it out with his foot. "Apparently he got hold of some pretty high grade heroin and shot himself up with it. The needle was still in his vein, when the uniformed officers found him."

"That's too bad," said Corrigan.

"Was Cobb a drug user?" asked Joiner.

"Why do you ask?"

"Well, I found it kind of unusual that he didn't have any other track marks on his arms," Joiner replied. "He just had the one injection site. The one that killed him."

"Yeah," Norwell concurred. "Most druggies have arms that look like Grand Central Station they've got so many tracks."

"That may not be as peculiar as it sounds," Corrigan responded as he cleared his throat.

"Why's that?" asked Joiner.

"While I'm still not a liberty to give you any specific information about Mr. Cobb," replied Corrigan with faked

162

reluctance. "But what you may have found was his first attempt to try and deal, in his own way, with the paranoia that was troubling him by using heroin." Corrigan knew Cobb self-medicated constantly, when he wasn't on his medication. But he wasn't going to tell Norwell that Cobb's drug of choice was alcohol. Thank God federal law didn't require Corrigan to reveal this piece of information to the detectives. For once the myriad federal, state and local laws and regulations about patient confidentiality finally worked in his favor.

"So this could have been his first attempt to try and self medicate with heroin?" asked Joiner.

"It appears that way," Corrigan replied with professional aplomb as this newest lie came easier than the last one.

"It seems strange, with his long history of psychiatric problems, that he never tried it before," Norwell voiced openly what both he and Joiner where thinking.

"Focus," Corrigan told himself. He then said to Norwell, hoping to deflect his unwanted inquisitiveness. "You have to remember he wasn't thinking rationally. It's one of the tendencies of our society when we try to understand an irrational act in a rational way. To try and make sense out a senseless act, you can't. That's why it's called irrational. That's why it doesn't make any sense. We may try and understand it the best we can, but we really, truly can't fathom some of the things people do." Corrigan hoped reciting the excerpt from his book would help convince the detectives to continue viewing Cobb's death as an accident. Then he added for effect. "Believe me, I should know."

"I guess you're right," Norwell said as he nodded his head.

Corrigan's cell phone went off. He retrieved it from his belt and looked at the phone number. It was the OB/GYN floor.

"Excuse me," said Corrigan as he answered the cell phone. "She is? I'll be right there."

The two detectives glanced at each other, then at Corrigan.

"That was the hospital," said an excited Corrigan. "My wife has gone into labor. I've got to go."

"Then get going," replied Norwell with a smile on his face.

"Do you need anything else from me?" asked Corrigan.

"Nah," said Norwell. "We got everything we need. It looks like Cobb did us a favor and saved the taxpayers a lot of money."

"Then I'll be on my way," said Corrigan as he stepped onto the porch and shut the door behind him.

Norwell and Joiner parted so Corrigan could pass between them. "I hope everything turns out all right," said Norwell.

"Give our best to your wife," added Joiner.

"I will. Thanks," Corrigan replied as the garage door opened.

"You can tell your wife she doesn't have to worry about Cobb any more," shouted Norwell as he watched Corrigan slide behind the wheel of his Mustang. Corrigan waved his hand in response.

Joiner and Norwell watched as Corrigan's Mustang sped down the street.

"I hope he doesn't get a ticket," said Joiner.

"Me too," Norwell concurred as he lit up a cigarette.

Joiner looked at him. "Well, what do you think?"

"I think we go back to the barn and close out this case as an accidental overdose." However, Norwell could see that Joiner was already ruminating. He'd seen that look before. It always meant more paperwork. "What?" he finally asked.

Joiner didn't respond. She was analyzing something and didn't want to be disturbed.

"Come on. Don't go Columbo on me."

"It might just be me," she finally responded. "But when you told Corrigan that Cobb was dead, he acted kind of strange to me."

"How did you expect him to react?" asked Norwell with a puzzled look on his face. "Jump up and down and shout for joy?"

"No. . .It seemed like," Joiner hesitantly replied as she searched to find the right word. She knew something wasn't right, but she learned the hard way you couldn't legally use, "woman's intuition," as a pretext for suspecting someone of a crime. A lesson she learned from a judge who tossed out a case when she testified she used intuition as her reason for questioning a man a few blocks from where an armed robbery had taken place. The judge told her she needed more than just her female psychic powers for probable cause to detain the man. As a result, she got into the habit of internalizing her, "women's intuition," debates rather than expressing them.

"Well?" asked Norwell as the two started towards their unmarked police car.

"Nothing," said Joiner, "Never mind." However, she continued to picture Corrigan's face when they told him about Cobb. How would she have responded to the news that the man who almost killed her and her husband was dead and no longer posed a treat to them? Pretty damned happy, that's for sure. Maybe that's what she saw in Corrigan's eyes, when they told him Cobb was dead. Joyous relief coupled with the sudden guilt for feeling that way. Norwell was probably right. There was nothing to it. She was reading way too much into his reaction, enough already.

When Norwell and Joiner reached their unmarked four-door sedan. Norwell got behind the wheel and Joiner sat in the passenger's seat. Norwell tossed his cigarette butt out the window before he started the car.

Joiner quietly shook her head in disgust, when she saw Norwell litter the street.

Norwell saw her gesture out of the corner of his eye but ignored it. He put the car in gear and they headed downtown. "Let's close this case. That scumbag got what he deserved."

Corrigan expertly maneuvered his car through the city streets and into the physician's parking lot at County General. After he parked his car, he sprinted to the south entrance of the hospital. Once inside he took the nearest elevator to the labor and delivery rooms. When the elevator doors opened, he ran to the nurses' station where he got the attention of an attractive young nurse behind the counter.

"I'm James Corrigan. My wife Diane is in labor. Where is she?"

"She's in labor room three," the nurse quickly replied. "Down there," she added as she pointed down the hallway.

"Thanks," said Corrigan as he dashed off in the direction of the labor room three. When he got there, he opened the door and found Diane in active labor.

"Oh, thank God you're here," Diane said, just as a contraction hit. Her face contorted in pain as she grimaced.

Corrigan quickly made his way to her side and took her hand. "Breathe," he said. They had taken a childbirth class together and learned different breathing techniques over the six week course to help ease the pain of delivery. It was now time to see if they really worked.

"Breathe. Just breathe," he repeated to his sweat drenched wife.

She looked up at him with nostrils flared and her teeth clinched and screamed. "You breathe! I just want her out!" She then moaned. "Oh, God, it hurts."

Undaunted, Corrigan continued to provide support. Even though his wife's normally pleasant personality had taken the day off. "Find your focal point," he encouraged.

"Focal point my ass," Diane cried. Then with a face so contorted it looked ready to explode, she shouted. "She's coming! I can feel her coming."

Corrigan stepped into the hallway and signaled for a nurse. A matronly looking nurse came down the hallway and quickly joined him. "She says it's time. She can feel the baby coming."

"Okay," the nurse calmly replied. "We'll move her into the delivery room."

A new life was about to begin. However, in Cleveland, Ohio a life was about to end.

Frank Wellington was the next name on this month's hit list to be paid a visit by chronic care team assassins, Kevin Doyle and Pete Hunter. They had already dispatched with comparative ease, George Cobb and one other victim as they moved east. Cobb was an easy accidental overdose, the other was a suicide. Doyle and Hunter preferred to work from the west coast to the east coast as they dealt out death to the patients who subscribed to the managed care companies that employed them. It was just geographical convenience. Only because Frank Wellington lived in Ohio, he would be the next to die. Doyle and Hunter often found it amusingly ironic that the premiums paid by their victims helped pay for their own demise. When the two arrived around dusk at Cleveland International Airport, Frank Wellington didn't know it, but he wouldn't live to see morning.

# CHAPTER 16

Frank Wellington, all six foot, three inches and two hundred and fifty pounds of him, stuck the key in the deadbolt of his third floor apartment. In his other hand, he gripped a 12-pack of beer. The cans were still cold thanks the chill night air. He was returning from his pilgrimage to the local convenience store to replace the twelve cans he had already consumed before the sun went down. He'd been celebrating ever since his discharge from the state hospital. He sold the medications he was supposed to taking on the black market and used the money to buy beer he consumed on a daily basis. The relief he sought for his paranoia could only be found in the shiny sixteen-ounce cans of beer that he consumed at a prodigious rate. Tonight he felt ten feet high and bullet proof with a blood alcohol level just a little over the legal limit.

Wellington opened the door to his government subsidized apartment and noticed all the lights were off. He thought he left at least one light on before he'd gone to the store. "I guess I didn't," he thought as he flipped on the wall switch and shut the door behind him. Wellington was startled to see a man sitting on the battered sofa in the middle of his sparsely furnished living room. "Who the hell are you?" he asked the man with the mustache, wearing rubber surgical gloves and blue paper booties over his tennis shoes.

"I am Captain Robert Teague of the Star Ship Andromeda," said Kevin Doyle. Before each assignment, Doyle and Hunt studied their targets medical charts to learn, which buttons they could push and which ones to avoid, to gain their target's confidence. It was easier to kill people when they cooperated. Wellington was a science fiction buff. So they based their strategy on convincing him that Doyle was from the future and he needed Wellington's help to return the star ship Andromeda to the 23rd century. If Captain Teague couldn't complete his mission, the star ship would be stuck in earth's orbit and trapped forever in the 21st century.

Wellington carefully set the twelve pack of beer on the ratty carpet next to the front door, "You the police?"

"No," said Doyle aka Captain Teague.

"Then what the hell are you doing in my apartment?" Wellington snarled.

"I need your help," Doyle calmly replied.

That's not what Wellington wanted to hear. "Get your ass out of my apartment before. . ."

Doyle cut Wellington off in mid sentence. He needed to establish a rapport with this irritable giant quickly or things could get ugly. "You are Frank Wellington of Cleveland, Ohio?" Doyle asked.

"Yeah, who wants to know?"

"I have been searching for you. I need your help."

"You already said that," Wellington tersely replied.

"You're one of only a handful of people we felt comfortable approaching about our problem."

"What problem?"

169

"You may find this hard to believe. But please hear me out," Doyle began. "As I said my name is Robert Teague, I am the captain of the star ship Andromeda that's currently orbiting 200 miles above your earth. Two days ago we passed through a time warp and entered your earth's orbit in this century. So far we have been unable to break free from our present orbit and return to the 23rd century. We need your help to return our ship to the 23rd century."

It took a minute for Wellington's alcohol soaked brain to process the stranger's information. When it finally did, Wellington smiled. He knew it. He'd been telling people for years there were advanced civilizations living in outer space. They thought he was crazy, well now, the shoe was on the other foot! Everyone else was crazy, not him. He had living proof of his claims sitting right here in his living room. What sweet revenge.

Doyle didn't know what to make of the giant's silence. He quickly continued from his memorized script. "We used our on-board computers to access several main frame data bases across the Northern American continent and found your name. It became apparent from the data we retrieved, that you had a unique ability to blend science fact with science fiction. Therefore we sought you out. Not many people would be able to understand what I am telling you. They might call the police. Or, heaven forbid, put me in a psychiatric hospital."

The latter sentence played right into Wellington's disorganized thought process. He had been hospitalized many times for saying he believed in people from outer space. He walked over to Captain Teague and extended his hand. "Welcome."

Doyle shook Wellington's hand, a rapport had been established. "I must apologize for the rubber gloves. But our

170

science officer made it very clear we must not contaminate your present day earth in the slightest way or it might disturb the space time continuum."

"I understand," Wellington replied. He really didn't but he wanted to remain friends with the time traveler in his living room. He was living proof that he was not crazy.

"Good," thought Doyle to himself. "It looks like the big guy has taken the bait."

Wellington sat down in a flimsy chair across from Doyle. "What can I do to help?"

"We need your help to set a clock located in Cleveland's City Hall back five minutes in time, he then looked at his watch in six point five hours from now. In doing so it will give us the five minute window we need to re-enter the time warp we slipped through and send us back to our own time."

Doyle's story seemed a bit strange even to a man used to having delusions. "Why the clock in City Hall?" asked Wellington.

"I don't know the specific details. But my first officer can explain it to you. Would you like to speak to him?"

"Sure," exclaimed an enthusiastic Wellington.

Doyle took out a science fiction prop he converted into a two way radio and opened it. He then spoke into the device. "This is Captain Teague calling First Officer Peter Stark."

"Go ahead captain," replied a male voice from the radio Doyle held in his hand. It was Doyle's partner in crime, Pete Hunter playing the part of First Officer Peter Stark. He was standing outside in the shrubbery beneath Wellington's balcony.

"I have made contact with Mr. Wellington and he has agreed to help us," Doyle said evenly into the hand held radio.

"Excellent," replied Hunter aka Peter Stark.

"However, he has a question about why we must turn back the clock at City Hall. Do you think you can explain it to him?" Doyle asked.

"I'll try," the voice of Hunter responded over the radio.

"Good," said Doyle.

Doyle then handed the radio to Wellington who looked at it in awe. He was holding a real piece of advanced space technology in his hands. However, in reality, it was plus or minus a few parts from Props Are Us in Hollywood and Radio Barn of West Burbank a complete fake.

"I'll try and keep it in layman's terms," began Hunter. "As you know, time and space can be altered. During these alterations, specific time resonates are established and dispersed into space much like a stone tossed in a pool of water. When these time waves hit an object, they're in harmony and they set up what is called a harmonic convergence. I'm sure you've heard of that?"

Wellington had to think for a minute. "Yeah, I remember them talking about that on an episode of Star Flash."

"Good," Hunter replied. "When a harmonic convergence is present it affects the space time continuum by setting up an anomaly called a time warp. A time warp is like a black hole, it can pull things into its core." As Hunter spouted his scientific babble, Doyle could tell Wellington was listening intently to every word. "We got pulled to this point in time by the harmonic convergence anomaly radiating from the clock in City Hall. And in order to reverse it, we have to go to the source and set it back to a time prior to the harmonic convergence. I hope this helps explain things."

Wellington might as well have been sitting in a class of advanced calculus. He only understood bits and pieces of what the phony first officer was telling him. But he wasn't about to show his ignorance and simply replied. "Yes."

"Good," Hunter replied over the radio. "I think we've found a good candidate to help us, captain." He added for effect.

"Good," said Doyle. He then extended his hand to take back the phony interstellar radio.

Wellington reverently handed the radio back to Doyle.

"Thank you Mr. Stark," said Doyle as he put the phony radio device away. He then looked at Wellington. "I'm glad you understand our mission."

"Oh, I do. I do." The bait had been taken.

"Good," Doyle replied. It was now time to set the hook. "I don't how we can repay you for your help."

The question caught Wellington off guard.

However, before Wellington could answer, Doyle suggested something guaranteed to reel in and land his victim. "How would you like to become a member of the crew of the star ship Andromeda?" asked Doyle.

Wellington's face lit up. "Would I?" he exclaimed. "I'd love to join your crew."

"It would mean leaving everything behind and traveling into the future," Doyle cautioned. "Once you make such a leap forward you won't be able to return to your present day life in Cleveland."

"No problem," Wellington quickly replied. His life in Cleveland hadn't been all that hot, two marriages, two divorces, several arrests and unemployed most of the time. When he did work, he never got along with any of his bosses. They were always out to get him. No, he wouldn't miss a thing, especially being locked up in psychiatric hospitals, just because he could communicate with people from outer space.

"I hope you understand. What I'm offering you is, what I believe you call in this century, a one-way ticket. You cannot come back," emphasized Doyle.

"There isn't anything holding me here," Wellington glibly replied.

"Very good then," replied Doyle. "One thing I might suggest before we go is that you leave a note behind so that people won't worry about you after you're gone."

"There's nobody going to worry about me after I'm gone," Wellington responded.

"How true," thought Doyle.

But he still needed Wellington to leave some kind of a hand-written suicide note. It made it much easier for the police when they found a suicide note near a dead body. While the police may give lip service to the concept that every suspicious death is treated as a homicide until it's declared something else, the reality is they have more important things to do than invest a lot of time and effort in something that's obvious a suicide. A suicide note left behind always helped.

"That may be true" Doyle continued. "But don't you want the satisfaction of letting the people who kept locking you up in those psychiatric hospitals to know that you were right?"

"Yeah, I never thought of that," said Wellington as his blood shot eyes danced with joy. "I'll show them, I was right. The bastards," he smiled, his face beaming. "Let me get a pencil and some paper."

Wellington stood and looked about the apartment until he finally found a sharpened pencil and a piece of notebook paper. He then walked over to the worn out kitchen table, pulled out a folding chair and sat down. He was going to write a letter to all those people who thought he was nuts and give them a piece of his mind. What he didn't know was that what he was writing his own death warrant.

When he finished the note Wellington left it sitting on the table. He then walked back into the living room and stood in front of Doyle. "Okay. Let's go."

"Would you mind if I read your note?" asked Doyle. He wanted to make sure, when they found his body, the contents of the note contained enough information for the police to reach the conclusion that Wellington had planned on checking out permanently and didn't mention his intervention. It didn't have to be a perfect suicide note, just one that got the point across.

"I guess not," said Wellington. He walked over, retrieved the note and handed it Doyle. "Should I pack anything?"

"No. Once you're on board the Andromeda, you'll be supplied with everything you'll need."

Doyle quickly read the note. It contained a lot of gibberish, as expected, and was peppered with epithets to show his displeasure at the people in the psychiatric field who doubted his sanity. But it got the point across that Wellington was pissed at the world and was leaving.

"Very good," said Doyle as he praised Wellington's fair well note.

"You think so?" asked Wellington.

"This will show them they should have never have doubted you," Doyle said with a confident smile as he handed the note back to Wellington.

Wellington set the note back on the kitchen table and returned to the living room where Doyle now stood. "What do we do now?" he asked.

"We go out to the balcony and make our way down to where my science officer is waiting for us."

"There are two of you here?"

"Yes."

"Man. This is way too cool," a giddy Wellington replied.

"We need to get going," said Doyle as he started toward the back bedroom where a sliding glass door opened to a balcony.

"How come we can't just go out the front door?" Wellington naively asked.

"Because if we leave together people would become suspicious," replied Doyle playing into Wellington's paranoia. "This operation has to be kept top secret," he added in the most conspiratorial voice he could muster. "Can you image the consequences if someone found out I was from the twenty-third century?"

Wellington couldn't quite put the two explanations together but he didn't want to ruin his chances of traveling through space on a star ship so he simply nodded and said. "Yes."

The two men walked through the messy bedroom and stopped at the sliding glass door that led to the balcony. Doyle slid the glass door open and they both stepped outside. The balcony was off the back alley of the apartment complex. It was secluded, had poor lighting and landscaping that made it easy for Hunter to hide. They couldn't have picked a better location for what they had planned. It was now Hunter's turn to play the role of star ship Andromeda's first officer. He was waiting for Doyle's signal before he revealed himself.

Wellington noticed a piece of clothes line tied to the guard rail of the balcony. "What's that for?"

"That's for us to climb down. My first officer is waiting for us below," Doyle replied without a hint of what the rope was really going to be used for.

"I don't know about this," a hesitant Wellington replied. "I was never much good at climbing ropes."

"You're not going to have to climb up. You're going to slide down. Let gravity do the work."

"Good idea," said Wellington as he bravely stepped forward. He'd come this far and wasn't about to miss out on the greatest adventure of his life. He would let gravity do all the work. Little did he know how well gravity would work?

Doyle walked to the edge of the guard rail and looked down. He then softly whistled like a bird. Hunter appeared from behind a tall box hedge and waved at Doyle.

Hunter waved back. "Good," thought Hunter. "Everything is going according to plan."

"My first officer is waiting for us," Doyle announced.

"No kidding," exclaimed Wellington.

"Look for yourself," Doyle pointed to the balcony.

Wellington leaned over the guard rail and saw Hunter, who waved to him. "I'll be damned," were Wellington's last words.

Doyle took the end of the clothes line and stealthy brought it up behind Wellington's back. The end of the rope was fashioned into a makeshift but effective noose, the kind a person might fashion if they didn't know how to tie a traditional hangman's noose. As Wellington looked down at Hunter, Doyle expertly slipped the noose around Wellington's neck and used the big man's weight to leverage him over the guard rail. The rope wasn't cut to reach the ground. It was cut to reach only ten feet from the top of the balcony. Wellington's body stopped abruptly at the ten foot mark, his neck snapping instantly. Wellington's big body now hung between heaven and earth.

Doyle went back inside Wellington's apartment and sanitized it so no one would know he had been there. He then made a silent egress from the apartment. As soon as he stepped outside, he stuffed his rubber gloves and blue booties into his coat pockets. He met up with Hunter down the block from the apartment complex. Together they causally strolled to their rental car and got in. As the car pulled away from the curb, they wondered how long it would take before someone found Wellington's body and reported it to the police. Hunter thought only a couple of hours, but Doyle thought the body wouldn't be discovered until morning. Either way both men would be on the next red eye with one more name scratched off on their list.

# CHAPTER 17

"Thank you for coming," a cordial Dr. Markus Lang greeted Corrigan as he walked into the director's office. It had been almost a month since Corrigan had stormed out of Lang's office in a fit of rage. A lot had happened since then. His daughter, Emily Ann Corrigan, seven pound, six ounces, had been born. George Cobb was no longer around and Corrigan had time, as they say, "to put things behind him." So when Lang called him to see how he was doing Corrigan took him up on his offer to meet today and discuss the possibility of returning to work. "Thank you for inviting me," a friendlier James Corrigan replied, he was feeling better about life in general.

"Please have a seat," Lang offered.

"Thank you," replied Corrigan as he sat in one of the comfortable chairs across from Lang's desk.

"How are doing?" came the opening question from a curious Lang. He wasn't sure what to expect from the man who stormed out of his office just a few weeks ago. However, Corrigan appeared to be acting more civil today, which held out hope that he could have an amicable conversation with him.

"I'm doing just fine," Corrigan replied. He honestly meant it and hoped Lang would see it as well. "I've also learned just how long I can go without sleep and still function thanks to our daughter."

Lang smiled. "Yes. Babies are a handful, aren't they?"

"Yes, they are," Corrigan agreed. "But worth every minute."

"I'm glad to hear it . . . How is Diane?"

"She's doing fine," Corrigan responded as he smiled broadly.

"Enough cordial banter," Lang thought to himself. It was time to determine, Corrigan's fitness for work. So he asked the first obvious question on his mind. "How did you feel when you heard about George Cobb's death?"

"Just like Lang," thought Corrigan. He can be friendly and affable for only so long. He anticipated the question about Cobb's death so he decided to tell the truth. After all, honesty is the best policy. "I'll be very honest with you," said Corrigan. "I didn't shed a tear."

"I see," Lang responded flatly. He wasn't surprised by Corrigan's answer. Knowing Corrigan as he did, he would have become suspicious if he answered any differently. The man was being honest and that was a good sign. It would be easier for him to assess Corrigan, knowing he wasn't holding anything back. Even with his abrasive manner, Corrigan was still a good psychiatrist and Lang wanted him back on his staff. "How do you feel about coming back to work?"

"I think I'm ready," replied Corrigan.

"Your objectivity," Lang asked skeptically.

"It's back."

And so it went for the next half hour. At the end of the grilling, Lang concluded Corrigan could resume his duties at County General.

"It will be a pleasure to have you back on staff, Dr. Corrigan," Lang finally said, as if bestowing the blessing of the Pope on him.

"Thank you. I'm looking forward to returning," a gracious Corrigan replied. "When do you want me to start?"

"Dr. Young is going to be taking a sabbatical starting tomorrow. Would that be too soon?"

"No," Corrigan replied enthusiastically.

"Good. You can take over his graveyard shift in psych triage starting tomorrow at eleven."

"Crap," Corrigan said under his breath.

"What?" Lang asked.

"Nothing," said Corrigan. "Of all places," he thought, psych triage. He had hoped to return to his regular duties working days, not stuck in psych triage five days a week, eight hours a night. Only Dr. Young, who was probably part vampire, enjoyed working the graveyard shift in psych triage. He had been doing it for so long most day people forgot he was on staff, as did Corrigan.

However, it was a win-win situation for Lang. He found an experienced staff member to take Young's place and with Corrigan in psych triage from eleven at night until seven in the morning he wouldn't have Corrigan around during the day to bother him.

"How long will Dr. Young be gone?" a crestfallen Corrigan asked, wanting to know how long he'd have to serve in purgatory.

"He received a grant from the National Institute of Mental Health to study the early symptoms of bipolar disorder in children and will be gone for six months."

Corrigan's felt his stomach fall. As it did, he thought he saw a mirthful crinkle in Lang's eyes. Lang was welcoming him back but also sending him a message. And Corrigan got the message, loud and clear. Lang wasn't welcoming him back with open arms, he wanted to punish him.

Corrigan was a good psychiatrist, but Lang felt he needed to teach this disrespectful subordinate a lesson. He enjoyed watching the change in Corrigan's expression when he announced he was going to be working in psych triage for the next six months. Welcome back, Dr. Corrigan, I'm still the boss around here.

Corrigan knew there was nothing he could do about his new assignment. There was one small consolation. Working nights in psych triage he didn't have to carry a patient load since they were all sleeping. If Corrigan refused the assignment, he could be fired. He resigned himself to not seeing daylight for the next six months. However, he wasn't going to give Lang the satisfaction of knowing how ticked off he was. "Thank you," said Corrigan, as if he had just received a promotion.

"Don't worry time should go quickly down there," Lang glibly promised. "And you'll be able to return to your normal duties in no time."

"Just smile," Corrigan kept reminding himself. "Thank you," said Corrigan as he stood to leave. He had to leave because if he didn't he might say something that would get him back in trouble.

Lang stood and extended his hand to Corrigan. "Welcome back."

Corrigan unenthusiastically shook Lang's hand and left.

The next night Corrigan kissed Diane and left for work around ten fifteen. He wanted to make sure he got to triage in time for report and to learn the subtle nuances of working the graveyard shift.

The graveyard shift at County General's psych triage is like psych triage on steroids. Everything is more outlandish, unbelievable and weird. For some reason it always seemed that when the sun went down the crazy people come out. During the

182

day a lot of psychotic people go unnoticed or are just ignored. However, at night it's a different story. When the sun goes down they're brought to psych triage by the bushel baskets, by friends, family members, relatives, the police, paramedics and even strangers. Some patients are glad to come to psych triage, others are not. As a rule, those brought in by the police on mental health warrants don't particularly want to be there. Not surprisingly they were always the meanest and most uncooperative of the lot. And they're not shy about telling you about it. Unfortunately, they also made up the bulk of the late night business at psych triage.

So it was with some trepidation, Dr. James Corrigan opened the door to psych triage to begin the next six months of his professional career in the psychiatric pressure cooker known as the graveyard shift. As the door shut behind him, the first thing he noticed was there were more patients in the waiting area than he'd even seen during the day. As he did his quick threat assessment he counted ten people sitting in the waiting room and one man pacing back and forth down the center of the room. He obviously had something flowing through his veins the others didn't. Corrigan made his way to the office door and was buzzed through. He was greeted by triage nurse Donna Sodabaker, mid-thirties, with short chestnut brown hair and blue eyes. She was seated behind the counter and was preparing to start her late night shift.

"Well, fancy meeting you here," smiled Sodabaker as she welcomed Corrigan to his new shift. "Welcome to the graveyard shift at psych triage." Sodabaker was a six-year triage graveyard shift veteran. She preferred working nights because her husband was a police officer and he worked the same late night hours.

"Thank you," Corrigan replied. "I've always wanted to see how the other half lived," he joked.

Dr. John Young was sitting at a desk finishing up an assessment. He looked up at his replacement and smiled. "Boy, I'm glad to see you. They've been bringing them in by the truck load tonight. If I didn't know any better I'd say there was a full moon out."

"There isn't," said Corrigan.

Corrigan pulled up a chair and sat down next to Young. As was the custom at the end of each hospital shift, Young briefed Corrigan on the status of each patient in psych triage. He pointed to one man and said. "Somehow that one got into the gene pool when the lifeguard wasn't looking. That one over there is as smart as bait. And the guy pacing back and forth probably has a room temperature IQ and is on something," Young joked before he started his actual briefing. Humor, even gallows humor, was a staple of the graveyard staff. It was one way to deal with the emotional carnage they had to sort through on a nightly basis.

"Why is he pacing?" asked Corrigan.

"He says its nervous energy. But, the police who brought him in say he's on speed. If I were a betting man I'd put my money on the speed."

Young then gave Corrigan a professional status report on each patient in psych triage that would soon become his responsibility. When Young finished briefing him, Corrigan asked the sixty four thousand dollar question that would determine what kind of eight hour shift he was going to have. "How many beds do we have?"

"We've only got three left," Young replied.

"Damn," said Corrigan. With only three beds left on the psychiatric floor that meant most of the people sitting in psych

184

triage at the beginning of his shift would still be there to greet the morning shift. It was already shaping up to be an interesting night.

Corrigan knew he was going to have to judiciously use the three remaining beds he had left. It also forced him into a position he didn't like. If he sent patients up to the psych floor now to fill the remaining beds and a violent or really crazy person showed up on their door step later things could get very dicey. Not having enough beds was always a challenge for the graveyard staff because patients were never discharged during the night. So the open beds they had now were going to be the only ones they'd have for the rest of the night. Corrigan decided he would hold back at least one bed, maybe two and prayed they wouldn't need more.

Young pointed to the assessment form he'd been working on and said, "This guy can wait until morning. He stopped taking his medications only three days ago. He should be okay until the sun comes up." He then pointed to a large stack of completed assessments. "These can wait until morning for beds to open up." He pointed to a smaller stack. "At least one or two of these people should be sent to up to the floor." Then before Corrigan could respond, Young quickly added, "I know. I know. We've only got three beds." He then pulled out two assessments from the smaller stack. "I'd recommend sending her and if you can, send him."

Corrigan looked at the names on the assessments. "But that'll only leave me with one bed."

"So what else is new?" said Young, as he placed the two assessments back on the stack and stood. Eight hours of unrelenting pressure was finally over. He wanted to get out while the getting was good. Because you never knew what the next knock at the triage door would bring. Young smiled as he said good-bye to psych triage for the next six months. He then quickly made his way to the triage door and was buzzed through. As he started to step into the hallway, Nurse Tammy Winslow walked up.

"Good evening, Dr. Young," said the pretty blonde nurse with the green eyes and the least amount of seniority and therefore assigned to the graveyard shift.

"Indeed it is," Young happily replied, "Now that my shift is over." Young let Winslow step inside and he and quickly departed.

# CHAPTER 18

Winslow entered the triage office and while putting her purse away spotted Dr. Corrigan. "Good evening Dr. Corrigan. Rumor had it you were going to replace Dr. Young."

"Well, the rumor's true. . . .I don't believe I've meet you before."

"Sorry. I'm Tammy Winslow. I've been working the graveyard for about six months now. I'm waiting for a position to open up on the day shift."

"Six months? Wow." Corrigan duly noted.

Winslow sat down next to Sodabaker who briefed her on the patients sitting in triage, just like Sodabaker had been briefed when she came on duty eight hours earlier. The end of shift report was important. Not only did it provide for continuity of care, it also kept patients from splitting staff. Splitting was usually done at the beginning of a shift by experienced frequent flyers who wanted something. When the two nurses finished, Corrigan pulled up a chair and sat next to them. "We've only got three beds left," he announced.

"Crap," Winslow grumbled. Even as a rookie it hadn't taken her long to become familiar with the harsh realities of the graveyard shift. And not having enough beds was one of them.

"So what else is new?" Sodabaker chimed in. She was starting a double shift and saw the warning signs were already in place for a long night.

"I don't need to tell you that with only three beds we're going to have to use them judiciously."

Sodabaker and Winslow both nodded their heads in agreement.

"What I'm going to do," Corrigan continued, " is admit one of the patients Dr. Young recommended then just keep an eye on the other one he felt should be sent to the psych floor. That way we can keep at least two beds in reserve. So I want both of you to watch the guy over there with the dirty hair and no shoes. If he starts to act out we'll send him to the floor, if he doesn't, it will give us another bed to work with."

"Sounds good," Sodabaker said approvingly.

"The way patients have been pouring in I'm going to try and hold onto those two beds as long as possible," Corrigan said as he finished laying out his strategy for the shift.

"I agree," replied Sodabaker.

"I can't argue with that," Winslow concurred.

"Before I forget," Sodabaker interjected. "Marlin isn't going to be here tonight. He's taking a couple of mental health days off."

"Marlin?" asked Corrigan.

"He's our crisis counselor. He works with families that come in. You'll like him," said Winslow. "He's a pretty easy going guy."

"I look forward to meeting him," said Corrigan.

"Okay, now that we've got our strategy planned. Would anyone care for a cup of coffee?" asked Sodabaker.

Coffee was the life blood of the graveyard shift and only available to triage staff. Patients waiting in triage were not allowed to have it because of the caffeine, so the drip coffee maker was hidden behind a filing cabinet. On average, a graveyard crew could drink two to three pots of coffee a night. However, if it was an especially busy night a pot of coffee could be left untouched until morning. The coffee pot became sort of a barometer for the next shift when they came on. They could look at the glass pot and tell what kind of night the previous shift had even before they were briefed. If the coffee pot was empty, that was a good sign. If it was full and smelled strong it was a bad sign. That meant it hadn't been touched all shift and that translated into a busy night.

"Since everybody has already been assessed, I'll have one," said Corrigan as he responded to Sodabaker's offer.

"I'll pass for now," said Winslow.

"All right then. Two cups of coffee coming right up," said Sodabaker as she stood. "What do you take in your coffee Dr. Corrigan?"

"Just one packet of artificial sweetener, it doesn't matter what kind."

Sodabaker went over to the coffee pot and poured two cups of coffee into Styrofoam cups.

"I might as well reach my therapeutic level of caffeine as soon as I can. I got a feeling it's going to be a long night for me," Corrigan quipped, knowing his body would soon be craving sleep.

"I know how you feel," Winslow sympathized. "It took me about three months before my body adapted to working nights."

"Great," Corrigan sardonically replied.

Sodabaker handed Corrigan a cup of steaming hot coffee.

"Thanks."

Before Sodabaker could sit down, there was a loud rap on the triage door. A quick look at the color monitor showed two police officers standing beside a man in a wheelchair. The man in the wheelchair was unkempt and from the dirty clothes he wore, it was obvious that he was a man of the streets.

189

"Not him again," Sodabaker lamented.

"Who is he?" asked Corrigan.

"He's one of our regulars," Winslow replied. "His name is Eduardo Sanchez. He's one of Doctor Welch's patients. He's an alcoholic. The police usually find him drunk somewhere along the side of the road in his wheelchair and getting in the way of passing cars. Then they bring him here."

Sodabaker buzzed the door for the trio to enter.

"Why do they bring him here?" Corrigan asked. "They've got a drunk tank at County Jail, don't they?"

"You'll see," Sodabaker replied with a flat grin.

A medium-sized police officer with black hair and a tattoo on his forearm pushed Sanchez's wheelchair through the door into the waiting area. The other officer, a sergeant named Moor, with short brown hair and a belly lapping over his Sam Brown, made sure the door closed behind them as they entered.

Eduardo was a drunk. He wasn't a mean drunk per se, but more of an irascible one. At the moment, everything was going his way so he was happy. It was then that Corrigan noticed the man in the wheelchair had only one leg.

The police officer with the tattoo parked Sanchez next to the wall. Moor entered the triage office and handed Corrigan the mental health warrant on Sanchez. "He's all yours." The tattooed officer also entered the office and joined Moor as Corrigan read Eduardo's mental health warrant.

When Corrigan finished reviewing Eduardo's mental health warrant, he couldn't believe what he just read. Eduardo was a danger to himself and others because he was a drunk.

"Why did you bring him here?" Corrigan asked Moor.

"Because he said he wanted to kill himself. And we can't take anyone to jail that's suicidal."

As Corrigan discussed the validity of Eduardo's mental health warrant with the sergeant, Eduardo took it upon himself to become mobile. He pushed his wheelchair over to a woman who sat in a chair along the wall minding her own business. She was depressed and felt like nobody cared if she lived or died. Then up rolls Eduardo the drunk, who begins to flirt with her.

"Hi baby," said Eduardo, with the combined odor of the twelve cans of beer he consumed tonight still on his breath.

He startled the poor woman. Her facial muscles twitched and her eyes became as big as saucers. All she could do was stare at him, "Hey, baby you want to boom, boom?" asked Eduardo as he made an obscene gesture with his hands.

"Oh, crap," said Winslow. "Sanchez is bothering that woman."

"I'll take care of him," said the police officer with the tattoo.

He entered the waiting room and walked briskly over to Sanchez. "You leave that woman alone."

Of course Eduardo didn't hear a thing the officer said. He continued to make amorous advances towards the frightened woman.

The officer pulled Eduardo's wheelchair back to the wall and parked it. "You stay here," he ordered. He then went back inside the triage office and listened in on the conversation still going on between Sergeant Moor and Corrigan.

"Did he actually make threats to kill himself?"

"Not exactly," the sergeant replied. "But he was a danger to others. We found him by the side of the road interfering with traffic."

"Like he always does right?"

"Yeah, but we just couldn't leave him out there. We'd get sued, if somebody hit him." Sergeant Moor protested.

"I agree," said Corrigan. "But, let me ask you a question. When did Mr. Sanchez begin to make statements about wanting to kill himself? Before or after you told him you were taking him to jail?"

"I guess afterwards," Moor replied.

"He knew you were taking him to jail. And being the clever frequent flyer that he is, he also knew that if he said he was suicidal before he got to jail, you were obligated to bring him here instead, right?"

All Moor said was, "Yeah." He didn't like the way this conversation was going.

Corrigan looked over at Sodabaker. "How many times does this make for Mr. Sanchez?"

"At least once a week for the last six months," Sodabaker replied.

Meanwhile, Eduardo pushed himself over to another woman sitting in the waiting area. He pulled up to a young Hispanic woman who had tried to kill herself and still had the superficial cuts on her wrist to prove it. He began to flirt with her and reached out and touched her arm. "My, you are very pretty."

"Shut up asshole!" The woman angrily shrieked. She was in no mood to have a drunk paw her.

"Oh, a feisty one," said an undeterred Eduardo, as he reached out to touch her again.

The woman slapped Eduardo hard across the face. She raised her hand again and waited, ready to deliver another blow if he tried to accost her again.

192

"For God's sakes," cried Winslow. "He's at it again."

"Call security," Corrigan ordered.

Both police officers quickly left the triage office to deal with Eduardo until the hospital's security guards showed up. Eduardo was no longer a happy drunk. He was angry. His amorous advances had been spurned, not once, but twice. Sergeant Moor wheeled Eduardo back across the room then parked and locked his wheelchair next to the triage office door. "You stay there and don't move. You got that asshole?"

The hospital security guards arrived. They were two guards Corrigan had never seen before. One was tall and thin with a sock of brown hair and the other looked like a body builder with muscles bursting from under his white shirt. When they saw Eduardo, they both shook their heads in disgust. They had dealt with this drunken frequent flyer many times. If Eduardo held true to form and wasn't admitted to the psych floor, he would be a pain in the ass the rest of the night. The guards walked over to Eduardo as he started to push himself across the room again. The taller of the two security guards stepped in front of Eduardo. "Whoa, Eduardo, you're not going anywhere."

Eduardo looked up at his new antagonist. "Get out of my way, man. Leave me alone." Eduardo tried to change direction several times. Each time, the guard blocked him. Eduardo was really pissed now.

"We can't have this guy sitting out there all night harassing patients. Especially the women," Corrigan said to Sodabaker and Winslow.

"Then we'll just have to admit him," said a frustrated Sodabaker.

"No. I need that bed for a real emergency. Not some drunk," Corrigan bitterly replied. He then looked at the two nurses and said conspiratorially. "I've got an idea."

Corrigan stepped into the waiting area, walked over and stood next to Eduardo's wheelchair. Even though Eduardo had only one leg, Corrigan remembered the mistake he made of getting to close to the wild-eyed U.N. / CIA /FBI special agent that kicked him in the shin so he stood along side Eduardo's wheelchair. "Mr. Sanchez. My name is Dr. Corrigan."

Eduardo looked up at Corrigan through the fog of having had way too many sixteen ounce cans of beer and tried to focus. When he finally made out Corrigan's white physician's coat, he smiled. He was talking to the man who could admit him to the hospital and keep him from spending the next twenty-four hours in the cross bar hotel. Eduardo simply wanted a place to sleep off his latest binge and do it in the relative comfort of a psychiatric bed rather than on the cold hard cement floor of the drunk tank.

"Mr. Sanchez," Corrigan repeated. "My name is Dr. Corrigan. How are you feeling?"

"Not so good," Eduardo replied.

"What's the matter?" asked Corrigan.

"I don't know."

"The police said you told them that you had a lot of beer tonight. Is that true?" Anyone standing within fifteen feet of Eduardo could smell he had been drinking.

"I guess."

"How many beers do you think you've had tonight?"

"Oh, I don't know ten or fifteen?"

"Could it be that you don't feel so good because you've had too much to drink," pressed Corrigan.

"Sí, it's possible."

"Did you tell the police officers you wanted to kill yourself?"

"Yes."

"Do you feel like killing yourself right now?" Corrigan asked.

"Not really. I'm tired. I just want to get some sleep. When are you going to send me upstairs?" Eduardo had just verbally tipped his hand. "Do you feel like hurting any one?"

"No," said Eduardo as he was getting tired of the doctor's game of twenty questions.

The security guards standing nearby shook their heads knowing Eduardo was only looking to stay out of jail and spend the night in a nice warm bed on County General's dime. While at the same time getting all the medications he needed to ease the pain of detoxification. Eduardo found out a long time ago they didn't give out medications at the jail unless absolutely necessary. The rumor on the street was the nurse in charge of the drunk tank didn't like to give out medications because her ex-husband was an alcoholic and she got some kind of perverse pleasure from watching the drunks suffer through detox.

"Do you still feel like you want to hurt yourself?" Corrigan asked as he needed to build his case for sending Eduardo to jail.

"No," replied Eduardo as a lucid moment bubbled to the surface in his beer soaked brain. "Why would I want to do that? I'm just tired. When are you going to send me up?" Oops, Eduardo verbally tipped his hand again.

"So you don't really want to kill anyone? And you don't want to hurt yourself. That's all I need to know."

After hearing Eduardo's confession, Corrigan stepped confidently back into the triage office. He sat down at a desk, took

Eduardo's mental health warrant and wrote a brief assessment on the bottom of the form. He wrote that in his opinion the patient was not suicidal nor a danger to himself or others and could be transported to the county jail. As soon as he finished signing his name to the form he walked over to the Sergeant Moor and handed him the mental health warrant. "Here you, go. You can take him to jail now."

"What?" The Moor blurted out. Nobody, at least since he'd been bringing drunks to psych triage ever told him to take one back.

"Why?" Moor demanded.

"Because he's not suicidal and jail's where he belongs."

"You're kidding?" The sergeant asked with a bewildered look on his face.

"No," Corrigan replied firmly.

The sergeant looked at Corrigan with a mixture of confusion and resentment. Corrigan had just made his shift a little harder and he didn't like it.

"Two can play at this game," Corrigan confidently thought.

"They're going to be pissed at the jail," Moor half threatened.

"Not when you show them my assessment and my signature at the bottom of the form."

The sergeant quickly read Corrigan's assessment. He also made sure that Corrigan signed his name. "I don't know," he said skeptically. He wasn't convinced the form he held in his hand would be seen by the jailers as legitimate.

"It's his go to jail do not stop at triage ticket. The guy's a drunk and he doesn't belong here," Corrigan added for emphasis.

This was totally unprecedented. In his nine years on the job, nothing like this had ever happened to Moor. Normally all he did was drop crazy people or drunks off at psych triage and leave. No questions asked. The old dump and run. However, this time they wanted him to leave with the same person he brought in.

"Okay, I'll take him to jail but my watch commander is gonna be really pissed," said Moor. He then stuffed the mental health warrant in his back pocket and went out to where his partner and the security guards were blocking Eduardo's wheelchair.

Corrigan could tell from Moor's animated conversation and the evil glance from his tattooed partner, the decision to take Eduardo to the jail wasn't going over very well. Apparently, Moor's partner was also a practitioner of the dump and run, just like Moor. Cops don't like to deal with mentally disturbed people, which is understandable. They're hired on to deal with criminals. Granted, a lot of criminals they come in contact with are mentally disturbed or full blown psychotics. However, it's not uncommon for San Salina police officers who come in contact with an unstable person to just dump him on the doorstep of psych triage like a bag of garbage left on the curb. They simply drive up and drop off anybody they have deemed worthy of placing on a mental health warrant and then leave.

This technique is particularly helpful during domestic disputes, when officers need to separate combating spouses. If during a domestic disturbance one of the spouses, inevitably the male, fails the field attitude test he will suddenly find himself placed on a mental health warrant and hauled off to psych triage. It's not exactly legal, but it gives the hothead a place to cool off.

When Sergeant Moor pushed Eduardo's wheelchair towards the triage door to leave, a bewildered Eduardo shouted, "Where the hell you taking me?"

"To jail," Moor's curtly responded.

"You can't do that," protested Eduardo.

"The doctor says you're not crazy, so you have to go to jail," said Moor's partner.

"That's it guys," thought Corrigan. "Pass the buck. It's my fault you didn't take him to jail in the first place."

The drunk problem was a sad consequence of the jail losing its liability insurance due to a rash of suicides, mostly by drunks, and the expensive legal settlements that followed. A frustrated Sheriff made the unilateral decision that any person considered a suicide risk, no matter how slight, would have to be taken to a mental hospital for an evaluation, rather than the jail. While it made the rank and file at the jail happy, psych triage took the brunt of the Sheriff's grand fiat.

When news of the directive hit the streets it didn't take long for the law of unintended consequences to kick in. Those in charge of the slammer had just issued, what was tantamount to, an avoid jail card. So Eduardo, like many of his frequent flyer buddies quickly learned that in order to avoid going to jail all you had to do was pretend to be suicidal and the cops would have to take you in for a psych evaluation instead of locking you up. And if you stuck to your story long enough you would get a nice bed to sleep in, three square meals a day and drugs to take the edge off your latest bender. So the jails' loss was triage's gain. Frequent flyers might be crazy but they're not stupid and they know how to exploit a weakness in the system when they saw it.

It reminded Corrigan of the time when he was an intern and was doing his first psych rotation. He had to do an assessment on a disheveled street woman in her late forties who had come to the clinic looking for help about a problem she wouldn't talk to anyone about except a doctor. Half way through his assessment he found out she wasn't looking for psychiatric help but a place to stay. She had been kicked out of every shelter in town because of her irascible behavior. It was now winter and she wanted a warm place to stay. Her temporary lodging problem actually fell under the auspices of the hospital's social work department and not the department of psychiatry. However, she had already been turned down by the social work department because she wasn't even a patient at the hospital. So the woman decided to try a different angle to find lodging.

Unfortunately Corrigan didn't know this piece of crucial information when he started his assessment. So he pulled out his copy of the county issued social services directory and began to thumb through it looking for a temporary shelter. When the street wise woman saw Corrigan had the latest edition of the directory she reached into her purse, pulled out last year's directory and wanted to trade him for it. It was also a little unusual for a street person to have her own personal copy of the directory since it wasn't made for public distribution. Yet, there she sat with her own copy wanting to trade up to the latest edition. When Corrigan refused to make the exchange the woman got upset. Before it was over hospital security had to be called to escort her from the premises. He learned a valuable lesson that day. Some frequent flyers not only know how to play the game, some of them even have their own copy of the play book.

With Eduardo on his way to county jail, Corrigan turned his attention to the patient Dr. Young recommended be admitted. The young lady had done some serious damage to her wrist in a suicide attempt and was clearly depressed. She was the kind of patient psych triage was set up to help. She was clearly a danger to herself and needed to be in a supervised environment. It took ten pages of forms signed by both Dr. Corrigan and the patient in order to finish her admission packet. After all the forms were completed, Corrigan called the psych floor and gave the charge nurse his transfer report. The mandatory transfer report consisted of giving the charge nurse a thumbnail sketch of the patient that included the results of the assessment, the diagnosis and any medications needed. It was a way for the staff on the floor to prepare for the patient's arrival as well as to prevent any surprises.

# CHAPTER 19

When the young woman's admission packet was finally completed, all that was left to do was call security and have her escorted to the psych floor. Winslow called security and ten minutes later the young lady was on her way up.

No sooner had the door closed, the phone on the triage counter rang and Sodabaker answered it.

"Psych triage, Nurse Sodabaker speaking. How can I help you?" she answered cheerfully. However, her smile quickly faded as the conversation continued. It was replaced with a look of irritation. "Uh-huh. She won't, huh? How old is she? And you can't do anything for her? Is she medically cleared? You're sure? Fine, send her over."

"What's up?" asked Corrigan.

"It's the ER," replied Sodabaker as she hung up the phone. "They've got a nineteen year old girl over there that either fell or jumped out of a moving car and hit her head."

"Sounds like a medical problem to me. What does that have to do with us?" asked Corrigan.

"She won't talk to anyone over in the ER so they're sending her over here."

"We can make people talk now? What are we now miracle workers?" Corrigan sardonically replied. "Where do they get off pulling stuff like that?"

"The long and the short of it," replied Sodabaker as she explained the ER doctor's decision. "In their opinion anyone who jumps out of a moving car and refuses medical treatment has to be crazy. My words, not theirs, so they put her on a mental health warrant and they're sending her over."

"The old punt, pass and kick routine," said Corrigan. "They do that on the day shift too. When in doubt, put a patient on a mental health warrant and pass the problem on to good old psych triage."

"Tell me about it," Sodabaker annoyingly agreed.

When the ER staff finds themselves in a bind, like the current one, it is standard practice to pass the buck. Although a patient legally has the right to refuse treatment and can leave the ER at any time. Being placed on a mental health warrant overrides the patient's decision. In doing so the ER staff is practicing their own brand of defensive medicine. Because they knew if they failed to treat a patient, even one that left voluntarily and they later developed complications, a lawsuit would soon follow. They frequently send uncooperative patients to psych triage instead of out the door to absolve the ER of any liability. Their hands were clean.

Once a person is placed on a mental health warrant they cannot be discharged from the hospital until they've had a full blown psychiatric assessment. A mental health warrant, while different from a criminal warrant, has the power to detain a person against their will. You can even admit a person to the hospital against their will if they are on a mental health warrant. It is a powerful tool. It can also be abused, as is often done in County General's ER where they issue more mental health warrants than any other department including psych triage

It seemed like Sodabaker had just hung up the phone, when there was a knock at the triage door. It never failed to amaze Corrigan how quickly a patient could be sent to psych triage from their ER. But, it took an act of Congress to get a patient sent in the opposite direction. The ER staff were masters at the punt, pass and kick game. A quick look at the color monitor showed there was a young Hispanic woman at the door with a hospital security guard standing next to her. It was hospital policy that anyone placed on a mental health warrant had to be watched at all times by staff or a security guard, especially when moved from one location to another. The door buzzed and the patient and the security guard walked in. The door closed loudly behind them.

"Here she is," said the muscular security guard to Sodabaker as he rolled up and passed through the hole in the Plexiglas window the ER papers that accompanied the new patient.

"Have her take a seat," directed Sodabaker.

The Hispanic woman walked over to an empty chair and silently sat down. Corrigan got the attention of the security guard and motioned for him to come into the triage office. The guard nodded his head and came around to the door and was buzzed in.

"What can I do for you Dr. Corrigan?"

"What do you know about this patient," he asked.

"She was brought in about an hour ago by her boyfriend. Apparently they got into an argument while they were driving in his car. And she decided to leave. Only trouble is the car was going about forty miles an hour at the time. She hit her head pretty hard on the pavement and has some bruises. Her boyfriend hung around for a while then apparently got scared and took off."

"And she didn't talk to anyone in the ER the whole time she was there?" Corrigan asked skeptically.

"She didn't say a word. Not to staff anyway," the guard replied.

"Is she mute?"

"I don't think so. Because when she found out her boyfriend left, she called him a couple of choice names."

"My, isn't true love wonderful?" Corrigan sarcastically quipped.

Corrigan then asked Sodabaker. "Did they run any tests on her?"

Sodabaker glanced through the ER forms both front and back before she replied. "It doesn't show any were done."

"Damn," thought Corrigan.

"I'll bet you I can tell why they didn't do any tests," the security guard volunteered. "When they couldn't get her to cooperate, they got madder and madder at her. The last time she didn't talk one of the ER doctors stomped out of her room and told one of the nurses that since she didn't want to cooperate he'd send her to psych triage and let them deal with her."

"How'd they get a mental warrant put on her?" asked Corrigan because he knew only the court or a police officer could issue such a formal document.

"They did it when a cop brought a guy in for stitches before he took him to county. One of the ER doctors pulled the cop aside and before we knew it there was a mental health warrant in her chart," the observant guard reported.

"Amazing," an exasperated Corrigan said as he shook his head. "It's amazing what they can get away with over there."

"I see it all the time," said the security guard.

Corrigan thanked the security guard for the much needed information on their new patient.

"No problem," said the guard. He then left triage and returned to roaming the halls of the sleeping hospital.

Corrigan made his way over to Juanita Hernandez a pretty, Hispanic young woman with long black hair and dark brown eyes. "Miss Hernandez, I'm Doctor Corrigan," he said to the drowsy looking woman. "I'd like to talk to you. Would you please come with me?" She silently nodded her head then stood. She caught her balance and slowly followed Corrigan to an interview room. On the way she suddenly became nauseous.

Corrigan could tell she was getting ready to heave so he pointed to the unisex bathroom across the room. "You can go in there."

Fortunately the bathroom wasn't occupied when she pushed on the door and went in. Even with the door closed it was plain to everyone within ear shot the poor girl needed to vomit. After a few minutes, Juanita came out of the bathroom. This time she looked weaker and paler than before she went in. Corrigan joined her and walked slowly beside her to the interview room in case he needed to catch her. When they entered the room, she sat down softly on the wooden chair across from the desk.

Instead of sitting behind the big metal desk Corrigan took the chair from behind the desk and placed it next Juanita, then sat down. From just a cursory glance he could tell the young girl was in distress. She was lethargic, had a flat affect and looked as if she wanted to throw up again. Sure enough Juanita got up from her seat, quickly scurried to the bathroom and shut the door. The unpleasant sound of her heaving quickly followed.

Corrigan left the interview room and walked over to Sodabaker who was sitting at her desk. He spoke to her through the hole in the Plexiglas. "She doesn't look very good."

"You can say that again," Sodabaker agreed.

"I don't like this," a worried Corrigan told her. "Who's the second on call tonight?"

"This month it's Dr. Fry or Dr. Rennet."

Corrigan knew both residents only by name. The hospital had residents work night shifts and weekends rather than regular staff physicians in order to save money. Residents were required, as part of their rotation, to also work graveyard shifts.

"Page whoever is on tonight and have them come down ASAP. I got a bad feeling about this girl."

Sodabaker quickly picked up the phone and punched zero for the hospital operator.

Juanita walked out of the bathroom again. She now looked haggard and tired. Corrigan went over and helped her back to the interview room. After she sat down Corrigan began a friendly conversation with her. This wasn't the time for a full blown psych assessment. This girl was clearly not feeling well and he needed to find out quickly what was causing her physical discomfort. Any emotional pain could wait, at least, for the time being. "How are you feeling?"

Juanita just stared at the floor.

"I know you fell out of a car," Corrigan softly probed. "It's okay. Nobody is going to arrest your boyfriend for what happened." Corrigan didn't know if that was true or not but he had a hunch she was protecting him. Even though she cussed him out for leaving the ER Corrigan knew that young lovers had great emotional swings. They could be mad as hell at each other one minute and then fawning over each other the next, such is the power of young love. "What you and I talk about stays here. Nobody else will know about it. Not the police. Not even your parents, unless you want me to tell them."

Juanita looked up at Corrigan. What he said got her attention. Evidently she was trying to protect her boyfriend. She now seemed more attentive despite her discomfort.

"I'm not going to tell anyone about what happened to you tonight. It's called doctor patient privilege. My main concern is that you're all right. Do you understand?"

Juanita barely nodded her head that she understood. Corrigan had gotten through to her.

"Thank God," thought Corrigan. Now that he could clearly see Juanita's eyes for the first time he thought one pupil looked smaller than the other, a classic sign of a concussion. "May I look at your eyes?"

Juanita slowly nodded her head. She was making an effort to cooperate but she was having a hard time staying awake. She lifted her head and Corrigan looked into her eyes. He flashed the beam of a small penlight at her pupils. The left one reacted and closed at the presence of the light. The right pupil didn't react. She has a concussion. "Those bastards in the ER," Corrigan silently fumed.

"Well, what are you doing here?" a surprised Dr. Ellen Stanley asked when she stepped into the small interview room with Corrigan and Juanita.

"It's a long story," Corrigan replied. "I'll tell you later. Right now I worried about this girl. She's got a concussion."

"Then send her over to the ER," came Stanley's quick solution.

"She came from the ER," Corrigan replied, his voice filled with animosity.

"What?" Stanley replied in amazement.

Corrigan quickly brought Stanley up to speed on the patient sitting in the interview room, ending with a strong recommendation that she needed to be on a medical floor.

"Let me take a look at her," said Stanley.

Corrigan got up and left the room. He shut the door to give Stanley and Juanita some privacy.

Stanley gave Juanita the best medical exam she could under the circumstances. When she ran her fingers through Juanita's hair she found the untreated wound where she hit her head on the pavement. Stanley exploded. "I can't believe this," she said to herself. "Those assholes didn't even clean out her wound."

After Stanley finished the exam she reined in her anger and spoke calmly and compassionately to Juanita. "When you hit your head, you got a concussion. That means your brain has kind of a bruise on it. That's what's making you feel bad. We won't know how serious it is until you've had an MRI."

Meanwhile Juanita started to throw up again. There wasn't time for her to make it to the bathroom so Stanley grabbed the plastic trash can from under the desk and held it in front of her. However, since Juanita had already tossed up everything in her stomach she only dry heaved. Stanley opened the door to the room and called Corrigan over.

"We need to get her an MRI stat."

"How," Corrigan asked. "I don't have any pull around here. You forget, I'm just a psychiatrist."

"Leave it to me," a determined Stanley replied. She stepped out of the interview room leaving Juanita stooped over the trash can heaving. She then walked briskly across the triage waiting area. When she reached the door, she was quickly buzzed through.

"Everything's going to be all right," Corrigan said soothingly to Juanita as he sat down across from her again. "I promise. Dr. Stanley is an excellent doctor and she's going to take good care of you."

For the first time since her arrival in psych triage, Corrigan saw a faint smile appear on Juanita's face. He then took the trash can from her but left it close by just in case.

A few minutes passed and Dr. Stanley re-entered the interview room. "I've got a gurney coming down to take her up for an MRI."

"You're a miracle worker," exclaimed Corrigan.

"Not really. I just called in a few favors," smiled Stanley as she accepted Corrigan's kudos.

"I'm glad you did," Corrigan replied thankfully. "By the way what are you doing here? You don't normally work eleven "P" to seven "A."

"I'm filling in for Dr. Fry tonight. He called in sick."

"Boy, I'm glad you did," Corrigan replied. He could only imagine the hoops he would have had to jump through to get Juanita an MRI if Stanley wasn't on duty. His medical diagnosis, while still valid, would not have had enough clout to get her an MRI in the middle of the night.

Two nurses entered the triage waiting room pushing a hospital gurney to take Juanita up to the fifth floor for her MRI. Stanley signaled for the nurses to bring the gurney over to the interview room. They pulled the gurney up to the door and waited. Stanley bent down and made eye contact with Juanita. "They're here to take you up for your MRI." The two nurses carefully placed Juanita on the gurney then pushed it towards the triage door with Stanley following behind them.

Corrigan looked at Stanley, smiled and gave her a thumb's up. Stanley accepted the compliment with a smile and a nod. The group was then buzzed out into the hall way.

Half an hour later Stanley called Corrigan and advised him the MRI showed Juanita had two bleeders in the brain. As a result Juanita was immediately taken to the intensive care unit and was now resting comfortably. Corrigan thanked Stanley profusely for her help. As he hung up the phone the theme from an old television western came to mind that he felt best described the ER's treatment of Juanita. "Moving, moving, moving, keep those patients moving'. Head um up, move um out, head um up, move um out."

Mercifully Corrigan's shift finally ended. After he gave his report to the doctor relieving him, he quickly made his way out the door. When the sliding glass doors opened he stepped out into a crisp autumn morning. However, the cold refreshing jolt wasn't enough to overcome his tiredness. He had just finished his first graveyard shift in more years than he cared to remember and it took its toll on him. He was ready for bed. He was emotionally and physically drained.

Very few people outside the helping professions know how physically exhausting it can be working with irrational patients in a highly charged emotion filled environment like psych triage. Having to maintain a constant state of alertness and objectivity so you don't miss something or make a mistake takes its toll both emotionally and physically. Many a mental health professional can be as physically beat after spending eight hours in a pressure cooker like psych triage as a marathon runner finishing a race. Corrigan made his way to the doctor's parking lot and looked forward to crawling into bed and putting the last eight hours behind him.

# CHAPTER 20

Since the birth of his daughter, the one thing Corrigan couldn't get enough of was sleep. Helping take care of Emily and adjusting to his new graveyard shift reminded him of his days as a resident when sleep depravation was a constant companion. Working 48 straight hours or more back then was normal. Sleep was a precious commodity and grabbed whenever possible, as it was now.

Corrigan had already slept eight hours and was sitting in the living room taking a cat nap when Dr. John Zilker called him on his cell phone. He wanted to remind him of the next chronic care team meeting.

"Good afternoon, Dr. Corrigan," a cheerful Zilker began. He then went on to advise the drowsy doctor the next chronic care team meeting would be held at the same location at seven o'clock this coming Monday night. When Corrigan told Zilker about his new schedule, Zilker simply replied. "We only have three cases to review. You'll be out in plenty of time to start your eleven o'clock shift."

"All right then. I'll see you Monday," Corrigan replied and closed his cell phone. "Damn," he thought. Until now he had been marginally successful at putting that ghastly night in the conference room behind him. Now it came flooding back. Zilker's phone call was a chilling reminder he was now a member in good standing of a coalition of fellow professionals who killed people. It made him shiver.

The last Monday of the month finally arrived and Corrigan still groggy even though he had slept eight hours got up and ate the equivalent of breakfast, a sandwich, an apple and some milk then relieved Diane in the living room of her baby sitting duties. Once relieved, Diane fell fast asleep in the recliner chair the moment Emily was in her husband's arms. As Corrigan paced back and forth patting Emily on the back to get her to burp he glanced at his watch. "It's going to be a long night," he said softly to himself.

He then remembered the check he received from Dr. Zilker's managed care company for his consulting fees after the first chronic care team meeting. The money more than made up for the inconvenience. Dr. Zilker explained after the meeting that their, "consulting fees," came out of a special account the four managed care companies set up for honorariums and bona fide consulting fees. While the bulk of the money in the account came from legitimate sources it also laundered the ten per cent remuneration the chronic care team received from the estimated money saved from the canceled policies of the patients they terminated.

Corrigan, in keeping with the secrecy of the chronic care team, opened a separate bank account to deposit his monthly consulting fee. After all, he rationalized; he could only put so much into his 401(k) at work. And considering his salary and benefits were totally dependent on monies levied from increasingly irritable taxpayers there may not be a pot of gold waiting for him at the end of the retirement rainbow. Therefore he planned to save all the money he made from consulting until his retirement, then surprise Diane with his apparent frugalness.

As he continued to pat Emily on the back his efforts were rewarded with a loud, "burp." "That's a burp a sailor would be proud of," Corrigan told his daughter. He then cradled his precious child and looked into her serene face. "You are the cutest baby ever born," he cooed. He enjoyed his time with Emily, which also included not shirking his parental duty of changing dirty diapers.

He had developed a strong stomach while in medical school and it served him well now that he was changing bulging diapers filled with odoriferous polychromatic surprises. Emily yawned and slowly closed her eyes. She was ready for her nap. Corrigan carried her gently to the master bedroom where they kept her crib. He tenderly placed her in the crib and then sat down on the edge of their queen size bed. He watched her sleep for a little while. He then decided it would be a good time to change clothes. However, before he knew it he was sound asleep.

Emily's crying woke him up. As if on automatic pilot, he sprung from the bed and made a bee line to her crib. However, when he reached down to pick her up she was gone. Not finding his daughter in her crib woke him from his stupor. He could still hear her crying and when he focused on where the sound was coming from, he saw Diane holding Emily in the doorway. "I've got her, you sleepy head," said Diane. "She probably needs her diaper changed. I'll get it."

"Was I asleep? I thought I was changing my clothes."

"I heard her crying from the living room and when I came in you were sawing logs."

"I didn't even hear her. Wow, I must've been tried."

"We both are, dear."

"I know," said Corrigan as he ran his hand thought his hair. He then looked at the digital clock on the night stand. It was after five o'clock. "I might as well get cleaned up and get ready for work."

It was a little after six o'clock by the time Corrigan finished his shower, shaved and put on a new set of clothes and walked out of the master bedroom. Diane was nursing her pride and joy in the new rocking chair they bought before Emily was born. Diane's mother insisted they buy one. She told the expectant couple a rocking chair was an essential piece of furniture that every new mother should have. It turned out she was right. Diane used it all the time. Corrigan walked into the living room and already had his coat on, which was a dead giveaway that he was leaving for work early.

"Are you leaving for work already?" The sleep deprived mother asked. From the tone of Diane's voice, Corrigan knew his early exit wasn't welcomed. Even though it had been less than a month since Emily was born, Diane and James Corrigan, like all new parents, fell into the trap that the opposite spouse wasn't holding up their end when it came to taking care of the baby. Naturally, Diane resented the idea of James leaving early, especially when she had other plans. Like taking a nap or just putting her feet up and watching a little television. She wanted some downtime.

"I have a meeting I need to go to before work," Corrigan replied knowing it probably wasn't going to placate his weary wife.

"What kind of a meeting?"

Corrigan's mind raced to come up with an appropriate answer. He silently reprimanded himself that he should have thought of something ahead of time. Some type of a cover story. But, he'd been too tired. His brain wasn't firing on all cylinders lately and he knew he should have anticipated Diane's question. Now he had to be careful how he responded. He needed to maintain the confidentiality of the group. Yet, he needed to satisfy the woman sitting in the rocking chair with the dark circles under her eyes. He finally blurted out what he thought would be the best way to handled the problem. "I took on a consulting job."

"What?" a surprised Diane sharply replied, "A consulting job. In the middle of all this you took on a consulting job. You never mentioned anything about a consulting job to me."

"I know. I agreed to it a couple of months ago," Corrigan began his half truthful confession. "It was going to be a surprise. Then everything happened and I forgot about it until I got a phone call a few days ago to remind me."

"You knew about this a couple of months ago and you didn't bother to tell me?" An even more aggravated Diane asked.

"Oh, boy, I shouldn't have said that," thought Corrigan as he regrouped.

"It's only one night a month," he said. "I just forgot. You can understand? Besides I felt we could use the extra money. You know, with the baby and all." He knew the last line was stretching it a bit, but he wanted to score as many points as possible before Diane took another shot at him.

"I'm disappointed you didn't tell me," said Diane as she placed Emily on her shoulder to burp.

"I know. I meant it to be a surprise," said Corrigan as he tried his best to convince Diane his motives were pure. "We just review a couple of cases once a month, that's all. I'm sorry I didn't tell you. I guess I blew it."

The look on Diane's face said it all. She was disappointed and angry. Then the guilt trip started. "That's all right," she replied innocently. "I'll stay home with the baby. You go to your meeting. We'll be all right." Her last words rang hollow and had the desired effect. Corrigan could feel himself being enveloped by an almost palpable cloud of guilt, which was Diane's goal. The old guilt trip was something she learned from her mother, the all-time master of guilt trips.

"I'm sorry," an apologetic Corrigan repeated as he tried to dig himself out of a hole.

Diane didn't respond. She suddenly became interested in something invisible on the ceiling and gazed at it to keep from looking at her husband. Finally, Emily's burp broke the silence. Diane got up from the rocker and walked across the living room. "I'll leave a light on for you," she said curtly as she passed her husband.

"Oh, come on, Diane," Corrigan pleaded. "Don't be like that."

"Like what?" said Diane as she started towards the master bedroom. "I'm just putting Emily down. After all she needs her sleep." Diane then disappeared down the hallway.

If looks could kill, Corrigan would have been a dead man ten times over. Diane made it perfectly clear with the emphasis she placed on, "she needs her sleep" the next layer of guilt had been applied. Corrigan knew he couldn't talk to Diane until she cooled off. Hopefully in the morning he would be able to do a better job of explaining himself. "Good-bye," he hollered to Diane who was now in the master bedroom. "I'll see you in the morning."

No response, another layer of guilt.

"I sure screwed that up," Corrigan said to himself as he walked to the front door. He slowly opened the door, looked outside then hesitated. He turned and shouted loud enough for Diane to hear him in the back bedroom. "I love you." He didn't wait for a response, because he didn't expect one. So he stepped outside, shut the door and missed Diane's reply. It was softer and filled with a twinge of regret as it came from the bedroom, "I love you too."

# CHAPTER 21

Corrigan was still feeling a little unsettled by his unpleasant departure as he pulled into the long driveway of Zilker's mansion. He parked his car and made his way to the front door. This time he didn't have to wait for someone let him in. The door was unlocked and he went directly to the study to join the rest of his colleagues. When he opened the door to the study, he was surprised to see empty champagne flutes in front of each member's seat and a magnum of champagne chilling in a bucket of ice in the middle of the conference table. As soon as everyone saw Corrigan they shouted. "Congratulations!"

Zilker broke out a box of cigars and handed one to Corrigan. "Congratulations to the new father."

"Congratulations," said Ozawa.

"Ditto," said Blair.

"That's all we need is another psychiatrist in town," joked Marapudi.

"Well, what's her name? Gatway asked.

"Emily Ann Corrigan," said the proud father as he made his way to his chair. "Six pounds, ten ounces, mother and baby are doing fine."

"That's a beautiful name," said Gatway.

"Thank you," Corrigan replied as he sat down.

"This calls for a toast," Zilker loudly announced. The magnum was quickly popped open and the empty champagne flutes filled. When everyone's glass was filled, Zilker raised his glass for a toast. "To the new father, his beautiful wife and, I'm sure, the cutest baby in town."

As one the table responded with. "Hear, hear."

Corrigan nodded his head and smiled appreciatively. The group drank the champagne and spent the next few minutes chatting like members of a social club.

It was Dr. Zilker who finally brought them to order. "We only have three cases to review tonight so I think we should get started." The friendly chatter dwindled away as everyone got down to business. Zilker opened the first medical chart for review. "The first patient tonight is Michael Anderson. A forty-two old white male admitted to Twin Lakes' hospital two days ago with a diagnosis of bipolar disorder. This makes his tenth admission in fifteen months and our managed care company has spent over six hundred and eighty thousand dollars on him. They've asked us to look into the matter."

"Why aren't his meds working?" asked Ozawa. "Bipolar disorder can be easily regulated with meds."

"I know. They do, until you stop taking them."

Ozawa rolled his eyes. "Damn not another one."

"Any known criminal history?" Dr. Blair asked.

"Most bipolar patients don't get into as much trouble as this guy," Zilker replied. "He's been arrested twice for assault, once for battery and, as to be expected, he's been arrested several times for shoplifting."

"How far apart were the assaults?" Marapudi asked.

Zilker flipped through a couple of pages before he replied. "Let's see. The first one was six months, the second one was two months ago and the last was just three days ago."

"It would appear the intervals between his aggressive episodes are becoming shorter. Which, means they'll probably even get shorter with the added potential he might really hurt someone," Marapudi openly speculated.

"I agree," said Blair.

"I agree," said Gatway. "He's like a time bomb waiting to go off."

"He has no support system, which doesn't help," added Zilker. "He's divorced, thankfully no children. . ."

"Thank God for small favors," Ozawa jokingly added.

Everyone around the table including, Corrigan smiled and nodded their head in agreement.

"As I was saying," Zilker continued with mock irritation. "The man has no support system and no one who will step up and help monitor his medications."

"What about putting him in a county program that will monitor his meds?" Corrigan asked optimistically.

"They already tried that," responded Zilker. "But he kept missing his appointments."

"Any alcohol or drug use?" asked Corrigan confident he already knew the answer. However, there was always a first time.

"He self medicates with cocaine and Jim Beam," replied Zilker.

"No wonder he can't get his meds regulated," said Corrigan.

"There you have it," Zilker concluded. "I think our patient has met the criteria for being referred to this group. He has had multiple admissions, he's had well over a half a million dollars spent on trying to straighten him out and he's not getting any better. If anything, in my opinion, he's getting worse and he's going to seriously hurt or kill someone if his pattern of behavior continues unabated. However, I'm open to any suggestions."

There was silence around the room.

"I concur with your analysis," said Ozawa breaking the silence.

"Same here," responded Blair. "He's not going to get any better. He's on a downward spiral and I don't want to see him take anybody with him."

"I don't see him getting any better, either," Gatway added. "I think we should cut our losses and give him a new diagnosis."

Zilker looked around the table, "Any objections?"

Everyone remained silent, even Corrigan, which surprised him how easy it was to talk about people in the abstract, especially when you didn't know them. Yet he knew his acquiescence meant only one thing, Michael Anderson was going to die.

"All right then," Zilker announced. "Michael Anderson's new diagnosis is terminus en extremes, any objections?" Silence again. "There being no objections, Mr. Anderson's name will now be placed on our referral list." This was another one of Zilker's euphemism.

Zilker set Anderson's chart down and picked up the next one for review. He opened the chart and began. "Our next patient is Gary Thompson. A thirty-eight year old white male admitted to Arbor Creek hospital three days ago. His admitting diagnosis was paranoid schizophrenia. This makes his 16th admission over the last 26 months. Our managed care company has spent over nine hundred thousand dollars on him. They've asked us to look into the matter."

"What's the patient's date of birth?" asked a concerned Corrigan.

"March tenth, nineteen sixty-five." Zilker replied.

"Is he a physician?" Corrigan asked with a sinking feeling in the pit of his stomach.

Zilker quickly thumbed through the chart and replied. "Why yes he is. He's a surgeon."

"Is he married to a woman named Betty?" Corrigan asked dreading the answer.

Zilker scanned the patient's psycho-social history. "Yes he is. Do you know this patient?"

"I'm afraid I do," Corrigan sighed. "We went to medical school together. He has two children, right?"

"Yes," replied Zilker. "Tom age nine, Gloria aged twelve."

"I'm their godfather," Corrigan sadly replied. "God," thought Corrigan. Just when he thought things couldn't get any worse.

"What a pity," said Zilker.

"We were pretty tight in medical school. He was a year ahead of me. I lost contact with him after he went into practice for himself. We said we'd keep in touch. But you know how that goes. I can't believe he's been referred to this group."

"Well your friend has apparently gone downhill since you last saw him," said Zilker as he sympathized with Corrigan. "According to his chart, he has a dual diagnosis of paranoid schizophrenia and alcohol dependence. He's made a mess of his life. And he meets all of our criteria."

"But he's a fellow physician," Corrigan offered in Thompson's defense.

"I know. That's what makes this all the more tragic," said a sympathetic Zilker.

"Damn," thought Corrigan.

Zilker flipped to another page in the chart and read out loud. "It says his license has been suspended. He's separated from his wife and according to some of the progress notes in the chart he apparently thinks he can cure himself."

"Well, that's obviously not true," Blair noted.

"What does it say about his alcohol use?" asked Corrigan, desperately searching for something to help mitigate his friend's circumstances.

"It says he drinks up to a pint of whiskey a day and at least half a case of beer on top of that. His liver enzymes show he's in the first stages of cirrhosis."

"But no drugs?" asked Corrigan.

"According to everything I've read, apparently not," replied Zilker.

"Does he take his meds?"

"Yes. But he drinks on top of them. So naturally they're not effective," Zilker replied.

"Couldn't his alcohol abuse be a form self medication because his meds are not working?" Corrigan asked as he hoped to plant seeds of doubt in the group.

"I know he's your friend. But, don't you think that's stretching it a bit?" Ozawa interjected. "His meds would work if he just gave them a chance."

"What's he on?" asked Corrigan.

Zilker flipped to the medicine page of the chart. He studied it briefly. "From what I can tell he's on a standard medication protocol for paranoid schizophrenia. They're the same meds I'd prescribe for any of my patients with a similar diagnosis."

"Has he been through any alcohol treatment programs?"

"Two."

"What happened after he left?" asked Corrigan.

Zilker was starting to bristle at Corrigan's questions. He reluctantly flipped through Thompson's progress notes until he found what he was looking for. "It says he stayed sober for three weeks after his first discharge and six weeks after his last program."

"I assume he was on his meds, while he was sober," Corrigan openly speculated.

Zilker unenthusiastically consulted Thompson's chart again. After he found the answer to Corrigan's latest irritating question he looked up at him and said with some testiness in his voice. "Yes."

Corrigan nodded his head. "Then he goes back to drinking, right?"

Before Corrigan could ask another question Zilker politely said. "Dr. Corrigan, as much as I'd love to play twenty questions with you. Would you please tell us what you're driving at?"

"It was now or never," thought Corrigan. He needed to interject some mitigating circumstances to the panel, with its singular mindset, so that his friend could be spared from their ultimate Draconian diagnosis. "The way I see it, the patient," Corrigan hoped the word patient would lend some objectivity to his presentation. "Has a dual diagnosis and it appears it has never been firmly established which is primary and which is secondary?"

"So?" Blair asked.

Corrigan ignored the interruption and continued. "His chart shows even before his meds have a chance to work he drowns them in alcohol. We can't say for sure if his schizophrenia is really being treated. We have no evidence he has been able to establish a therapeutic level of anti-psychotic medications, which would suggest to me that alcohol may be his primary problem. And until the alcohol problem is treated he may never get better. Either way I feel it is imperative to establish his primary diagnosis before we dismiss the patient's lack of progress out of hand."

"Oh, please," said Gatway.

"Then what would you suggest?" asked Zilker knowing Corrigan was upsetting the apple cart.

"That the patient be monitored after his discharge to make sure he's fully detoxified and that his meds have a chance to work for at least six months. Then we might be able to arrive at a working diagnosis."

"I see," was all that Zilker disdainfully said. What Corrigan just suggested was unprecedented. Once a patient was sent to the chronic care team it was understood the patient was written off. Money saved and the chronic care team got its cut.

"You have presented a very strong argument for your friend," Zilker told Corrigan hoping to placate him.

"Thank you," said Corrigan as he accepted the compliment and gave Zilker a professional smile.

"I understand how you feel," said Zilker now sounding almost fatherly. "But we still have a job to do . . . If you'd like to recuse yourself while we review his case, I think we'll all understand."

Everyone around the table nodded their head in affirmative agreement. They truly felt sorry for Corrigan but they also resented the fact he had introduced cognitive dissonance into the group for the first time since they started meeting.

"This couldn't have happened in a million years," thought Ozawa as he watched Corrigan.

"Damn, this is really uncomfortable," thought Blair as she avoided eye contact with Corrigan.

"I would like to stay," Corrigan began.

"I don't think that would be wise," said Zilker as he tried to hide his irritation. "I know how you feel and you've presented an admiral defense of your friend, which we will take into consideration when we make our final decision. But I think it would be best if you were to recuse yourself and not be present for this review."

"We'll treat him fairly," added Ozawa.

"They're professionals," thought Corrigan. "They'll take everything into consideration. Beside, I think I made a good argument for an alternate treatment plan. They have to respect that. They surly aren't that locked into the process."

"Well?" Zilker courteously pushed.

Corrigan stood. "I'll wait outside." He then walked towards the door.

"We'll let you know when we're finished," said Zilker as Corrigan put his hand on the door knob to leave. He then opened the door, stepped outside and closed the polished wooden door behind him.

"I don't care if he is Corrigan's friend," Blair began. "We still have a job to do."

"We shouldn't give him any special consideration," Marapudi added, his nose almost upturned. "He's as bad as any patient we've reviewed."

"I agree," said Gatway. "Besides this is a one in a million fluke. It'll never happen again."

"But he's a fellow physician," offered Zilker. "That should count for something."

"Lots of physicians lose their licenses every year because of alcohol and drugs. This guy shouldn't be treated any differently," Blair countered.

"The man meets all the criteria," Marapudi pointed out.

"And he's cost your managed care company a boatload of money," Blair reminded Zilker and everyone around the table. A couple of heads nodded in agreement.

"The man has been given chance after chance," said an exasperated Ozawa. "And yet he still thinks he can heal himself. This could go on for years."

"Or until his liver gives out," Gatway said with gallows humor.

"I think I hear a consistent theme in all of your opinions," observed Zilker. "It seems you want to give this man no quarter and treat him like every other patient we review. Is that what I'm hearing?"

Everyone around the table nodded their head.

"Then if we are all of one mind, I will ask if there is any further discussion."

The room fell silent. They were ready to vote.

Ozawa then spoke up, hoping to assuage any reservations the group might have. "I think Corrigan would objectively agree with what we are doing if he were voting."

"That's true," Zilker agreed. "Do I hear any recommendations from the floor?"

"The same as the last one," Blair bluntly recommended.

"Any objections?" asked Zilker.

The panel remained silent.

"Then it's unanimous. We will give Dr. Gary Thompson a new diagnosis: terminus en extremes." Zilker then spoke in confidence to the panel members. "After Dr. Corrigan re-enters the room we will review our last case and then adjourn. I'm sure he will suspect the worse despite his spirited defense so I will talk to him after the meeting. So please remain professional and do not reveal our recommendation."

Zilker stood and walked to the door. He opened it and asked Corrigan to come back in.

As soon as Corrigan sat down he asked Zilker. "What did you recommend?"

"We have one more case to review," said Zilker as he sat down. "I think we should get it out of the way first." He then looked directly at Corrigan. "I will talk to you about Dr. Thompson's recommendation after the meeting. I think you'll be pleased." Zilker threw in the lie at the end to keep Corrigan at the table and to placate him until the end of the meeting.

Corrigan smiled appreciatively.

Zilker picked up the last chart and opened it. "Our last patient is a twenty-eight year old African-American male named Ted Washington." Zilker looked over at Corrigan. "He's not a friend of yours too, is he?"

"The name doesn't ring a bell," Corrigan smiled.

"Good. Then we'll proceed."

When the meeting concluded, everyone said their good-byes and quickly left, expect for Corrigan who remained seated. After seeing his last guest out, Zilker returned to his seat at the head of the conference table. Corrigan expected, as he watched Zilker settle in, that since Zilker told him he would be pleased with the group's action, that the group followed his recommendation. After all, it made sense. However, he became a little worried by Zilker's protracted silence.

227

"About your friend," Zilker finally began. "There is no easy way to put this, but the panel went against your recommendation and voted that Thompson be referred to our friends in the field."

"What!" a shocked Corrigan exclaimed. "God damn you. You said. . ."

"I know what I said. But, I didn't think it was the time or the place to discuss the recommendation. Please forgive me."

"How could you do this?"

"I didn't do it the panel did," said Zilker as he deflected the blame. "The panel took your recommendation under consideration, however they felt it was inappropriate considering the mission of the group."

"The mission," Corrigan shot back. "The only mission of this group is to kill people."

"One of whom you personally disposed of yourself, if I might add," Zilker caustically countered, as he purposely brought up the not so subtle reminder. He let Corrigan know his hands were just as dirty as anyone else who sat in judgment around the table. He then added. "Didn't you understand after the first night? You're just as culpable as anyone here for the recommendations we make?"

"But I never thought. . ."

"We never thought this would happen either," said Zilker now actually sounding apologetic. "I know it probably will never happen again, but just in case I'm going to establish a new screening protocol to prevent a repeat of this unfortunate incident."

"But he's my friend. He deserves a chance," Corrigan found himself pleading.

"I understand. It's not personal. It's just business. The people who pay our salaries expect certain things from us and we have to deliver."

"What you're saying is that no matter what I say or do my friend is still going to be murdered?" This time Corrigan had no trouble using the word, murder.

"Such a harsh word," said Zilker. "But, yes, I'm afraid the die is cast."

"What the hell have I done," thought Corrigan as he chastised himself for ever having met with these Godforsaken people. All the patients he reviewed with them until now were just faceless names on a medical chart. What had started out as an abstract exercise suddenly became personal after his friend's chart was opened for a deadly review. Thompson had a real face and a real family with kids. Unlike Cobb, who Corrigan felt deserved to die, Gary Thompson was salvageable. "This has gone too far," Corrigan thought to himself. "I've got to get off this panel."

As if reading his mind Zilker said. "I know this has been rough. But I hope you're not thinking of quitting."

"Now that you mentioned it I would like to resign my position effective immediately."

"Isn't that a little rash?"

"No," replied Corrigan. "I think I've gotten in way over my head and I want out."

"Really," said Zilker with a critical squint.

"You can trust me not to tell anyone about the chronic care team," Corrigan quickly added hoping to assuage Zilker's biggest fear.

"This man is becoming a pain in the ass," thought Zilker, "So much for my research." Corrigan, on paper, was the perfect replacement and now he wanted out. Let some damn fluke happen and suddenly Corrigan shows his true colors. Zilker never anticipated such a problem and now the secrecy of the group was

229

at stake. He couldn't just let Corrigan walk away. No matter how many times Corrigan promised he wouldn't reveal the existence of the panel, Zilker knew it wouldn't be fair to the other members to live in constant fear of being exposed. He had to think of something quickly in order to buy some time.

"I understand how you feel," Zilker said smoothly. "But we don't meet again for another month. If you still feel the same way, then by all means resign, fair enough?"

"I want to resign now," demanded Corrigan.

"Please. I know this has been very trying for you," said Zilker apologetically. "This will never happen again."

Corrigan just stared at him.

"I promise," Zilker said as he tried to get Corrigan to agree to his proposal.

"I don't know."

"Please just think about for a month," Zilker implored.

"I already know what my answer will be," Corrigan tersely replied.

"Please. Give us the courtesy of a month. A lot can happen in a month."

"All right," Corrigan sighed, "One month and not a day longer."

"That's all I ask," Zilker smiled.

Corrigan stood to signal the meeting was over. Zilker remained seated as Corrigan silently left the room.

As soon as Corrigan was gone, Zilker reached for his cell phone. He punched in a number, waited for a response and then said. "We've got a problem."

Corrigan walked briskly to his car. He opened the door and slid behind the wheel. After he shut the door and put the key in the ignition, he suddenly felt sick to his stomach. His friend was now under a sentence of death. The more he thought about it, the more he felt he needed to do something. He couldn't let his friend be put down like a stray dog. He pulled out his cell phone and dialed the number for Arbor Creek Hospital. "Hello. This is Dr. James Corrigan. Could you please tell me who the attending is on a patient of yours? His name is Gary Thompson. Sure I'll hold." The person on the other end of the line found the information. "Dr. Masterson," Corrigan parroted back. "Thank you. Good-bye."

Corrigan closed his cell phone and started up the Mustang. He had taken the first step. As he drove the car onto the street and headed to psych triage he thought. "What could Zilker really do to me anyway? Kick me off the panel? Big deal." Little did Corrigan know what Zilker was actually capable of?

After putting in another eight hours at psych triage, Corrigan was glad to be pulling into his garage. On the way up the drive he noticed the porch light was still on. Diane, true to her word, must have turned it on before she went to bed. Seeing the porch light also reminded him of their little rift before he left the house. As the garage door closed, he wondered how Diane would greet him this morning. Would he get the cold shoulder or did she mellow out during the night? He unlocked the front door and walked in. Corrigan could hear Diane in the kitchen and could smell coffee brewing. "Maybe she forgot about last night," he thought optimistically.

# CHAPTER 22

After he shut the door, Diane walked into the living room carrying Emily. "Good morning dear," Diane said cheerfully. "How was your night?"

"Pretty busy, I don't think I'll ever get used to the freak show that comes through there every night."

"I made some decaf coffee if you want some," Diane offered pleasantly. She then sat in the rocker and began to slowly rock Emily.

"Thanks. I think I will," Corrigan replied, wondering if he had walked into a trap. Diane had either forgiven him or she was up to something. Corrigan fetched a cup of coffee and returned to the living room.

Corrigan sat down on the sofa facing Diane. "You wouldn't believe the patients that came in last night. One young girl cut her wrist to show how much she loved her boyfriend."

"What?" Diane replied as her nose wrinkled with disgust.

"She found her boyfriend with another woman, so she decided the best way to show him how much she loved him was to cut her own wrist."

"That doesn't sound like love. That sounds stupid," Diane replied.

"I know. But, she felt it was the only way to show him how serious she was about their relationship."

"Some relationship," Diane remarked sarcastically.

"I know," Corrigan agreed. "But, I read a paper about the hormonal changes during love and there is a point where the brain's chemistry can cause a reaction like that around the second or third month of a relationship. It's total biochemistry."

"If I were her I would have shot the son of a bitch rather than cut myself," Diane said matter of factually. "How old is she?"

"The sad news is she's only nineteen. She's still got many more years of disappointments ahead of her."

"Jeez," Diane sighed, "So young and so dumb."

"I know," said Corrigan as he patiently waited to see if the other shoe from last night would fall. "The other patient was a woman who decided to stop taking her medications because she saw her favorite movie star on some talk show say psychiatric medications were bad for you. He encouraged the use of vitamins and jogging."

"And she bought that line of crap?" asked Diane.

"Yep, the police found her standing on a street corner downtown screaming at the top of her lungs at people. According to her sister, who called the police, she was doing just fine until she saw the TV show and stopped her meds.

"That's really sad," said Diane. She paused and looked at her husband. It seemed like forever before she spoke, but it was only a couple of seconds. "About last night."

"Uh-oh, here it comes," Corrigan said to himself. He would soon learn his fate.

"I'm sorry about the way I acted."

Corrigan couldn't believe his ears. It sounded like she was forgiving him.

"I thought about it after you left and I can understand your point of view. You had good intentions but bad timing. I'm sorry."

"I'm sorry too. Especially for the way you found out. I didn't mean to spring it on you like that," Corrigan replied truthfully. "But it won't be a problem anymore. I had some time to think about it and I've decided it's not worth it. I'm going to quit the consulting job so I can spend more time around here where I'm really needed."

Diane wanted stand up and shout hallelujah. But she stayed calm and remained seated. "Are you sure?"

"Yes. I'm sure. I need to be here for you and Emily."

"I hope my temper tantrum last night didn't have anything to do with you changing your mind," Diane demurred.

"No," Corrigan only half lied. It did to a small degree. But, he really wanted out because of what happened at last night's chilling meeting.

"I'm glad to hear that," Diane smiled.

"I'm Emily's father and I need to be here for her. I can get a consulting job anytime." Corrigan got off the sofa and walked over to Diane. He stretched out his arms. "Here, let me take her."

Diane handed Emily over and watched as her husband cradled their precious bundle in his arms. Emily yawned and slowly fell asleep.

Corrigan carried Emily down the hall to the bedroom. Diane followed him and watched him gently place Emily in her crib. When he finished, Diane put her arms around his neck and kissed him deeply. "I love you."

He returned the kiss with equal passion. "I love you too."

The two kissed and embraced with an ache and inner longing only those who have been intimate can truly understand. Corrigan hands wondered over Diane's breasts as he kept his lips pressed against hers. She undid her bra to allow him freer access. They both gently lay down on the bed facing each other. They continued to kiss and caress each other until their bodies were ready to ignite. "I've missed your touch," moaned Diane.

"I've missed touching you," Corrigan tenderly replied as his hand wandered down toward her panties.

Diane gently took his hand away and tactfully reminded him it was to early for them to make love because she still needed time to heal.

Corrigan mentally scolded himself. He knew better but in the heat of the moment he forgot. "Sorry," he said.

"That's all right," she seductively whispered. "I'll be open for business soon."

They continued to kiss until Corrigan couldn't stifle a yawn. He was horny but he was also very tired. "Sorry," he apologized.

"Hey," Diane chuckled. "Aren't you supposed to do that after we make love?"

"Sorry. I couldn't help it." The moment was broken.

"You need to get some sleep," a sympathetic Diane said as she sat up and slipped back into her bra.

Corrigan sat up. "I love you."

"I love you too. That's why I want you to get some sleep."

"Thanks," Corrigan gratefully replied. He slipped out of his shoes and began to undress.

"I want you fully rested when you wake up so you can watch Emily."

"I had a feeling you weren't letting me sleep for purely altruistic reasons," Corrigan smiled.

Diane left the room to let her husband get some much needed rest.

As soon as his head touched the pillow it seemed like the alarm clock went off. "I must have set it wrong," he thought as he tried to focus on the digital numbers on the clock radio. When they finally came into focus he saw that he had been asleep for eight hours. He reached over and silenced the alarm. He sat up, rubbed his eyes and looked over at the crib. Emily was gone. He tossed off his covers and went to the bathroom where he relieved himself and got ready for what was left of the day.

When he walked into the living room, he found Diane lying on the sofa sound asleep with Emily sleeping next to her. Taking advantage of the situation, he quietly walked into the kitchen to make himself something to eat.

As he sat eating at the kitchen table, he heard footsteps approaching. Diane entered the kitchen carrying Emily. "Well, good morning," she said cheerfully. She then handed Emily to him. "She's been fed and burped. I need to take a bath." Diane then quickly left.

Corrigan cradled Emily in his arms. "I guess it's just you and me, kid." Corrigan continued to eat with his right hand, while Emily nestled quietly in the bend of his left arm. When he finished eating, they moved to the living room. He sat down on the sofa and flipped open his cell phone. He punched in a number and waited. Emily watched fascinated at what he was doing. "I dread the day you get one of these," Corrigan said to his little angel.

Dr. Masterson didn't answer his phone but his answering service picked up. "Could you page, Dr. Masterson for me please? This is Dr. James Corrigan. I need to speak with him. He has my cell phone number. Thank you."

Corrigan was making goo, goo sounds and playing with Emily's fingers when his cell-phone rang. He picked it up and

236

flipped it open. "Dr. Corrigan," he professionally answered. "Hey, David how are you doing? Diane and the baby are doing fine. Thanks. The reason I called is that I need to ask you a favor . . . I heard you've got a patient named Gary Thompson over there and you're his attending. . . .You know. From a nurse who knows a nurse who knows a nurse. You know how that works. Seriously though, I went to medical school with Thompson and wanted to know if I can be of any help. . .Sure I'd like to visit him. . .When are you planning on discharging him? . . Could I help you with his discharge planning? I know it's a bit unusual. But I feel I owe it to the guy. I'm his kid's godfather. . Thanks. I knew you'd understand. I owe you one. I'll drop in and see him first thing in the morning. Thanks. Bye." Corrigan closed his cell phone and set it on the coffee table. He did it, he was now officially involved in trying to save his friend's life. Any sense of relief he felt was tempered by the realization Zilker and the death panel wouldn't like it.

Diane walked into the living room and sat in the rocking chair. "Well, how you two doing?" she asked.

"We're doing just fine," Corrigan replied buoyantly. "Although I think she might be ready for a nap."

Diane got out of the rocker and picked up Emily. She returned to the rocker, sat down and began to rock her precious bundle.

"You remember Gary Thompson?" asked Corrigan as he unknowingly opened up a conversation that would dramatically change both their lives forever.

"I think so."

"I went to medical school with him. He was a surgeon. He's married to Betty. They have two kids."

"Oh, yeah, now I remember," said Diane as the name finally rang a bell. She hadn't known Gary as long as her husband, but remembered Betty was pregnant with her second child when Gary was lured away from private practice by a prestigious surgical group and they had to move. Diane and Jim were there for the second baby's christening and became godparents. After that they lost touch, except for the occasional Christmas card. Then the cards dwindled away. Life has a tendency to get in the way, even with the best of friends. "Aren't we their kid's godparents?"

"I believe so."

"Whatever happened to him?"

"Well, Gary's in a psychiatric hospital."

"Oh my God, what happened?" Diane asked with genuine concern.

"I talked to his psychiatrist, Dr. Masterson," said Corrigan as he began his tale of woe. "It appears he's been diagnosed as a paranoid schizophrenic with alcohol dependency and they're having trouble telling which one is his primary problem. Betty left him. He's no longer practicing medicine. And he's on the verge of losing his license, if he doesn't straighten himself out."

"That's terrible."

"I know. I asked Dr. Masterson, if there was anything I could do to help," Corrigan continued. "He said if I could visit him, it might help."

"What hospital is he at?" Diane asked.

"He's at that new private hospital, Arbor Creek. The one they built on top of North Pines. I haven't been there but I've seen their brochures and it looks pretty nice."

"Poor Gary," Diane sympathized.

"I told Masterson I'd stop by in the morning and see him. If that's all right with you." He didn't want a repeat of last night.

"Good grief. Sure. Go see your friend."

"Thanks," replied Corrigan. He then went over and kissed Diane forehead. "Are you hungry?" He asked.

"I could use something to eat."

"Good. I'll go nuke you a TV dinner."

"My, aren't you the gourmet cook," Diane laughed.

"Dinner will be served in a matter of minutes," Corrigan chuckled. He then disappeared into the kitchen.

After dinner, Corrigan spent the rest of the evening with Emily and Diane. When it came time for him to leave for work, Diane put Emily down for the night. She then joined her husband at the front door as he prepared to leave. She didn't want a repeat of the previous night's testy good-bye so she hugged him around the neck and kissed him passionately.

"Wow," a surprised Corrigan said as their lips parted. "What's that for?"

"It's just my way of saying thank you," purred Diane.

"Well, you're welcome," a perplexed but appreciative Corrigan replied. As he walked out the door Diane surprised him again by playfully slapping him on the butt. He turned and shot a glance at her before he responded. "You better watch out. You might be biting off more than you can chew."

"I hope so," Diane roguishly smiled. She then slowly shut the door.

Corrigan slid behind the wheel of his car and as he shut the door he thought to himself. "I wonder what that was all about." He then just shook his head, "Women."

Corrigan spent the next eight hours in psych triage dealing with the usual cast of characters that paraded through the buzzing door. When it was time to leave, he wasted no time getting to his Mustang and heading out to Arbor Creek hospital. It took about forty minutes for him to get to the two lane blacktop that would take him up the winding hill to the private for-profit psychiatric hospital. "It's almost cold enough for snow," thought Corrigan as he snaked his way up the road.

# CHAPTER 23

In between assessments at psych triage, Corrigan came up with a simple, yet bold plan to keep his friend from being murdered. He was going to blackmail Zilker into calling off Ozawa's hired assassins. He was going to demand Zilker stop his hired killers or he would go to the police and expose the chronic care team and its entire covert operation. He knew Zilker had him on tape ordering Cobb's death, so he knew it would be a huge gamble. But, he felt Zilker and the chronic care team had more to lose, if they were exposed than he did. He sensed it while talking to Zilker at their last meeting when he wanted to quit the team. He was going to play on Zilker's fear and gamble that his fear of being exposed would save Thompson's life.

Corrigan didn't feel as tired this morning as he pulled the Mustang into the parking lot of Arbor Creek Hospital. He wasn't yawning or falling asleep at the wheel as he usually did on the way home each sunrise. Maybe his body was finally adjusting to becoming a night owl. It definitely wasn't the caffeine because he swore off it completely at work when it started to interfere with his sleep during the day. Or maybe it was the adrenaline rush from knowing that by helping Thompson, he going was to upset the chronic care team's plans. There was an element of danger involved. Whatever it was, he felt pumped.

After he parked his car in the physician's parking lot, Corrigan made his way to the front door of the contemporary single-story facility. The hospital grounds were well manicured and displayed patches of green despite the weather. The mountain air was fresh and clean, with a hint of pine. There was no fence around the hospital because the buildings were strategically interlocked to prevent escape. The building had been designed to look like a comfortable hotel rather than the public's perception of a psychiatric hospital. Egress from the hospital was denied by a series of overlapping walls that blended into the landscaping, a real contrast to County General. When Corrigan stepped into the hospital's foyer, his jaw dropped.

The lobby could easily pass for the entrance to a four star hotel. It was well lit with both natural and artificial light. Two sets of waiting areas with matching sofas and chairs and dark wood coffee tables were set at opposite ends of the room. It provided privacy for people while they waited. The walls were painted in cheerful pastels with paintings of landscapes hanging in strategic locations to enhance the ambiance. The floor had expensive throw rugs under each sofa grouping with high-priced tile throughout the rest of the area. Artificial plants in earthen adobe planters were artfully placed about the room. The whole effect said "Welcome." "So this is how the other half lives," thought Corrigan as he walked over to the receptionist.

The pretty young woman behind the mahogany desk looked up at him. "May I help you?"

"Yes, I'm Dr. James Corrigan. I'm here to see a patient named Gary Thompson. Dr. Masterson left authorization for me to see him."

The receptionist looked through a blue three ring binder, and found the authorization. "Yes. Here it is. When I buzz you through the double doors, go down the hall and turn to your left. The interview rooms are on the right. I'll have Mr. Thompson brought to interview room three."

"Thank you," Corrigan graciously replied.

"You'll need to sign in," said the receptionist as she handed Corrigan a red three ring binder.

Corrigan wrote his name along with the date and current time in the binder. As soon as he finished, the receptionist handed him a plastic visitor's identification badge.

"Be sure to wear your badge at all times," she instructed.

"Thank you, I will." Corrigan clipped the badge to his breast pocket and walked over to the locked double doors that lead to the hospital's psych units. The door buzzed, he opened it and then walked through. The carpeted hallway coupled with the clean pastel walls seemed like a world away from the worn neutral floor tiles and dull walls he was used to at County General.

When he reached the first left, he turned and followed the hallway to the third interview room. He opened the door and found a room similar to the one where he assessed patients at psych triage. However, it was cleaner, had better lighting and was furnished with a nice polished desk and two chairs rather than the recycled stuff used by the county. Out of habit Corrigan sat behind the nicely polished desk as if he was going to conduct an assessment. He didn't have long to wait before a psych tech opened the door and stuck his head in. "Are you Dr. Corrigan?" asked the young male psych tech with the ratty looking mustache.

"Yes I am."

The psych tech then stepped aside and Gary Thompson entered the room. Although Thompson was only a year of ahead of Corrigan in medical school, the ravages of his dual diagnosis had taken its toll on him and he looked much older. He stood six foot one, his brown hair was oddly combed and he had dark circles under his brown eyes and was unshaven. Despite his clean clothes, he could pass for a typical psych triage patient. Thompson sat down across from Corrigan and the psych tech closed the door. Thompson was alert despite the fact he was still on his detox meds.

"James Corrigan," said Thompson as he started the conversation. "That's a name out of the past. What the hell are you doing here?"

"I heard you were in the hospital and I wanted to see if there was anything I could do to help," Corrigan cheerfully replied.

"Well if that don't beat all," Thompson chuckled, "A surgeon needing the help of a psychiatrist."

"Gary, I'm here as a friend not as a psychiatrist," said Corrigan. "A friend," thought Corrigan, "who doesn't want to see you murdered."

"You still pissed off at me?" Thompson asked out of the left field.

"Why would I be pissed off at you?" asked Corrigan.

"The bar fight you know, the one where you got that scar over your eye."

Corrigan unconsciously touched the scar above his eye. "You mean this?"

"Yeah, I yelled at you to duck, remember?"

"Well, I was kind of busy at the time," said Corrigan as the memory of the bar fight played out in his head. "It needed six stitches to close."

"I could have done it in five," Thompson boasted.

"Spoken like a true surgeon. But what the hell does that have to do with anything?" asked Corrigan.

"You never said if you were still pissed at me or not," Thompson countered as he pressed for an answer.

"Well, to be honest with you. Yeah, I'm still a little pissed," Corrigan begrudgingly admitted. "It did mar a beautiful face." The latter said with an impish grin.

"Good," Thompson said soberly.

"Good?" Corrigan was really confused now. His friend wasn't making any sense. Maybe he was too far gone.

"I just wanted to see if you'd be honest with me. That's why I brought it up," said Thompson as he divulged the reason for his obtuse question.

"Haven't I always been a straight with you?" asked Corrigan feeling a little disappointed his friend would say such a thing.

"Yes, you have," Thompson honestly replied. "I guess you've always been a straight arrow."

"I wouldn't go that far," said Corrigan with a twinge of guilt knowing the real reason why he was there.

"I'm sorry James. But, I've been treated by a hell of a lot of psychiatrists since I was diagnosed with schizophrenia and alcoholism and none of them have been worth a damn. Forgive me if I'm just a little leery of psychiatrists, even if one happens to be an old friend."

"I understand," replied Corrigan. He couldn't blame his friend. He'd be suspicious too if someone he hadn't seen in years suddenly popped back into his life offering to help him, especially a psychiatrist.

"Those quacks have put me through hell," Thompson cursed. He then began a diatribe about everything he felt was wrong with the field of psychiatry in general and psychiatrists in particular.

Corrigan thought it would be best to let his friend vent so he quietly listened. However, as he did the thought surfaced again that maybe his friend was already beyond help. He couldn't help but hear the echo of a frequent flyer in Thompson's voice, as he rambled on about the way the field of psychiatry had mistreated him.

Then just as suddenly as Thompson started his rant, he stopped, made eye contact with his old friend and asked. "How can you help me?"

Corrigan was used to dealing with patients like Thompson and was unfazed by his erratic behavior. "I have a treatment option that might have been overlooked," Corrigan calmly replied.

"What?"

"It's based on the chicken and the egg theory."

"Great," Thompson smirked. "I knew you guys were into voodoo but, this is the first time I've heard any one of you admit it."

"It has nothing to do with voodoo," Corrigan replied seriously. "What I want to do is find out which came first your drinking problem or your schizophrenia. You know, which came first, the chicken or the egg?"

"Oh, I get it."

"I feel the key to helping you is to determine conclusively what your primary diagnosis is and then treat it. Then deal with the secondary one."

"Well, I've always had a taste for the drink," Thompson admitted. "That's why you always found me at the Red Garter after a hard day at medical school." Then he chuckled. "As far as the schizophrenia, I don't know when I caught that."

"I'm serious," Corrigan said to his friend. "I'm hoping if we can treat your primary diagnosis you'll be able to get back on the road to a real recovery."

"Sorry," said Thompson as he lowered his head like a scolded child.

"Gary, I want to help you," Corrigan reiterated. "Please believe me. I want you to get better."

Thompson slowly raised his head and looked at Corrigan. "Well, I guess if any psychiatrist can do it, James, it's probably you. What have you got in mind?"

Corrigan then explained to his friend what he had in mind. When he finished he looked at Thompson to see whether or not he thought his plan had merit. Corrigan could see Thompson's analytical mind working just like it did when he was in medical school. That was a good sign. It meant Thompson's brain was still functional even though it had been subjected to massive amounts of alcohol over the years. Thompson continued to ruminate then finally spoke. "I only have one problem with your plan."

"What's that?" asked Corrigan.

"The half way house."

"What about the half way house?" asked Corrigan wondering what kind of monkey wrench Thompson was throwing into his plan.

"Have you ever been in one of those places?" Thompson challenged. "That would be the last place I'd stay to get off of drugs or alcohol. They mean well but, it's hard to keep an eye on 20 or 30 guys living under one roof. The last place I stayed at I went into the kitchen to help with dinner and found one of the residents drinking pure vanilla extract. He was stone drunk. No, it has to be some place else."

"Okay then," Corrigan replied, "How about a friend or a relative?"

"No good. I'm the black sheep of the family now. Oh, everything was fine when I was the doctor in the family. But, as soon as I hit a few bumps in the road, I immediately become persona non-grata. You won't find any takers there. As far as friends, I don't have any left."

The line of questioning was beginning to sound vaguely familiar to Corrigan. "What about your apartment?" asked Corrigan as he now began to grasp at straws?

"No good either. Too many bad memories there, besides I've still got lots of booze there."

"Crap," thought Corrigan. His plan was unraveling before it even started. As much as he hated to admit it, his friend had turned into a typical frequent flyer with all the concomitant problems associated with their peculiar breed. But he couldn't give up. The stakes were way too high. He would have to think of something or his friend would be killed shortly after he left the hospital.

"Sorry James, I didn't mean to be such a pain in the ass."

"Don't worry," said Corrigan. "I'll find a place for you to stay."

"I hope so. Your plan sounds like it might work."

"Good," said Corrigan as he stood to leave. "Let me get started and see what I can come up with."

Thompson remained seated. He looked up at Corrigan, cleared his throat and said. "There's one more thing I think you should know.

"On, no," thought Corrigan as he sat back down. "Please don't screw this up now with some bizarre confession you're a serial killing or something."

"It happened before I was admitted," Thompson confided. "I didn't tell the intake staff and I lied to Masterson about it."

"What about," Corrigan asked apprehensively.

"I tried to kill myself."

Corrigan tried not to be jaded by Thompson's disclosure since he'd heard the same confession hundreds of times before from the galaxy of patients that paraded through County General.

"I had a gun in my mouth and was ready to pull the trigger," Thompson said soberly as he lowered his head. He was ashamed and embarrassed to admit to his old friend that his life had spun so out of control he actually planned on ending it. "I felt Betty and the kids would be better off without me. I even felt the whole world would be better off without me. I was tired of living. I was about to pull the trigger when the doorbell rang. It was some kid selling candy bars for his school. His mother was standing behind him. They reminded me of Betty and my son. I bought a couple of candy bars from the kid, tossed the gun in the trash and called the hospital." He then placed his thumb and index finger only a few millimeters apart for emphasis and said. "I was this close to pulling the trigger."

"I'm glad you didn't," Corrigan replied sincerely.

Thompson looked at Corrigan with eyes haunted by inner demons and confessed. "If I relapse again when I get out of here, then screw it. Life isn't worth living anymore. It's too hard. I'll do everybody a favor and check out permanently."

"Don't worry. My plan will work," said Corrigan confidently.

Thompson didn't respond. He had said all he needed to say. So he stood and said quietly. "I appreciate what you're doing, James."

Corrigan stood and they shook hands. Corrigan pulled open the interview room door and saw the psych tech still standing in the hallway. "We're done," he told him.

The psych tech walked up to the door and waited for Thompson to exit. Thompson casually stepped out into the hall way.

"Hang in there, buddy," said Corrigan as he patted Thompson on the shoulder.

"I will," Thompson replied. He was then escorted back to the adult psych ward.

Corrigan watched as Thompson entered the locked part of the hospital and disappeared behind two heavy metal doors. Now that his friend was gone, he didn't have to pretend that Thompson's suicide attempt deeply concerned him. Friend or not, he was obligated by law to tell Dr. Masterson about Thompson's attempt. Little did Corrigan know that it would turn out to be a fatal mistake?

Corrigan back tracked to the lobby, turned in his visitor's badge, entered his log out time and left.

Driving back down the mountain Corrigan mentally went through a list of potential places where Thompson could stay after his discharge. As he went down the list he realized just how few places that were available for people like Thompson. "No wonder there's such a failure rate for people struggling with chemical dependency and mental illness," Corrigan concluded as he left the two lane blacktop and got back onto the main highway.

When Corrigan finally pulled into his garage and parked the Mustang he hoped Diane would be receptive to the plan he concocted on the way home. As he made his way to the front door he wrestled with the best way to present the plan to his lovely bride. Or better yet, make her think she came up with it on her own. When he entered the living room, he found Diane taking a nap on the sofa. Even though she was in her bathrobe and had no make up on she was still attractive. He tried not to wake her because she was a light sleeper.

Diane sat up and ran her hand through her hair. "Good morning."

"Sorry I woke you."

"That's all right," said Diane as she yawned. "Did you see Gary this morning?"

"Yes I did," Corrigan replied as he sat down next to her. "He's doing pretty good considering all that he's been through."

"That's good to hear."

"He'll be discharged in a couple of days," said Corrigan as he began to lay down the rationale for what he was about to propose. "Unfortunately it's looks like he's got no place to stay after he's discharged. Betty's left him. The place where he was staying has refused to allow him back," the latter obviously was a lie but he needed to lay it on thick and make the situation look as desperate as possible. "Dr. Masterson has already checked into half way houses and some other places where he could stay but they're all full."

"That's terrible," Diane replied with appropriate sympathy.

"I know," said Corrigan as he looked at the floor and shook his head. "I wish there was something I could do. Dr. Masterson feels Gary may only have one more chance before he becomes a full blown frequent flyer. I'd hate to see that."

"That's too bad," was all Diane said. However, she could sense something was on her husband's mind.

"She's not taking the bait," thought Corrigan. Look's like he would have to up the ante. So he looked sadly into Diane's eyes. "Gary hasn't lost his license, but he's close. And there's a chance he might be able to reconcile with Betty, at least according to Dr. Masterson. I'd hate to see him lose everything just because he didn't have a place to stay after he left the hospital."

Diane gave her husband a look that let him know she was on to his blarney. The last time he acted this way was when he bought the Mustang sitting in the garage without telling her.

"Damn," he thought when he saw Diane's expression. "I must have laid it on too thick."

"You sound like our insurance agent. What are you trying to sell me?"

He couldn't think of any thing else to say so he blurted out the truth. "I'd like Gary to stay here for a couple of weeks after he's discharged."

He could tell from Diane's look of gawking disbelief, what he had proposed wasn't exactly what she expected. She expected they might have to lend him some money or subsidize a place for him to stay, but not live with them. "What?" exploded from Diane's mouth?

"It would be only for a little while . . . Until he gets back on his feet. That's all. He's not violent or anything. He'll be on his medications. And I can monitor him," Corrigan implored. Then he decided to play the sympathy card. "After all, we are his children's godparents."

"But, after they moved to Riverside we lost touch with them," Diane countered. "So don't give me that." She didn't want a mental patient living in her house, especially now that they had a baby.

"But he needs our help."

"What about the baby?" Diane challenged.

"What about the baby? Corrigan countered. "Diane, he's not the devil incarnate. He's a doctor just like me only he's been through a rough time. And he's trying to deal with it."

"I know. But he's still a," Diane didn't finish the sentence but it was too late. She now regretted it.

"What? You can go ahead and say it a mental patient. A psycho," said Corrigan as he found himself raising his voice. "Of all people, I thought you would understand."

"I do. Believe me I do. But that all changed when that son of a bitch, Cobb, tried to kill me and my baby. Or have you forgotten?" Diane turned her head away. Her eyes got misty.

George Cobb had come back to haunt him again. "Damn him," Corrigan said under his breath. He now felt bad for raising his voice. Having worked with mental patients for so long it was second nature for him to gloss over even the most bizarre behavior they exhibited, the kind of behavior that would give other people nightmares. You had to develop a thick wall of professional detachment or you couldn't work in this field. Diane didn't have the benefit of such a wall and was upset.

"I'm sorry. I understand how you feel," Corrigan said softly. He really did. But, he also couldn't really tell her the truth. If she knew his real motive for wanting Thompson to stay with them she'd never let him step within a hundred mile radius of their house. "What do I do now," Corrigan anxiously thought to himself.

However, it was Diane who came to the rescue. She wiped her eyes and looked at her husband. "Jim, you've got such a big heart."

Corrigan looked embarrassingly at the floor. Despite his sometimes gruff exterior, he did care an awful lot about his patients. Diane saw that in him when they first met.

"I know you wouldn't have asked me if it wasn't important," Diane continued. "If you feel he needs your help that badly, then he can stay here for a little while."

"You really mean it," Corrigan asked cautiously.

"Yes. But, I want to lay down some hard and fast rules before he does."

"That goes without saying."

"I also want something else understood," Diane said firmly. "If at any point during his stay I feel he is threat to me or the baby, I will call the police and have him yanked out of here. Day or night, with or without your permission, understood?"

"Yes, completely understood."

"Good."

He took Diane's hand. "Thank you." He then leaned over and kissed her on the cheek.

"When does he get out of Arbor Creek?" Diane asked.

"He's scheduled to be discharged Monday morning," Corrigan replied. "He can sleep on the sofa bed in my office."

"Fine," she replied.

"I want you to tell him the rules of the house before he gets here. Understood?"

Corrigan nodded his head.

"Good," said Diane even though she was still apprehensive about having Thompson stay with them.

Corrigan was glad that was over. Now all he had to do was convince Zilker it would be in his best interest and the group's to leave Thompson alone. He felt confident he could do it. "After all," he naively thought. "He was dealing with fellow psychiatrist not the Mafia."

# CHAPTER 24

Dr. John Zilker sat behind the big mahogany desk of his well appointed office, an office befitting his title as medical director of the nation's largest psychiatric managed care company. It had plush carpeting, a conference table and chairs, a credenza that matched his desk and windows that looked out on a well manicured green belt and man made lake. On the wall behind his desk hung his medical degrees along with plaques and awards for outstanding service to the community. Zilker's blue blazer was draped over the back of his leather swivel chair as he started the day shuffling through the stacks of paperwork that always seemed to accumulate on his desk while he was gone. The phone rang, "This is Dr. Zilker," he answered perfunctorily. It was one of his operatives at Arbor Creek. "He did what?" he exclaimed. Zilker couldn't believe what he just heard. The operative informed him Thompson had just been discharged to Corrigan and he was taking him home.

"That son of a bitch," Zilker said to himself. "How long ago?" he asked. The operative told him about an hour age. "No," Zilker responded to the operative's next question. "There's nothing you can do. Thanks for letting me know." Zilker replaced the phone and uncharacteristically slammed his fist on the desk. "Damn him!"

He had underestimated Corrigan. He honestly hoped having the tape of him ordering Cobb's death would keep him in line. But, apparently Dr. Corrigan was going to be a problem after all. He had to find out what in the hell was going on. Thompson's name was already on this month's list of patient's to be permanently discharged. More troublesome for Zilker was that he had already made the financial commitment to his own managed care company to write Thompson off. Zilker stood and walked over to a floor to ceiling window and looked outside to compose himself. "Damn him and his stupid friend."

As he watched the wind blow across the water of the man made lake below he reflected on how everything had been going so smoothly since the inception of the chronic care team. It had been in operation for almost a year and no one was aware of its existence and the cost savings were beyond what they had projected. He shuddered to think what the owners of the managed care companies that sponsored them would do if they found out their covert cost containment program had suddenly developed a complication, one that could possibly land them in prison.

Zilker walked back to his leather chair and sat down. Like any corporate executive faced with a dilemma, he began to think of ways to cover his ass. He mentally considered various scenarios. Unfortunately they all arrived at the same unpleasant conclusion. He was in deep trouble, if he didn't do something about that self-righteous asshole, Corrigan. Corrigan could compromise the whole operation with his unauthorized intervention. If left unchecked Zilker's world, as he knew it, could crumble around him. His expensive house, the cars, his bank account and all the material things he loved so much would evaporate. He reached for his cell phone, flipped it open and punched in Corrigan's phone number.

Corrigan was sitting at the kitchen table when his cell phone went off. Sitting across from him enjoying a bowl of cereal was

Thompson. Diane and the baby were in the master bedroom sleeping.

"Nice of you to let me stay here," said Thompson.

"You don't have to keep thanking me. What are friends for?" Corrigan said as he reached for his cell phone. He flipped it open. "Dr. Corrigan."

"What the hell do you think you're doing?" the caustic blast from Zilker shot straight into Corrigan's ear. "No one gave you the authority to overturn the panel's decision."

Corrigan, although stunned by Zilker's angry outburst remained calm. He silently stood from the table and looked over at Thompson. "I need to take this in private." He then looked at his watch. "Jeez," he thought. He picked up Thompson from Arbor Creek only two hours ago. Zilker must have some pretty good spies at the hospital.

"No need for you to leave," said Thompson. "I'm the guest, remember?" Thompson stood, picked up his bowl of cereal and walked out of the kitchen.

Corrigan waited to make sure Thompson was out of ear shot before he spoke to Zilker. He wasn't ready to confront Zilker right now, much less spring his blackmail plan on him. He had hoped to have more time to prepare before he confronted Zilker. However, Zilker's phone call had forced his hand and left him little choice.

"What the hell do you mean, what am I doing? He's my friend." Corrigan shot back. "Did you think I was going to just stand by and let your guys murder him in cold blood?" It was not exactly the opening line he would have used to begin a negotiation but he didn't like being verbally attacked especially by Zilker.

"You knew we made difficult decisions," Zilker countered.

"I know. But this is different," Corrigan calmly replied as he regained his composure. He had to remain in control because he knew, with the tape, Zilker had the upper hand. He would also lose whatever advantage he had if he got angry. It happened once before and look where it got him, inducted as the newest member of Zilker's version of the Spanish Inquisition.

"Sounds like the good doctor has found himself a conscience," Zilker scoffed.

"We all have one. Some of us just choose to use it once in a while," Corrigan bristled.

"Funny. You didn't mention a conscience in your book, or maybe I missed that."

Corrigan listened silently. He was fuming inside but knew he better stay calm and not take the bait.

"So what's good for the goose in not necessarily good for the gander, I take it?" said Zilker, his voice dripping with contempt. "Too bad, you looked like you had such a promising career with us."

"You don't understand," Corrigan finally implored. "This hits to close to home."

"So much for professional detachment," Zilker taunted.

"I don't know why I got mixed up with you guys in the first place," Corrigan confessed.

"Sure you do," Zilker replied smoothly. "You just don't want to admit it."

"Bull!" Corrigan shouted. "Easy now," Corrigan said to himself. "He's getting the better of you."

"You wanted to see the logical extension of your theory and how it would operate in the real world. That's why you joined us."

"Did you even read my book?" asked Corrigan his voice now strained. "I never promoted killing patients. I just wanted patients to be held accountable for their behavior." Zilker was making it hard for him to control his temper. Corrigan took a deep breath and slowly exhaled to calm down. "Damn, he's good," he thought to himself.

"And we made them accountable for their behavior, didn't we?" Zilker continued with measured arrogance.

Yes, Corrigan wanted frequent flyers to take responsibility for their behavior, even more so after what Cobb did to him and his family. Maybe Zilker was right. "Stop it!" Corrigan mentally shouted to himself. Zilker was expertly manipulating the conversation again. He had to change the subject quickly.

"Let's cut to the chase, okay?" Corrigan bluntly tossed out. "I want to make a deal."

"You want to make a deal with me?" Zilker laughed. "You're in no position to make any deals."

"I think I am."

"You do?" Zilker replied with patronizing skepticism. "You seem to forget something."

"I know you've got the tape of me and Cobb."

"Yes, I do," Zilker replied smugly. "I'm glad you remembered. I'm sure the police would be very interested to hear what's on it."

"I know. But just hear me out."

"Why should I?" Zilker questioned arrogantly.

"Because two can play at this game," countered Corrigan.

"What are you talking about?" Zilker cautiously demanded.

"You can give the police the tape. That's true, but I can beat you to the punch."

"Beat me to the punch?" asked Zilker.

"If you try and give the tape to the police, I'll go to them first and tell them about you and the chronic care team," said Corrigan as he laid out the essence of this plan. "Your tape will only validate what I've told them."

"You don't seem to understand," Zilker began.

Corrigan cut him off. "You don't seem to understand," said Corrigan as he tried to regain the upper hand. "The bottom line is that we both want something concealed, right?"

"Yes. But, you'd be a fool to go to the police. You'd be charged with murder," Zilker countered.

"Maybe so, but you would too."

"Oh God," Zilker thought to himself as he paused to think about the consequences of what would happen to the chronic care team if Corrigan was foolish enough to go the police. "First a conscience, now he's getting ethical, what's wrong with this guy?"

Corrigan wondered why the long silence.

Zilker finally spoke, this time with a little less confidence in his voice. "I really think you should reconsider such a drastic move."

Corrigan could sense the change in Zilker's resolve. Now was the time to bluff him. "Why? Who's going to stop me?"

Zilker didn't respond. His face grew pale. All he could say in response was a feeble. "I wouldn't do that if I were you." Corrigan noticed the subtle change in Zilker's voice and knew his strategy was working.

"It's my choice," Corrigan said firmly. He knew that deep down Zilker feared exposure of the group more than anything else. The damage would be disastrous for him and his fellow psychiatrists. "You're a fool," Zilker admonished.

"Maybe, maybe not, that's for you to decide," Corrigan said knowing he had now turned the tables on Zilker. "You willing to listen to what I've got to say or not?

"All right I'll listen," Zilker angrily spat. He knew he'd better start taking Corrigan seriously.

"I promise not to go to the police and promise not to tell anyone about the chronic care team if you call off your partners in the field. I'll quit the panel, as I already planned to do and you'll never hear from me again."

"I don't know," Zilker cautiously replied.

"What do you mean, you don't know? What have you got to lose?" pressed Corrigan.

"More than you can imagine," Zilker replied cryptically as he felt beads of perspiration form on his forehead.

"You can keep the tape as an insurance policy that I'll never go to the police," offered Corrigan.

"You're damned right I'll keep the tape and I'll sure as hell use it if I have to," Zilker shot back as he tried to regain the upper hand.

Corrigan smiled. He had made Zilker angry, perfect. "Think about it," said Corrigan as he pressed his advantage. "If you go along with my plan, you'll never have to give the tape to the police and you'll never hear from me again. And no one will be the wiser."

"Hmm," was all that Zilker said as he thought about Corrigan's proposition.

Then Corrigan added for effect. "I think we've got each other by the short hairs, don't you?"

"Why are you doing this?" Zilker demanded.

"I told you he's my friend," Corrigan replied firmly.

"Where is Thompson now?" asked Zilker.

"He's with me."

"What do you plan to do with him?"

"I'm going to keep him here until I can determine his primary diagnosis and then treat him just like I told you and the panel."

"What does your wife think about what you're doing?" Zilker probed. Hoping he might find a place to drive a wedge.

"She's in complete agreement with me."

"Hmm, interesting," Zilker responded somewhat skeptically. But, he was really thinking two steps ahead. "Damn," thought Zilker. "His wife appears just as foolish as her husband." His plan to divide and conquer doesn't seem like it's going to work.

"What do you say?" Corrigan pressed again. "My silence and you get to keep the tape. Just stay away from Thompson and you'll never hear another word out of me. I promise."

"I need some time to think about it," said Zilker as he felt a vein throbbing at his temple.

"What's to think about?" Corrigan demanded.

"Dr. Corrigan what you're proposing has to be sanctioned at a corporate level much higher than mine. You've thrown a monkey wrench into a something you cannot fully grasp," Zilker replied knowing Corrigan had not just upset the apple chart he tipped it over.

"How much time do you need?"

"A couple of days," Zilker said sourly.

"Two days and that's it," Corrigan quickly replied not letting Zilker off the hook. "If I don't hear from you by Wednesday then you'll leave me no choice. I'll go to the police."

"It would be a sad day if you did," Zilker mildly threatened.

It was time to spring his final bluff on Zilker. "Try me," Corrigan said coldly as he tried to sound like a man with nothing to lose. He then snapped his cell phone shut. He prayed Zilker would get back to him by Wednesday because he knew he really couldn't go to the police. Being arrested for murder was the last thing he wanted.

It took a second for Zilker to realize Corrigan had hung up on him. When he did, he fumed, "That bastard." Zilker hit speed dial on his cell phone.

Ozawa was driving to work when his cell phone rang. "Dr. Ozawa."

"It's Zilker. Thompson was discharged to Corrigan this morning and he took him home."

"You've got to be kidding," replied Ozawa.

"I wish I were. He thinks he can save his friend."

"I had a feeling he might pull something," said Ozawa as he kept his eyes on the road.

"He threatened to go to the police, if we don't call off Doyle and Hunter," Zilker quickly added.

"How can he threaten us? We've got the tape of him and Cobb."

"I know," Zilker irritably agreed.

"You don't think he'd really go to the police, do you?"

"I don't know. But from the way he sounded, it was like he was a man who didn't have anything to lose."

"Oh, man!" an aggravated Ozawa spat.

"I know."

"God, I'd hate to think of what would happen if he went to the cops," a worried Ozawa replied.

"Tell me about it."

264

Ozawa pulled his car to the side of the road and parked. He didn't want to be distracted. There was too much at stake.

"I don't know about you but, I have no desire to go to prison for murder," Zilker said dryly.

"You think I do?" Ozawa quickly replied. "What should we do?"

"We definitely need to take care of Thompson," replied Zilker sounding now more like a Mafia boss than a mental health professional. "We're already committed."

"Damn right we are," Ozawa agreed. "There'd be hell to pay if we didn't.

"I know," Zilker sighed.

"What about Corrigan?"

"I'm going to call his bluff," Zilker replied in a cold ominous voice.

"Do you think that's wise?" asked Ozawa.

"I don't think so. I've got a hunch," said Zilker.

"A hunch," Ozawa blurted out. The idea of a hunch determining whether or not he was arrested for murder and carted off to prison sent a chill down his spine.

"I can't see a man, especially one with a new baby, going to the police and asking them to arrest him for murder. I think deep down inside Corrigan's afraid of going to the police," Zilker speculated with a hint of optimism in his voice.

"What about Thompson?"

"I think we should move on Thompson and wait to see how Corrigan reacts."

"Don't you think we should move on Corrigan too? We can take them both out at the same time." Ozawa offered.

"No," Zilker sagely replied. "I think our best course of action is to eliminate Thompson and see how Corrigan reacts. I'm hoping that once his cause célèbre is dead he'll lose his reason for going to the police and keep his mouth shut."

"I hope you're right," said Ozawa.

"Me too. Tell Doyle and Hunter to be careful because we've never been down this road before, okay?"

"Okay," Ozawa relented. With that settled the two men ended their conversation.

Ozawa hit the speed dial on his cell phone. It took a couple of seconds before Doyle answered. "This is Ozawa," he said curtly. "I need to see you and Hunter ASAP."

Corrigan and Thompson were enjoying Monday Night Football in high definition on the sofa in Corrigan's living room, unaware of the forces that were being aligned against them.

"Can you believe they called a stupid play like that on third and three?" Corrigan complained.

"It wouldn't have mattered what play they called. They would've got stuffed. Their defense is tough."

"Oh, yeah," Corrigan challenged.

"Yeah," Thompson countered. "Your team's offense sucks. Or haven't you noticed? The score is twenty-one to nothing and it's the fourth quarter."

"They'll come back," Corrigan replied confidently. "They always start out slow. Then 'Bam!' they hit you with the long bomb."

"Start out slow? They've had three quarters to warm up. They better start warming up they're running out of time."

"Don't worry. They will," Corrigan said as he tried to sound convincing.

The losing team called a time out and instantly a beer commercial filled the big screen. Corrigan scanned the messy coffee table until he found his soda. As soon as he picked it up he could tell it was empty. "I'll get us another round of sodas?"

"I'll get this round. That's if you don't mind," offered Thompson.

"Sure, be my guest."

Thompson gathered up the empty soda cans off the coffee tale and made his way to the kitchen.

Three minutes and fifteen commercials later the game came back on. Suddenly over the din of the football game a horrible scream could be heard coming from the kitchen. Corrigan nearly tripped over himself as he rushed to the kitchen. When he entered the kitchen he saw Thompson shaking uncontrollably in front the sink, his eyes transfixed with horror at the window in front of him.

"What's the matter?" asked Corrigan.

"I saw it. It was staring at me in the window," Thompson cried.

Diane entered the kitchen seconds behind her husband and stopped in her tracks. "What's wrong?"

"I don't know. I heard him scream and found him like this," Corrigan replied.

Diane couldn't help wondering if her worst fear had already come true, Thompson was losing it. From the back bedroom they both heard Emily start to cry.

"You go take care of Emily," Corrigan strongly suggested to his wife. "I'll take care of Gary."

"Do you want me to call the police?" asked a now worried Diane.

"No. Let me talk to him first," Corrigan replied optimistically.

"Okay, but I'm going to keep my cell phone with me. If you need help just holler," said Diane as she left the kitchen to take care of Emily.

Corrigan slowly inched his way towards his friend. He didn't want to frighten him any more than he already was. When he finally stood next to Thompson he took a quick glance out the kitchen window and saw nothing but darkness. Corrigan was concerned his friend might be hallucinating so he calmly asked him. "What do you see?"

"I saw a ghost," his terrified friend replied.

"Where," Corrigan calmly asked.

"In the window, it was staring at me."

Corrigan slowly placed his hand on Thompson's shoulder. "It's gone. You don't have worry about anything now." This was not the time or place to have an intellectual debate about the existence of ghosts. Whatever Thompson saw, it was real to him. "It's all right," Corrigan continued soothingly. "There's nothing to be afraid of now. It's gone."

Thompson turned and looked at Corrigan. "Did you see it?" He asked, his voice trembling. Whatever he saw had made this former bar room brawler shake with fear.

"No," Corrigan honestly replied. "Maybe it was just the refection of a car's headlights or something."

"No, Jim it was real. Swear to God. It looked right at me."

"Well, it's gone now," Corrigan replied calmly. "Let's sit down, okay?"

"You think I'm crazy, don't you?" said Thompson, his voice still filled with fear as he looked to make sure the ghost wasn't in the room.

"No. I don't think you're crazy. You obviously saw something or you wouldn't be so upset. I just want to find out what it was."

"I told you it was a ghost" Thompson repeated as he continued to look around the room.

"I believe you."

"You do?" asked a skeptical Thompson as he focused his attention on Corrigan. "You really do?"

"Yes," said Corrigan firmly.

Thompson had been told so many times before it was his imagination playing ticks on him that it took him a couple of seconds to realize Corrigan had agreed with him.

"It's obvious you saw something. So let's talk about it, all right?" Corrigan offered again. For the time being he would tactfully not bring up that he suspected Thompson may have been hallucinating. First he needed to calm him down.

"All right," said Thompson as he took a leap of faith and trusted his friend. He took a deep breath and slowly began to regain his composure.

Corrigan led Thompson to the kitchen table and they both sat down. "Can I get you anything?" asked Corrigan.

"No thanks," replied Thompson as the blood started to return to his ashen face.

"So what did this ghost look like?" Corrigan asked as he began his delicate assessment.

"It looked awful. It was black with a distorted white face and mouth. It was all twisted up."

"You mean like the one in those scary movies?" Corrigan cautiously asked.

"Yeah, kind of like that, but this one was real. It was in the window and under some supernatural control because it just floated there."

"Hmm," thought Corrigan as he wondered what kind of hallucination may have been triggered in Thompson's still recovering brain. "Have you ever seen a ghost like that before?" Corrigan inquired.

"Not exactly like that one, but I've seen ghosts before, usually when I was drunk. I've also seen a lot of weird things coming off the booze too. But this was different. It was real. I've never seen anything like it before."

"You haven't stopped taking your meds all ready, have you?" Corrigan knew from experience that some patients, even in a hospital setting, were experts at, "cheeking" or concealing their meds in their mouths to avoid taking them. So he felt compelled to ask just to make sure.

"No," Thompson replied. "Cross my heart and hope to die if I'm not." He then crossed himself with his right hand for effect.

"Good. I knew you were, but I had to ask."

"I don't blame you," said Thompson. Then as he finished his sentence a new fear griped him. "You don't think I had a psychotic break, do you?" asked Thompson. His face then turned cold stone serious. "I'm not going back to that hospital. I told you I'd rather die before I let that happen again."

"I think your brain is still detoxifying, that's all. It's to be expected," replied Corrigan as he tried to put the best possible spin on what just happened.

"You really think so?"

"Yes I do," Corrigan replied trying not to betray his own concerns. "It takes months for the brain to fully detox down to the cellular level. I told you the most critical time of your recovery would be the first couple of months after you were discharged, didn't I?"

"Yeah," Thompson agreed.

Corrigan could see the fear slowly fading from Thompson's face. Thompson sighed, his body stopped trembling, his color was back to normal and his affect was better.

"How do you feel?"

"Better," Thompson replied, now that he was back in control. The fear was gone. "It looks like I'm going to have to reevaluate my position on psychiatrists," he quipped.

"You want to finish watching the game?" asked Corrigan, hoping the diversion would help get things back to normal.

Thompson looked at his watch. "No. I think I've had enough excitement for one day. I think I'll turn in."

"Okay. But, if there's anything you need just let me know."

"Thanks. I'll be okay," a grateful Thompson replied. Both men stood. "You're a good friend, thanks."

Feeling a little guilty Corrigan just nodded and smiled. As Thompson left the room Corrigan thought, "What have I gotten myself into?"

There was no way Corrigan could have known that Doyle and Hunter were responsible for Thompson's ghost. They had hoped to trigger a psychotic break that would send Thompson over the edge. Doyle and Hunter appreciated Corrigan telling Dr. Masterson about Thompson's suicidal ideations. Dr. Masterson dutifully added them to Thompson's progress notes. They judged that Thompson's fear of returning to a psychiatric hospital was tantamount to a career felon who would rather go down with guns blazing than return to prison. This little tidbit helped them with their strategy to scratch Thompson's name off their list.

When Corrigan returned to the messy living room, Diane and Emily were already in bed so he cleaned up the Monday night football mess. When he finished, he made his way down the hall to the master bedroom. As he passed his office he checked in on Thompson. Thompson was sound asleep on the sofa bed. The Ambien he prescribed for him had taken effect. He quietly closed the door and made his way down the hall to join Diane.

# CHAPTER 25

When Corrigan finally crawled under the covers, Diane automatically curled up next to him even though she was sound asleep. He enjoyed the closeness of her body. He snuggled up next to her and yawned. Before he knew it, he was asleep.

The faint sound of whistling woke Corrigan from his sleep, it was Diane. Whenever she was in a deep sleep, she would breathe through her mouth and make a soft whistling noise. He glanced at the clock on the night stand. The digital numbers read two fifteen in the morning. Corrigan softly nudged Diane onto her side and the whistling stopped. He laid his head back down but as soon as he closed his eyes he heard a blood curdling scream, it was Thompson.

Corrigan bolted from the bed and ran down the hall to his office. He opened the door and turned on the light and saw Thompson on the sofa bed curled up in a fetal position. He was trembling and his eyes were filled with terror. The sight made the hairs on the back of Corrigan's neck stand up like porcupine quills. He quickly scanned the room. Except for the half-open window, nothing was out of place and there was no obvious clues as to why his friend was so terrified. Corrigan walked over to the sofa bed and knelt down next to Thompson. He softly placed his hand on Thompson's shivering shoulder. "Gary, it's me. What happened?"

"The ghost, I saw it again," Thompson cried. "It was in the window."

Corrigan looked at the half opened window but there was nothing, only darkness. He calmly stroked Thompson's head like a frightened child. "Calm down. Whatever was there it's gone now." Corrigan looked up and saw Diane standing in the door way.

Diane had a look of concern mixed with a tinge of fear on her face. She silently mouthed the words. "What happened?"

Corrigan silently mouthed the words back to her, "The ghost again."

Diane shook her head in disgust and left the room.

Corrigan could tell from her reaction that, as far as she was concerned, Thompson had just worn out his welcome. He couldn't blame her. It was only Thompson's first day and he already had two episodes of erratic behavior. Maybe his noble experiment wasn't such a great idea. But the consequences of failure were much too high so he had to press on.

Thompson struggled to regain his composure. As his trembling slowly subsided Corrigan spoke softly and reassuringly to him. When the shivering stopped he asked. "Are you okay?"

"Jim, I'm scared."

"I know," replied Corrigan.

"Not that kind of scared, Jim," Thompson replied with a combination of anguish and despair in his voice. His eyes had a haunted look. "Jim, it's starting all over again. I'm losing it. I can feel it. I'd rather die than go back to that hospital again."

As a psychiatrist, Corrigan understood why people wanted to commit suicide. Emotionally, the person felt like they didn't have any options left and had simply given up hope. The person had systematically narrowed their focus down to one deadly option.

274

They were not able to see any other solution to their problem other than ending their life. He also knew from experience if a person really wanted to kill himself there was practically no way, short of a 24-hour guard, to keep them from doing it. Sometimes, that even didn't help.

Thompson finally sat up in bed. He put his face in his hands. "God, I'd hoped this time it would be different. I really did, Jim."

Corrigan pulled his black leather office chair next to the sofa bed and sat down. For some reason this simple act made him feel like he could handle the situation better. Then it dawned on him. Sitting in his leather chair across from Thompson was similar to being in an individual therapy session with a patient. It allowed him to wear his armor of professional detachment and protect himself from the slings and arrows of a patient's outrageous behavior. "How interesting," he thought.

"I mean it Jim. I don't want to go on living like this. It's not the life I want," Thompson continued, his voice having deteriorated into a whimper.

"It's all right," Corrigan said soothingly as he went into therapeutic mode. "I understand." However, he wasn't prepared for Thompson's response.

Thompson looked straight into Corrigan's eyes. "Do you?" he asked bitterly as his fear quickly turned to anger. It was basic psychiatry. Fear, frustration, hurt and a sense of helplessness were all progenitors of anger. And Thompson was scared to death and never felt so helpless in his life.

"Do you really?" he snarled. "I've gone through hell the last five years. I've lost everything that was important to me. I've been hospitalized more times than I care to count. And I've been put on more medications than you can find in the Physician's Desk Reference, and for what? I'm still the same screwed up person."

"Of course I can't understand how you actually feel," Corrigan countered knowing again from experience what was motivating his friend's sudden outburst. "Only you can. But I can understand what you're going through better than most people. You seem to forget I'm a psychiatrist. I think that counts for something. Plus I want to help you."

The scowl on Thompson's slowly faded as he listened to his friend. He knew he shouldn't be mad at Corrigan, but he couldn't help himself. "I'm sorry, Jim. I know you want to help." But, a nagging feeling still plagued Thompson, "Can he, really?" He thought.

"You had a small set back that's all," Corrigan replied, trying not to sound to Pollyannaish. However, he knew his plan to help his friend was going to have to be modified. "Everybody has set backs. It's par for the course."

"You sure?" Thompson asked skeptically.

"Yes," Corrigan responded more firmly. "But, I want to ask you few questions in order to get to the bottom of this."

"You wouldn't be a shrink if you didn't," Thompson wisecracked.

Corrigan saw it as a good sign that Thompson apparently felt comfortable enough to joke with him. He was beginning to sound like him self again. Maybe his plan wouldn't have to be modified.

"What I'd like do is find out why you saw a ghost twice in one night."

"Okay."

"First off was it the same ghost?" Corrigan began.

"Yes," Thompson's quickly replied.

"Okay," said Corrigan. "Did you open the window?"

"Yes. It was a little stuffy in here."

"How did you know the ghost was there?" Corrigan continued.

"The damned thing was brushing something back and forth against the window screen. I heard the noise, woke up and there it was."

"So the ghost had to get your attention before you saw it." This was Corrigan's first clue the ghost might not be of an ethereal nature.

"Yeah," said Thompson.

"Did it do or say anything while it was at the window?"

"Not that I can remember. I kind of flipped out when I saw it again. I don't remember too much after that. All I know was I was really scared."

"So it just stood there and looked at you, right?" asked Corrigan.

Thompson's face suddenly blanched as he remembered. "Oh, God, it was making a cutting motion across its throat." Thompson started to breath rapidly and his eyes widened with alarm. "It was telling me to kill myself. That ghost was showing me the way out."

"That's nonsense," Corrigan said as he tried to keep his friend from hyper-ventilating. "There's no such thing as ghosts. You're a doctor, you know that." It was time to take off the gloves and deal forcefully with Thompson before he had a complete breakdown.

"Bull," screamed Thompson. "What I saw was real."

"No it wasn't!" Corrigan shouted back.

"How can you be so damned sure?"

"Because I think you were hallucinating," Corrigan countered hoping to end the escalating war of words.

"You think I was hallucinating?" a startled Thompson asked.

"It's possible. But I don't think you were," replied Corrigan cryptically.

"Oh, that's just great," Thompson said sarcastically. "First you tell me it's not a ghost. Then you tell me I'm hallucinating. Then you tell me I'm not. Damn it, Jim. Talk straight to me, will you?"

"Hallucinations generally don't act like the one you were describing. And neither do ghosts."

"Then what was it?" an exasperated Thompson asked.

"I don't know for sure, but I'm going to stick around and see if it shows up again." Corrigan had a hunch, a bad hunch about Thompson's ghost, and it made his stomach tighten. For the first time in his life he regretted not having a gun in the house. He silently prayed the mysterious visitor that appeared in the window didn't have one either.

"What better way to find out what's going on than to meet this ghost of yours up close and personal."

"What about me?" asked Thompson as he regained control of himself.

"You can go back to sleep. After I turn off the lights I'll sit over in the corner and watch the window."

"You really think it will come back?" asked Thompson.

"I don't know. But if it does I want to be here." Corrigan could tell from the look on Thompson's face, he wasn't convinced about his plan. "Don't worry. You can go back to sleep. I'll keep an eye on everything."

"You promise?"

"I promise," repeated Corrigan for his friend's sake. He then raised his right hand, "Scout's honor."

"I don't know."

"Trust me," said Corrigan. "I won't let anything happen to you. You can take that to the bank."

"Okay," Thompson reluctantly sighed. "I guess you know what you're doing. You're the doctor." Thompson then laid down on the sofa bed, pulled up the covers and tried to go to sleep.

Corrigan stood, turned off the lights then pushed his office chair into a darkened corner of the room and sat down. The book case hid him as he kept an eye on the open window. Despite Thompson's concern he wasn't going to fall sleep he was snoring within minutes of his head hitting the pillow. The ten milligrams of Ambien, Corrigan had prescribed earlier no doubt helped.

Corrigan found it rather easy to stay awake now that his body had adjusted to working nights. However, with nothing to do he was bored out of his skull. He couldn't turn on a light to read and he couldn't make any noise or the ghostly apparition might not reappear. So he just sat there trying to figure out what to do if Thompson's ghost was actually in his head. Or worse yet, his suspicions were right. He was pretty sure that Thompson wasn't hallucinating, but without any hard evidence the jury was still out. However, he didn't have long to wait before some hard evidence showed up.

Corrigan heard what sounded like a fingernails being drug quickly back and forth across the window screen. Apparently the ghost was back. "How about that," Corrigan thought. "The son of a bitch is back."

Corrigan quietly slipped out his chair and crept along the wall towards the window. When he pulled up alongside the window, he could see there was indeed a ghost in the window. Thompson was right the ghost did look like the one in the movies.

279

No wonder he freaked out. The grotesque mask would have scared anyone at first glance. However, Corrigan could tell there was flesh and blood behind that store-bought costume. The sound of the scrapping finger nails across the window screen started to wake Thompson.

Corrigan didn't want Thompson to overreact at the seeing the ghost again so he made a fist and violently smashed his left hand into the face standing in the window. His fist caught the ghostly apparition by surprise and it pushed the plastic mask up against the human nose underneath. Corrigan jumped in front of the window and punched out the window screen and grabbed the ghost by its costume. The ghost pushed back.

"I knew it," a not-so-astonished Corrigan said to himself as he kept trying to pull the mask off the struggling specter. The ghost had warded off Corrigan's attempts to unmask him, but when he saw he was the losing the battle, he decided it was time to leave. However, when the ghost stepped back to flee, Corrigan's grip on the fright mask pulled it off revealing the man with the acne-scared face he saw at the gun range. "Why, you!" Corrigan cursed, as he recognized the man.

Capitalizing on the momentary distraction, Pete Hunter smashed his right fist into Corrigan's nose.

"Ouch!" cried Corrigan, as he saw stars. Corrigan then stumbled backwards from the impact and fell against the sofa bed.

Hunter picked up his mask, crashed through the shrubs and quickly ran to his rental car parked down the block.

Corrigan's hand instinctively went to his painful nose and found it covered with blood.

"What's going on?" Thompson shouted as he sat up in bed. He saw Corrigan at the foot of the bed. "Jim, what happened?"

Corrigan looked up at his friend with blood running from both nostrils and said. "That was no ghost that you saw." He then tipped his head back to help staunch the flow.

Thompson jumped out of bed. "I'll get something for your nose," said Thompson as left the room.

Before Thompson returned, Diane walked into the office. "What's going on?" she cautiously asked. She flipped on the light switch and screamed when she saw the blood streaming down her husband's face. "Oh, my God, what happened?" She quickly ran to her husband's side. "Are you all right?"

"Yeah," he weakly joked. "I bleed like this all the time." He wanted to put on a brave face and not upset Diane any more than she already was.

Diane surveyed the damage to her husband's face and saw that it was not life threatening and asked again. "What happened?"

"Gary's ghost came back," Corrigan said, as he still acted brave.

Thompson entered the room carrying a bath towel and a wet wash cloth. He gave them to Corrigan who began to clean himself up until Diane took over.

"Let me do that," she insisted.

When his nose finally stopped bleeding, Corrigan told Gary and Diane about his encounter with the phony ghost. Of course, he left out any incriminating information. When he finished, they were more puzzled than before he gave his explanation.

"Who would what to do such a thing?" Diane honestly asked.

Corrigan had a pretty good idea, but he couldn't tell Diane or Gary. So he lied. "I don't know."

"Someone's got an awfully warped sense of humor if you ask me," said Thompson.

"You should call the police," said Diane.

"And tell them I was attacked by a ghost?" Corrigan sarcastically replied. "Yeah sure, they'll think I'm the one who needs to see a psychiatrist."

"But you were attacked," said Diane as she held up the bloody wash cloth. "We've got the evidence to prove it."

"I'll survive," Corrigan quickly said to change the subject. He definitely didn't want the police involved, especially now that he knew who the ghost was. They would ask too many questions. Questions he didn't feel like answering right now, questions that might put him in jail. "I need a drink," Corrigan painfully announced as he felt his nose starting to swell.

"What would you like?" Gary asked.

"Something strong," he replied.

"I don't think you should drink any alcohol right now," Diane strongly suggested.

"I'm the doctor. And I want something to numb the pain, okay?"

"Okay," Diane acquiesced.

Corrigan stood and started towards the door. Diane knew her husband well enough that she wasn't going to be able to stop him. And Thompson sure wasn't going to stand in the way of a man who wanted a shot of whiskey.

As Corrigan walked down the hallway to indulge in a few ounces of painkiller, all he could think about was that rat bastard Zilker. He would call him first thing in the morning and ream him a new one.

John Zilker sat behind his desk at Multi-Group Managed Care sipping his first coffee of the morning. He had already plowed through a mound of paperwork left on his desk from the

282

previous day and was attacking another stack when his cell phone rang.

"You son of a bitch," Corrigan yelled at Zilker over his cell phone. It was his turn to explode. "I know what you tried to do last night." Corrigan had slipped into the garage and was seated behind the wheel of his car so no one could hear his conversation.

"I don't know what you're talking about," Zilker lied.

"Bull! You sent one Ozawa's goons over to my house last night dressed like a ghost to scare Thompson."

"Why would I do that?" asked Zilker.

"So he'd decompensate and try and kill himself," Corrigan fired back.

"That's preposterous," said Zilker.

"Oh, yeah," Corrigan countered. "Then how do you explain the fact the guy I saw wearing the ghost mask looked a hell of a lot like the guy I saw at the gun range when I met Ozawa?"

"Are you sure it was him?" Zilker smugly challenged.

"Yes! Cause I pulled his damned mask off! That's how I know for sure."

"Oh," Zilker replied. But he really thought. "Damn it."

"If you don't leave Thompson alone," said Corrigan, as he slowly ground out each word between clenched teeth. "I'll. . ."

Zilker interrupted Corrigan in mid sentence. "You'll what? Go to the police. I don't think so. You've got too much too lose." Because Corrigan called him first rather than the police he felt it validated his belief about Corrigan's need for self preservation. So Zilker felt confident he could spar with Corrigan again.

"Listen asshole. I'll do it. I really mean it," Corrigan threatened. "As far as I'm concerned I've already sold my soul to the devil so I've got nothing else to lose."

"Too bad you feel that way. I'd hate to see the tape of you ordering Cobb's execution fall into the wrong hands."

"You give that tape to the police and I swear I'll take all of you down with me," Corrigan said ruthlessly.

"Are you really sure you want to do that?"

"Try me," Corrigan coldly taunted. "In fact, I might as well call the police right now since I'm not getting anywhere with you." It was a bluff, but one he hoped would work.

Zilker began to feel uneasy about Corrigan's latest threat. Even if he was correct about Corrigan's need for self preservation, he also knew that an irrational man could be dangerous and do stupid things. That was the last thing he needed right now. He didn't want to push Corrigan into doing something stupid. Too much was at stake. "Let's not get rash," Zilker replied as he tried to placate Corrigan. "We can work this out." He sensed he better not push him too far.

"There's nothing to work out. Either you leave Thompson alone or I'll go to the police it's that simple."

"Then I guess you leave me no choice. I'll call Ozawa," said Zilker as he pretended to concede. He needed to buy time. He'd call Ozawa all right. But, not to honor Corrigan's demand.

"You better," Corrigan said forcefully. "You tell Ozawa to call off his hit men. Then everything will go back to the way it was. I'll forget I ever met you guys and you can forget about me."

"All right, Dr. Corrigan. You have my word," Zilker lied.

"Good," replied Corrigan. "I want to see Thompson live to a ripe old age."

"I understand," said Zilker.

"Then this should be the last time I'll ever need to talk to you, so good-bye." With that Corrigan ended the conversation. As he closed his cell phone a smile appeared on his face. "I did it," he smugly said out loud to himself. He had pulled the tail of the tiger and had gotten away with it.

When the line went dead, Zilker quickly punched the speed dial on his cell phone.

Ozawa had just finished parking his Jaguar in the executive parking lot in front of Global Behavioral when his cell phone rang. He answered it and quickly got an ear full from Zilker.

"Calm down," was the first thing Ozawa was finally able to squeeze in as he listened to Zilker's diatribe. He already knew about the botched attempt because Hunter called him right after it happened and also told him about the mask. Ozawa was pissed, but there was nothing he could do about it.

"Why in the hell did he use a ghost?" Zilker demanded.

"After they read Thompson's chart, Hunter felt a ghost would be the most effective way to scare him into an appropriate end."

"Well, it backfired," Zilker shot back. "Corrigan is screaming that he'll go to the police."

"I assume you reminded him about the tape?" asked Ozawa.

"Of course you idiot," an exasperated Zilker replied. "Unfortunately it seems he's also developed a backbone."

"That bastard," growled Ozawa. "We've got too much at stake to let him screw things up."

"I know. It seems I've greatly underestimated him," Zilker irritably replied.

"So what do we do now?" asked Ozawa.

"I'm afraid we have no choice," Zilker replied, his voice as cold as death. "We have to permanently discharge both of them." Sadly, he wished Corrigan would have been a team player and gone along with the group's recommendation. But it was too late. Corrigan had sealed his own fate.

"I'll call Doyle and Hunter and tell them about the change in plans," said Ozawa.

"Also tell them to make sure whatever they do, especially when it comes to Corrigan, to make it look like an accident. It'll be bad enough when the police learn there's a connection between the two. We don't need to give them anything more to be suspicious about."

"I'm sure they can come up with something special," Ozawa smiled.

"Good," replied a relieved Zilker. With that Zilker ended the conversation, spun his chair around towards the wall and stared into space, then sighed. "What in the hell have I gotten myself into?"

# CHAPTER 26

Corrigan sat in the opulent lobby of Arbor Creek Hospital waiting for Thompson to finish his appointment with Dr. Masterson. When the double doors finally opened, Thompson walked out with a smile on his face. Corrigan stood and greeted his friend.

"How did it go?"

"Masterson said my meds are at therapeutic levels."

"Good."

"And except for this damned dry mouth I'm not having any other side effects," Thompson's smiled continued.

"That's great."

After Thompson turned in his visitor's badges, both men left the lobby. The cool, crisp air felt good. They could see their breath as they walked down the sidewalk towards the parking lot. Corrigan couldn't help but notice again the stark contrast between County General and Arbor Creek. All the pigs in the entire barnyard would have to fly before County General looked anything like Arbor Creek.

Being a physician had its privileges, Corrigan parked in the physician's parking lot. When he got to his newly polished red Mustang, he slid behind the wheel, buckled his seat belt and put the key into the ignition.

Thompson got in the passenger side and shut the door. After he buckled his seat belt he looked at Corrigan. "I want to thank you

287

for helping me. I was feeling pretty shaky the other day after that ghost thing. I don't know what I would've done if you weren't there."

"What are friends for?" Corrigan glibly replied.

"I can't believe you still consider me a friend after all I've put you through," Thompson said with a mixture of gratitude and disbelief.

"I'm sure you've got a lot of friends who feel the same way. Don't worry about it."

"Yeah, right," Thompson replied dismissively. "You become mentally ill and see how fast your friends disappear."

"Fair weather friends are always the first to leave."

"But that old saw doesn't explain why Betty and the kids left me though, does it?" Thompson cynically replied.

Corrigan didn't have a handy platitude for that one.

Fortunately, Thompson answered his own question. "I guess I can't blame her. Living with a drunken schizophrenic can be hell."

"You think she'd be receptive to seeing the new you?" Corrigan asked optimistically.

"James, my boy, she's seen the new me and the new me and the new me before that. The woman's a saint, but I don't think she's ready yet."

"I understand," said Corrigan as he started the engine of the high performance vehicle.

Thompson looked at his watch. "It's almost noon. No wonder I'm hungry. You feel like getting something to eat?"

"Sure," replied Corrigan. "What are you in the mood for?"

"Would you believe a hot dog? I haven't had one in ages," said Thompson.

"Oh, man. Have I got the place for you," Corrigan smiled as he put the Mustang in gear. When he drove the Mustang out of the parking lot, neither man noticed the small drops of brake fluid leaving a trail on the blacktop behind them. Doyle and Hunter had paid Corrigan's Mustang a visit while he was inside. "I'm going to take a short cut. I think you'll like it. It goes by the river."

"Fine by me, as long as we don't get wet," said Thompson. As the two set out for the river road, Thompson had no idea just how prophetic his words were.

Corrigan took the pine-tree-lined trail from Arbor Creek to the bottom of the hill then turned left, and went two more miles. He then connected with the road that would take them into town and avoid the main highway. After a few minutes, the cold rushing waters of Crystal River came into view.

Corrigan caught himself smiling for the first time in a long time as he drove the Mustang effortlessly down the two lane blacktop that followed the shoreline of the river. Maybe the chronic care team fiasco was finally behind him and things were looking up. However, his smile quickly disappeared when he pressed down on the brake pedal and it felt mushy. As they approached the crest of the steepest hill along the route Corrigan pressed on the brakes again. "What the hell?" Corrigan shouted out loud.

The Corps of Engineers planned to fix the dangerous almost ninety degree turn at the bottom of the hill and it was always on their list of things to do. However, there never seemed to be enough money leftover in the budget at the end of the year so again it went un-repaired. Most locals knew about the hazardous curve and drove accordingly so they didn't wind up in the river. Although the occasional drunken teenager hell bent for leather still wound up in the icy water. Some miraculously survived but, more often than not they drowned and their bodies were recovered down stream. The picture in newspaper of the last teenager pulled out of the river flashed through Corrigan's mind as his Mustang crested the top of the hill. He tried the brakes again. They barely slowed the car. He could see the hairpin turn below as the car angled downward.

"Jim, I think you better slow down," said Thompson as he also saw the dangerous turn at the bottom of the hill.

"I'm trying," replied Corrigan.

"Try harder."

Corrigan felt the fluid drain from the lines each time he pressed on the brake peddle. Momentum was now imposing its will on the car as it accelerated down the hill. The Mustang's speed increased with each passing foot of blacktop.

"Jesus!" Corrigan cursed as he pumped furiously on the useless brake pedal. "The brakes are gone."

"Oh, man," Thompson groaned, "just as I was starting to get my act together."

The speedometer now registered 35 miles an hour. Corrigan pressed down on the emergency parking brake. It went all the way to the floorboard and failed to engage. There was only one thing left to do. "We need to jump."

"What?" Thompson shouted in disbelief.

"Just get out of the damned car!" Corrigan shouted. He glanced at the speedometer again. This needle registered just under 40 miles an hour. Corrigan unfastened his seat belt and looked at Thompson. He was frozen with fear. "Come on move!" he shouted. "Or you'll be fish food."

Thompson sat there, his mouth was moving but no words were coming out. His face was ashen and his eyes were as big as dinner plates.

Corrigan reached over and unhooked Thompson's seat belt. "Open the door!"

Thompson looked out the window at the fast moving scenery and shook his head. "I can't do it."

"Like hell you can't!" Corrigan screamed. He reached across and pushed the door open. "Get your ass out of here!"

Thompson hesitated. Corrigan glanced at the speedometer. It was close to 50 miles an hour. "Move!" he exploded.

Thompson slowly leaned toward the open door. As soon as he did, Corrigan shoved him out onto the pavement. Thompson went bouncing along the road until he hit the dirt embankment and rolled under some bushes.

Corrigan quickly followed suit and rolled out of the speeding Mustang. Fortunately, the first part of his body to make contact with the asphalt was his buttocks. He tumbled several yards down the road before he finally stopped. When he sat up, he slowly took stock of himself. Nothing seemed to be broken but he was going to be black and blue in the morning.

Corrigan then sat and watched helplessly as the driverless Mustang swerved back and forth across the road heading for the turn at the bottom of the hill. The car, however, didn't make it to the bottom. The last time it swerved to the left, the Mustang plowed into the guardrail, spun back onto the road and flipped over. Corrigan watched in disbelief as his precious Mustang flipped over. He shut his eyes and groaned. Unfortunately he could still hear the sound of breaking glass and crunching metal. The

Mustang he had dreamed of owning since high school landed in a heap of metal in the middle of the road.

"Jim, are you all right?" asked Thompson as he walked up behind Corrigan.

Corrigan opened his eyes, stood and dusted himself off. "Yeah," he said dejectedly. He then looked to see what was left of his beautiful Mustang. Steam rose from under the crushed hood as broken coolant lines poured their contents onto the hot engine block. Every window was smashed and pieces of debris littered the road.

Thompson looked at the twisted metal in the middle of the road. He tried to cheer up his friend. "Well, at least we got out alive."

"Yeah," Corrigan replied without much enthusiasm. "You, all right?"

"Yeah, nothing broken, but I'll be sore in the morning. Sorry about hesitating back there," Thompson apologized.

"That's all right. It's the first time I've had to bail out of a car too . . . Corrigan then said to no one in particular, "I don't understand it. I keep that car in excellent condition".

A police car appeared at the bottom of the hill with its red lights flashing and siren wailing. As it started up the hill, a second police car fell in behind the first car. "Well, I guess we've got some explaining to do to the local constabulary," said Corrigan as he started walking towards what was left of his car.

A black two door sedan rolled to a stop at the crest of the hill. The driver and passenger could see the carnage sitting in the middle of the road half way down the steep slope, both men smiled. However, Doyle and Hunter smiles quickly disappeared

292

when they saw Corrigan walking with Thompson toward the Mustang they had tampered with. "Damn it," Doyle angrily cursed.

When Hunter saw the two police cars at the bottom of the hill he calmly said. "We better get out of here."

Doyle nodded and wasted no time in turning the car around. The two men quickly drove off in the opposite direction of the oncoming police cars.

Corrigan was allowed to call a tow truck after he explained to the police officers what happened and then only after passing a field sobriety test. By the time the police had finished their accident report the tow truck arrived. The pile of twisted metal that once was a beautiful Mustang was unceremoniously loaded onto the bed of the tow truck and carried away. The police officer in charge of the scene, a young man with freckles, was kind enough to give Corrigan and Thompson a ride home.

As they drove through the city, Corrigan prayed no one would recognize him in the back seat of the police car. He breathed a sigh of relief when the police cruiser finally pulled into the drive way of his home and parked.

The young police officer let Corrigan and Thompson out of the caged back seat. "Sorry about having to put you back there," he said.

"That's all right. I'm just glad you were kind enough to give us a ride home," Corrigan gratefully replied. Although he still felt self-conscious about getting out of the back of a police car, despite having done nothing wrong. He hoped there weren't any snoopy neighbors watching.

Corrigan and Thompson shook the police officer's hand.

"Thanks for the ride home officer," said Thompson.

"You're welcome," the young officer graciously replied. He then slid behind the wheel of his black and white and started the engine. The car then slowly backed out of the drive way.

The front door opened and Diane saw the police car backing onto the street from the drive way. She then saw her husband and Thompson. They both looked a little ragged. "What's going on?" She asked as she shifted Emily from one arm to the other. "And what's that police car doing here?"

"We had an accident," Corrigan said as he tried to minimize the sound of the word: accident.

"Oh my God, are you all right?" She asked.

"I'm fine," Corrigan replied. "No broken bones. Just a few scrapes and bruises."

"We're gonna both be real sore in the morning though, I can feel it," Thompson volunteered.

Diane hugged her husband to make sure he was all right. Reassured that he was still in one piece she asked. "How's the car?"

"It's totaled," Corrigan gloomily reported.

"Oh, my God," Diane replied as her jaw dropped.

"It's a mess," Thompson added.

"Come on inside and sit down, both of you," ordered Diane. Both men obediently followed her into the house. After they made themselves comfortable in the living room Diane asked. "Can I get you guys anything?"

"I could sure use something cold to drink," Corrigan requested.

"Same here," Thompson chimed in. Then he quickly added, "As long as it's non-alcoholic."

"You got it," said Diane as she left for the kitchen.

"Any idea why the brakes went out?" asked Thompson.

"I don't know. It didn't feel like the master cylinder went out. Cause each time I pressed on the brake pedal it felt like I was squeezing the fluid out of the lines. When the master cylinder goes out you instantly lose your brakes. It was almost as if…" Corrigan stopped in mid-sentence. He finished the sentence in his head. "The lines were cut."

"As if what?" Thompson asked as he waited for Corrigan to finish his sentence.

"Oh, my God," thought Corrigan. Suddenly a shiver went down his spine.

"Earth to Corrigan," said Thompson as he tried to get his friend's attention.

"Sorry. It's as if there was a leak somewhere in the lines," said Corrigan as he finished his sentence. He hoped his face didn't betray what he really thinking.

"It's been know to happen," said Thompson as he tried to console his friend. "It's just too bad it happened at the top of a hill."

"Here you go," said Diane as she entered the living room. She handed her husband a large glass of ice water with a twist of lemon and handed one to Thompson. "Have you called the insurance company yet?"

"No," Corrigan sullenly replied. "I better call them and give them the bad news." He polished off his glass of water and set it down. "I'll call them from my office. I've got the insurance papers in my desk. I'll be right back." He stood, left the living room and disappeared down the hall.

When he entered his office, Corrigan shut the door and sat down at his desk. He pulled out his cell phone, punched in a number and waited.

Dr. Zilker had just finished signing a managed care review form and was placing it in his out-basket when his cell phone rang.

"Dr. Zilker," he perfunctorily answered.

"What the hell do you think you're doing?" A very angry Corrigan asked as he tried to keep his voice down so his wife and friend couldn't hear him.

"What do you mean?"

"Don't play games with me. Ozawa's men just tried to kill me and Thompson."

"What!" said Zilker, as he pretended to be surprised?

"You son of a bitch," Corrigan said angrily.

"What are you talking about? That's impossible. I told Ozawa to leave you alone."

"Well, he obviously didn't get the message."

"How do you know for sure it was him?" asked Zilker.

"How do you explain my brakes conveniently going out at the top of a hill with Thompson in the car with me?" Corrigan quickly fired back.

"The brakes on your car went out?" Zilker condescendingly replied. "Dr. Corrigan, please. The brakes on a car can go out at anytime. Accidents happen, you know that. That's why they're called accidents. I must say you're acting a little paranoid."

"Don't give me that crap," Corrigan fumed.

"Do you know for a fact your brakes were tampered with?" asked Zilker hoping the answer would be no.

"No," Corrigan sheepishly replied. "But they felt like the lines were cut."

"They felt like they were cut," Zilker replied condescendingly.

"Yes, but. . ."

"I suggest until you have proof to support such an outrageous accusation that you please not call me again," Zilker said in a huff. "Or I will take such a libelous allegation to court." Zilker then abruptly hung up on Corrigan.

Corrigan looked at the cell phone in his hand. "That's not exactly the how I expected that conversation to go," he thought to himself. "Maybe he's right. Maybe it was just an accident."

As soon as Zilker finished talking to Corrigan he placed another call. He needed talk to Ozawa immediately.

Ozawa was walking into the executive's men's bathroom at Global Behavioral when his cell phone went off. He unclasped the cell phone from his belt and looked at the caller identification. He shook his head, "Now what?"

"This is Ozawa," he said curtly as he answered the phone.

"I just got off the phone with Corrigan. Your guys screwed up again," an irritated Zilker began. "He and Thompson are still alive."

"Give me a minute," said Ozawa. He looked around the bathroom to see if he was alone. He then quickly went down the line of toilet stalls to see if any of them were occupied. They were empty and he was alone.

"Look. Doyle told me what happened. They did their best to get both of them at the same time," Ozawa replied indignantly. "It wasn't their fault they were able to get out of the car somehow."

"Well obviously their plan didn't work as well as they thought it would," Zilker snapped.

"Well, if you want them dead so badly, then why don't you do it yourself," Ozawa angrily challenged. "I'll tell Hunter and Doyle to move onto the next person on their list." He was tired of being yelled at for incompetence, especially when it wasn't his fault.

"No. No. No," replied Zilker as he back peddled. "I'm just upset. Sorry." He sure as hell didn't want to personally kill anyone. That's why they hired Hunter and Doyle.

"Then let them do their job, okay?" said Ozawa. "They're the experts. They'll figure out something."

"Okay, okay," Zilker relented.

"What did you tell Corrigan when he called?"

"I told him he was getting paranoid and that accidents happen," Zilker replied.

"Do you think he believed you?"

"I don't know," Zilker responded. "But, I think I may have bought us some time. Your men had better act quickly because if he suspects were after him too, he'll definitely go to the cops. And then we're all screwed."

"I understand. Don't worry. They won't fail."

"I hope for all our sakes you're right. If not, we're all going to jail," Zilker emphasized.

"I know," Ozawa replied. The image of him in prison garb standing behind iron bars flashed through his mind. It made his bowels loosen.

"Good-bye," said Zilker.

"Good-bye," said Ozawa as he hung up. He quickly entered a stall, pulled his pants down and sat on the toilet. He then hit speed dial on his cell phone and waited.

Kevin Doyle was sitting on a bar stool in a seedy establishment that reminded him of a few he frequented while stationed at Ft. Benning. Except this place had bar flies so ugly, the tide wouldn't take them out. He had already put down two beers

298

and was nursing a long neck in front of him. When he lifted the beer to take another swallow, his cell phone went off. He took the cell phone off his belt, glanced at the incoming number and answered it, "Doyle here."

# CHAPTER 27

The LED clock on the dashboard read three fifteen in the morning as Doyle pulled the rental car over to the curb and parked. From the front seat Doyle and Hunter both scanned the deserted residential street in front of them. Like the rest of the houses up and down Corrigan's block the lights were off. Both men looked at each other and silently nodded their heads, their mission was a go. They were both dressed in black from the top of their watch caps to the tips of their sturdy combat boots. They had evil on their minds and were dressed for it. They both quietly got out of their two door sedan and walked briskly down to the street to Corrigan's house.

When they reached the driveway, they quickly dashed to the side of the house and silently disappeared into the darkness. After making sure they hadn't been spotted, they carefully crept up to a window hidden by a tall hedge and peeked inside the living room. The room was dark and unoccupied just as they had hoped. It was a good sign. Both men then slipped on surgical gloves. Hunter took out a diamond cutter and etched a circle in the window pane near the lock. With a suction cup he pulled out the circle, reached inside and opened the window lock. He carefully pushed the window open and then like a ghost slipped into the living room. He then helped Doyle quietly enter the darkened room.

Their plan was simple. They were going to loosen the gas line to the water heater then place a small incendiary device hooked up to a detonator cell phone near the leak. They would exit the house and wait for the house to fill with gas. Then with the latest in bomb making technology they would call the cell phone and trigger the incendiary device attached to the gas line. The resulting explosion would take care of people inside of the house and destroy any evidence they were involved.

Meanwhile Thompson tossed and turned on the sofa bed in Corrigan's office. He was having a fitful night's sleep, even his pajamas felt uncomfortable. He finally opened his eyes and stared at the ceiling, his mouth feeling like it was stuffed with cotton. It was the side effect of his meds again. He looked over at the small end table where he kept a bottle of water. It was empty. "Damn," he said to himself. "I better get another one or I'll never make it through the night."

Thompson tossed off his covers, got out of bed, stepped out into the hallway and started towards the kitchen. As he turned the corner to enter the kitchen, he thought he heard voices. He stopped to listen. "Wait a minute," he thought. "Was someone really talking or were his symptoms coming back?" He pondered the question for a moment then shook his head. "Nah, it can't be," he said softly to himself. "I'm on my meds."

Doyle and Hunter were on their knees in front of the water heater when Thompson stumbled upon them.

"Hey, what are you doing?" Thompson benignly asked.

The answer came quickly in the form a single bullet from a nine millimeter Beretta. The bullet entered Thompson's chest just below the sternum and tore a gapping hole in his heart muscle. He was dead before he hit the floor.

Their cover blown, Hunter and Doyle quickly tightened the gas line and sanitized the area before shutting the door. "We need to make it look like a burglary," Hunter whispered loudly over the ringing in his ears. "Grab some stuff on the way out."

The sound of the powerful handgun woke Corrigan. Startled from his sleep Corrigan bolted up and tossed off his covers. He was at the bedroom door and opening it before he realized what he was doing. Then it hit him. "Oh, God, no," he apprehensively thought. Did Thompson shoot himself? "I don't own a gun," he quickly remembered, but Thompson did. How did he get it out of his apartment? That and a million other questions raced through his mind as he opened the bedroom door and he stepped into the hallway. As he did he heard the sound of someone running through the house then the sound of the front door flying open.

Diane was awake and alert with eyes wide open. "What's going on?" She asked.

"I'm not sure. But, call 911."

Diane obediently grabbed the phone off the nightstand and punched in the number. "What do want me to tell them?"

"I think we've been burglarized. And I thought I heard a gun shot."

In their haste to escape, Doyle and Hunter took a short cut across Corrigan's sprinkler-soaked front lawn. It was a critical mistake. When they got back to their rental car both men quickly jumped inside. Doyle slid behind the wheel and Hunter plopped down on the passenger seat.

"Who did you shoot?" asked Hunter.

"I don't know. I didn't get a good look at his face," Doyle responded. Then he added with a grin. "But, I'm sure we'll find out in the morning."

"One down and one to go," Hunter added with a grin.

Doyle put the car in gear and slowly made a U-Turn. Then the two assassins nonchalantly drove away.

As Corrigan cautiously made his way towards his office, he saw Thompson lying on his back in the middle of the hall, his motionless body not making a sound.

"Gary, are you all right?"

No answer.

Corrigan ran to his friend's side and got down on his knees next to him. "Gary, are you all right? Talk to me." When he checked for a carotid pulse he saw a pool of blood in the middle of Thompson's chest and one forming on the floor under his back. "Oh, my God," Corrigan cried. He then screamed. "Diane, tell them to send an ambulance!"

The Corrigan household was a crime scene again, just like the night George Cobb tried to kill them. Yellow police tape was up, the house lights were on and uniformed police officers were milling around. However, this time Gary Thompson had a sheet over him in the middle of the hallway.

Detectives, Norwell and Joiner, who were on deck for the next homicide, stood in the hallway looking down at Thompson's covered body. The sheet that covered the upper torso was soaked in blood. Corrigan stoically stood beside the detectives looking at mortal remains of his friend.

"I know this is a bad time," said Norwell. "But I need to ask you a few questions."

"I understand," Corrigan somberly replied.

"You told the first police officer to arrive you heard what sounded like a gun shot and that's when you woke up, right?"

"Yes. I was sound asleep. I heard the gun shot and then came down the hallway and found Gary lying on the floor. When I went to check for a pulse, that's when I realized he'd been shot."

"Did you get a look at who did it?" asked Norwell.

"I didn't see anyone. All I heard was footsteps running out of the house as I left the bedroom," replied Corrigan knowing his answer wasn't much help.

"Did it sound like one or two people running?" Norwell asked trying to glean more information.

"I'm not sure. I was a little preoccupied to be counting footsteps."

"I understand," Norwell replied sympathetically.

Two men from the Corner's office gently put Thompson's body in a black body bag. They then placed it on a gurney and rolled Thompson's body outside where they would load it into a white van.

"Burglars don't normally carry guns, do they?" asked Corrigan directing his question at Norwell.

"Normally they don't. But you never know these days. We've even found shoplifters carrying guns. We live in a very violent society."

"I imagine if the way things keep going, everyone will be carrying a gun before long," Corrigan mused out loud.

"I hope not," Norwell sighed. "We've got enough people killing each other already as it is."

"You said that from what you could tell the burglar or burglars didn't take very much stuff, right?" asked Joiner.

"Yeah nothing of value anyway, it's like whoever it was just grabbed things on the way out."

"I guess whoever it was must have just entered the house and was looking around when your friend unfortunately interrupted him," said Norwell speculating from years of experience. This wasn't the first time a homeowner or house guest had stumbled into a burglary in progress and suffered the consequences. Nor would it be the last.

A heavy-set man wearing a dark blue wind breaker with Crime Lab written on the back walked up to Norwell. "Where did you want me to dust for prints?"

Norwell pointed to the window with the neatly cut circle in it. "Over there."

"You got it," the lab man replied. He made his way over to the window and began the meticulous process of trying to lift prints from the obvious point of entry.

A uniformed police officer entered the house and walked up to Norwell. "We found two sets of what look like boot prints on the sidewalk out front. Whoever they were they cut across the wet grass and left the prints behind."

"Make sure you get pictures of them before the dry up," ordered Norwell.

"We're already on it," replied the police officer.

"Good," acknowledged Norwell. He then turned to Corrigan. "Well, now we know for sure there were two of them."

The information that it was two men who took his friend's life didn't make Corrigan feel any better. Then it suddenly struck him. "No, it couldn't be," he thought to himself.

"We'll be here for a while," said Norwell.

"Uh, yeah, okay," Corrigan replied awkwardly, as he kept his suspicions to himself.

"It was a good idea to send your wife and baby to a hotel for the night," said Joiner.

"She didn't need to be here," Corrigan replied. "She's already been through enough."

Both Norwell and Joiner nodded their heads in sympathetically agreement.

"Diane's mother will be here in morning. I'll let Diane decide what she wants to do after that."

"Good idea," said Joiner.

"If you don't need me for anything I'd like to go be with her," said Corrigan.

"Go ahead. We've got your cell phone number if we need to reach you. And we'll lock up when we're done."

"Thanks," said a grieving Corrigan.

Dr. John Zilker greeted the new day like most mornings at his stately mansion. He showered and shaved and then entered his walk in closet, put on a $1,000 tailor-made business suit, expensive black leather shoes and made his way downstairs to the kitchen. He polished off a bowl of heart healthy cereal and two cups of decaffeinated coffee before heading off to work. As he was driving to work in his silver Mercedes his cell phone rang. He answered the phone, it was Ozawa.

"Thompson's dead," said Ozawa.

"Good," Zilker cheerfully replied. "What about Corrigan?" he asked hoping their worries were finally over.

"He's still alive."

"Crap!" an irritated Zilker cursed. "What happened?"

Ozawa quickly summarized for Zilker the events that transpired during the night from the briefing Hunter and Doyle gave him.

306

"I see," said Zilker as he mulled over the information.

"Don't worry, though," Ozawa quickly added. "They're already working on a plan to take out Corrigan."

After a brief moment of silent reflection Zilker finally said, "I don't think that will be necessary now."

The mysterious response confused Ozawa. "What?" he asked.

"Think about it," said Zilker. "If Corrigan believes it was a burglar who shot his friend, then we're home free. Thompson's out of the way and there's no need for Corrigan to go to the police."

"But what if he does suspect us?"

"Then we'll have to take him out. But, right now I feel we should wait and see what happens. There's no need to create any more problems unless we have to."

"That's easy for you to say," a nervous Ozawa replied. The image of him in prison garb flashed through his mind again.

"Look," said Zilker as if lecturing a student. "If we don't have to kill him, it'll be better for all concerned. There's already an established connection between Thompson and Corrigan. So let's don't give the police an excuse to look any deeper if Corrigan should turn up dead, okay?"

"Okay," a reluctant Ozawa agreed.

"For the time being let's just keep an eye on him and see what happens."

"All right," Ozawa signed.

"Where are Doyle and Hunter now?" Zilker asked.

"They're still in town."

"Good," Zilker replied. "Have them follow Corrigan for a couple of days and see what he does. The next couple of days are going to be critical."

"I'll call them as soon as I get off the phone."

"Good. I'll call you tonight and see how things are going. Good-bye."

"Good-bye," said Ozawa as he ended his conversation with Zilker and quickly punched in the number for Doyle's cell phone.

The next morning, James Corrigan sat behind his desk at home, alone with his thoughts. He had just returned from the airport, where he dropped off Diane, Emily and his mother-in-law. Diane decided it would be best if she and the baby stayed with her mother for a while. Corrigan couldn't fault her decision. Lightening had struck their home twice. He definitely understood why Diane felt safer some place else. "Who knows?" he thought. "She may never feel safe here again."

Corrigan reached over and picked up the phone on the desk and punched in the number of Dr. Markus Lang.

Lang answered his phone on the third ring.

"Dr. Lang. This is Dr. Corrigan. . . .Yes. I know. He was a friend. . . . Thank you. The reason I'm calling is that I need some time off."

After he got Lang's approval, he hung up the phone and leaned back in his chair and let his mind reflect on what had happened the last few days. Why two burglars? Although, according to Norwell, it was not that unusual. Corrigan still felt it was significant considering Ozawa had two assassins. Another fact that bothered him was the burglaries were armed, at least one of them anyway. According to Norwell, this was still not unusual. Ozawa's men were proficient with firearms. Something he knew first hand after watching them shred targets at the pistol range. Both burglars wore combat boots. At least one of Ozawa's men had a military look about him and Ozawa said they were both ex-military. "Maybe that's stretching it a bit," he thought. Then again, "Maybe not."

He wrestled with the problem most of the afternoon before he realized there was only one way to find out if Ozawa's men were responsible for Thompson's murder. He would have to find them and then ask them. He knew it would be dangerous, but he had no other choice. He couldn't go to the police and he knew Zilker would deny everything. His only problem was where to find them. "I'll begin at the beginning," Corrigan said optimistically to himself as he rose from his chair to start a dangerous journey with an uncertain outcome.

# CHAPTER 28

Corrigan waited until after dark before he drove to the gun range where he first saw Ozawa's assassins. He hoped to find Bill behind the counter so he could ask him a few questions. When he parked his wife's Mercedes along the curb, he saw Bill inside the well-lit store helping a customer. "Good," thought Corrigan as he turned off the ignition.

"I'll be with you in a minute," said Bill when he saw Corrigan walk in.

"Take your time. I'm in no hurry," Corrigan replied. He then pretended to be interested in some holsters hanging on the wall while he waited. When Bill finished selling his customer a box of shotgun shells and some clay pigeons, he came over to wait on Corrigan.

"What can I do for you?" asked Bill with the chrome plated 44 still strapped to his hip.

"I don't know if you remember me or not. I was in here a while back looking for someone. They weren't out here and you directed me to the shooting range in back."

"Oh, yeah," smiled Bill. "You thought whoever was looking for you would walk up and say, hi. But the store was empty. Yeah, I remember, why?"

"Well, I did find the person I was looking for," said Corrigan as he began his bogus story. "As it turned out he helped me get a great job. I wanted to thank him by getting him a present. And since I know he's a gun enthusiast I figured what better place to buy him something."

"You've come to the right place," Bill said happily. "Got any idea what you'd like to get him?"

"Well, I know he does a lot of shooting. So I was thinking of maybe buying him some ammunition."

"Sure. What kind?" asked the affable old clerk?

"I was hoping you could tell me. I don't know much about guns myself so I wouldn't have the slightest idea of what kind of ammunition to buy."

"Do you know what kind of gun he uses?" asked Bill hoping to narrow the field.

"All I know is that he uses a small semiautomatic pistol," Corrigan replied. "I was hoping you might have a record of any ammunition he may have bought the night I was here. Then I could buy the same kind."

"Well, if he bought any ammo here, I should have a record of it," Bill confidently replied.

The two men walked over to the glass counter stocked with dozens of gun metal blue and chrome plated pistols. Bill slipped behind the counter while Corrigan stood in front of the glass cabinet. Bill found his receipt book, placed it on the counter and thumbed through it. "Here we go," said Bill. "Looks like I sold two different types of ammo that night. Four boxes of nine millimeter and one box of seven point, six, five millimeter."

"Would you be able to tell me what kind of pistols would use that kind of ammunition?" asked Corrigan.

"The nine millimeter stuff is normally used in handguns like a Glock or a Beretta, something along those lines. The smaller ammo is for a pocket-type pistol."

"That had to be Ozawa's gun," thought Corrigan. "Do you have the names of the people who bought the bigger ammunition?" asked Corrigan hoping to get his first clue.

"No. Don't need to keep names for selling ammo, yet. But, you wait and see. The way those damn gun control freaks are acting it won't be long before I'll have to take down the name of anyone who just walks in front of the store."

"That's too bad," Corrigan replied as he hid his disappoint.

"Those damned government types will be regulating everything before long," replied Bill thinking Corrigan was agreeing with his anti-gun control sentiments.

"Well, thank you for your time," said Corrigan.

"Don't you want to buy any ammo?" asked Bill.

"No. Not until I'm sure of what kind to buy. When I do, I'll come back," said Corrigan as he disengaged from the unproductive conversation. "But thanks for your help."

"I'll be here," said Bill as slipped the receipt book under the counter and watched Corrigan leave the store.

"What in the hell do you think he was doing in there?" asked Hunter. Doyle and Hunter were parked down the block from the gun store. They had been tailing Corrigan ever since Ozawa called them. They watched as Corrigan exited the gun store and got behind the wheel of his Mercedes.

"You got me," replied Doyle. "But I don't like it. He's up to something."

Corrigan's car pulled away from the curb and merged with the street traffic.

When the Mercedes was far enough ahead, but still within view, Doyle put his rental car in gear and began to follow Corrigan again. He used the traditional car surveillance techniques the government taught him when he worked for military intelligence.

"Do you think he's trying to find out who we are?" Hunter asked.

"If he is, that can only mean one thing. He suspects we killed his friend," Doyle replied as he continued to expertly follow Corrigan's Mercedes through the city traffic.

"Even if he found out who we are, what good would it do? He can't go to the police," said Hunter.

"True," replied Doyle. "But, there's one thing that bothers me about him."

"What's that?"

"He's a loose end," Doyle replied. "And I hate loose ends. An Op is never over until all the lose ends are tied up." It was another lesson drilled into him, courtesy of the U.S. Military.

"Even if he is a lose end," Hunter reminded his cohort in crime. "We can't do anything to him without Ozawa's authorization."

"To hell with Ozawa," Doyle snarled. "He's not the one out here putting his ass on the line, we are. If I feel Corrigan is about to compromise us, I'll take him out. Then I'll tell Ozawa."

Hunter didn't respond. However, his silence spoke volumes because he agreed with Doyle. He didn't want to wind up on death row because of Corrigan. If it meant killing Corrigan to keep from getting a lethal injection so be it. Hunter valued his own life far too much to allow some jerk like Corrigan to compromise it.

Hunter and Doyle tailed Corrigan's Mercedes in their innocuous rental car through the city and out into the suburbs. All the while, Corrigan had no idea he was being followed.

When he made a right turn onto Quail Lane Corrigan was almost home. Less than a minute later, Doyle's car made the same right turn. As Corrigan continued down Quail Lane toward Hummingbird, he finally noticed there was a car behind him, but he didn't pay any attention to it. However, he did when he glimpsed in the rear view mirror and saw the outlines of two figures sitting in the front seat. He was now concerned.

Instead of making the usual right turn onto Hummingbird Drive, he drove an additional block and made a left turn onto Sparrow Lane. When he reached the middle of Sparrow Lane, he looked in his rear view mirror and saw the same car turn onto the street. "Are they following me?" thought Corrigan as he suddenly felt a little unease. "Only one way to find out," he said under his breath. He then quickly made a left turn onto Bluebird Street and slowed down. This time he was only a quarter of the way down the residential street when the same car appeared. A chill went down his spine.

"What the hell is he doing?" an exasperated Doyle asked as he continued to follow Corrigan's Mercedes. "Is he lost or something?"

"No!" Hunter shouted. "Turn off your lights and pull over!"

Doyle quickly complied. Having worked together as a team for so long both men had come to trust each other's instincts. Their lives depended on it. Still, Doyle looked over at Hunter with a quizzical expression.

"He's trying to find out if he's being followed," Hunter enlightened his friend. "Let's wait here and let him leave. We know where he lives. He'll show up there eventually."

"This is not good," said Doyle as he turned off the car's engine.

314

Corrigan continued down the street then turned onto Bluebird Lane anxiously expecting car headlights to appear at any moment. But, as he made his way down the street no headlights appeared. He slowed the Mercedes to make sure, still no headlights. With a sigh of relief he took the next left and headed for home. "Man, I'm getting paranoid. I've got to watch it," Corrigan cautioned himself.

When he turned into his driveway, he thought he caught a glimpse of car a coming down the street with its headlights off. However, when the garage door opened, he was temporarily blinded and lost sight of the car. After he parked and stepped out of the garage, he looked up and down the street, nothing. When the garage door closed, it was dark again and that's when he noticed three parked cars down the street instead of two. He wasn't sure, but he thought he saw movement in the dark sedan parked farthest down the street. Rather than stand out in the open and continue to stare at the car, Corrigan went inside his house.

Once inside he turned on more house lights than necessary. Satisfied it looked like he was home for the evening, he went to the kitchen where he retrieved a cold bottle of water from the refrigerator. After quenching his thirst he sat down at the kitchen table. Who was following him? Maybe Norwell had put him under some kind of police protection. "No," thought Corrigan. "I'm sure he would have told me if he had." What if they were Ozawa's men? If they were, it meant Zilker had been lying to him all along. His stomach tightened at the thought. Had the hunter become the hunted? There was only one way to find out. He was going to have to take a look inside that car. If everything was just coincidence and he was just being paranoid then no harm done. However, if they were Ozawa's men it meant Zilker was out to permanently discharge him.

Corrigan slipped out of the kitchen and into the darkness of the backyard. He cut across the lawn and opened the wooden gate to the alley. He then made his way quietly down the trash-can-lined alley and when he reached the street, he cautiously surveyed the area. Like a commando, he used the shadows cast from street lamps and the concealment of trees to draw closer to the car. As he did he was able to confirm that there were definitely two men inside the car. However, he was knew he was as close as he dare get, without being detected.

"Damn it," he thought. He still couldn't tell for sure if they were Ozawa's hit men. The distance and the darkness conspired against him. Since it wouldn't be prudent to advance any closer he decided to retreat. As he reentered the alley an idea came to him. He quickly took out his cell phone and punched in a number.

"911, please state your emergency," said the 911 operator in response to Corrigan's call.

"Yes," Corrigan said softly. "I'm with the neighborhood watch on Mockingbird Lane and I'd like to report two suspicious people parked in a car down the street."

After taking the necessary information the emergency operator promised to send a patrol car over to check out it. "Thank you," said Corrigan as hung up the cell phone and opened the gate to his backyard.

After he entered the house, he made his way to the master bedroom and changed. He put on an old Harvard sweat shirt, slipped on some sweatpants and a pair of jogging shoes. He couldn't remember the last time he went jogging. He had worked his way up to five miles a day before he stopped. It seemed liked ages ago when he went out and pounded the pavement before dawn. He left the bedroom and turned off all the house lights. He then slipped out the back door again and prayed that his legs would hold up long enough for his plan to work.

Both Hunter and Doyle saw the lights go off in Corrigan's home. "I think he's in for the night," said Hunter dropping more than a subtle hint they could now leave. Hunter didn't relish the idea of an all night stake out. He knew that no matter how you twisted or turned as you sat in the front seat of a car it eventually became uncomfortable. And even with a heavy jacket it was hard to stay warm.

"Maybe you're right," Doyle replied. Suddenly the interior of the car lit up as if the sun had suddenly dropped out of the sky behind them. Doyle quickly glanced in the rear view mirror and saw the high beams and spot light of a police cruiser parked directly behind them. "Grab a map out of the glove compartment!" Doyle quickly shouted. "It's the police."

Hunter complied and slowly opened the glove box, retrieved a road map and carefully opened it.

Officer Jerry Knight, a ten-year veteran of the San Salina police department got out of his patrol car. He carefully approached the driver's side of the parked car with his right hand resting on his holstered service pistol. When the burly six foot four, two hundred and fifty pound officer reached the driver's side window he pointed his five-cell, heavy-duty flashlight directly in the face of the driver.

"Roll your widow down," ordered Knight.

The window immediately came down. "Can I help you officer?" Doyle asked in the politest way he knew how.

"We got a call from the local neighborhood watch about two people parked in a car on this street," replied Knight as he now targeted Hunter with the flashlight. "I was sent to check it out."

"We're just lost, officer," Doyle lied. "We were in town on business and thought we'd look up an old friend. But dick weed over here can't read a map."

Hunter smiled stupidly and held up the map for Knight to see.

"You guys got any I.D.?"

"Sure officer," Doyle responded as he retrieved his wallet from his back pocket and quickly pulled out his driver's license.

Both men normally had lots of phony identification for such an emergency, but they had grown complacent. The pair had never even seen a police officer, much less stopped by one as they crisscrossed the country killing people. They not only had become complacent, they also became careless. With some reluctance, Doyle handed Officer Knight his real driver's license.

Knight studied Doyle's driver's license. The picture on the license matched the driver and it did show the man was from out of town. Knight then looked at Hunter. "You got any I.D.?"

"Yes, officer," Hunter courteously replied. Hunter retrieved his wallet from his back pocket and handed his real driver's license to Doyle, who in turn handed it to Knight. It would turn out to be a mistake all three men would soon regret.

Knight studied the license. As he did, Corrigan, in his jogging outfit, appeared out of the darkness and was bathed in the lights of the patrol car. Knight looked up to see who was approaching. When he saw that it was just a jogger who presented no immediate threat, he turned his attention back to the occupants of the car.

Hunter also saw Corrigan and turned his head away. However, it was too late and both men recognized each other. When Corrigan saw Doyle behind the wheel his knees went rubbery for an instant. "It's them!" Corrigan exhaled under his breath. He then tried to jog nonchalantly past the car. Despite being out of shape and sucking wind, he passed the car with increased speed. He wanted to put as much distance between him and Ozawa's killers as possible.

"You boys won't mind if I run a check on these licenses, would you?" asked Knight.

"No officer, go right ahead," replied Doyle with a smile. The two men had one thing going for them as professional assassins, neither one had a prior criminal record under their real names. Therefore they had no fear of the police officer's wants or warrants check. They knew it would come back clean and they would soon be on their way.

Knight returned to his patrol car. He squeezed back into the front seat and called in the names of the two men he'd stopped. When the report came back negative, he returned to the parked car.

"Well, I guess you two guys haven't been up to anything," quipped Knight as he handed both drivers licenses back to Doyle.

"I could have told you that officer," Doyle replied with a cordial smile as he handed Hunter his driver's license. Hunter then made the mistake of opening his jacket to put the license in his shirt pocket instead of back in his wallet. When he did the grip of his nine millimeter Glock 17 in his shoulder holster stood out like a cordless electric drill. Knight saw the pistol and immediately reacted to the threat.

"Freeze, don't move!" he shouted as he drew his own nine millimeter service pistol and pointed it at both men. "Keep your hands where I can see them!"

319

"Oh, damn." Doyle fatalistically sighed. They were almost home free. He could hear Knight call for backup on his epaulet microphone.

"Officer, I can explain," said Hunter.

"Shut up! And keep your hands where I can see them," Knight ordered.

Doyle then did something really stupid. He knew when the police got around to searching the trunk of their car they would find lots of stuff that would be hard to explain, if they were just business men from out of town. Things like a black bag that contained a set of forged passports and credit cards along with some extra boxes of nine millimeter ammunition, not to mention several thousand dollars in cash. Out of fear or panic or a combination of both, Doyle's survival instincts took over. He slowly reached down and grabbed the inside door handle. He then pushed the car door open and slammed it into Knight as hard as he could. Knight doubled over from the impact and dropped his pistol on the pavement. Doyle started the rental car, shoved it into gear and peeled out. As the car accelerated, the left rear tire ran over Knight's ankle breaking it in two places.

"What the hell are you doing?" screamed Hunter as he looked back and saw Knight lying on the ground holding his ankle in pain. "You ran over a cop!"

"Shut up!" shouted Doyle.

"Do you realize how much trouble we're in now?" asked a rattled Hunter.

"I guess it's time for Plan B then," shouted Doyle as he tightened his grip on the wheel of the speeding car racing down the street. Doyle was already thinking two moves ahead of the police. But plan B seemed to be the only viable option now.

Plan B was something both men hoped they'd never have to implement. However, they were also realists. They were in a dangerous profession and things happened. They knew if anything hit the fan, they would need a back up plan. At first they jokingly called it Plan B then the name stuck. The plan was simple. Pete Hunter and Kevin Doyle would cease to exist. They would leave the country under assumed names with just the clothes on their backs and the numbers to their Swiss bank accounts. Plan B sounded good on paper, now it was time to find out if it worked.

Unfortunately for Corrigan as he jogged onto Mockingbird Lane, he was unaware that Hunter and Doyle were speeding towards him. His legs ached and his feet hurt as he slowly jogged down the sidewalk. "Damn," he thought as he sucked in air. "I'm really out of shape." He was two doors from his house when he saw a rapidly approaching car with its high beams on. He stopped and held up his forearm to shield his eyes from the bright glare.

Doyle couldn't believe his eyes when he saw the car's headlights fall on the man standing on the sidewalk half way down the block. His lip curled in anger. "There's the son of a bitch that started all this." Doyle took his foot off the accelerator and let the car slow down.

"What are you doing?" a shocked Hunter demanded. This was no time for Doyle to slow down. There had to be dozens of cops swarming to their location.

"I got a loose end to tie up," replied Doyle as he reached for his nine millimeter Beretta. Doyle didn't want the specter of Corrigan following him into their self-imposed exile. Or worse yet, having to worry about the potential damage he could do to the chronic care team. Doyle whole-heartedly believed in the goals of the chronic care team. His only regret was that he wasn't going to be able to continue to avenge the loss of his wife. He hoped Ozawa would find another pair of skilled assassins to continue punching the tickets of frequent flyers. It was a noble undertaking as far as he was concerned. Right now, the only way to insure the continued success of the chronic was to eliminate Corrigan and there he stood.

Corrigan noticed the speeding car suddenly slow down and within seconds draw along side him. Although the driver's window was down, he couldn't make out the driver. Then he thought he saw the driver point something at him. Before he could register what it was, he saw a muzzle flash. Then it felt like someone hit him in the chest with a baseball bat. Doyle fired two more times at his hapless target. Corrigan's knee buckled from the impact of the second bullet entering his leg, which caused the third bullet to miss his head and lodge in the front door of a neighbor's house. Corrigan could see the cold hard sidewalk quickly coming up to meet him.

"I got him!" Doyle shouted. "That son of a bitch won't bother us any more," he bragged. Doyle then slid the Beretta back into his waistband and stomped on the accelerator. Before long, all that was left of the escaping duo were the tail lights of their car.

Corrigan tried to move. But, his body refused to respond. He remembered being hit by something and then he felt the cold hard sidewalk slam against him. As his body started to go into shock, he heard someone scream. Then he heard someone shout, "Call 911!"

"My, it's getting cold," Corrigan heard his own disembodied voice say as consciousness fled.

Corrigan would have died from loss of blood, if the ambulance that responded to the 911 emergency hadn't been returning to its nearby fire station from another call. The ambulance was able to respond in half the time. Corrigan was taken to County General because the ambulance crew couldn't find any identification on him. They knew from experience, that if they took him to a for-profit hospital without any identification it would create problems. The for-profit hospital would treat the patient in the emergency room, as required by law, but they would demand mounds of paperwork to justify the ambulance crew's decision to bring him there. The life or death of the patient didn't enter into the equation, only the bottom line: reimbursement. It cost them money to treat an indigent patient, money which they most likely would never recoup.

The ambulance or the box, as it is affectionately called by the paramedics because of its bulky square shape, was backing up to County General's ER entrance within minutes after picking up Corrigan. Corrigan was quickly unloaded and wheeled inside. Dr. Mack immediately recognized his latest trauma patient and gave Corrigan priority treatment. After he was stabilized in the ER, Corrigan was sent up to surgery. While he was under the knife two bullets were removed from his body, one from his chest and one from his left leg. He spent the rest of the night and the better part of the next morning unconscious in the I.C.U.

When the haze finally lifted and Corrigan was able to focus he saw Detectives Norwell and Joiner standing beside his bed. Corrigan felt the tug of a morphine drip taped to his arm as he slowly moved.

"Your doctor said you'd be coming around," said Joiner. "We wanted to be here when you did."

"You know we've got to stop meeting like this," Norwell chided when Corrigan looked at him.

"What happened?" asked Corrigan.

"You were the victim of a drive-by shooting," Norwell flatly replied. "You were shot twice."

"The hospital was able to get a hold of your wife. She should be here by tonight," Joiner thoughtfully added.

"Tonight?" a bewildered and groggy Corrigan asked. "How long have I been here?"

"They brought you in yesterday night," replied Joiner. "It's late afternoon now."

"I know this is not the best time to be asking you questions but we need to piece some things together," Norwell said as he began his formal interview.

"Piece things together?" thought Corrigan. Even in his groggy condition that didn't sound good.

"We think we might have the guys that shot you," said Norwell. "I'm waiting for forensics to call me as soon as they know something."

The unsettling revelation surprised Corrigan but he remained silent. Even in his drugged state he knew the consequences of being associated in any way with Ozawa's assassins would not bode well for him, even as a victim. Assassins required a motive and a potential motive was something he didn't feel like discussing with the police now or ever.

"Last night one of our patrol officers responded to a neighborhood watch call about two suspicious men in a car parked down the street from your house. The two men were armed and they fled in their car in the direction of your house."

Corrigan listened intently. What Norwell was telling him didn't sound good.

"And apparently you were jogging on Mockingbird Lane at the same time." Norwell said more as a statement of fact than a question.

It was now becoming obvious to Corrigan that one of Ozawa's men had shot him. Zilker did want him permanently discharged. Yet, Corrigan knew he couldn't be linked to the two assassins. The consequences would be disastrous and he could find himself facing the death penalty.

"Did you see who was in the car?" Norwell asked.

"The last thing I remember is jogging home," Corrigan coughed weakly hoping Norwell would stop asking him questions.

"Do you go jogging the same time every night?" Norwell asked.

"I used to jog. But, I stopped. I just started up again last night," Corrigan half lied. "I thought it might help reduce some of the stress I've been under," Corrigan flat out lied.

Norwell knew more about last night than he was letting on and wanted to see how Corrigan would react to the information as he slowly disclosed it. "The officer who got the neighborhood watch call was injured but was able to put an APB. That resulted in a pretty nasty car chase through half the county. After the two guys wrecked out they put up a fight. A guy named Kevin Doyle was killed. His partner named Peter Hunter wisely decided to surrender. He's in custody but, he's not talking."

"Oh, jeez," thought Corrigan.

"Both men were armed with nine millimeter handguns," said Joiner.

"Interestingly, the same caliber weapon used on you and your friend Thompson," Norwell added. "I'm waiting for a call from forensics to see if any of the bullets match."

"Oh crap," thought Corrigan. If the bullets did match, which he had a sinking feeling they would, he was going to be in big trouble. He was going to have to quickly come up with a fairly convincing explanation for why two perfect strangers would want to kill him, fake a burglary and murder Thompson. He also had the sinking feeling that if he tried to deceive Norwell the man would see through him. Corrigan felt queasy and it wasn't from his injuries.

Norwell then asked the sixty-four dollar question. "Do you know Hunter or Doyle?"

Corrigan remained silent. He couldn't tell the truth. But, he also knew when the results of the ballistics' tests came back it would be obvious there had to be some connection between him, the two killers and Thompson. He was in a terrible bind and his silence spoke for him.

Norwell decided it was time to toss out a few more facts to see how Corrigan would react. "Did I mention the police officer who was injured remembered seeing a jogger while he was talking to Hunter and Doyle? And we also found out the phone call placed to 911 about the two suspicious men was made from your cell phone." Norwell let the latest pieces of information hang in the air for effect. Norwell was good at reading faces and catching criminals in lies. So he watched Corrigan's face and waited. Corrigan silently looked down and averted his eyes, an obvious sign he knew something but wasn't telling.

The silence was broken when Norwell's cell phone rang. "This is Norwell. A match huh, both bullets. Interesting, thanks for getting back to me so quick. . . . I know. I owe you one. Okay, bye." Norwell clipped the cell phone back on his belt. He then

326

looked at Corrigan and bluntly asked. "Why would Hunter and Doyle want to kill you?"

"I don't know," Corrigan weakly replied. His words sounding hollow, even to him, as they came out of his mouth. "Crap," Corrigan thought. If his own response didn't even sound convincing to him, Norwell sure wasn't going to buy it.

"The bullet recovered from your friend Thompson and the slugs they took out of you were fired from the same gun. A gun that belonged to Kevin Doyle, if you ask me that's one hell of a coincidence, don't you?"

Corrigan remained silent. He knew it was over and a new nightmare was about to begin.

Norwell moved closer to the bed, looked straight into Corrigan's eyes and asked bluntly. "Why don't you cut the crap and tell me what's going on?"

Corrigan thought long and hard about what Norwell said. He didn't want to admit his involvement with anything associated with the chronic care team but the shootings wouldn't make sense without it. He also knew he'd better start telling the truth or things would only get worse. The only chance he had to save his own skin was to cooperate and tell the truth. "Maybe I can turn state's evidence," he thought. He'd seen it done countless times before on television and the guy always seemed to be given leniency by the court. So Corrigan loudly sighed, looked up at Norwell and finally said. "I'll tell you what's going on." It was time to come clean and sing like the proverbial canary.

Norwell took out his notebook. As he did he briefly glanced at Joiner. He remembered the sixth sense she had about Corrigan when they met him at the front door of his house. Joiner saw the glance and gave Norwell a smug look of satisfaction.

Corrigan gave Norwell all the sordid details. How the group of malevolent psychiatrists operated. How they ordered patients killed to save money. He explained that although he never really met Doyle or Hunter officially, he knew they carried out the death sentences ordered by the group. He told him how he got pulled into the psychiatric star-chamber and his involvement in Cobb's death. He then told Norwell that when Thompson's case came up for review and they wanted to kill him he tried to stop them. After Thompson was killed he honestly didn't know why they wanted him dead. Except they might be afraid he would still talk to the police. When Corrigan finished confessing, all Norwell could do was shake his head in disbelief and say. "My God, I've seen and heard a lot of things in my day but I never heard of anything like this."

"What you've told us is unbelievable," said the street wise Joiner.

"I know," sighed Corrigan.

"You know, I'm going to have to place you under arrest," Norwell reluctantly said. It was his duty.

"I figured as much."

"You said they meet locally, right?" asked Joiner.

"Yes," Corrigan replied. "They meet at a mansion over in West Grove. It's Zilker's place."

"And they're all there at one time?" Joiner wanted to confirm.

"Yes. Zilker and Ozawa live in town. The others fly in for the meeting."

"When's their next meeting?" asked Norwell.

"Like I said they meet the last Monday of each month."

"That would be the twenty fourth," Norwell calculated. "That gives us plenty of time to set things up. We should be able to catch them red handed."

"What now?" Corrigan asked.

"I'm going to take this information to the District Attorney's Office and then proceed from there. It sounds like their business venture also crossed over state lines so the FBI might get involved. But, whatever happens I'll tell the D.A. you cooperated fully and were responsible for bringing this horrible business to an end."

"I'd appreciate that," said Corrigan sincerely. "And I wouldn't mind if you kept repeating to him as often as possible."

As Joiner and Norwell prepared to leave, Joiner whispered something in Norwell's ear. Norwell briefly thought about it and nodded his head. He then looked at Corrigan. "Even though you are formally under arrest, we're not going to post a police guard at your door unless you want one."

"I appreciate that," said a thankful Corrigan. "It'll make it a little easier for me to tell Diane when she gets here."

"I hope she understands," Norwell said honestly.

"So do I," Corrigan glumly replied.

Norwell and Joiner then left the room.

As Corrigan lay in bed he gathered his thoughts, the guilt and shame was unbearable. How was he going to break the news to Diane that her husband was a murderer? He knew no matter how gently or tactfully he told her it was going to be devastating. There was no way to sugar coat murder. He wouldn't be at all surprised if she left him. His only hope was she loved him enough to stay by his side as they went through this horrible nightmare together.

# CHAPTER 29

"Too much has happened. We can't meet," an agitated Ozawa said as he spoke to Zilker over his cell phone. "Doyle is dead, Hunter is in jail and God knows what Corrigan's been telling the cops."

"We have to meet," argued Zilker. "We're committed."

"I don't think it's wise," said Ozawa. "We still don't know if Corrigan has said anything to the cops."

"Look. It's been over a week. If he's said anything to them about us don't you think we'd be in jail by now?

Ozawa thought about it. "Yeah, I guess you're right," he reluctantly agreed.

"I think when it came down to it, Corrigan wanted to protect his own hide like anyone else," Zilker said cynically. "If he hasn't said anything to them by now I don't think he ever will."

"I hope so," Ozawa replied optimistically.

"Trust me," Zilker said arrogantly. "We don't have to worry about him."

"What about Hunter?" Ozawa asked.

"I spoke with the attorney we got for him," said Zilker as he continued to calm his concerned colleague. "The one I told you about that can't be traced back to us."

"Yes, I know who you're talking about," said Ozawa.

"He assures me that Hunter will not say anything about the chronic care team as long as we take care of him."

"He's blackmailing us?" A shocked Ozawa inquired.

"Wouldn't you?" Zilker replied with narcissistic candor.

"I guess so," said Ozawa as he was also a firm believer in self-preservation.

"The attorney also told me with any luck they can plea bargain him down to assessor to an assault with a deadly weapon."

"What about the burglary and murder at Corrigan's place?" Ozawa asked.

"The attorney said they tried to pin that on him, but without any witnesses they've got nothing. Their evidence isn't strong enough to sustain a murder charge. Besides, the actual known killer is dead, so they're not pursuing it that hard."

Then Ozawa asked the sixty-four million dollar question, "They don't know about the other discharged patients, do they?" Hoping the long list of patients who died at hands of their assassins was still a secret.

"Of course not," Zilker replied scornfully. "Do you honestly think Hunter would blurt that out to the cops. 'Oh, by the way did I mention I've killed about 60 other people?' I don't think so. He'll stick with the assault charge. At the most he'll get five years. That's a hell of a lot better than facing the death penalty."

"So I guess the meeting is still on then?" asked Ozawa.

"Of course, we'll meet this coming Monday. But, just to be on the safe side, I think we should postpone our next two meetings to let things settle down. It'll also give you time to find replacements for Hunter and Doyle."

"That's an excellent idea," Ozawa whole heartedly agreed.

"Do you have anyone in mind?" Asked Zilker.

"I know two men with similar backgrounds as Hunter and Doyle. I'll contact them."

"Excellent. I'll see you Monday. Bye." Zilker was so pleased with himself that when he got off the phone he smiled. He knew there were always unforeseeable problems with any new start up and the chronic care team had just survived its first major crisis. He couldn't believe his good fortune. Hunter was going to remain silent and his worst fears about Corrigan had not been realized. He congratulated himself again. A major catastrophe had been averted. After taking a couple of months off the chronic care team would be back in business, as if nothing had happened.

It was well after six o'clock in the evening by the time Assistant District Attorney Roger Nelson rang the door bell to Corrigan's house. The tall, handsome bachelor had spent the last ten days working with his boss to hammer out at strategy that would insure those associated in any way with the chronic care team would be tried and convicted. Nelson had spent hours with Corrigan taking copious notes at the hospital and then after his discharge home.

Diane opened the door. "Mr. Nelson. We've been expecting you." She let Nelson in and closed the door behind him.

"I'll go get Jim," said Diane as she led Nelson into the living room. "Please have a seat." She then disappeared and returned with her husband.

"Good evening Mr. Nelson," said Corrigan as he greeted the young district attorney sitting on the sofa. Corrigan walked with a slight limp as he entered the room. He sat down on the recliner chair across from Nelson.

"I know the last ten days have been hard on both of you."

Diane and her husband silently nodded their heads. Of course the last ten days had been hard on both of them. They had been the hardest days of their lives and strained their marriage to the breaking point.

"I wanted to let you both know that the District Attorney, my boss, has a proposition for you Dr. Corrigan," Nelson continued. "So I wanted to deliver it to you in person."

"What kind of proposition?" Corrigan asked warily.

"He would like to give you immunity in exchange for your testimony against the members of the chronic care team including the one we've got in jail."

"You've got to be kidding," Corrigan replied incredulously. Then he quickly asked. "Why?" Not that he was looking a gift horse in the mouth, but he had been responsible for a man's death and needed to know why he wasn't going to be prosecuted. The District Attorney might be able to wipe the slate clean but he still had to live with the fact George Cobb was no longer alive because of him. Plus a couple of other people. Knowing why they didn't feel he wasn't culpable might help, especially on the nights when he lay in bed thinking about what he did.

"Since the chronic care team was a covert operation, we need an insider to make our case. Someone who knows its inner workings and can name names. Your testimony is crucial. Also after reviewing your short tenure with the group, and your lack of physical participation in Mr. Cobb's death, whose loss I can truthfully say hasn't been mourned by anyone in our department, we felt your participation with the group was minimal compared to the rest of those on the team."

Corrigan was stunned. He felt light headed for a moment. He was being given a pass, even after all that happened. Diane hugged him around the neck and kissed him. She was thrilled he wouldn't be going to jail. For the first time in days, she saw a glimmer of hope. They now might be able to put their shattered lives back together again.

"Well, what do you say?" asked Nelson.

"Of course I'll take it," replied Corrigan as he felt like the weight of the world had just been lifted off his shoulders. "I'll do anything I can to help."

"Good," smiled Nelson. He then added. "I think you should know that the police are going to arrest the chronic care team on Monday."

Mindful of how dangerous the members of the group could be Corrigan asked. "Do you think any of them will make bail after they've been arrested?" He didn't want Zilker, or for that matter, any member of the group running around loose once they found out he was the one who put them behind bars. They tried to kill him twice already. He didn't want to give them a third chance. He didn't want to be like the old saying goes, "The third time is the charm."

"Probably not considering the number of murders they'll be charged with. A judge would be out of his mind to let them out on bail. The public out cry would be humongous," replied Nelson.

"I hope so. I don't want my family put in any more danger," said Corrigan as he put his arm around Diane's waist and drew her close to him.

Diane smiled at her husband's tender gesture. She then asked Nelson if she could get him anything.

"No thanks," Nelson replied. "But thanks for the offer." Nelson then stood. "If you don't mind it's been a long day and I've got someone waiting for me at home." Her name was Betty, a court reporter with long blonde hair and the body of a goddess.

Corrigan and Diane stood and walked Nelson to the door. "Thanks for coming," said Corrigan.

"No problem," Nelson said happily. "It's not often I get to deliver good news."

"You don't know how good it is," Corrigan replied as a genuine smile appeared on his face for the first time in days. Both men then shook hands. After Nelson left, Corrigan shut the door and turned to his wife standing next to him. Without saying a word, they hugged each other and started to cry.

# CHAPTER 30

Norwell thought it was overkill to have the entire S.W.A.T. team on hand to raid the Zilker estate. They were just going to arrest a bunch of psychiatrists not a gang of street thugs. But it was department policy so Tonelli and his men where there in force. It was a moonless night and the S.W.A.T. team members were almost invisible in their black uniforms. Norwell was in charge of the operation along with Captain Tonelli. They waited until the last psychiatrist's car arrived before they deployed. A small S.W.A.T. detail was positioned around the perimeter of the stately mansion just in case anyone tried to escape. While the bulk of the S.W.A.T. team gathered by the front entrance for the signal to bust down the door and rush in. Tonelli came out of the darkness like a black apparition and walked up to Norwell and Joiner who were standing in the drive way. "Everyone's in place," he announced.

"Okay," replied Norwell. "Let's do it."

The trio walked over to the front door where six heavily armed members of Tonelli's expert entry team waited. One of the men was holding a heavy metal battering ram with both hands. Tonelli looked at the man and nodded his head. He raised the battering ram and aimed it at the deadbolt on the door. However, before he swung the battering ram at the door, Norwell raised his hand and stopped him.

"What's the matter?" asked Tonelli.

Norwell reached for the door knob, turned it and quietly opened the door. He smiled, looked at Tonelli and said nothing as he pushed the door all the way open. Tonelli exhaled sharply and shook his head. He then whispered to his men to follow him quietly into the house.

Tonelli and his men entered the mansion followed by Norwell and Joiner. Working from the information provided by Corrigan, the entire squad quickly made their way to the study. It was going to be like shooting fish in a barrel.

Except for Corrigan, all the psychiatrists of the chronic care team were seated in their usual places when the doors to the study suddenly burst open. Seven heavily armed police officers quickly entered into the room followed by shouts of, "Freeze! Nobody move! You're all under arrest!"

The S.W.A.T team members expertly took control of the room and surrounded the doctors who sat in shock around the conference table. All six members of Tonelli's entry squad had their short version M-16's pointed at the psychiatrists, daring any of them to make a move. All the psychiatrists, except for Zilker, quickly raised their hands.

"The room is secure," shouted Tonelli.

"What is the meaning of this!" demanded Zilker. He decided his best defense would be a good offensive. He angrily challenged the authority of the men pointing the rifles at him. "You have no business being here. My colleagues and I are reviewing private medical records."

When Norwell and Joiner entered the room, Norwell deliberately walked over to Zilker.

Zilker looked up at Norwell with contempt. "You have no right to be here," he said, his face turning red with anger.

Norwell reached for and picked up a medical chart from the stack sitting in front of Zilker. "This is your next victim?"

"I don't know what you're talking about," Zilker responded indignantly.

"Bull!" Norwell snapped. "We know everything about you and your chronic care team."

"I've never heard of any chronic care team. We're a managed care review panel," Zilker lied. "This is outrageous. Do you have a warrant?"

"Well, that's too bad," Norwell smugly replied as he placed a warrant on the table in front of Zilker. "We know all about you and you're under arrest." Norwell then signaled for the S.W.A.T. team members to lower their weapons and they complied. He then turned to Captain Tonelli. "I hope we brought enough handcuffs."

"Don't worry. We've got plenty," Tonelli smiled.

"All right everybody stand-up," ordered Norwell. Everybody including Zilker stood. Zilker angrily stared at Norwell.

"All right boys cuff 'um," ordered Tonelli. The members of the S.W.A.T. team pulled out their handcuffs. However, just as the first pair of handcuffs were about to be clamped down, a group of men barged into the room.

Six men all wearing smartly tailored business suits quickly walked into the room. The S.W.A.T. team members immediately focused their guns and attention on them. The men had their coats unbuttoned revealing each one had a pistol clearly visible in a shoulder holster.

"Whoa, boys," said the man obviously in charge of the group. "We're on your side. I'm Tom Brubaker. I'm with the Justice Department. We mean you no harm." Brubaker then held up his badge for everyone to see.

338

"What the hell are you doing here?" asked a stunned Norwell.

"We're taking jurisdiction over this case," Brubaker calmly announced.

"What?" Norwell angrily replied.

"We got a tip from the FBI about this case and so we did a little investigating of our own. It appears these guys broke all kinds of federal laws."

"So?" Norwell replied.

"So, that means we get first crack at them," Brubaker smoothly countered.

"No way," said Norwell as he raised his voice another octave. "We put this case together and we're not going to let some Johnny-Come-Lately Feds waltz in here and take it away from us."

"Oh, but I'm afraid that's exactly what you're gonna have to do," Brubaker replied smugly. "They're federal prisoners now. And there's nothing you can do about it."

"Oh yeah?" snarled Norwell. "I'm calling my watch commander."

"Go right head. You can even call the District Attorney if you want. He was pretty pissed too when he found out we were taking over. But there was nothing he could do about it either." Brubaker then looked at Tonelli. "It's Captain Tonelli, right?"

"Yes," replied Tonelli cautiously.

"You can tell you men to lower their weapons. We're not going to use ours. And you look like you've got us out-gunned anyway."

Tonelli looked at his men and nodded his head to signal it was okay to lower their weapons. Each man obeyed Tonelli's silent command and lowered his M-16.

Norwell flipped open his cell phone and punched in the number to the watch commander's direct line. Captain Brandies answered the phone. "Captain Brandies?" Norwell began. "This is Norwell. What the hell is going on? We've got a room full of Feds here saying that they're taking over the chronic care team case." Norwell didn't expect Brandies' response. "Damn it, captain. They've got no right to do this. We're the ones who put this case together."

Brubaker smiled as he watched Norwell learn the sad truth that he was no longer in charge. No matter how much he argued, he wasn't going to get his case back. The Feds had usurped his authority and he was learning the painful truth that whatever the Feds' want, the Feds' get. Some call it taking the initiative, others call it plain old bullying.

"But sir," Norwell still argued over the cell phone. After a few more minutes of fruitless conversation Norwell finally relented. "Yes sir. Yes sir. We'll cooperate," said a defeated Norwell. With controlled anger, he closed his cell phone.

Brubaker could see the defeat in Norwell's face. So he just shrugged his shoulders and said. "Sorry."

Norwell mouthed the word, "bastard," back to him.

"Okay guys. We've got to leave," Norwell bitterly announced to Tonelli and the S.W.A.T. team. "The Feds' have screwed us. We've got to turn the case over to them."

"You've got to be kidding!?" asked a pissed off Joiner.

"I wish I were," replied Norwell.

"Are you serious?" asked Tonelli.

"Yes," replied Norwell.

"You absolutely sure about this," Tonelli asked again.

"Yes," Norwell replied bitterly.

"Damn it," spat Tonelli.

"I know," said Norwell as he shot Brubaker a dirty look.

"Come on guys, let's go," said Tonelli through clenched teeth as he addressed his men. He then shot Brubaker a dirty look. "The stink in here is getting pretty bad anyway."

Being the well disciplined unit they were, the entire team left the room without saying a word. However, they did make obscene gestures with their hands as they walked past Brubaker's men. After the team left the room they back tracked down the hall and filed out of the mansion.

Brubaker looked at Norwell. "Sorry about all this, but I'm just following orders."

"Screw you and your orders," Norwell icily replied. He then walked briskly past Brubaker and out of the room. Joiner gave Brubaker an "if looks could kill stare" as she passed him on the way out.

Brubaker waited a few seconds then stepped out into the hallway. He watched Norwell and Joiner leave. When he was satisfied everyone was gone, he returned to the study and addressed the group of bewildered psychiatrists who were still standing around the conference table. "Please have a seat," he cordially invited.

The panel members complied. As they sat down, they looked at one another as if to ask, "What's going on?" But no answer was apparently forthcoming at least not from Brubaker.

Brubaker reached into his coat pocket and pulled out a cell phone. He punched in a number and waited. All he said was, "They're ready," and then quickly hung up. He then addressed the group. "Everybody relax. I've got someone I want you to meet."

A couple of minutes later a well-dressed man in his late forties with short brown hair and an administrative air about him, walked into the room carrying a briefcase. He went directly to Brubaker and said. "If you'll please, excuse us for a few minutes?"

Brubaker nodded his head, turned to his men and signaled for them to leave the room. One by one the clean-cut agents walked out of the room. Brubaker was the last man out. Before he shut the doors to the study, he said to the man with the briefcase. "We'll be just outside if you need us."

The man simply nodded his head.

Brubaker closed the doors and left, leaving the stranger holding the briefcase in charge.

"I demand to know what this is about?" asked Zilker in a huff.

The man with the briefcase ignored Zilker and silently walked to the opposite end of the table. He pulled the swivel chair away from the table and stood in its place. Without saying a word, he set his briefcase down on the polished conference table and sized up the group in front of him before he spoke. "I am Dr. Raymond Marshall." Marshall was a controversial recess appointment made by the president some ten months ago. "I'm the chairman of the newly created Independent Payment Advisory Board."

The bewildered psychiatrists silently looked at each other. However, Zilker recognized Marshall's name and said, "You mean the Death Panel we've been hearing so much about?"

"If that's what you want to call it," said Marshall. "But we're about saving money just like you."

"But, what does any of this have to do with us?" asked Zilker.

"It has come to my attention," Marshall continued. "That you have been, "treating", the air tweaked with his fingers for sarcastic emphasis, "chronically ill mental patients with, shall we say, a radically different approach."

"I think I can speak for all of us when I say, I don't know what you are talking about." said Zilker as the rest of the members nodded their heads in agreement. .

"Oh come now," said Marshall as he brushed aside Zilker's lie. "Are you saying names like Frank Wellington, George Cobb, Michael Anderson and Gary Thompson don't mean anything to you?" Marshall saw some of the psychiatrist look down and squirm in their seats. Even Zilker now had a worried look on his face. "Good," thought Marshall, his revelation apparently had the desired effect.

"When I got a tip from a friend over at the FBI about the investigation, they were coordinating with the San Salina police department about your operation I did a little research of my own," continued Marshall. "When I found out how effective you were at saving mental health dollars for your respective managed care companies, I was very impressed."

The psychiatrists remained silent. They sat frozen in their chairs as Marshall revealed one revelation after another about their once secret operation.

Marshall could tell from the stoic expressions on the faces of the psychiatrists sitting around the room, they knew their draconian sentences were now coming back to haunt them. "Oh, come now," he light-heartedly admonished. "You didn't think you could keep your little star chamber a secret forever, did you?"

Zilker finally got up the nerve to ask. "So why are you here?"

343

"I'm glad you asked," smiled Marshall. "With the coming implementation of the government's new health care initiatives, there is going to be a tremendous need to find ways save money. We are looking at establishing effective cost-containment strategies in both the medical and psychiatric fields. As you know a lot of people who are mentally ill are also on Medicare or Medicaid. And they cost the taxpayers a bundle of money. Most of them, like the ones you review, will never get better and will remain on the public dole for the rest of their lives." Marshall then paused for dramatic effect. "The goal of our advisory board is to develop strategies to put an end to such a waste of money."

The psychiatrists looked at each other in disbelief. They couldn't believe what they just heard.

"To put it in the simply, my board wants to engage your services," said Marshall.

This time Dr. Blair couldn't restrain herself. "You've got to be kidding?"

"On the contrary," replied Marshall.

"What about the diagnoses we use?" asked Zilker, his eyes narrowing with suspicion, "I've been told they're quite harsh?"

"As long as you remain cost effective and save the government money, the diagnoses don't matter," Marshall replied candidly.

"Let me get this straight," said Zilker. "You want us to continue reviewing our managed care patients while at the same time reviewing Medicare and Medicaid patients for you."

"Not exactly," replied Marshall.

"What do you mean by not exactly?" Zilker asked ominously.

"You'll review chronic cases, yes. But, only for us," replied Marshall. "You'll work exclusively for our advisory board."

"But what about the managed care companies we already work for?" Zilker asked.

Marshall opened his briefcase and pulled out five sheets of letter-sized paper. He handed them to Dr. Blair who was sitting closest to him. "These are resignations we've prepared for you to submit to your respective managed care company. All it needs is your signature at the bottom. Please take the one that belongs to you and then pass them down." Blair found her resignation letter and passed the rest to Ozawa.

After the letters made their way around the table, Marshall watched as each doctor studied their individual resignation letter. When he saw they'd finished he addressed them again. "Just so everyone will know. The basis for all your resignations is that you have been given a unique opportunity to work for the government on a special project and as patriotic Americans, you felt it was your duty to serve your country. The rest of the letter is about you having to leave the country and being unable to talk about the project until it is finished. That was added to give the assignment an air of mystery and to also discourage any further contact from your companies."

"What happens after we sign this letter?" Zilker asked.

For Marshall, Zilker's question was a good sign. It was inquisitive rather than adversarial. Which meant the idea of working for the government apparently didn't sound all that bad. Maybe the rest would follow his lead. It would make it a lot easier for him if they did. Because his orders were very specific, they all had to agree or they would all be sent to prison. Zilker and his fellow psychiatrists didn't know it yet, but what they were being offered was an all or nothing proposition.

"If you decide to join us, you will become employees of Health and Human Services," Marshall proudly announced.

There was some mumbling around the table as the doctors saw their careers taking a new direction. A direction none of them would have taken voluntarily.

"You will then enter into what is tantamount to a witness relocation type program. Before you arrive in Alexandria, Virginia you will be provided with a new name, new identity social security number the whole nine yards. You will also have your choice of two residential neighborhoods to live in."

"What about our families?" Marapudi asked.

"They will be able to come with you," replied Marshall. "And except for the real reason you are leaving you can tell them anything you want about why you have to move. However, it would be easier if you stick with the reason in your resignation letter."

"What about the police?" Zilker asked. "Won't they become a little suspicious if they don't hear we've been prosecuted or sent to jail?"

Marshall replied with a conspiratorial voice for dramatic effect. "When you leave this room you will all cease to exist. If down the road anyone bothers to ask about you, they'll be told that you got off on a technicality. It happens all the time."

"And they'll buy that?" a skeptical Zilker asked.

"The whole time you've been sitting here has anyone read you, your Miranda rights?" asked Marshall.

"Come to think of it, no," responded Zilker. Everyone else in the room nodded their head as they agreed with Zilker. Not a word had been mentioned about their rights.

"There's your technicality," Marshall told them.

"Very interesting," Zilker smiled wryly. He immediately began to think of a way to get out of his current predicament based on Marshall's statement.

However, Marshall was one step ahead of him. He looked directly at Zilker and said sternly. "Don't even think about it. You're still a murderer."

"Perish the thought," Zilker replied.

Marshall scanned the room again to make sure he had everyone's attention. It was time to hit them with his ultimatum. "What'll it be? Come work for us or do I let Agent Brubaker take you all to Leavenworth or whatever federal prison they lock up murderers these days." Marshall was offering them paid servitude or life sentences behind bars. He hoped, for their sakes, they would chose government paid servitude. Marshall watched as the group fell silent. He let them ponder their fates.

Each cornered psychiatrist, no doubt, wondered what the other was thinking as their professional careers, as they knew it, were coming to an end. However, they avoided eye contact with each other. This was an agonizingly individual decision each one of them was going to have to make on their own. The downside was they had been caught and faced murder charges. The upside was they were being given an unprecedented opportunity to avoid the consequences of their actions.

When enough time passed Marshall impatiently broke the silence. "Ladies and gentlemen, what it comes down to is I believe I'm making you an offer you can't refuse."

Marshall hoped they would all agree. The department's plan wouldn't work otherwise. He knew H.H.S. couldn't legally or ethically train mental health professionals to do what this group had been doing with such ruthless efficiency for so long. Therefore it was imperative they all joined. The chronic care team was already operational and best of all they could be blackmailed, it was perfect. Ironically it was their cold-hearted efficiency and cost savings that made their operation so appealing to H.H.S. It fit right in with the new health care law. Marshall prayed they would all agree and come to work for him.

Again after what seemed a long time, but in reality was less than a minute, Zilker finally spoke up. "I for one have always been a patriot."

"I don't see how it could hurt to save the government some money," Ozawa rationalized.

"We are running a deficit," added Gatway.

"I think it's every citizen's duty to try and balance the budget," offered Marapudi.

Marshall smiled. The votes were going his way. Only one left to go.

"Oh, cut the crap," Blair said bluntly. "Let's get real. We're going to do it because we don't want to go to jail."

"I'm glad you all see it my way," a grateful Marshall replied.

By now everyone in the room had deduced it was Corrigan who had turned them into the police. And they all wished that he would rot in hell.

"I have a question Dr. Marshall," Zilker asked.

"What is it?"

"What about Dr. James Corrigan?

"Yeah," groused Ozawa.

"What's going to happen to him?" Zilker continued.

"He was a part of this operation like everyone else," added Marapudi.

"We're going to give Dr. Corrigan an offer similar to yours," replied Marshall. "Except that he's not going to work for H.H.S. He will be relocated to a place where he can continue practicing psychiatry either in public or private sector."

"Why?" demanded Zilker. "He's just as guilty as any of us."

"Yeah," railed the angry chorus from the rest of the psychiatrists around the table.

"Because he'll be our key witness in any future criminal proceedings if anyone here thinks they can renege on their agreement with us. He's our ace in the hole."

"What if Corrigan doesn't accept your offer?" asked Zilker. "The man thinks of himself as a paragon of virtue."

"He already has," Marshall responded.

"Damn it," Zilker cursed as the rest of the room grumbled. "I have a tape that you might be interested in," Zilker offered up cheerfully. He wanted to do anything he could to get back at Corrigan. "It has Corrigan ordering George Cobb's death."

"Excellent," smiled Marshall. "You can give it to me later."

"With pleasure," Zilker snarled.

Marshall then looked around the room again. "Are there any other questions?"

"Yes. Who is going to replace Hunter and Doyle?" Ozawa asked.

"Do you have any candidates?" asked Marshall.

"No, not right now," replied Ozawa. He consciously decided not to tell Marshall about the two men he was thinking about asking because he hadn't contacted them yet, and because the whole dynamic of the operation had just changed.

"That's okay," said Marshall, "the less contact with anyone outside the group the better. As for their replacements I have some highly motivated, Special Ops people who wouldn't mind picking up where Hunter and Doyle left off." Marshal waited a few moments then asked, "Anything else?" The group remained silent.

"Good," Marshall cheerfully replied. "From this point on I will be in charge. I will also be your liaison with H.H.S., since none of you will have any direct contact with them. Everything will go through me, is that understood?"

The psychiatrists as one nodded their heads in agreement. They were now officially government employees and they had better learn to start taking orders.

"When do you want us to start" asked Zilker.

"I'm glad you asked," replied Marshall as he pulled the swivel chair back to the table and sat down. He reached inside his briefcase and pulled out a half a dozen medical charts and set them on the conference table in front of him. He then closed his briefcase and set it on the floor. Then with cold calculating eyes he looked at everyone around the table and with a modest smile announced, "You start tonight."

The psychiatrists were taken back by the announcement. This was happening faster than any of them had expected. However, no one protested because they knew better. They also knew from this point on their lives would never be the same.

Marshall opened the first medical chart. "Okay ladies and gentlemen. Let's start saving the government some money, shall we?" And with that opening statement, the chronic care team re-adjourned under new management.

# EPILOGUE

Dr. James Corrigan agreed to Marshall's offer. Self-preservation won out over principle. He is currently in private practice in the Northwest. Diane got a job at a local television station and is working her way back up through the ranks and is pregnant with their second child. As for James Corrigan, there isn't a day that goes by when he doesn't curse the day he meet George Cobb.

The chronic care team still has an undetected and flawless track record and has saved the American taxpayers a substantial amount of money. It remains to this day the only Black Ops program ever funded by the department of Health and Human Services.

Made in the USA
San Bernardino, CA
18 October 2015